WHEN ALL GOES BRIGHT

JESS MOWRY

Copyright © 2011 - 2021 by Jess Mowry

PRINT ISBN-10: 0-9980767-9-1
PRINT ISBN-13: 978-0-9980767-9-9

EBOOK ISBN-10: 0-9977379-0-5
EBOOK ISBN-13: 978-0-9977379-0-5

First Anubis Edition 2017

This is a work of fiction. Names, characters, businesses, products, places, events and incidents are either the manifestations of the author's imagination or are used in a fictitious context.

OTHER BOOKS BY JESS MOWRY

Rats In The Trees
Children Of The Night
Way Past Cool
Six Out Seven
Ghost Train
Babylon Boyz
Bones Become Flowers
Voodoo Dawgz
Tyger Tales
Phat Acceptance
Skeleton Key
Knights Crossing
The Bridge
Reaps
Midnight Sons
Drawing From Life
Magic Rats
Double Acting
The Coyote Valley Railroad
In The Dead Of Night
Ghost Ship
Spencer's Spirit
The Insiders
The Light

FOR ALL THE KIDS
IN WARS

WHEN ALL GOES BRIGHT

PROLOGUE

It could have been called a not-quite land.

It was not quite in the center of Africa, though far enough south so it wasn't steamy, and yet it was not quite a veldt. Although it was tiny in terms of a nation its borders had never been quite defined – some said it ended here at this river, others said it began at those hills -- for its people knew when enough was sufficient, and more than they needed was too much to have.

The not-quite land wasn't much of a prize when the Europeans came to conquer; it was too far away from an ocean to be a convenient source of slaves -- who inconveniently tended to die if forced to march for weeks in chains -- and it didn't have anything valuable like diamonds, gold or oil.

Since the land contained nothing exploitable and its people pro-

1

vided no profit, it was merely taken because it was *there* and anything that wasn't possessed was a threat to those who didn't posses it.

Some said the French had first stolen this land, but were not quite sure what to do with it. Then, as a sort of colonial joke, they bargained it off to the British for someone else's purloined home.

The British loved to colonize -- at least they did at the time – because even possessing a worthless place meant one less threat to their empire.

It was rather like moving into a house with a family who already lived in the attic, and of never taking the trouble to go up and make their acquaintance. Whoever they were they caused no disturbance and never complained if the roof might have leaked. And while it was true they didn't pay rent, they never asked for anything, like running water, electric lights, or telephones to call their friends, so they weren't a bother to keep.

One might have imagined a retired British Major reading his paper in robe and slippers and hearing something go bump in the night. He might pause for a moment, puffing his pipe, and wonder about those people up there, but perhaps it was better to just let them be rather than risk some unpleasantness.

One day the Major passed away and left the house to his children. He hadn't done much to keep it up, and repairs would have been expensive. Besides, there was nothing of value inside and the neighborhood wasn't desirable. No one else wanted the worthless house, so it was returned to its free-living tenants.

So the not-quite land was forgotten again, and decades passed away in peace while the rest of the world made various wars. But, far away was a powerful land ruled by those who still believed that whatever wasn't possessed was a threat to those who didn't possess it. These rulers had been put in power by people who'd never learned to be satisfied with what was sufficient: they were only five percent of the world, yet they gobbled up twenty-five percent of everything the world possessed. The purpose of power was power (they said) and the more you possessed the more you should want because that was the natural order of things… or so they had always been taught.

The house of Earth could not be enlarged, but its privileged children demanded more room -- or at least more possessions to put in their rooms -- because that was the natural order of things, or so they had always been taught.

So, they started to think of remodeling, and began to measure the house to capitalize on its limited space and make everyone pay for their privilege.

ONE

The not-quite land was mostly flat, but here and there were huddles of hills like scattered camps of sleeping camels. Much of the country was dusty and dry, and yet it was not without life; there were groves of acacia trees, African oak, and thorny bushes, though never quite abundant enough to really be called a forest. There were even some places of not-quite jungle surrounding occasional waterholes and lining the banks of slow-running streams, which were never quite rivers except when it rained and meandered their way across the plains in lazy loops with ox-bow lagoons, adding sinuous stripes and shadings of green to an otherwise gold and brown palette.

Some might have called the land barren in places, and yet it was never quite naked: there was hardy grass of amber hues that grew as high as a lion's shoulder. ...Yes, there were lions in this tiny place, though not quite as large as in other lands, and therefore not as interesting to those who studied such things. It had also been this way in the past for those who came to Africa to murder something noble: one wanted the true king of beasts for a trophy, a lion who *looked* like a worthy opponent when seen in the sights of a high-powered rifle.

It was not quite the end of a long hot summer, but not quite time for the hard winter rains. One of the not quite worthy lions had just downed a small antelope -- another species of life in this land that had never quite been worthy of notice -- and was dragging it into the shade of a tree when a distant droning invaded the peace. The lion paused to listen a moment, then returned to his meal.

The approaching hum was faint at first like a distant swarm of migrating bees. (One might think African killer bees, if that was the way they'd been taught.) Then an airplane appeared in the southern sky, which today was as blue as a porcelain bowl and as clear as the eyes of a smiling child. The plane skimmed the hump of a slumbering camel, thereby crossing an ancient border and blatantly breaking a brand new law.

The plane was a Douglas C-47 painted a tawny-golden shade very much like the coat of a lion. This wasn't a color one might have imagined for something created to fly in the sky, but it would have been hard to see from another airplane flying above. At the moment there weren't any other airplanes for a hundred miles in any direction, but far overhead, unseen up in space, the all-seeing eye of a spy satellite had spotted an unexplained shadow below and was searching its memory files for a possible threat to its masters.

The C-47 was flying so slowly a hawk could have passed it with ease in a dive and laughed at the foolish pretensions of men who created such clumsy and noisy machines to go where they didn't belong. About every three minutes the plane's port side engine would sputter and spew out gray smoke. This would continue for several seconds and sometimes the engine would backfire, but at last it caught up with its starboard brother to finally resume their droning duet.

The airplane's skin looked as crinkled as the foil of an old cigarette pack, while riveted patches showed here and there, and the flanks of the forward fuselage were dented and scarred in a thousand places by ice being thrown from the spinning propellers in higher, colder altitudes. The engine nacelles were lathered with oil, and carbon soot blackened the wings' undersides, but there was a saying about these aircraft: they could possibly crash but would never wear out.

Painted on either side of the nose was the face of a friendly-looking lion wearing old-fashioned flying goggles above the words

5

SIMBA AIR FREIGHT

The cockpit was like a tin camp stove with the sun blazing down on the lion-colored roof, though the windows were open and wind rushing past with the soothing sound of a waterfall. Dust seemed to coat every surface inside, including the glass of the instruments, their needles twitching and quivering, while the air was a stew of leather and sweat, hot engine oil and hydraulic fluid.

A man lay asleep in the co-pilot's seat, a fine-boned man of not quite thirty. He was shirtless in trousers of lionish brown, while his skin was a dusky, lusterless shade like the satin-black of the instrument panels. He seemed a bit taller than only six feet, partly because of the cramped surroundings, but mostly because of his cheetah-like build where every tight muscle was starkly defined like an artist's anatomy model. His chest was a pair of high jutting bricks above a belly like ripples of stone, his biceps as solid as river rocks even while resting relaxed. His face looked youthfully peaceful in sleep, with rounded cheeks and a wide snubby nose. His lips were full and reposed half open, revealing the gleam of large white teeth. His hair was bushy, indifferently kept, and powdered with dust to a lion's-mane color. His feet, resting clear of the rudder pedals, were clad in what seemed to be native-made boots with antelope uppers and truck tire soles. Unlike most pilots he wore no watch; and a tuft of brown fur on a slim leather strip loosely encircled his neck. At his side was a heavy utility knife in a sheath decorated with beads.

In the pilot's seat was a boy of thirteen who was reading a book titled, *Fate Is The Hunter*, while a primitive, mindless, mechanical thing composed of gyros, gears and wires, with oil for blood and a pump for a heart attended the business of flying, mysteriously moving the twin steering yokes as if a ghost was guiding the plane. The boy, like the man, was deep dusky black, shirtless and shiny with sweat in the heat, which had muddied the leather beneath him. His hair, like the man's, was bushy and wild, shaded by dust to a lion's-mane brown and crowned with small yellow headphones. His face wasn't quite the same as the man's, disregarding their difference in age, but mostly due to plump round cheeks and the hint of a small second chin. The boy,

6

like the man, had slender bones, which made his softly rolly body look like it weighed a twice as much as it did. Sprawled in the narrow pilot's seat as only a boy of his age could sprawl, his belly spilled over his ragged jeans and quivered like pudding contained by skin, his navel overlapped by fat and forming a sort of wide cheeky smile, while his chest was a proud pair of spherical shapes that some might have called voluptuous, their nipples inverted like soft little slits and about the same shade of the rest of him so to be almost invisible.

The boy had youthfully large feet and hands, the former encased in boots like the man's with antelope uppers and truck-tire soles. The latter were chubby and possibly clever when not resting paw-like and loose. His nose was wide, basically bridgeless, and rather impertinently snubbed. His full lips were at rest in a half-open pout, displaying a pair of startling teeth that might have opened bottle caps. His large onyx eyes had long silky lashes and were slightly upturned at the corners, which gave him a rather foxy look, though they couldn't be seen at the moment, concealed by a pair of pilot's sunglasses designed for a larger face than his as well as a drastically different nose.

Unlike the man, the boy wore a watch that was almost cartoonishly huge and complex. On his opposite wrist was a souvenir bracelet that might have come from a carnival. It was nickel-plated but now showing brass, and engraved with the name, DAKOTA. Around his neck was a slim leather strip, and a tufted lock of lion's mane nestled between the spheres of his chest. He wore a headband of antelope skin, skillfully woven and beautifully beaded, which only partially tamed his hair but channeled the sweat from his eyes. A knife in a sheath, also beautifully-made, was secured to a loop on his jeans.

Like all things cherished in this tiny land, the plane was protected by charms: a lion's fang dangled above the compass, along with a doll in the *Akan* tradition that smilingly swung and regarded the sky. A souvenir photo was taped to the roof, looking down at the man and boy, the kind that were taken at carnivals. The boy there was holding an ice-cream cone, his belly half bare in an underwear shirt that would have been tight on a much slimmer youth, while the man was clad in brown coveralls and looked like a bumpkin come to a fair.

Dakota's headphones were plugged to a Diskman and the volume

7

was high with African rock, yet he glanced out about every three minutes whenever the port engine sputtered. Then he would lower his book and scan the dusty instrument panel. The airspeed was steady at 130 knots, but he'd fondle the port side throttle a bit and tinker with the mixture control. Then his large and foxy eyes would roam the faces of other gauges -- revolutions and temperatures, oil, fuel, and manifold pressures, altitude (about 3000 feet), flick to the compass (north by northwest) -- then return to the port side engine, which usually steadied and stopped spitting smoke as if sensing the boy's annoyance. Then Dakota would gaze ahead through the bug-spattered glass of the grimy windscreen. Finally, he'd reach between his legs where a bottle of Coke was nestled upright and take a sip of the warm contents. He also munched on Simba Chips bought that morning in Johannesburg.

The port side engine sputtered again, belching a burst of gun-metal smoke as if sipping a beverage that didn't agree. The sleeping man stirred whenever this happened as if the malfunction invaded his dreams, but Dakota performed his ritual of fondling the throttle and pampering the mix, and the engines resumed their droning duet. Finally he drank the last of his Coke, tossed the bottle out the window and gave the compass another glance. Then he studied the landscape ahead and a huddle of hills in the distance. He checked the altitude again, then lay his book on the instrument panel, slipped the head-phones off his ears and hung them next to an ancient pair, huge and heavy, Bakelite and steel, that served the airplane's radio.

Leaving his seat was an undulant struggle of dynamic muscle against static mass, and complicated by ergonomics designed in the 1930s when pilots had seldom been fat. Finally reaching an upright position, his body rearranged itself obeying the law of gravity, his belly cascading over his jeans in a pair of pendulous teardrop shapes com-pletely concealing his crotch, his navel tunneling upward between them and smiling cavernously, the orbs of his chest like bobby bal-loons. Muddy sweat drained from his navel to spatter the worn metal floor, while more trickled down from under his arms, beneath which were squeezed chubby rolls. The soles of his boots made potato chip sounds in the gritty carpet of dust on the floor as, leaning backward

8

to balance his belly, he entered the sweltering cargo bay.

Sunlight streamed in through the rows of small windows while dust motes danced in the broiling beams to the battering beat of the engines. The cylindrical space was crowded with things, cardboard boxes of various sizes, many displaying labels of food, flats of tinned milk, a stack of rice sacks, barrels of fuel and kerosene, and a 1943 Willys jeep born the same year as the airplane. The freight included roofing tin, lengths of plastic water pipe, a restless roll of chicken-wire, a truck engine banded to rough wooden skids, along with shovels, axes, hoes, and a dozen machetes bound in a bundle that looked like a primitive killing machine.

There was also a British style "toe-pincher" coffin, which gave off a rather ominous scent suggesting the plane had a passenger whose body should have been on earth... more properly six feet below it. If scent had it color this would have been bronze, a dry and acrid but tolerable smell.

Dakota's jeans sagged cartoonishly low, baring much of the moons of his bottom and covering all but the toes of his boots beneath their ragged tumble of cuffs, the latter dragging over the floor and leaving a trail behind in the dust as he wobbled his way through the quivering cargo.

Reaching the double doors near the tail, he unlatched and pushed the forward door open an inch against the rushing wind, held it there with one hand, hoisted his belly with the other, revealing a dusky puff of chub protruding from his unbuttoned fly and engulfing all but the tip of his shaft, and relieved himself in the sky.

The port engine sputtered again.

"Bother!" he said in Swahili, which might have meant damn or probably worse, and wobbled his way back to the cockpit to pamper the throttle and mixture controls.

He scanned the instrument panel, then pulled another warm bottle of Coke from a rusty ice chest as dry as a desert, then settled into his seat once more and was slipping the headphones back on his ears when he noticed a rising column of smoke beyond the humps of hills ahead. He squinted a bit in the savage sun-glare despite the deep green of his oversize glasses, and noted circling vulture shapes skirting the dirty-gray pillar. He frowned a little, leaning forward, his breasts lolling over the steering yoke, and even his teeth seeming eager to see as his mouth slowly opened in wonder. Then he reached over the throttle quadrant and prodded the sleeping man's shoulder, his fingertip leaving an ebony spot in the coating of tawny-brown dust.

"Nathi."

The man was awake in an instant. His eyes were as foxy and black as the boy's, flicking first to the instrument panel, checking the compass and altitude, then giving Dakota a questioning look. The boy only pointed ahead. The man also frowned, then said in Swahili, "Take her up a little," and reached for a pair of binoculars which had once belonged to the British Army.

Dakota unlocked the auto-pilot and took control of the plane, planting his boots on the rudder pedals and gripping the steering yoke. He set the mix on auto-rich and slowly advanced the throttles. The port side engine faltered at first, but quickly recovered and roared again. The airplane's nose tilted up. Clearing the hills by a thousand feet, Dakota lowered the throttles once more while the man scanned ahead through the windscreen.

Some might have said it was not quite a village but only a huddle of mud-plastered huts surrounded by fields of native crops: millet, maize, beans, and yams. It looked even less like a village today; the huts were roofless and smoking within, while flames still flickered here and there like angry red eyes in soot-blackened faces.

The vultures scattered away from the plane as it churned through the column of smoke. The smells of charred thatch and smoldering wood, of baking clay and burned possessions, blew into the cockpit then faded away as the plane burst again into sunlight.

"Shall I circle?" asked Dakota.

"I don't see anyone," said Nathi, still intently scanning the ground. "No cattle, no goats. Not even a chicken."

Dakota scowled. "The Army would have taken them."

Nathi shifted the glasses. "They didn't bother to burn the crops. ...Maybe the people escaped to the hills." Then, his muscular body tensed, and a finger fine-tuned the binoculars' focus. "Bring her around and come in low."

Again Dakota reached for the throttles, but paused to point ahead. "That must be the Army trucks."

Nathi aimed the glasses northeast, where a cloud of dust rose in the heat-shimmered distance. "Probably two," he said. "Maybe fifteen kilometers. I doubt they can see us through all their own dust or hear us above their engines." He glanced at the fuel level gauge. "Bring her around."

A few minutes later, the C-47 swooped over the village at seventy knots with man and boy scanning the ground.

"I see someone," said Dakota, half upright with his head out the window, his jeans abandoning his bottom. "There in the shade by the chicken house, the one with still part of a roof."

The man only sighed. "A boy, and he's dead."

"Are you sure?"

Nathi lowered the glasses. "Yes."

"Was he theirs, or ours?" asked Dakota.

"It doesn't matter to him anymore."

Dakota reached for the throttles again, about to pull up, but said, "They always welcomed us with a feast."

Nathi considered then nodded. "Take her down."

There wasn't an actual airstrip, but the ground was flat and fairly smooth. The boy brought the plane to a thousand feet, gently banked to circle around while carefully losing more altitude and lowering the wing flaps. Then he lined up the nose with faint wheel tracks that marked their previous landings.

"Cross feed," he called, a hand on the throttles.

Nathi reached for the fuel selectors.

"Cowl flaps open, gear down." Dakota pulled back a bit on the yoke as the landing gear lowered with shuddering thumps and the airplane balked with the drag.

"Green and latched," said Nathi. "Tail wheel locked." He peered ahead at the oncoming earth. "Someone has been digging there, but not enough for graves."

Dakota checked the airspeed again, noted the smoke still rising straight up, then lowered the flaps to full position, easing a bit on the trembling yoke as the airplane flared on ground-effect.

11

It was a perfect approach, but Nathi's eyes seemed troubled as he gazed ahead at the place of digging. *Too small for graves.*

The main wheels touched with a firm double-bump, spewing twin clouds of tawny dust that fanned away behind the tail. Dakota reached to lower the throttles.

"Mines!" yelled Nathi.

"Full throttle, full rich!" yelled Dakota, straining back on the yoke. "Gear up!"

Nathi considered for less than a second, then jerked the landing gear lever, yanking the wheels from under the plane, which desperately fought to stay aloft, seeming to strain every creaking rivet, engines roaring at full RPM, gushing out solid black streamers of smoke, propeller blades pitched for maximum bite, frantically clawing the precious air so terribly close to the ground. Machine and boy battled together to fly, and then they were past the digging.

"Gear down!" yelled Dakota.

This time the thumps of the landing gear locking echoed the thuds of the wheels hitting dirt.

"Green and latched," called Nathi.

"When all goes bright, don't look," puffed Dakota, an expression newly come to this land, though no one seemed to know why.

Dust billowed over the ground once more as the airplane rattled and jolted along, a thing from the sky now awkward on earth. Dakota gently toed the brakes. The tail wheel dropped with a lesser thump, tilting the cockpit skyward again so he had to stretch up to see over the nose. Finally, the airplane creaked to a halt a few hundred feet from the side of a hill and the village's ancient burying-ground. More tawny dust drifted in through the windows, furring the glass of the instruments and dimming the glare of the sun. The doll and lion's fang swung to and fro. Dakota bowed his head to the doll and murmured a "thank you," echoed by Nathi.

Dakota retracted the flaps, lowered the engines to clattering idle, studied the oil pressure gauges a moment, then stretched to reach the ignition switches above the windscreen frame. The engines sputtered and coughed to a stop and silence settled around the plane except for the ticking and clicks of hot metal. Dakota flashed a sudden smile, displaying his bottle-opener teeth.

"How was that?"

Nathi sighed, stirring dust in the air. "We were ten knots below stall speed, yet you flew."

"Perhaps we had help from the Lion?"

"Or ground-effect," said Nathi. "Though it shouldn't have worked in this heat." Then he smiled. "I couldn't have done any better, but please never do that again."

Then, both faces, youthful, mature, hardened into grimmer lines.

"Do you think those mines were for us?" asked Dakota.

"Now they are for everyone."

Dakota squiggled out of his seat and hoisted his recalcitrant jeans. Secured to a bulkhead by rubber cords was a pair of AK-47s with most of the blackness worn off their metal, leaving a dull silver-gray. Their bolts and triggers were shiny from use, their wooden stocks darkened by oil and sweat. He took down one of the weapons while Nathi uncradled the other.

Like Dakota's ragged jeans, Nathi's trousers clung low on his hips as he slung his rifle over a shoulder and followed the boy down the now-slanted floor, their boots crunching dust in the sweltering silence. He wrinkled his nose as they passed the coffin.

Dakota cocked his rifle, setting it to full-auto fire and crouching close to cover the man as Nathi opened the doors. The squeak of hinges was loud in the quiet. Nathi blinked in the savage sunlight, shading his eyes as he scanned the hills, while Dakota poised ready to shoot.

"They would have known it was us," said Nathi.

"Should we wait?" asked Dakota, his eyes turning to study the village.

"They would have known," Nathi repeated. "And the trucks have been gone at least an hour."

"Do you think the Army took the people to a relocation camp?"

"There were only two trucks." Nathi unslung and cocked his weapon.

It was in the boy's nature to jump to the ground, but he comically landed and almost fell, his jeans slipping down to his knees, while

Nathi landed as light as a cat. Dakota recovered his jeans and adjusted his glasses, which scorned his nose, while Nathi studied the port landing gear, where leaking oil was spattering dust like tiny atomic explosions.

"Shall I put in the pins?" asked Dakota.

"We may have to leave in a hurry," said Nathi.

Rifles held ready, man and boy moved cautiously off toward the smoke-shrouded village, pausing once to look back at the plane, well camouflaged by its lion-colored paint... though far up in space the dust had been noted and pictures were being transmitted.

The vultures, disturbed by the landing, were now returning to earth. They hadn't quite reached the boy on the ground, who lay in the shade of a smoldering henhouse, the smoke casting rippling patterns around him. He was deep dusky-black and might have been twelve, naked and showing no body hair, and looked well fed and round-tummied. His eyes, pure midnight and not yet sunken, gazed off in that strange and disturbing direction that no living eye can follow. His chest had been riddled by full-auto fire, though mercifully now it was covered with flies and the gleaming bones mostly concealed. One of his teeth was slightly chipped, which somehow made him look younger. Around his neck was a beaded steel chain and a pair of shiny aluminum tags, the only things left to him in this world except his glossy, feasting shroud.

Dakota's eyes kept flicking about behind their lenses like emerald tears, scanning the scatter of smoking huts, the camel-like humps of the lion-colored hills, and the empty amber sun-shimmered land. His chubby fingers roamed the gun, though seldom strayed far from the trigger. But the only sounds were the buzzing of flies, the croaking and caws of the impatient vultures, the campfire crackle of burning wood.

"I thought they took one?" he said at last, his gaze coming back to the bright metal tags, which made the boy's body look like a possession... left-luggage, perhaps, to be called for later, though it seemed clear that nobody would. "To give to his family at least."

"Only an army with honor," said Nathi. "Which wouldn't have stripped him and left him for vultures."

"Maybe they need the uniforms? That could be useful information."

"Someone fought back," said Nathi, kneeling to pick up a cartridge case from a scatter of many others. "This is from an AK."

One of the vultures, hungry or boldest, made a scuttling dart toward the body. Dakota swung his rifle, slamming the bird away. It retreated in fury, hissing, screaming, shitting itself. The others watching seemed to laugh.

"We should bury him," said Dakota.

"But, he's not one of ours."

"His spirit should not be left to wander."

Nathi nodded. "For now..." He handed his gun to Dakota, then pulled a sheet of rusty tin from what remained of the chicken house and arched it over the body. The vultures gave him angry glares. Then, man and boy moved through the smoke-shrouded village, weapons ready, eyes alert, peering into each smoldering doorway, one always guarding the other's back, tensing at every soft sputter of flame or the crack of a charred rafter falling. Hut after hut lay gutted and empty except for the ashes of household things. Bullets had ripped the mud-plastered walls, and the Army had used incendiary grenades to set every dwelling afire. Nathi noted this, saying, "They seem to have more weapons than fuel."

"That is useful information." Dakota went to the well and looked down. "They had enough fuel to poison the water."

"A few liters would have been sufficient."

"Why didn't they use grenades on the crops?"

Nathi was scanning around again. "Perhaps they hoped to harvest them before the rains begin. But they seem to have left in a hurry, and that's why we saw the mines." He aimed a finger here and there. "Most of these cases are M-16, though an AK or two fired back."

On the ground near the last of the burned-out huts, Dakota spotted an Army cap in a camouflage pattern of desert tans, which didn't quite work in this lion-colored land.

"The General has many new toys," Nathi warned.

Dakota studied the sun-baked dirt before lifting the cap with his AK muzzle and flipping it into his hand. A tag inside read

BARRYMORE CORP.
HOUSTON, TX, USA

Dakota flung it away and pushed up his slipping glasses again. "Maybe the people crossed the border? Or, maybe Rashawn took them to safety."

Nathi studied the cartridge cases. "A few hundred rounds, and maybe two rifles. Short bursts to conserve ammunition. Then they ran... there..."

Man and boy faced the last smoking hut. Then they approached it, weapons on point.

Two more dead boys lay inside, one maybe ten, while the other was close to Dakota's age, wearing a tuft of lion's mane on a leather strip around his neck. Unlike the round-tummied soldier, these boys were as lean as cheetahs. Both wore tire-tread antelope boots, though their only clothes were loincloths in a camouflage pattern of ambers and golds randomly striped with shadings of black.

Dakota's hands clenched on the gun. "I should be fighting with them!"

Nathi touched Dakota's arm. "A truly great general once said that the three things most useful in winning his war were bulldozers, trucks, and the C-47... none of which were created to fight."

TWO

"Mom? I think Freddy's dead."

"...Oh," said Nicole after a moment of not knowing anything else to say. She paused in her fight with a lipstick tube -- she knew there was still quite a bit left inside, but the dammed thing wouldn't unscrew anymore as if cunningly crafted to cheat and retreat -- and turned from a mirror steamed from her bath to the near-naked boy in the doorway.

Zackary was nearly thirteen, with sandy blond hair in an unruly mop that sheep-dog-like covered indigo eyes almost down to his small snubby nose and tumbled shaggily over his shoulders. He'd always been charmingly chubby with chipmunk cheeks and a cute double-chin, and his fearsome buck teeth had at least been aligned thanks to a year of expensive braces, but seeing him now clad only in boxers, and those seemingly about to fall off in a state Nicole's mom would have called "droopy drawers," Nicole realized he had gotten quite fat and wondered when that could have happened. His belly cascaded over his shorts in a pendulous pair of teardrop shapes, his navel a wide-smiling cavern between them that tunneled upward to shadowy depths, while his chest was a duo of bulbous balloons that jutted somehow aggressively and constantly quivered with each move and breath as if over-inflated with something like Jell-O and on the verge of explosion. His skin was un-sunned peaches-and-cream, his nipples almost invisibly pale, their tips inverted instead of protruding, which didn't do much to define his sex.

Nor did his chrome-plated necklace, which looked like an oversize bathtub chain, though they were currently "in" for boys... as well as green hair, which she'd promised tomorrow. He'd dropped out of soccer the year before, indifferently settled for D's in P.E. -- his school gave no F's for physical failure -- and now spent most of his time in his room sprawled on his bed watching TV or playing violent video games that featured mass-murder and nuclear wars, with blood and guts in stark Technicolor and shockingly grisly sound-effects. Nicole wasn't sure how to deal with that -- or even if she should try -- any more than with Freddy's apparent demise.

She tossed the lipstick into the wastebasket, telling herself to remember the brand and never buy it again. ...Or, could its commercial chicanery be used to advantage somehow? *Ours gives you all you deserve?* But her company didn't make cosmetics... at least no division she knew of. And what was the crap anyhow, she reflected; colored grease to smear on her mouth to make it look wet and willing to males.

"Er..." she said, feeling out of her depth, a rather familiar sensation of late. "Are you sure, honey?"

Zackary shrugged as if half asleep, though he'd looked that way for most of this year, even engaged in genocide on rampaging hordes of terrorist orcs... sub-human things motivated by hate that one only wanted to kill. Orcs never had any families, no cute little orclings to cry for their daddies, or wives to weep for their slaughtered breadwinners, so nobody felt the slightest remorse about bombing them all into nuclear hell. Nicole had suspected drugs for a while as the source of Zackary's lethargy, and had read somewhere that heavy dope smoking in pubescent males could cause their breasts to become... well, breasts. But she'd never smelled any weed on Zack so she'd settled for lack of motivation and probably too many carbs.

"He's all stiff, mom," said Zack.

Nicole glanced again at the misty mirror, patted her golden-brown hair into place and wondered if it was getting too long... too late to

18

worry about that now. She almost guiltily checked her watch: Freddy had picked a bad day to die – assuming there were any good ones -- and she hoped it wasn't an omen. But she made herself smile in a hopeful way. "Maybe he's just sleeping late."

"He's all stiff, mom," repeated Zack, without the slightest degree of hope in a squeak-punctuated androgynous voice like a choirboy about to age-out.

Nicole took her son's chubby hand, noting his sloppily wobbling walk with jiggles, shimmies and undulations as if he was pudding draped upon bones, breasts bobbing about as if questing for something, him leaning way backward to balance his belly in an awkwardly comical sway-backed stance as it plunged and rebounded with every step as if determined to bounce on the floor, as she tried to hurry him down the hall without seeming overly stressed. Her morning commute was looming ahead like its own kind of video game from hell... Road Rage X, perhaps.

The house seemed depressingly dark and still, suggestive of a funeral home. The air conditioner murmured low, sounding a bit like sad organ music, combating the heat of a Houston June. Their feet were silent on deep pile carpet, Zackary's bare – and none too clean -- Nicole's in new shoes that were stiff, unforgiving, and bought yesterday along with another moderate suit. She caught sight of herself in a closet door mirror while passing the huge master bedroom; still rather attractive at thirty-four years, certainly not a Barbie doll, but she'd never bought into the health-nazi hype that skinny was some kind of master race.

Her eyes were sky-blue, her cheekbones high, and her chin was determined and firm. Her complexion had always been clear and smooth, easily tanned with a touch of sunlight to the honey-bronze shade of a Malibu bunny; a look that Texans seemed to favor as much as the surfer-boys in L.A., though Nicole declined the blue eye-shadow. Her lips had a natural fullness and color, her lashes needed no lengthening, and her makeup was usually minimal.

Zackary's room was also immense and featured lots of free space, mostly thanks to Maria the maid, who shoveled it out three times a week, though a litter of fast-food and candy bar wrappers again defiled the floor. The shelving system was sagging with things, comics, CDs, and model airplanes, almost a hundred little aircraft, the older of many different types, the newer all fighters or death-dealing bombers. There was a fifty-inch TV, a new X-box, a million games, DVDs and assorted software, along with a massive stereo and a few old toys from Zackary's past... action-figures of muscle-bound males equipped with weapons of mass-destruction in every conceivable form.

Several were sold by her company; the Defenders Of Democracy series with "fully authentic uniforms," though ironically made in Communist China. One Defender was African, stripped to the waist in camouflage pants with a feral pattern of amber and black. Nicole had suggested a few less muscles and a more realistic physique, but had been overruled by Marketing... "Boys want masculine mass," they'd said.

There was also a Barney, an old Tonka truck, and a well-tickled Tickle-Me-Elmo, along with a maxi-size mini-fridge Zach had asked for a few months ago and kept massively stuffed with sodas and snacks from an on-line delivery service. The room's walls were defaced with gothic posters, some almost seeming satanic, while others depicted bombers in flight with savage explosions erupting below.

The cable box clock showed 7:13, sparing Nicole another semi-guilty glance at her watch as she went to the Hamster Habitat, a plastic mini-universe of pipe-like runs and transparent chambers that probably gave an illusion of freedom while keeping its occupant safely contained. There wasn't much doubt that Freddy *was* dead, a very rotund little ball of fur now sprawled beside his brimming food dish. But she opened the cage to make sure, forcing her finger to stroke, not prod, as Zack looked on with a sleepy expression. *Rigor Mortis* seemed to have passed, and the flabby furball was room temperature.

"I guess he was getting old," said Nicole, though she wondered how old was old for a hamster. Could you overfeed them like goldfish? If so that was probably cause of death, but at least he'd passed looking happy. ...Or was that *rictus sardonicus?*

"I guess," said Zack.

"I'm sorry, honey," murmured Nicole, giving her son a comforting hug and almost expecting a squeeze-toy squeak. He felt like Freddy

20

without the fur. "How do you feel about that?"

Zackary shrugged. "He *was* gettin' old. Maybe I'll get me a rat."

"...We'll... talk about it," hedged Nicole, who had never liked rodents in any disguise. Rats smelled, she had heard, but so did Zack; that bright bitter bite of young adolescence, which seemed to saturate the room. He also jacked-off constantly, and with such blatant carelessness it was hard not to catch him at it -- he never locked his door -- and she pictured Maria crossing herself when washing his seminally-soiled sheets or vacuuming the crusty carpet underneath his workstation/desk, which looked like the bridge of a slovenly star-ship... or maybe a space-going garbage scow. She had done her own version at his age, of course, but had concentrated on quality while Zack seemed to go for quantity and never seemed to have enough. The last time they'd been at a mall he'd excused himself to go to the bathroom and returned with flushed cheeks and panting a bit, and hadn't even washed his hands.

He'd obviously done it this morning, as evidenced by wet on his shorts that showed beneath his belly lobes as well as the strongly obvious scent; and it suddenly occurred to Nicole that most of what he'd done this year was eat, play games, masturbate and sleep; and boys of his age were nasty things, dirty, randy animals, who should have been housed in a backyard box with a beware of something sign, washed with a hose, fed from a dog dish, and handled with care wearing HazMat gloves.

She noted with a bit of surprise the few wispy curls under his arms, or rather sprinkling the small rolls of fat squishily squeezed where there should have been pits, though it would likely be several more years until he'd start shaving his face. She supposed she would have to read up on that rite and be ready to offer advice.

"Guess we should bury him, huh?" said Zack. "Like, before he starts to smell?"

"We might have to do it this evening, honey. I have a meeting this morning, remember?"

"They gonna give you more money?"

"I suppose it's possible. But we're not doing badly right now, are we?"

Zack reached for a half-eaten Milky Way bar on his beside table. "Guess we gots enough."

That was certainly speaking the truth: the settlement terms had been more than sufficient, mostly due to Roger's abuse -- vicious and vile but thankfully verbal, as Zack had testified in court -- and Nicole had opened a Cayman account, investing her present in Zackary's future. "We could put him in the refrigerator. Like they do in a... morgue."

"With the *food?*" Zack asked with his mouth full of chocolate.

Nicole took note of the "u" in food. Zack had asked for a "pin" last week, and after she had found him one he'd given her a baffled look and said he needed to write.

"We'd put him in something," Nicole improvised. A disposable Tupperware tub came to mind in lieu of a hamster casket. She wondered if anyone made such an item. Surely there were coffins for pets?

Zack's accent reverted to Thousand Oaks: "Mom, that's gross!"

Nicole glanced again at the fat ball of fluff and mentally wished it in hamster hell for skewing her mind from important things. "We can bury him in the flower bed. There's a shovel in the garage. But we'll have to hurry so you won't be late. You don't want to miss graduation practice." Nicole realized with a new flash of guilt she hadn't yet bought him a gift.

"I gots a box," said Zack. "The one my ol' G.I. Joe came in. I guess it's okay to touch him all dead?"

Nicole smiled, as much at Zackary's innocence as the double-syllable he'd given to "day-ed." Like most Californians she thought of herself as having no accent, regarding a drawl with amused reserve and a drawler as slightly inferior -- maybe more than slightly -- though of course she kept this under cover, dwelling here in drawler land.

She refrained from correcting his "gots," which sounded redneck and/or retarded. "I don't see why not," she said. "He's still the same Freddy, just... not all here." She glanced around the raunchy room: the big new Dell PC was on, and she chose to ignore a soft-porn site... at least they were gothic girls, so Zack wasn't drifting *that* way. ...Or, were they called Emo these days? She made a mental note to check his browsing history -- assuming he hadn't deleted it -- but, maybe like his

22

masturbation, he just wouldn't care if she knew. "I'll get breakfast started."

"Okay, mom," said Zack, licking chocolate from pudgy fingers that obviously hadn't been washed, then casually cupping and lifting a... breast... to lick a sweet smear from a nipple. He hoisted his belly to scratch underneath, revealing a pendulous puffball of fat that lolled down over his sagging shorts, and from which just the tip of his pink shaft protruded like some sort of timid something-or-other peeking out of a pouch.

Nicole sophomorically thought of cream-puffs; and though surely his member extended at least a little more when aroused, she wondered how he got a grip. She also noted his bottom had become a pair of pale moons colliding and the waistband of his shorts looked ready to rip any moment.

Leaving him to the lay out the deceased, she hurried down the shadowy hall and into the cavernous kitchen, a ranch-style room with a Spanish tile floor and a huge island range in the center. The fridge was a monstrous stainless-steel box that might have served well in a morgue with huge double doors and a rabid ice-maker she couldn't seem to control. The kitchen faced out on a vast patio through a virtual wall of thermal-pane glass, overlooking an almost olympic-sized pool with a tall water slide and a huge Jacuzzi in which a hippo might comfortably wallow. The sun, still brassy and low in the east, struck glittering sparks off the turquoise water, reflecting from rows of bright copper pans that hung above the eight-burner stove. Maria polished them every week, though Nicole had little time to cook and usually brought home take-out meals or texted Zack to order his own.

She took a "ranch breakfast" out of the freezer and slid it into the microwave. The Mr. Coffee had already started, set to her usual schedule. She poured a cup of Chock Full O' Nuts, tumblers of milk and orange juice for Zack, then switched on the wall-mounted flat-screen TV.

The face of THE FEARLESS LEADER appeared, the red-white-and-blue at his back as if in attempt to prove his allegiance to something besides a dollar sign. Raised by disillusioned hippies -- a term her mother often used -- Nicole wasn't very patriotic: a country was a concept and she hadn't asked to be born in one.

Still, she tried to keep up with the score; who the current terrorists were – according to the government -- why they threatened her way of life and had to be bombed off the face of the earth so she could have freedom and Ronald McDonald. Not to mention plenty of gas at whatever price the traffic would bear.

She tried not to think about things like that, though she understood them well enough, being in propaganda herself. She usually recognized liars and lies, but *her* terrorist threats were closer to home in the constant intrigues of the office. She daily dealt with the petty dictators who plotted and schemed to destroy what she'd built, dropping their bombs in boardrooms and lounges, booby-trapping her office PC -- or trying to give it a virus -- and setting trip-wires in her projects in hope they'd blow up in her face. Everyone mined her road to success in a savagely civilized way.

She had once made a stab at "saving the world" and had found it rather ungrateful. In fact, it had booted her square in the butt and sent her running for home. Still, no one had given her anything, and she'd given back more than her share: it was time for her slice of American pie and she wanted it creamy and sweet.

She pulled her notebook out of a pocket and typed, *pet coffins, lying lipstick, and graduation gift for Z.*

Zack wobbled in wearing baggy blue-jeans that gave a new meaning to "saggers." Their pockets were nearly down at his knees, while their cuffs dragged the floor in puddles behind him and hid everything but the toes of his sneaks. Their rather ridiculous volume -- enough overpriced denim to cover three kids -- did manage to slim his appearance a little despite all the fat hanging over in front and spilling way out on each side, or at least seemed to give it a stable base. I-Buds were plugged in his unwashed ears somewhere under his messy mop, and his feet were encased in the latest sport shoes, which seemed rather oxymoronic given the shape of his still-shirtless body. He was puffing a little – surely he hadn't done it *again* – but maybe just from the trek up the hall; though Nicole had another realization that he breathed a lot though his mouth these days, maybe due to gaining weight, which gave him a slack-jawed vacuous look… though he'd

24

always seemed an intelligent boy. Still, she remembered reading somewhere that parents were often in denial in regard to mentally-challenged children.

Zack set a small box on the counter top and raided a cupboard for Pop-Tarts.

"Er," said Nicole. "Put him out on the patio, honey."

"It's pretty hot, mom," Zack replied – which seemed an astute observation -- while locking and loading the four-slice toaster. He snagged a box of Mud & Bugs and switched the TV to Cartoon Network where villains were more comprehensible, their evil motives transparent enough for even a child to discern. "I sealed him in plastic," he added, while plopping down at the table and filling a Lion King cereal bowl.

"I hope you washed your hands."

"Sure 'cause he's day-ed.'"

Nicole wondered if he was teasing her with that ludicrous dialect... but what could have been his motive? She eyed the analog clock on a wall – though just about every kitchen appliance flaunted the hours, minutes and seconds in gaudily glowing digits -- a 1950s amber lion who twitched his tail and rolled his eyes to mark the relentless march of time... which seemed to be marching much faster these days. It had once belonged to her grandmother back in the decade of *Leave It To Beaver*. Then it had hung in her parents' kitchen, seeing Nicole through her Wonder Years from kindergarten to U.C.L.A. Her mom had been going to throw it away when it started succumbing to senior moments, but Nicole had had it cleaned and repaired... at an astronomical cost by a jeweler who thought she was missing a marble for wanting to save such a stupid old thing.

She hoped Freddy's funeral wouldn't take long: she normally left the house by eight, and the drive was at least thirty minutes... assuming no wrecks or road-rage attacks. Her meeting was scheduled for ten, which gave her a margin of safety: still she decided to cover her butt, and took out her company-furnished phone as Zackary drowned his Bugs in milk.

She got her boss's receptionist, who always seemed to be at her post with a finger firmly on company pulse. Jenny knew where the bodies were buried, yet seemed content with what she had, never back-biting or playing for power, which often puzzled people.

"Hi, Jenny," she said. "I'm having a problem... I know, it would be today. ...No, not stuck in traffic again... not yet anyhow. ...It's... a... death in the family. ...Thank you. But I'll be there in time for the meeting. I wanted to let Dwane know. ...Yes, it's sad to lose a loved-one."

She glanced at the box on the counter as Zack masticated his muddy bugs and glassily gazed at the TV screen while dribbling milk from his chins to his breasts, which lavishly lolled on the table top. She noted another Amber Alert, the third in two weeks; and though kidnapping kids was a horrible thing it was starting to seem as commonplace as terrorist threats, school massacres, and all the anti-obesity hype.

"But, we weren't very close," she added. "Thanks, Jen."

The microwave beeped, and she took out Zackary's plastic-sealed breakfast of eggs, link sausage, and hash-brown potatoes -- "Made country-fresh on the farm every morning" -- as the toaster ejaculated Tarts, and set it beside his bowl of bugs along with a fork and napkin.

"Don't forget the Eggos," said Zack.

Nicole reloaded the microwave, set out butter and a bottle of syrup – genuine maple from Vermont -- and said, "I'll go find the shovel."

Zack began intaking scrambled eggs as Nicole went into the three-car garage, her footsteps echoing hollowly across the spacious concrete floor, which was large enough for a Texas barn dance with only her Chrysler Cruiser inside. The emptiness still surprised her without Roger's Lexus and Hummer H-2, prudently flaunting American flags, though the stickers were made in China. Her car was unpatriotic, which had likely been noted by parking lot cameras.

Her yard was maintained by a weekly service -- a Mexican man, she assumed, assisted by his two chubby sons, who were capitalistically paid in cash -- and her big riding mower was shrouded in dust, along with her own garden tools. Nicole glanced down at her shiny new shoes as she picked up a cobwebby shovel. She wondered if she should change for this job, but how deep a grave did a hamster need?

She found old sneaks in a box of clothes that Roger had left... she'd been meaning to call the Salvation Army but always seemed to forget.

The garage was still fairly cool from the night, but the outside air was a sauna from hell when she opened the door to the patio, and she hoped her antiperspirant worked as well as its claims on TV. A six-foot wall of *faux* adobe defended her sprawling back yard from its neighbors, each big enough for a small soccer game, with turquoise pools and brown-skinned servants to tend yellow roses and kelly-green lawns.

Her grass was wet from the auto-sprinklers, making her grateful for changing her shoes, as wisps of steam like infant ghosts puppied around her ankles. She selected a spot in a flower bed still in shade near the wall, and found the earth was thankfully soft as her shovel clove deeply beneath Roger's sneak.

She heard a rumble of sliding glass and Zack jiggled out on the patio, bearing the box and a Pop-Tart. He started to sweat almost instantly, and reached her all shiny and twice as smelly. He'd shown an increasing reluctance to bathe, though Jenny had said that was normal, having raised three sons of her own. The gardener's boys were around his age, but seemed to possess no particular scent -- flowers and earth more than anything else -- whenever Nicole had offered them Cokes. She often felt guilty, seeing them sweating while skimming the pool and probably longing to go for a swim, but they *were* getting paid by the hour. Three shovelfuls later the grave was dug, and Zackary, plopping onto his knees, solemnly lowered the coffin. Amusingly -- or maybe not -- the box displayed an American flag.

Here lies Freddy, thought Nicole, a patriotic American rodent who gave his all for consumerism.

Zack added a bit of Pop-Tart to see Freddy through on his journey beyond.

Nicole said, "He was a nice hamster," feeling a few words were needed.

"See ya, Freddy," said Zack, and saluted.

The wireless beeped in Nicole's pocket.

"I'll do it, mom," offered Zack, as Nicole extracted the phone. Except for his toddler days at the beach, this might have been the first time in his life he'd ever used a shovel.

Dwane Barrymore's face appeared on the screen, Texas-tanned and steely-blue eyed with just the right etchings of weathered crows feet to remind everyone of the Alamo. Naturally he "ran a few cows" and threw barbecues on his "acre or so."

"Y'all havin' some trouble this mornin'?" he asked. He wouldn't have *said* "little missy," – at least not to her -- though it seemed implied.

"No problem," said Nicole, while noting the digital time on the screen. "I'm just getting ready to leave."

"Jenny told me you lost a relation. I'm sorry, Nicole. Are you all right?"

"Thank you, Dwane, but I'm fine." Nicole glanced at Zack, who panted and shoveled and shimmied all over, his raunchy sweat smogging the atmosphere. "We weren't very close."

"When's the service? I'll send some flowers."

"...Er," said Nicole. "He didn't want one."

"Well, I don't want you drivin' bereaved so I sent somebody to pick you up."

"...Oh," said Nicole, as Zackary, puffing, completed the grave. His jeans were dragging the shorts off his bottom, now soaked and al-most transparent with sweat, which had activated a seminal smell above and beyond what seemed normal these days. "I'm really all right," she insisted.

"It's already done, so you just never mind. Matter of fact, he should be there by now. We can't have you missin' this meetin'."

"...Oh," Nicole echoed, a little surprised and doing the math... an ambulance couldn't have made it that fast. Then she heard an approaching drone, and the whopping chop of propeller blades. Zack looked up, wiping sweat from his eyes, as the small silhouette of a helicopter appeared above the suburban horizon.

"Woah, mom!" he cried. "Check it out!"

"Y'all better wave," chuckled Dwane. "Them houses out there pretty much look alike. Hope you don't have any clothes on the line."

Zack was already waving, his boxers and jeans at an indecent level, though his belly concealed his well-padded privates.

"...Oh," repeated Nicole. Her mother still hung out her clothes on a line, but in this neighborhood that was likely illegal. "This is too much, you shouldn't have, Dwane."

Dwane only chuckled again. "Enjoy the ride, Nicole. Might be a lot more in your future."

What did that mean, Nicole wondered? She took hold of Zack's flabby bicep, mindful of the menacing blades as the aircraft settled itself on the lawn with the pompous grace of a fat bumblebee. **BARRYMORE** showed bright on its side, along with a gaudy American flag.

"This is so cool!" exclaimed Zack, displaying more life than he'd shown in a year. "Hey, mom, you're really important!"

Nicole kept her grip on Zackary's arm until the rotors had slowed to a stop. She admitted to feeling a *little* important, knowing the neighbors were all taking notes. No one had actually *said* anything, but it seemed to have been assumed in these parts she wouldn't be able to keep the house without a man to win her bread. Even the director at Zackary's school had tactfully mentioned "other schools with reasonable fees, whose standards were *almost* as high as their own."

Zack had been scanning the aircraft. "It's only a Eurocopter, mom. An' kinda old, but it's still cool."

Well, thought Nicole, old or not -- and that was a relative term to Zack in a world where things were obsolete by the time you got them home from the store -- this was still an impressive perk. And all because Freddy was dead. She suddenly wished him in hamster heaven with brimming food dishes of rodent delights and effortless treadmills that powered themselves.

The pilot looked like every pilot -- mostly from movies or striding through airports -- Caucasian, of course, and inspiring trust; a rather indefinite young middle-age, with closely-cropped hair and a lightly-tanned face. His eyes were concealed by shiny sunglasses, reflecting the world in bright mirror tears. He was clad in blue slacks and a spotless white shirt. His narrow knit tie, of the type pilots wore, was pinned with a tiny American flag, and his Rolex chronometer gleamed in the sun, as did his professionally pleasant smile as he opened the door

29

and stepped down.

"Miz Neale?" he asked in a southwestern voice above the idling whine of the engine, which left a kerosene scent in the air that thankfully overpowered Zack's.

"Yes," said Nicole, stepping forward as if to receive a diploma. Then she glanced down at her ratty old shoes. "I'll just be a minute.'

"Mom!" yelped Zack, breaking loose.

"You're going to be late for school," warned Nicole, restraining herself from making a grab that might have looked overprotective.

The pilot smiled at Zack... and didn't look like he thought him too fat or otherwise anything less than normal. "How far is your schoolhouse, son?"

"I dunno," said Zack, his eyes roaming over the flying machine. "The bus takes about twenty minutes."

"They have a big playin' field?"

Comprehension lit Zackary's face. "Yeah! Cool!"

"Is that all right?" asked Nicole. Maybe it was paranoid, but she wondered if she was being tested.

"Oh sure," said the pilot easily, as if he could do what he damn well pleased as free as a bird in the sky. He glanced at his watch, which had multiple dials. "We'll have you there in no time. ...Name's Ted Baxter."

"Nice to meet you, Mr. Baxter." Nicole took his hand. He smelled like soap and aftershave... so civilized compared to Zack.

"Ted."

"Ted." Nicole felt cool air flowing out of the cockpit, where Zack was raptly peering inside. It was good to see him excited again after months of virtual apathy. "I'll change my shoes and get my things. ...Come on now, Zack. Go get a shirt and your books. Hurry up."

"Okay, mom." Zackary lumbered back to the house as fast as he'd moved in his soccer days, though he had to hold onto his jeans with a hand and looked like an earthquake in flubber. Nicole hurried after him, leaving the shovel upright in the earth over Freddy's sealed-in-plastic remains.

30

THREE

The sun had grown ruddy and low in the west but the heat of the day hadn't lessened. The earth had been hard and defiant, resisting shovels and even a pick as if weary of death and accepting more children. Attacker, defenders, it made no distinction, giving no quarter to iron and steel, or the dreary labor of man and boy to return what it had nurtured.

Dakota and Nathi were muddied with dust, and even their sweat couldn't wash it away, though the earth seemed eager to drink of them, maybe accepting that as payment as they filled in the last of three small graves in the village's hillside burying-ground. The site was extensive, centuries old, and most of its mounds were ancient and weathered, telling a tale of long tenancy and lives lived out in not quite abundance but seldom with less than sufficient. The headstones were pyramid shapes, some built of rocks, others of clay, the oldest melting back into the earth like empty castles of termite cities after their empires had fallen. Most of the graves were adorned with treasures, a beloved pot, a favorite basket, a knife, a machete, a necklace. One grave boasted a radio, a first-generation transistor type. On another small mound was a toy airplane still hopefully poised to fly.

Dakota shoveled the last of the dirt and wiped tawny sweat from

31

his eyes. Then he measured the sun, which was nearing the hilltops. Neither he nor Nathi had spoken while working, and the only sounds had been their digging, their panting breaths as they'd open-ed the earth, and a few murmured curses encountering rocks. They had often paused to scan the horizon and listen for voices or engine sounds, but nothing had broken the sultry silence except the sighing of breeze through the grass. Then they would drink from a battered canteen as the earth was thirstily drinking of them. The vultures had sulkily watched their work, surrounding the site in a rustling circle and muttering curses beneath their own breaths as the young boys' bodies were covered. Even then a few had remained, eying the diggers in speculation as if it was only a matter of time.

Dakota cleared the dust from his throat, spitting brown mud between the two graves, then sloppily gulped more water, spatters running down his chest and leaving bright stripes in the dust. "It will be dark when we get there," he puffed, passing the canteen to Nathi.

Nathi drank, then splashed his face. "You need the practice of landing at night."

"I still find it scary."

"So do I. But a little fear is a healthy thing." Nathi smiled. "Some pilots are old and some are bold, but very few live to be both."

He turned to look down at the ravaged village where yesterday's children had waved at the plane while chasing its southern-bound shadow. The fires had all burned out by now, though smoke still ghosted from blackened doorways and wafted through windows like empty skull eyes.

Dakota frowned. "Even if the people return they will never rebuild on this site."

Nathi nodded sadly. "A thousand years of tenancy ended in less than an hour."

"Perhaps that's part of the General's plan?"

"Perhaps," said Nathi. "We should leave a warning. The Army may have laid mines in the crops."

Dakota scanned the hills again, while sweat trickled brightly from under his arms to channel the mud on his body and more dribbled out of his navel to water the earth of the graves. "Where do you think the people have gone?"

"Rashawn must have known there would be an attack or he wouldn't have left defenders. Maybe he did help the people escape. Took them across the border, perhaps. He has a few trucks and a Land Rover now."

Dakota looked down at the airplane, a tawny shape in the amber grass beneath the redly sinking sun. "And soon he will have a jeep, along with the engine he needs."

"Thanks in part to you," said Nathi.

Dakota hoisted his low-slipping jeans and pulled something out of a pocket. "I took one," he said, displaying a shiny aluminum tag.

Nathi sighed. "Maybe some day there will be an accounting, when the world has learned the value of life."

"He must have been brave," said Dakota, looking down at one of the mounds. "He was shot in the chest, not in the back."

"Or just boyishly bold." Nathi gathered the shovels and pick, then slung the canteen by its hand-woven strap. Dakota studied the tag for a moment, then lay it on one of the graves. He slung Nathi's rifle over a shoulder but kept his own in hand. They walked down the hill through the whispering grass, both scanning the ground for mines.

A few minutes later they reached the airplane, its wing shadows stretching out graceful and long. Far up in space those shapes had been noted, waiting for someone to correlate them with the dust of the landing a few hours before.

Dakota went to the port landing gear and peered up into the wheel well. "It's still leaking a little," he said, ignoring the oil that dripped from the engine.

"It should be all right," said Nathi, sliding the shovels and pick through the doorway. The coffin now gave off a horrible stench after baking for hours in the cargo bay. Assuming a scent could have a color, the bronze-hued reek, which had seemed rather dry, had turned a slimy and wet yellow-white.

"We'll put in the new seals tomorrow," he added, backing away and catching his breath. "I'll get the engines warmed up."

"What of the mines in the crops?"

"There's some red paint in the tool box. Leave a few warnings and hope nobody goes into the fields."

"A hungry child might."

"Speak then as a child to a child." Nathi boosted Dakota aboard by grabbing the back of his jeans. "We'll deal with the other mines ourselves. Hurry before it gets dark."

Dakota clamped finger and thumb to his nose, leaned from the doorway to suck a deep breath, then wiggled his way through the jumble of cargo. He quickly returned with a can of spray paint and trotted away to the village. He tagged the warnings on bullet-pocked walls... a disk-like shape and a menacing skull. On the disk he painted

U.S.A.

The engines were idling, spitting out smoke, as Dakota came panting back to the plane. Nathi took him under the arms and hoisted him through the doorway again. Both held their breaths as they squeezed past the coffin and crunched their way up the sloping floor. The sun was sinking behind the hills as Nathi slid into the pilot's seat and checked the various gauges.

"Tail wheel unlocked," said Dakota, plopping into the co-pilot's seat. "Cowl flaps, trail. Mix, auto-rich."

The port engine sputtered a bit as Nathi turned the plane around, the toe of his boot on the port side brake, and lined up the nose with a distant hilltop, avoiding the place where the mines were laid. He held both brakes while testing the engines and running up the pitch controls. Dakota watched the instruments, calling out pressures and RPMs, switched fuel tanks to draw from the fullest, then locked the tail wheel.

"Twenty-seven-hundred," he called above the rumble of rising power.

Nathi took his boots off the brakes. The plane surged forward, gathering speed, rocking and jolting over the ground, propellers eagerly clawing the air, engines roaring, rivets creaking, a cloud of dust fanning away from the tail. Dakota called more instrument readings, holding the throttle handles while keeping an eye on the gauges. The clatter of cargo and creaking grew louder. The doll and lion's fang

capered and danced. The ancient aircraft gained more speed, bouncing across the dusty terrain. The tail rose gently off the earth, tilting the cockpit level again. The plane rattled past the corpse of a village and finally climbed thundering into the sky.

"Gear up," called Nathi.

Dakota pulled the landing-gear lever as Nathi eased back on the steering yoke and the airplane cleared the hilltops.

"Get ready," said Nathi, banking to starboard. "The light's going fast."

Dakota centered the lever, then took one of the rifles. He set the selector to full-auto fire as Nathi circled the plane around, adjusting the flaps and coming in slow, banking gently to starboard again as Dakota took aim out the window. The rifle bucked in Dakota's hands, its butt driving deep in his shoulder. Orange muzzle flame licked out toward the earth. Smoking brass spewed from the hammering gun, bouncing off the quilted padding that lined the inside of the fuselage. One of the mines exploded below with a muffled WHUMP and a scarlet flash. Dirt and metal blasted skyward, jolting the plane in the air. Another mine burst like a flower of death, erupting more dirt and flinging up rocks, along with slashing shreds of steel designed, devised, by civilized men to razor flesh and shatter bones, to kill and maim, to cripple and blind.

A third mine exploded, and finally two more as Dakota grimly reaped a harvest. The stink of gunpowder, the reek of cordite, the smells of hot steel and bright bitter brass, filled the cockpit and burned his eyes.

They circled around for another attack and three more mines were destroyed. The eye in the sky took note of them all as if fretting over the waste. Now recognizing a definite threat in the fiery blossoms erupting below, it frantically signaled its masters.

The light was too dim for a third approach, though the sun reappeared for a lingering moment as Nathi climbed to three-thousand feet and brought the airplane back on course, north-by-northwest in the deepening dusk.

"How was that?" asked Dakota, pulling the empty clip from the gun.

35

"It should be sufficient." Nathi lowered the engines to cruising speed and their throbbing subsided a bit. "The craters will be a warning." He switched on the instrument panel lights as the sun disappeared below the horizon, but left the wing tip and tail lamps off.

Dakota reloaded the smoking gun and racked it back in its cradle. "There are two Cokes left."

"Maybe you should check the jeep, I feel it shifting around."

Dakota switched on the cargo bay lights and went back to tighten the nylon straps that held the jeep to rings in the floor. He inspected the other restless freight, including the hideous coffin, returned to the cockpit and uncapped the Cokes, handing a bottle to Nathi while plopping into the co-pilot's seat. The auto-pilot was back in control, sensing the world through its gyros, the airspeed steady at 130 knots. The nearly-full moon had not yet risen, and the sky was black velvet studded with stars. The engines sang their droning duet, the port side sputtering now and again but soon catching up to its brother. The wind rustled past with its waterfall sound, cooler now as night settled in, and the ruby lamps of the instrument panel provided the only light. Dakota trailed a hand out the window, the other fingered the charm on his chest. The coffin's reek was fainter behind the wind like an unburied ghost, masked by the smells of hydraulic oil, upholstery leather and weary sweat.

"Sometimes I wish we could stay up here."

Nathi glanced at his son, a scarlet-eyed demon with bloody red teeth. "I often wish that."

"Who started the war?"

Nathi sighed, at ease in the seat, his boots resting clear of the rudder pedals, the steering yokes making their ghostly moves. He gazed ahead at the ebony sky beyond the ruby glow of the compass. "If you mean who fired the first shot, then it's easy to blame the General. Still, he's only a puppet whose strings are pulled from far away."

Dakota drank from his bottle. "He dances for America. But, why does America help him? And what does it want from us?"

"Greed wants whatever it doesn't possess."

"But how did the General come into power?"

36

Nathi regarded the airplane's charms as they gently swung on their leather strips. "Mostly because we let him." He sipped from his Coke and considered again. "There was no violence at first. Laws were passed with no one's consent. Laws the General said would protect us, but really just gave him more power."

"And we did nothing to stop him?"

"At first the laws seemed reasonable to make us more secure. He said we needed an Army to defend ourselves from terrorists."

Dakota scowled. "Instead he brought us terror!"

The port engine sputtered again. The instrument needles quivered and twitched. Then the starboard engine faltered. The airspeed needle began to drop, along with the nervous altimeter. The auto-pilot creaked in surprise, sensing a wrongness as best it could and mindlessly trying to right it. Nathi unlocked it, taking control, while Dakota's hand went to the mixture knobs.

"Use the auxiliary tanks," said Nathi, dropping the nose to bring up speed while sacrificing altitude.

Dakota clicked the fuel level gauge, reading each of its quadruple faces. "The auxiliary tanks are almost empty."

Nathi searched the horizon ahead as both engines spit and backfired, blowing out fistfuls of yellow-orange flame that flared beneath the wings. The moon was slowly rising now, silvering the nighted land, and a huddle of hills had appeared in the distance. "It should be sufficient. We'll filter the main tanks tomorrow."

Dakota fussed with throttles and mix. The port engine steadied and roared again. Then its mate rejoined it. "Do you think they gave us bad fuel on purpose? Perhaps in league with the General?"

"I don't want to believe it," said Nathi, returning the plane to cruising speed. "You can't live your life thinking all are against you. Then you become your own enemy, suspicious, hateful, and frightened of shadows."

Dakota regarded his father. "You don't like fighting, do you?"

"A boy wants to die for a noble cause, but a man wants to live for one."

"The British said we were children. Fila said that in a history lesson."

37

"The British were giving up their empire. They had taken all they could from us, and children are an obligation. But, other lands are building new empires, and greed is never satisfied."

Nathi adjusted the trim wheel and guided the airplane in silence a while, both engines droning steadily now, sipping their untainted fuel. The moon had also gained altitude, lighting the land and the hills ahead with its softly silvery glow. "Do you want to land?"

Dakota drank the last of his Coke and tossed the bottle out the window. "I still get scared landing at night."

Nathi got up. "Take me to your scary place."

Dakota squeezed into the pilot's seat, took hold of the yoke, put his boots on the pedals, and studied the slowly approaching hills. "Should we cross-feed again?"

Nathi clicked the fuel gauge selector, reading the port and starboard tanks. "There should be enough. ...If you make it the first time."

Dakota snorted. "Please note the amused expression that didn't cross my face." He rechecked all the instruments, then eased the yoke forward a little, descending toward a gap in the hills that widened into a valley. Lights shone ahead amongst shadows of trees, pale glimmers of kerosene lamps and yellow flickers of cooking fires. The silvery sparkle of moonlit water traced the vein-like course of a stream. Dakota maintained a slow descent, aligning the nose with the stream, and flashed the landing lights once.

At the valley's far end stood the tallest of hills in this little land, a huge rounded bulk that was not quite a mountain but towered impressively under the moon. A tiny spark winked from its crest for an instant, maybe a flashlight aimed at the plane. The altimeter needle showed eight-hundred feet as the plane descended into the valley, the not-quite mountain looming ahead. Dakota peered out though the bug-spattered windscreen, his chest overlapping his hands on the yoke. "Bother, dammit! Where are the lights?"

Nathi replied, "One should not rely on lights. The world has often been dark in the past and may be again in the future."

Dakota's eyes stayed aimed ahead. "Are you taking me to *your* scary place?"

"They will have heard us," said Nathi. "The children are probably having their suppers."

Dakota's eyes flicked to the fuel gauge, then to the towering not-quite mountain, its mass now cutting off part of the sky. "I wish I was." He shot a glare over his shoulder. "I could probably smell it except for that stink!"

"All the more reason to make it the first time."

"Maybe we should switch tanks again? Bad fuel is better than none."

"You're the pilot," said Nathi.

"No, wait," said Dakota.

Below in the valley, to the left of the stream, other small sparks were flaring to life, one by one in a line.

"There are still lights in the world," said Nathi.

"Not funny," muttered Dakota, his face gleaming wet in the instrument lights while trickles ran shiny from under his arms. "Am I allowed to use ours?"

"In light of the fact we're low on fuel."

The plane was well into the valley now and below the tops of the smaller hills. The brawny bulk of the not-quite mountain seemed to be blocking escape. Dakota switched on the landing lights, their bluish beams stabbing the darkness ahead. "Auto-rich. ...Gear down." He glanced at the speed, easing back on the yoke as the landing gear lowered with thumps. Then he reached for the flap control. The stench from the coffin was mounting again as the airspeed continued to drop.

Nathi centered the landing gear lever. "Green and... No green on port."

"Not funny, dammit!"

"Please note the amused expression that didn't cross my face."

"Shit!" cried Dakota, darting his eyes to a red panel light above one that should have been green. He scanned the rapidly uprushing earth, then the looming not-quite mountain. "Maybe the light switch is stuck again?"

Nathi half rose to look out his window. "The starboard gear is down."

Dakota peered out his window. "So is the port, but did it latch?

Maybe because of the oil leak?"

"No way to tell."

Dakota's eyes narrowed. "Dammit, I'm tired and hungry! It's not the time to be testing me!"

"One is seldom able to choose the time for being tested by life," said Nathi. "But this is not one of mine. I want to be home as much as you. You can still pull up and circle around. We can raise and lower the gear again. We may hear the sound of it latching."

"It made the same sound it always makes. The lamp switch is probably stuck."

"You're the pilot."

Dakota's eyes went to the ground once more. Then to the airspeed. Then to the mountain. "To pull up and circle we'll have to switch tanks and use the bad fuel."

Nathi glanced at the fuel gauge. "Yes."

"Should I be bold?"

"A good pilot makes quick decisions. If they happen to be the right ones sometimes he lives to be old."

"What would you do?"

"Trust my pilot."

Dakota spit out the window. "I hate that bloody coffin!"

"So do I."

Dakota's hands clenched on the yoke. "Put out that light, it bothers me."

Nathi turned the lens control, dimming the lamp to a tiny red dot. "It's still there, a possible danger."

Dakota frowned. "The world is full of possible dangers, I can't waste my life being scared of them all."

FOUR

The helicopter settled to earth at the edge of the huge playing field. Nicole had been worried about the kids, who'd been staring up with open mouths when they realized the aircraft was landing, but all seemed aware of the dangerous blades and didn't approach until they had stopped.

"TV and movies," said the pilot as if he'd been reading her mind. "Kids learn a lot and they don't even know it."

He scanned the digital displays on the pulpit-like instrument panel, while Zackary noted his every move as if watching a superhero at work. Ted had seated Zack in front, crowning his mop with a pilot's headset, while Nicole had been cradled in soft luxury back in the well-padded passenger section. The leather was real, she'd found, but re-minded herself this *was* Texas. Ted had professionally made her feel welcome, pointing out seatbelt and satellite phone, the built-in bar -- also furnished with snacks -- stereo, TV, and a port for laptops.

"This is quite a command post," she'd said.

Ted had smilingly replied, "Gotta keep you VIPs in touch, the world can change a lot in a minute."

"I've noticed that," Nicole had agreed, thinking of airplanes bring-ing down buildings.

Zack had beamed at her with pride, and Nicole had passed him a Hershey bar just to prove she could.

Now back on earth, Nicole leaned forward to kiss her son, forgetting that might not be cool in front of his crowding contemporaries. But Zack seemed too happy to care, allowing Nicole to buss his cheek -- soft as down but salty with sweat -- then struggling with his safety belt beneath his wobbly sprawl of belly.

"I won't be late," said Nicole.

"It don't start till seven." Zack traded the pilot's headphones for the smaller pair of his I-pod, then paused with a hand on the door latch. "An' my party tonight with Austin an' Dillon?"

"I haven't forgotten," said Nicole, recalling her own junior-high graduation, which hadn't exactly been sober. She wasn't sure about Zackary's plans, though hers were to keep him safely contained. "I'll order the pizza before I leave work and have it delivered at ten."

"Three extra-large combos," said Zack, taking his pack with its laptop and phone, spare batteries and power converters, along with candy bars and snacks like a civilized kid's survival kit. "See ya, mom." He saluted Ted. "Thanks, Captain Baxter."

Ted returned the salute, and Zack climbed rather clumsily out, almost missing the step on the landing gear strut because he couldn't see his feet. But none of the other kids laughed, probably awed by his airborne arrival. His jeans had slipped to hazardous lows by the time his feet were on the ground, and the lobes of his belly hung blatantly bare despite his triple-X *Warcraft* shirt.

While none of the children were less than well-off, and many were much more "weller" than Zack, arriving by air was the *coup d'etat* and several young faces showed envy. Most were boys who'd been on the field, possibly sharing things to smoke that probably weren't tobacco, though a handful of girls had joined them. There were two green heads, plus a purple and blue, which the school had finally permitted this year... though painting one's face like a corpse was still "out." A soccer game had been in progress, and most of the players were shirtless in shorts. Few of the kids looked less than well-fed, and none were skinny except two girls who might have been anorexics in training. Four kids were more than a little chubby, and one of the boys was so

42

mammothly fat that, puffing and panting, his face glowing red, he still hadn't reached the landing site.

He was Austin Colt, one of Zack's BFFLs, and a savage slayer of video foes. He was kin to the famous gun-maker whose products had proudly slain millions of people, though his father owned a herd of McDonalds, which only slew billions of cows. Austin slept-over with Zack every weekend, installing himself in front of a screen -- PC, TV, or electronic carnage -- and staying immobile while eating all day, though from the passionate puffing and panting Nicole overheard while passing Zack's door he seemed to share Zack's other primary pastime.

Zack seemed to fit well in this well-off place of the more than sufficiently well-fed and wealthy, though Nicole wasn't sure what to think about that now that it came to mind. On one hand, he wouldn't be dissed for his weight, the latest American terror threat... there was Dillon Barrymore, shirtless and muscled in soccer team shorts, a boy-god of gold despite his green hair, and Zackary's other BFFL, trotting proudly to stand with Zack and bask in his airlifted status. On the other hand, what of Zackary's health? He'd seldom been sick in Nicole's memory, but he'd *really* gotten fat this year and a checkup might be wise.

She also saw with some surprise that, besides being nothing less than well-off, none of the kids were less than white. The school had been recommended by Dwane, but Nicole hadn't noticed its lack of color and wondered why she noticed it now.

"Ready, Miz Neale?" asked the pilot.

"...Oh," said Nicole, who hadn't imagined she'd be in command. "Yes. And please call me Nicole."

"Have you there in a jiffy, Nicole." Ted checked the door latch then gripped the controls. "Mighty nice boy, your son," he added, above the engine's rising whine. "Knows a few things about aircraft, too."

"He builds model airplanes."

"Built a fair number myself," said Ted. "Teaches a boy a lot of things an' keeps him out of trouble. 'Idle hands,' you know?"

"Yes," said Nicole, though thinking Zack's hands were seldom idle with keyboards, controllers, remotes, and himself.

43

She raised a hand to wave to Zack, actually feeling a little surprised when he and the other kids waved back.

"Looks like a nice bunch of kids," called Ted, as the helicopter tilted a bit and seemed to rear backward into the sky. The earth dropped out from under the skids as if the planet was spinning away, while the children shrank to colorful dots on a small patch of green in a toyland town and then just seemed to disappear.

America's future elite, thought Nicole, and doubtless mostly Republican. She settled back into buttery leather that gave off a manly aroma above the scent of hot kerosene. The latter awakened old memories of warm summer evenings in Thousand Oaks; a breeze drifting down from the grassy hilltops, charcoal lighter, tiki torches, and sizzling steaks on the backyard grill... her parents had been into love and peace, but that hadn't included beasts of the field. In fact, they owned a shop at a mall that specialized in leather goods; trousers, coats, and hand-made boots.

She tried to get her bearings by searching for landmarks below, but she wasn't very familiar with Houston even after nearly two years, and wasn't sure if that teeming freeway was where she might have been trapped right now if not for the opportune death of a rodent. She remembered this wasn't a sight seeing tour and was costing her company money. She pulled out her notebook and typed a memo: *pizza and checkup for Z.*

Then she ported her laptop, noting its time agreed with her watch. A search for pet coffins got hundreds of hits with thousands of models and styles, including caskets for rats and mice. That probably wasn't surprising in a nation that loved its pets. Fido was more than fertilizer.

Most of the stuff was from home workshops, and the quality varied widely. There were ostentatious caskets for dogs, some with crosses or Stars of David, even one with a crescent moon, while others were only rough pine boxes for budget disposal in pet potter's fields. A few were advertised as Green, which seemed to imply, recycle Rover.

She wondered about a retail chain with mass-production overseas and tasteful outlets at upscale malls. Maybe The Happy Hunting Ground? Or would that sound too predatory? Nice people buried their pets in coffins, and nice people didn't go hunting these days.

WHEN ALL GOES BRIGHT

On the other hand there was Walmart, and a lot of its customers did go hunting, though they probably dealt with their furry friends' deaths in less extravagant ways. But, people could always be taught to want things even when they didn't need them.

"Here we are."

"...Oh," said Nicole, surprised again. She peered from a window, slightly confused, not recognizing her building at first in the glittering jungle of glass and steel that seemed to be rising to meet her. She saw an obvious helipad, and also a huge American flag, which many other buildings displayed. Was it patriotic pride? Or more like chips on corporate shoulders daring somebody to knock them off?

Or, to knock them off again.

"That was fast," she added, fighting a moment of vertigo as the aircraft tilted and sank toward the roof a little faster than she would have liked.

Ted plied the controls with no more concern than a limousine driver curbing his car. "The only way to travel."

"That's for sure," agreed Nicole, thinking of all her time lost in traffic... hours, days, months of her life, wasted in getting from here to there. Like pitiful motorized lemmings.

"I know what you mean," said the pilot; and Nicole realized she had spoken her thought... like a senior moment.

Suddenly the sky went white!

A stab of terror shot down Nicole's spine! She remembered something her parents had said, being children of the Atomic Age trained to hide under their desks at school in the event of THE BIG ONE... *When all goes bright, don't look!*

But she frantically blinked and found she could see, though fireballs danced on her retinas. She braced herself for she didn't know what... bombs bursting in air, a shattering crash, the end of all life as she knew it.

But Ted apparently hadn't been bothered, his eyes defended by silver tears. He muttered something that sounded like bastard and brought the aircraft murmuring down.

Nicole saw another helicopter, smaller, sleeker, and gleaming gloss black, off to one side of the landing pad. Its windshield and

45

windows were blazing mirrors, probably silvered to keep out the sun but creating a visual hazard. It bore no company markings, and reminded Nicole of a kid's muscle car, a little self-consciously arrogant and adolescently menacing. Compared to its lean and dangerous shape her ride was a nerdy family sedan. She pictured it pulling up alongside and challenging Ted to a drag.

Ted gave it a glance of annoyance as his machine touched gently down, and Nicole decided to buy sunglasses before going corporate flying again.

She unplugged, cased, and shouldered her laptop as Ted dismounted to open her door. "Thank you," she said as he helped her down. "And for dropping off Zack."

"No problem, Miz Neale. Hope to see you again real soon."

Nicole was about to remind him of their former informality, but then considered surveillance cameras and probably microphones: people tended to let down their guard in parking lots and garages, often discussing results of meetings or planning last-minute strategies. Her suspicion seemed confirmed when she answered with, "thank you, Ted," and he gave her a wink of conspiracy from behind his inscrutable mirrors.

She gave him a quick appraisal... athletically trim with a confident stride, he might have played tennis or handball. Despite the sweltering rooftop heat, he didn't seem to be sweating as he ushered her to a small boxy structure a hundred feet from the helipad. It was an elevator shaft, topped with enclosed machinery and guarded by armored doors. One of the building's security staff, packing a pistol, a club and Mace, smiled a greeting then tapped a keypad. A few moments later the doors slid open.

"Have a nice day, Miz Neale," said Ted, who seemed to be staying on duty up here or maybe soaring away on a mission. Would he be flying her home, she wondered? But, a company car seemed more realistic.

The Barrymore Building was only ten stories, which wasn't impressive for Houston, though Nicole seldom soared above floor number nine, above which one needed a privileged key card. But, that was normal security in a nation threatened by terrorists; religious fanatics,

46

usually faceless... though their complexions were generally brown.

The guard, whose face was brown and cheerful, his name tag reading, J. Sanchez, inserted a key in a panel and tapped a button for floor number seven, sending Nicole on her way. Just for grins she punched number ten -- after all she was descending -- but wasn't surprised to be ignored, the elevator continuing down without the slightest hesitation. She supposed her defiance had been recorded.

"Habari ya asubuhl, Bibi Neale."

"...Er...?" said Nicole, as the doors slid back with a *Star Trek* sound, opening into a large, pleasant room with a lush profusion of tropical plants where there was a big impressive desk in a virtual glade of green rubber trees. As when Zack had reported Freddy was dead, the words awakened an old memory. Then she smiled. *"Habari ya asubuhl, Bibi Walker."*

Jennifer Walker was fifty-five, proudly full-figured and still quite attractive despite growing gray at her post. Her complexion was glowing ebony, enhancing the snowy-white of her smile. But, except for a necklace of red, black and green, and providing the room with its African flora, she had never shown any ethnicity.

"Hey, Jen," said Nicole. "I don't know why I remember that. It's been almost sixteen years." She wondered a moment how Jenny had known, but of course it was in her resume.

"I guess it's like riding a bike," said Jenny.

"I never thought I'd use it again so I haven't kept in practice." Nicole had a feeling of being appraised, just as she'd rated the pilot.

Then, Jenny's face showed concern. "I'm sorry about your loss, Nicole."

Nicole hesitated, but she trusted Jenny. They seemed to have clicked nearly two years ago, like one of those met-in-another-life things. Nicole flicked a glance to a small panning camera mounted discreetly high in a corner, though warning it watched with a tiny red eye. Jenny's eyebrows arched a bit. She powered up her pencil sharpener, feeding it a new Number Two as Nicole crossed the room and leaned close to the desk beneath its concealment of foliage.

"It was a hamster. Zack's."

Jenny laughed. "Oh, my god!"

"Dwane wanted to send flowers."

"No!"

"I swear. Then I couldn't tell him the truth. Not after he sent the helicopter."

Jenny, chuckling, wiped an eye. Then she pulled out the stub of a very short pencil, composing her face as the camera swung back. "Do you need any help with the arrangements?" she asked with a suitably somber expression.

"We've already taken care of that, but thanks anyway."

"Burial at sea?"

Nicole almost cracked. "Old family plot."

"How's Zack holding up?"

"He doesn't show his feelings much."

"Boys don't at that age," said Jenny. "When they're young they have womanly qualities, and usually the best of those. But then they're taught men don't express... except for mass-murders now and then." She glanced at the pictures adorning her desk, some showing three boys, others young men, in various poses at various ages.

"Well," said Nicole. "I always got the impression that Freddy..." She glanced at the camera. "Uncle Fred... really meant more to Roger than Zack. A stab at quality-time that missed, though a pit-bull would have been more his style." *Let Security figure that out.*

"Zack's graduating tonight, isn't he?"

"Yes, and his friends are sleeping over. They're having a pizza party." Nicole glanced again at the camera. "I'm sure that will help ease the sorrow."

"Only pizza?" asked Jenny.

Nicole dropped her voice. "Dillon is probably bringing beer, but it's better than all the alternatives."

"Crazy, isn't it," said Jenny. "We make it hard for kids to get beer, but they can buy drugs anywhere."

"Especially at his school." Nicole wondered if anyone actually listened... they would have to be pretty damn bored if they did. "Half those kids are on something, though some of it's probably prescribed, but, so far I guess he's just said no. ...And I still haven't bought him a gift."

48

"I'll cover that," said Jenny. "You might be in the meeting past lunch."

Nicole glanced up at the ceiling. "Nobody's said much about it, which makes me think it's important."

Jenny's eyes, like liquid obsidian, held Nicole's blue for a moment. "It could be," she said, then smiled. "But no one tells me anything. ...Nice outfit."

"Thanks," said Nicole. "But the shoes pinch a little. I should have gotten the next size up."

"Any ideas?"

"About the meeting? Not a clue."

"I meant Zack's gift."

"I don't know. He already seems to have everything."

"How about a watch?"

"Three. ...At least."

"Shoes?"

"Tons. But they go out of style every week, and I wouldn't dare buy him something like that unless he picked it out."

"Has he given you any hints?" asked Jenny. "It might be hard to believe, but boys can be subtle at times."

Nicole tried to recall conversations with Zack... intelligent talks, anyway. "Sometimes I think he'd like a..." She caught herself before saying "machine gun." And even something completely absurd like "stealth bomber" or "nuclear missile" would probably rattle Security. "A rat," she finally finished.

Jenny faced the camera. "Most of them are running the country."

Nicole laughed. "I have to think about it. They smell, don't they?" Then she almost kicked herself... why would Jenny know about rats?

"They poop their own nests," said Jenny, not seeming the least offended, "along with everyone else's."

"Zack wants to dye his hair green."

"Go Emo like Dillon?"

"I guess. But I promised him that after graduation."

Jenny scanned her pictures again. "I went through the same things with Keeja back in the days of eraser-heads. Does Zack like sports?"

"Not since he dropped out of soccer."

49

"Games?"

"Sometimes I think they're his anti-drug. Games, food, and model airplanes." She stopped before adding his other main interest. "He did say something the other day... Death Merchant, I think."

"We've come a long way since Pong, haven't we?"

"I remember Pac Man... first generation."

"It's the same with my grandsons," said Jenny. "Violence, war, and killing things. Everything we claim to abhor but teach our children by example. I can pick it up if you want? Our new game's out, too; Defenders of Democracy based on the action figures. Got a Parental Advisory so naturally all the kids want it."

"Thanks, Jen," said Nicole. "And anything else you might think of. ...Here's my Visa."

"Terrorist Threat Ten is out."

"I guess he'd like that, he's got all the others. ...Oh, and maybe a model airplane. Something with bombs and missiles."

"Consider it done. How did you like your ride?"

"It's the only way to travel. ...I guess he's married?"

"Ted? Very. White picket fence and two-point-five kids."

"The good ones always are." Nicole saw her reflection in the glass of Jenny's pictures. "Especially at my age."

"You're still a kid to me." Jenny sharpened another pencil. "He's not your type, anyway... beat the Bible and bomb the bastards. Don't get him started on terrorists or he'll probably foam."

"Oh well." Nicole glanced again at her watch. "I'd better check my mail."

"Dwane's in a breakfast meeting."

"Thanks. ...Do we have a cosmetic division?"

"Not yet." Jenny inspected her menacing Mongol and fed it to the machine again. "But we might be branching into shoes."

Nicole raised an eyebrow. "That doesn't seem very smart. There must be a million brands already. Just like jeans. Hard to be new and different. And even harder to sell."

"There was the Pet Rock," said Jenney. "And Mood Rings back in the '70s. Those were new and different."

"We studied those in Marketing. But the timing was right for happy things." Nicole considered the camera, then added, "People were sick of a war without end."

"And rats in high places pooping their nests."

The elevator softly bonged like the stewardess call in an airplane.

"Mornin', ladies."

Dwane Barrymore could have played J.R. in the 1970s *Dallas* soap; though Nicole remembered the actor more as the rather charming but slightly buffoonish master of a nubile genie and could never take him seriously as a calculating villain. Dwane's suit was, naturally, western-cut, his dagger-toed boots like mahogany mirrors. His watch, belt buckle, and silver-tipped tie were adorned with Indian thunderbirds in coral, onyx and turquoise. Of course he doffed his Stetson and bowed a bit from the waist, still rangy and lean at forty-eight years though showing the bulge of a cowboyish pot from too many Lone Stars at lunch.

"How y'all holdin' up, Nicole?"

Nicole exchanged glances with Jenny. "I'm fine, thanks, Dwane. Really. Like I said, we weren't very close."

"If there's anything I can do, just ask. ...Enjoy your ride?"

"It was very considerate, thank you."

"Didn't want you drivin' upset. Lost me a second-cousin last month. We wasn't close but I darn near cried." Dwane glanced at his watch. "Meetin' was scheduled for ten, but since I knew you were on your way I sent everybody up. ...No calls, Jenny, 'less they're impor-tant."

"Right," said Jenny.

"Oh..." Dwane drew a key card I.D. from a pocket and handed it to Nicole. She had seen a few Visitor cards, but this was brand-new and her very own. Even her company photo looked good. Jenny smil-ed significantly.

"Sorry about them things," said Dwane. "I never wanted to bother with 'em, but Security insisted after we got that government contract."

"Do I need anything?" asked Nicole. "I've got the new stats on Defenders."

"Nope," said Dwane. "Just your own capable self. But how are our soldier-boys doin' these days?"

51

"We haven't slaughtered G.I. Joe, but Mattel might be getting nervous. Of course we don't have their distribution or their advertising budget. But since we got into Walmart..."

"Them sales are thanks to you," said Dwane. "Them nifty little uniforms. You were right about boys bein' real clothes-conscious. We been sellin' an average of three new outfits for every doll off the shelf. An' that African Ally Defender of yours has been our best-seller in toys this month."

"Captain Keto was Jenny's suggestion."

"An' she's gettin' the standard bonus for productive employee ideas." Dwane smiled at Jenny. "Accordin' to the customer cards there's just as many white boys buyin' it as... well, anybody else's kids. I even gave one to Dillon, though 'course he don't play with dolls."

"Er?" said Nicole. "How do we know that?" She glanced at Jenny. "We don't ask about race on those cards."

"Research figured it out," said Dwane. "Names, addresses an' parents' jobs. Other toys, hobbies an' music." He chuckled. "If your name is Leroy Washington an' you live in ghetto-town, your daddy is a janitor, an' you don't buy nothin' but rap CDs, we're pretty sure what you are. ...Guess we better be goin' up before the natives get restless."

"How'd you come up with that uniform pattern?" asked Dwane as the elevator stopped at nine and requested its occupants prove who they were or there would be a security lock. Dwane inserted his card in a slot and punched the button for ten. "Real eye-catchin', that yellow an' black. Jumps right off the shelf at you. It's been the best sellin' outfit for all the Defenders this month, so we best get a trademark on it pronto."

Old memories awakened again. "I saw it in Africa," said Nicole, making a mental note about trademarks. "It seemed to fit Captain Keto."

"When you were in the Peace Corps?" asked Dwane. "Saw that in your file."

"Yes," said Nicole.

"An' you still speak the lingo?"

Nicole remembered Jenny's greeting and wondered again what was up. "I'm not sure anymore."

52

"Probably like ridin' a bike," said Dwane.

FIVE

Dakota's body was gleaming with sweat that glistened like blood in the instrument lamps, its muskiness masking the coffin's reek as he brought the airplane gently down, aligning its nose with the flickering sparks that beckoned to safety below. The approach appeared to be perfect, and the artificial horizon agreed, but then he tilted a wing to the left.

Nathi turned his eyes to his son as the moonlit ground came rushing up, defining itself in the landing lights as dun-colored dirt and amber grass unrolling at 70 knots. But Dakota's gaze was fixed on the fires, the line of yellow sparks ahead. His chubby hands clenched on the steering yoke, overlapped by the lolling spheres of his chest. His mouth was open, his eager teeth bright, the sunglasses riding high in his hair. Not taking his eyes off the oncoming earth, he replied to Nathi's silent question.

"Welcome to my scary place. We still may need to switch tanks."

Nathi reached for the fuel selectors.

The port wheel struck with a jarring thump, spewing dust and clumps of grass that tumbled away behind the tail. The airplane tried to roll to the left, but Dakota corrected instantly. He bumped the port side wheel again, then yanked the steering yoke back to the right, bringing the starboard wheel to earth with another thud and a billow of dust. Finally, he lined up the nose with the lights as the airplane jolted and rattled along.

"It seems to be latched," he puffed.

"Sufficiently," Nathi agreed.

The tail wheel touched with a lesser thump, and Dakota gently toed the brakes as the plane neared the last of the flickering lights that paralleled the stream. Ahead was a village of softly-lit huts with cooking fires glowing before them. Dakota brought the plane to a stop, its brakes protesting with dusty squeals, then swung it around by gunning an engine, which backfired loudly and died. Then, the other engine quit, clattering into silence.

"The last of the good fuel," said Nathi.

Dakota switched off the ignitions. "How was that?"

"Any landing you can walk away from is usually sufficient."

Both bowed their heads to the still-dancing doll as children's voices were heard outside and small figures ran to surround the plane, along with the romping shadows of dogs.

The stench of the coffin was horribly vile, flooding the cockpit with death and decay like a loathsome vapor of liquid putrescence.

"Never mind the rest," said Nathi, shutting off other switches. "We'll check things out in the morning."

The air itself seemed slimy and wet in the small glaring globes of the cargo bay lights as Dakota and Nathi, holding their noses, made their way back to throw open the doors.

A group of children and youths awaited, along with a capering pack of dogs, their teeth gleaming bright in the moonlit shadows, their eyes reflecting electric glow as it spilled in a fan from the doorway. All, from the smallest, five and six, to the tallest, no more than a few years older, were similar shades of lusterless dusk, their bushy hair adorned with bands and some decorated with feathers. Most of the younger had prominent tummies carried on gracefully sway-backed builds, and none were skinny or frail. The dogs were also sufficiently fed, of medium size and lionish tan, their loops of tails fanning a welcome.

All the children wore antelope boots, and some little else but bracelets and beads. Some older boys wore trousers or jeans, while

55

others were clad in canvas shorts, though their small-bottomed, long-bodied, narrow-hipped builds were seemingly never created for clothes. The girls were dressed in colorful skirts, though bare as the boys above the waist.

The boys had gathered around the doors, the dogs darting joyfully here and there, but the girls remained at the edge of the group. They were just as eager to greet and be greeted, but bound by ancient and sensible custom; pretending, at least, they were being protected behind the milling mob of males.

But the crowding suddenly changed to retreat as the coffin's stench burst into the night like a blast wave from an explosion of death. If smell had a sound, this sound would have roared! The younger boys scattered like leaves in the wind, unashamedly joining the girls in everything but horrified cries. Each boy was armed with an AK rifle, but smell was a terror that couldn't be fought. Only the two eldest boys stood against it... and only to rescue Dakota, who'd leaped from the doorway and almost fallen while comically losing his jeans. They grabbed Dakota and dragged him away. The dogs also bristled and fled.

"Bloody hell!" cried one of the boys, the oldest who looked like a bushy-maned god in nothing but jeans and beaded boots. He wasn't actually massive, only approaching his fifteenth year, but seemed to be made of nothing but muscle, his chest jutting starkly like small paving stones and deeply entrapping his lion's-mane charm in the shadowy cleft of its valley. His rifle was slung by its strap on a shoulder, and a heavy knife hung at his side.

The other boy made a hideous face. "What in god's name do you have in there?" He was fourteen and well-muscled, though his belly ballooned like a beachball and far overlapped his uncertain shorts so he had to lean backward to balance. His rifle was also slung by its strap, and like his companions he wore the charm. He kept hold of Dakota like something precious, gripping him under a sweat-slicked arm.

"Rashawn's coffin," panted Dakota, his jeans at his knees while he sucked fresh air. The two other boys pressed tight to him as if they were bound in a bundle of three.

The stark-muscled godlet glanced at the airplane, where Nathi was checking the landing-gear. The younger children were venturing back, all of them holding their noses. The dogs seemed less inclined to return. "It never stank like that before!"

"We were delayed," puffed Dakota. "It sat in the sun for several hours."

"It smells like several bloody weeks!"

"What happened?" asked the big-bellied boy.

Dakota sighed. "I'm tired and hungry, news can wait."

The godlet called to the children. "Put out the lights!"

The kids hurried out on the landing field to douse the line of flickering lights... food tins filled with gasoline.

"Did you get all the things?" asked the godlet.

"Everything, Thabo," Dakota replied.

"And the beer?" asked the big-bellied boy.

"Yes, Kobe."

"And cigarettes?" queried Thabo.

"Yes," said Dakota. "Now do let me breathe."

Thabo and Kobe released him.

"Are you sure you remembered it all?" prodded Thabo.

"You didn't ask for much," said Dakota. "And there was money left over." He pulled a bundle of Rands from a pocket.

Kobe's mouth dropped open. "Is all that for us?"

Thabo's jaw had also fallen. But then he frowned. "What good is that here? It's nothing but paper."

Dakota shrugged. "What else could I bring you?"

"You could have gotten more beer," said Kobe.

"You didn't ask for more beer," said Dakota. "Am I expected to read your minds... simple as they are?" He took Thabo's hand and plopped down the money.

"What can we do with this?" grumbled Thabo. "Use it to wipe our asses?"

"Put it somewhere safe," said Dakota. "I'm sure you'll find a use for it when you're in Johannesburg."

"My sisters made more boots," said Kobe.

"You don't need them now," said Dakota. "Because you have money to buy what you want."

"Anything?" asked Thabo, looking down at his money-filled hand.

"If you know when enough is sufficient."

"You keep the money for us," said Kobe, taking the bills from Thabo and holding them out to Dakota. "My sisters allow me no secrets."

"Nor does my wife," said Thabo. "She tidies worse than my mother."

"Do you keep secrets from her?" asked Dakota, not taking the bundle of money.

"Nothing of any importance, but with money I would. She would want to buy something 'useful,' like a green enamel teapot."

Kobe slowly counted the bills. "I'm sure you could buy many teapots with this."

"One will be sufficient," said Thabo.

Dakota said, "Everyone keeps their own money. If not, it causes trouble." He took the bills from Kobe's palm, divided them into equal piles and slapped a stack in both boys' hands. "There, you have money. Buy each other while I go eat."

"No, no," said Thabo, taking Dakota's arm again. "First get the things."

"Yes," said Kobe. "I'm tired of maize beer."

"More likely you drank it all," said Dakota. "But first unload that bloody coffin and take it far away."

Thabo turned to the group of kids, who were walking and chatting with Nathi while moving off toward the fire-lit village beyond the glimmering stream. "Tindo! Bilal! Malik!"

"Good," said Dakota, as three smaller boys came running back, rifles bouncing on their shoulders. "I'll go eat while you're doing that."

"Bother!" muttered Kobe.

Another voice spoke. "I brought you supper, Dakota."

All the boys turned as a girl approached. She was around Dakota's age, clad in boots and a knee-length skirt of amber, black, and leafy green. Her hair was adorned with a beaded band, and a cowrie shell bracelet encircled a wrist, but her dusky body was otherwise bare. Her breasts were proudly round and full, her midnight eyes upturned at the corners, and dimples accented her welcoming smile. She carried a wooden platter piled with juicy slices of meat, a mountain of beans, and two sweet-potatoes.

"*Salamu*, Akili," said Dakota.

"Oh, I think he will melt," Kobe cooed.

"Shut up, hyena-face!" growled Dakota.

Akili ignored the other boys' grins. "I knew you'd be hungry." She glanced at Thabo and Kobe. "But, the business of men is much more important."

"Attend to it, men," said Dakota.

"Bother!" said Thabo, then added, "Come on," shooing the smaller boys off toward the airplane, then nudging Kobe, who lingered and wistfully regarded the plate. "The sooner it's out, the sooner our things."

"And the beer," Dakota reminded, when Kobe still seemed reluctant to leave.

"I need to wash," he said to Akili, after Thabo and Kobe had gone. "I smell like a vulture's banquet."

Akili took Dakota's hand. "Let's go to the pond."

They walked around the airplane's tail, hearing muffled curses inside as the other boys battled the coffin.

The stream was only a few meters wide and less than knee-deep to a child in most places, flowing slow and quietly from a cave within the not-quite mountain, past the village and through the valley to dwindle away on the dusty plain. Its shallow banks were lined with trees, mostly scrub-oak and acacia, grown uncommonly large, while bushes, ferns, and leafy foliage spread out in the grass on each side. An earthen dam had been built long ago to guard the people from summer drought, and its pond provided a peaceful place.

Thorn bushes also cherished the water, gorging themselves to magnificent size with splendidly ferocious spikes, and these had been tempted away into hedges, protecting the village's crops. They also defended the quiet pond from all but the smallest of creatures, while wooden-slat gates with leather hinges guarded various paths.

Dakota opened such a gate and entered ahead of Akili, who followed him to the tree-shadowed pond. Patches of moonlight dappled the water, filtering down through branches and leaves. A mossy sluiceway out on the dam provided a background of liquid music, while insects chittered and clicked in the foliage. Somewhere in the surrounding hills a lion's roar trembled the air, but Akili only smiled at Dakota, waiting for him to choose the place, a moon-silvered spot by the trickling sluice. "What do you think he's roaring about?"

Dakota washed his hands in the pond. "Maybe he smelled your delicious cooking." Dakota sat down with his back to the sluice and accepted the platter, then sank his teeth into well-seasoned meat.

"Perhaps he is young?" said Akili, settling beside Dakota. "And calling for a mate?"

"Probably several mates," said Dakota, caught between ripping and chewing. "That's how it is with lions. And some people in other lands. For them it makes sense because children die."

Akili's face saddened. "Here our children kill each other."

Dakota sighed. "We buried three more today. At the village near the border. The Army attacked and burned it. Two of them were Rashawn's."

"I hate this war!" snapped Akili.

Dakota looked up at the moon. "The sky is always so peaceful and pure, but men taint the earth with hate and death. Sometimes it makes me ashamed to be one."

Akili touched Dakota's arm. "You're not like them, you're a real man. ...What of the village's people?"

"I don't know. Rashawn may have helped them."

"Is that why you were late?"

"Yes."

"You must be tired, I saw the landing."

"That was a mechanical problem. My landings are usually much better, even at night." Dakota set the platter aside and reached into a pocket. "I brought this for you from Johannesburg."

He pulled out a small piece of cloth and unwrapped a necklace of glittering beads that looked almost black in the silver moon glow. Then he dug in his pocket again, producing a little pilot's flashlight.

Akili drew a breath of surprise as the necklace burst into crimson brilliance. "How beautiful! Are they rubies?"

"I would they were, but only glass."

"Who would care?" said Akili, holding the necklace up to the light so it sparkled like drops of red wine.

Dakota smiled. "A 'civilized' girl knows the value of things."

"I only know what is beautiful. Does that make me a savage?"

"No, it makes *you* beautiful." Dakota leaned close to fasten the beads around Akili's neck, the orbs of his chest softly brushing her breasts. The feeling was mutually startling, as if an electric spark had jumped. They hesitated a moment. Then their arms went around each another. Their lips met gently, their breaths grew quicker.

"Dakota!" called Thabo's voice. "Hurry up!"

"We want our things!" Kobe's voice added.

"Bother!" muttered Dakota.

SIX

Nicole had seen many corporate boardrooms and wasn't impressed by Barrymore's. Its paneling of walnut veneer could have come from a mobile home, and its western decor of leather and wood had been tamed to a more international taste, except for a pair of Texas longhorns and an oversize painting of End Of The Trail. There was also a portrait of Seth Barrymore, who'd converted his "little ol' blacksmith shop" to manufacture railroad lanterns back in 1883. He was holding one of his products and seemed to be searching for an honest man. The company still had a Brightway division producing flashlights of various types, though now they were made in Myanmar. Of course there was Lone Star beer at the bar, but also Kirin and sake, plus vodka, scotch, rye and gin, as well as fruit juices and bottled waters.

The table could have seated twenty, but only five people were present this morning and sipping bland generic coffee supplied by a mid-range catering service. Four Nicole knew from working acquaintance and Dwane's barbecues on his ranch; a flabby and fortyish balding man, Pete McCoy from Development; a late-twenties lean and cowboyish type, Jefferson Brill from Marketing; and a pale and furtive Aaron Steele who oversaw Foreign Production.

Steele resembled Uriah Heep with reddish hair and sun-yellow eyes, the former longish, the latter alert and usually paranoiacally rolling. He set up children's sweatshops, and gave Nicole a defensive look as if she might not approve... she didn't.

There was also a fiftyish woman, Meg Tanner, who resembled Belle Star on a bad hair day and chain-smoked unfiltered Camels. Her smile was an open wound with teeth, and she jealously guarded the corporate coffers as if every cent was a pound of her flesh. "Nice job on Defenders, dearie," she rasped.

"Thank you, Meg," replied Nicole.

The fifth figure looked like a Man In Black, except he was dressed in moderate gray. His blond hair was short but not severe, his face well tanned and not from a tube, and he surely must have lifted weights, though he wasn't cartoonishly bulked. His black sunglasses seemed over-the-top, but Nicole forgave him for that. She wished she'd been wearing a pair herself so she could have checked him out on the sly. He was maybe mid-thirties and drop-dead handsome, a perfect example of Caucasian male. A more stylish suit would have made him look flashy and he seemed to have the sense to know it. Even his watch was gunmetal gray with a simple strap of black nylon webbing.

Dwane introduced him as Tom Reynolds -- "no relation to aluminum" -- a joke he clearly found lame. He rose to maybe six-feet-three in a wide-shouldered, narrow-hipped athletic wedge, and smiled at Nicole with perfect teeth that had probably never worn braces. She assumed his hidden eyes were blue. His hand was firm, neither rough nor soft, though he might have climbed mountains or done extreme sports. His watch was a twenty-four hour type, and his manly scent was neutrally nice with a slightly mysterious hint of leather.

"Tom's with the government," added Dwane. "He consults with us on our overseas work."

Nicole asked, "Like our Defenders uniforms?" ...And caught a frown from Aaron Steele.

Tom's accent was also neutral, though maybe with shadings of mid-Atlantic. "I approved that arrangement, Ms. Neale. It helps our relations with China. ...I hear you've lived in Africa. Namibia, right?"

"Only about a year. There was a revolution."

"I know," said Tom. "You were lucky to get out alive."

Nicole resisted raising an eyebrow. "Was I?"

"Yes, Ms. Neale. Other Americans weren't so lucky."

"...Oh," said Nicole. "I'm... sorry to hear that." Tom's tone of voice had been matter-of-fact, but she wondered if he was being dramatic.

"Well, that's Tom," chuckled Dwane, while pouring two cups of coffee. "Always Mr. Gloom an' Doom."

Tom's smile stayed neutral; a man possessed of confident power without any need to prove it. "It's my job to look on the dark side."

"An' he does it real good," said Dwane. "I been tempted to call him the Grim Reaper the way he's killed some of our projects. ...Oh, sorry, Nicole." He handed Nicole a steaming cup, though she would have preferred a Snapple. "Nicole lost a loved-one today."

There were appropriate murmurs.

"We weren't very close," said Nicole.

"Y'all know everyone else?" asked Dwane.

"Yes," said Nicole, nodding to all and feeling appraised. She took a chair across from Tom, where she hoped to do some appraising herself.

"All right," drawled Dwane. He took his place at the head of the table below the portrait of Seth Barrymore, who seemed to regard him doubtfully, as if his heir should have done a lot better than only ten stories and walnut veneer. Dwane nodded to Aaron Steele, who seemed to be guarding a box. "What do you think of these, Nicole?"

The box was surrendered and passed to Nicole, a Nike box that looked well-traveled. She lifted the lid, smelling leather and rubber, a rather primitive, earthy aroma. Inside was a pair of ankle-high boots, maybe U.S. size 10 or 11. Their uppers were crafted of supple suede, soft as kid but tough as buckskin. She thought of Native-American work, but they didn't have moccasin toes. The soles were made of truck tire rubber, reminding her of Mexican craft and tire-tread *sandalias*, but their upper edges were decorated with beautiful ebony cowrie shells, suggesting another culture. She thought of her parents' leather goods shop with its wide selection of imported footwear as well as American Indian boots, but she'd never seen anything quite like these. They were very nice things, she thought. They'd be perfect with jeans, out in the woods, or strolling along a seashore.

Everyone seemed to be watching her, so she inspected the boots a bit more. She had seen enough tourist-trap junk in her life -- "Indian moccasins" made in Taiwan, "Eskimo Mukluks" from Singapore -- to know these were the real deal in whatever culture they came from. Maybe Finland, or Tibet? But, they would have been made of reindeer hide... or possibly yak with the fur still on. Aleuts worked with sealskin, and cowrie shells weren't used in Peru. The stitching was heavy like sailor's twine, natural fiber instead of nylon, and seemingly waxed so it wouldn't rot. Attaching the soles had been difficult, requiring effort with an awl. A machine could have done it easily, but all the work had been done by hand. By children, she wondered?

Her eyes flicked to Aaron Steele: there were rumors he liked children very much -- especially boys in Thailand -- but that might have been back-biting envy; his expense account was legendary.

He seemed to be watching her carefully, while Tom, she noted, was looking attentive behind his Men In Black glasses. What was this all about, she wondered? Why would the U.S. Government have any interest in somebody's boots? Had they been made in a terrorist country? Surely not in Iran... though their style was rather desert boot, and their soles would offer good traction in sand.

Well, she thought, since her opinion was obviously wanted -- an opinion considered important enough to fly her in by helicopter -- she'd better get on with the show. Donning a carefully critical face, she removed her shoes and put on the boots. In the way of most primitive footwear they didn't differ from left to right, yet they welcomed her feet like long-lost friends. She rose and walked across the room. Even though too large for her, they were comfortable and surprisingly light. They had a natural kind of feel as if made by someone who understood feet and what they were intended to do. She felt as if she could run in them, though she hadn't run anywhere in years.

She noticed Tom was smiling, as if guessing her dog-and-pony show, but the five other faces -- six counting Seth's -- seemed to await a judgment call.

"They're very well made," she said, sitting down and replacing the boots with her brand-new hundred-dollar shoes, which now felt like torture devices. "Attractive in a rustic way." She examined the stitching again. "They must have been labor-intensive to make."

"Definitely," said Aaron. "I know good work when I see it."

"And unique," added Nicole. "Where did they come from?"

"I picked them up in Johannesburg," said Aaron while glancing at Dwane. "I'm always looking for original things. Even on unscheduled stopovers. But, I wasn't able to trace the source." He seemed to give Tom a look of annoyance.

"They were made in Kiwanja, Ms. Neale," said Tom.

"Is that one of the newer African countries?"

"Might be one of the oldest," said Tom. "If you could actually call it a country. We don't know much of its history prior to British colonization in 1897. Like most of the little mud-hut states, the people never learned to write, so they didn't keep any records."

Nicole found herself resenting this as classic American arrogance, but Tom's tone of voice had been neutral again, though everyone else cracked smiles. Tom's hidden eyes seemed to search her own in an almost apologetic way.

"They must have an oral tradition," she said.

"I'm sure they do," said Tom. "But that doesn't work with computers." He took a remote from the table and lit up a titanic plasma TV. A map of Africa appeared. Rising, he went to the screen, zoomed in the focus and pointed.

Nicole leaned forward and squinted a bit despite her laser surgery and 20-20 vision. "I don't see it."

Dwane, who was closer, chuckled. "Looks like somethin' a fly left behind."

"It's an old map," said Tom. "About the size of Los Angeles, though."

"How big is that?" drawled Jefferson Brill.

"Around 469 square miles."

"How big is Houston?" Dwane demanded.

"About 594. And Kiwanja is sparsely populated."

This seemed to bring several sighs of relief.

"Oughta be enough people to make a few boots." Dwane swung around in his chair to Nicole. "Supposin' we bought a bunch of these things, what do you think we could sell 'em for? I remember you sayin' your folks had a shop."

Nicole warned herself to tread with care. "That would depend on the wholesale price."

"I paid twenty dollars," said Aaron.

"That was retail?" asked Nicole.

"Yes," said Aaron testily as if admitting a shameful thing. "And I couldn't get the shop owner to tell me how much he paid."

"Y'all sweeten the pot?" asked Dwane.

"It was a black slum district. You never know what offends those people."

Dwane laughed. "Who'd get offended by money?"

"It wasn't a place to flash it," said Aaron.

Nicole studied the TV screen, buying time to make calculations. Who might wear these beautiful boots? "I'd have to do some research."

"'Course," said Dwane. "But give us some women's intuition like you did with Captain Keto."

Tom spoke: "You said they were good boots, Ms. Neale."

He was trying to help, thought Nicole. But he'd only increased the pressure on her to make a decision without enough data. "They are," she said with sudden conviction, picking one up and enjoying its feel. "But they're probably common wherever they came from... made for everyday use. With a little more trim they'd be artifacts. African souvenirs, at least. But, what we have here are someone's work or everyday boots."

"Well," said Jefferson Brill. "Lots of rich folks like poor people's stuff. We sold tons of Mexican ponchos."

Dwane nodded. "My daddy sold coonskin caps back in the 1950s, after that Davy Crockett movie."

"Anyway," Nicole went on, "I'd market them as exotic but practical. ...Maybe call them Lion Hunters. ...Just off the top of my head."

"I don't know about that," said Brill. "The animal lovers might get upset. We sure couldn't sell coonskin caps these days."

Dwane chuckled. "Guess we couldn't call 'em Jungle Bunnies."

Nicole smiled politely while others laughed, though Tom might have rolled his eyes. She tapped the boot's sole with a fingertip. "The

67

recycled rubber is environmentally friendly and that would appeal to a lot of people."

"Call 'em Tree Huggers," quipped Pete McCoy.

"But let's have some figures," said Dwane, after laughing.

Nicole had been using the time to think. "We might price them at around eighty dollars, competitive with mid-range sport shoes, and they might catch on with younger consumers. Possibly alternate teens." She wondered if Zack would wear such things: he was definitely drifting toward alternate something.

Dwane frowned. "You talkin' about that 'Emo' stuff?"

Pete, Meg Tanner and Brill looked blank, but Dwane seemed slightly annoyed. "My boy Dillon's been messin' with that, but I guess it's one of them teenage phases."

"It's a growing market," ventured Nicole.

"I'm listenin'," said Dwane.

"They'd probably wear pretty good," said Pete, who'd been inspecting the other boot. "My kids go though shoes like a hurricane in a trailer park."

"Of course," Nicole added, "the price would depend on what they cost us, plus import duties and advertising."

"Don't forget distribution," said Brill. "An' we sure couldn't sell 'em for eighty bucks if they're costin' us twenty a pair."

Aaron spoke: "I'm sure I could get them made for much less." He glanced at Tom. "In China."

"Well, yes," Nicole said carefully. "And that's a good point, Mr. Steele."

"Aaron," said Aaron, with a graciousness that sounded ironic.

"Aaron. But then we'd lose their exotic appeal."

Dwane took the boot from Pete. "Couldn't ride a horse in these things... no heels. Probably not a zebra, either." He waited for the chuckles to die, mostly from Pete and Jefferson. "But, who's gonna pay eighty bucks for Chinese copies of African boots? Like Nicole said, African sounds exotic... like a safari an' shootin' lions. Made in China just sounds cheap, even if everything is these days."

"I agree, Dwane." Pete faced Aaron. "Too bad you didn't find out where they came from and what the retailer paid."

"We know where they came from... now," said Aaron. "Thanks to Mr. Reynolds." He waited a moment for Tom to say Tom. When Tom said nothing, he added, "I wasn't sure there would be any interest. I pick up a *lot* of things in my travels. Those candle lanterns from India..."

"Right," said Dwane. "A mighty fine seller."

"Great profit margin," agreed Meg Tanner. "Even at Walmart."

"Thank you," said Aaron. "But I hadn't been going to Africa. The plane was rerouted." He frowned at Tom. "More terrorist threats. It's getting harder for Americans to travel. Everybody hates us."

Tom shrugged. "It's the price we pay for our freedom." He smiled slightly and added, "And prosperity."

Dwane held up a hand. "Now let's not get into politics, folks, this is good ol' American business here."

"Well," said Aaron. "I don't imagine the shopkeeper paid much more than five dollars a pair, considering his slum location."

"Now that's more on target," said Dwane.

Nicole asked, "Were there children's sizes?"

"There were smaller ones, yes," said Aaron.

Nicole turned to study the map. "Johannesburg is a long way from... er..."

"Kiwanja," said Tom, who'd been standing with arms crossed over his chest in a classic action-figure stance.

And he would have made a cool action-figure, stripped to the waist in camouflage pants, a sight Nicole would have liked to see. He was probably bored, she decided; a man of action surrounded by sloths... and maybe that included herself. "Thank you, Mr. Reynolds."

"Tom."

"Tom. ...It's a long way from Johannesburg. And I don't see any roads."

"None that show on this old map."

"Aren't there government satellite photos?"

"We don't watch that part of the world," said Tom. "It's basically still in the stone-age, and they can't throw spears across the ocean so they aren't a potential threat." He turned to the map again. "The British built a rail line from what used to be Rhodesia... Kiwanja had

69

some coal reserves. But the trains aren't reliable anymore and the roads all flood in the rainy season." He seemed to pause significantly. "Which will probably start in a week or so."

"They must have an airport," said Aaron.

"Dirt," said Tom. "And a lake when it rains. In the capital city... the *only* city. But it's hardly even a town. Used to be called Victoria's Hope. Should have been called Victoria's Secret."

There were chuckles from all.

"It's called N'dila now," said Tom, "in honor of the President."

He clicked the remote to show a photo; an incredibly fat and dusky-black man who was stuffed in a camouflage uniform that must have been specially made. Its mottled colors of sand-and-tan were familiar to most Americans thanks to the war in Iraq. He was probably in his early thirties, but looked like a fat kid playing soldier.

"He looks more like a general," said Nicole.

"Good observation: President-General N'dila," said Tom.

Nicole smiled. "Or Baby Doc in his younger days."

Everyone looked confused except Tom. "I thought so, too, when I saw his picture, but we believe his intentions are good."

"Not like ol' what's-his-name?" asked Dwane. "The one who ate his own people."

"Idi Amin," said Tom. "And that was never proven, though he killed 400,000 of them."

"Population control?" said Dwane, drawing some rather nervous looks, though Tom's expression stayed neutral.

"Opposition control." Tom clicked the remote and a wide view appeared of a dirt-streeted town. It looked like a set from an old western movie, partly Dodge City and part Mexico, yet somehow foreign to both. There were a few wooden buildings, sadly weathered and crying for paint, but most appeared to be plastered brick, and rusty tin roofs were the norm. Tumbleweeds would have completed the picture, along with horses hitched to posts, but a cargo truck was parked in the street; obviously an Army truck and painted desert camouflage.

"Population about three-hundred... no census, of course," Tom continued. "No scheduled flights from the airport. Small-time freight and bush pilots mostly. ...Might be how those boots got to Johannesburg."

"Sounds like the ass-end of nowhere," said Dwane. "Beg pardon, ladies."

"I take it Kiwanja is poor?" asked Aaron.

"By our standards, destitute." Tom glanced at Nicole. "Like an African Haiti. No exploitable resources. ...There *was* some coal, but barely enough for the railroad, and it's still dug by hand. Subsistence farming... yams, corn, African stuff. Cattle, goats, and chickens. Supplemented by hunting and fishing. Not the kind of population a government can tax, which keeps a country poor." He seemed to consider, then added, "We've been sending some aid."

"Tourism?" asked Pete McCoy.

"You've just seen the capital city," said Tom. "I think there's one hotel, and I doubt if it's a five-star. No rivers or lakes of any size." He glanced at Nicole again. "Except when it rains. Land mostly flat and semi-arid. Animal life pretty ordinary, at least for that part of the world. Even their lions are small. No phones, except in the 'city,' and I doubt if they work half the time. No paved roads. Hardly any transportation. A few old British trucks and cars."

"No industry at all?" asked Aaron.

"They seem to make beautiful boots," said Nicole.

Everyone laughed, but Nicole went on, "What I meant was, if someone makes something this well, they can usually make other nice things."

"Good point," said Meg.

Nicole turned to Tom. "What kind of aid are we sending?"

Again Tom seemed to consider. "At the moment it's mostly military."

"Are they having a revolution?"

Everyone looked surprised except Tom. "Just normal internal affairs, Ms. Neale. Policing their little country. We're mostly giving them trucks and fuel so their Army can get around." He looked at Dwane. "And uniforms made by your clothing division... I wasn't supposed to tell you that."

Pete McCoy looked thoughtful. "Are they pygmies?"

"Pygmies?" asked Dwane.

Pete consulted his laptop. "Most of those uniforms are small."

"But they cost just as much to make," added Meg.

Tom shrugged. "Guess they are small by American standards. Environment tends to shape a people... natural selection. Small people don't need a lot of food."

Nicole asked, "What *about* the people? Small or not, don't they need anything besides trucks, fuel, and army supplies?"

Tom shrugged again. "They haven't asked for anything else. They could probably use more productive crops, and we've sent them a few tons of seeds, but they don't seem to have any problems with food."

"I'd guess not," said Jefferson Brill. "After seeing the President. He's sure as hell no pygmy."

Even flabby Pete laughed, but he looked anorexic compared to the General.

Nicole said, "It's fairly common in Africa for a chief or elder to be fat. If a leader is wise and his village prospers the people reward him with shares of their crops. And/or cattle or goats."

"Then he must be a helluva leader," laughed Brill.

"Here they just take our money," said Dwane. "An' whether we like 'em or not."

"True," said Tom. "But they never had an Army before, and that's expensive for any country."

Nicole didn't want to press the point, but asked anyway, "Why do they need an Army now?"

"They never had a government. At least in the way we know it." Tom clicked the TV back to the map. "Consider the size of the country, Ms. Neale..."

"Nicole."

"Nicole. ...Scattered villages, each with its chief, and all apparently lived in peace. More like a feudal system, though there never seems to have been a king to centralize a government."

Nicole felt like asking, *So, why a general?* But this was a business meeting.

"Is the government stable?" asked Aaron.

"We intend to keep it that way," said Tom.

Dwane asked, "So, what's your advice on this one, Tom? Should we go an' set up a boot factory?"

"It would help our relations," said Tom. "Give them something to export, and open up a new market."

"Pretty small market," said Pete McCoy, squinting at the map. "Even if they're not pygmies."

"Every little bit helps," said Tom, drawing several chuckles.

"What about power?" asked Brill. "They can't play games or watch TV unless they've got electricity."

Dwane winked at Nicole. "They could always play with Captain Ketos."

Tom said. "The British built a plant for the town. ...In 1917. But you'd probably want your own generators."

"Costly," said Meg.

"'Specially with air-conditioning," said Pete.

"Those people are used to heat," said Aaron.

"I'm sure Uncle Sam would help," said Tom.

"What about shipping?" asked Brill. "If they don't have a decent airport and their railroad isn't dependable...?"

"We're planning to help them improve the airport. And probably the railroad. But not until after the rainy season." Tom looked at Nicole. "I'm sure you know what those rains are like?"

"Yes," said Nicole, though wondering why he'd asked. "Everything comes to a stop for months."

"Any other incentives?" asked Dwane. "Like a break on import taxes?"

"I'm sure we can work something out," said Tom.

Dwane faced Nicole. "Y'all think you could sell them boots?"

Everyone's eyes had turned to her. Aaron Steele's looked predatory. Of course, she couldn't see Tom's... but had he nodded encouragingly? Nicole still held the boot in her hand; it just felt good somehow. "I'd like to give it a try."

"Glad to hear it," said Dwane. "How soon can you leave for Kwanzaa?"

"Kiwanja," said Tom.

"...Er?" said Nicole, and Aaron looked as stunned as she felt. "You'd

73

want me to set up production?"

Dwane waved a hand. "That would be jumpin' the gun, Nicole. All we got here is one pair of boots, which could have been made by an ol' shoemaker all by himself in a little mud hut." He looked around the table. "I think it'd be wise to scout things out, an' our Miz Neale speaks the lingo."

"I've never had any problems," said Aaron in a tone somewhere between servile and snappish.

"Aaron, you've done a fine job," said Dwane. "An' nobody's tryin' to steal your thunder. But I think we should see if the natives are friendly before sittin' down to palaver."

Tom nodded. "I agree with Mr. Barrymore. We know very little about Kiwanja, and we've made a few screw-ups in foreign relations that started with misunderstandings." He faced Nicole. "You've read *The Ugly American?*"

"Back in college." Nicole thought for a moment. "Ignorant, arrogant American Imperialism. Complete disregard for another culture." She glanced around at questioning faces. "It was written in the 1950s. About how America makes itself hated."

Tom nodded again. "We haven't gotten prettier since then." He took off his glasses, revealing blue eyes. "There are some people in government who want to change that image. Dwane and I talked it over at breakfast. We think it would be a good idea if someone like Nicole, someone familiar with African culture, would go in and... well... see if the natives *are* friendly."

Dwane laughed. "Just don't end up in a stew pot."

Tom looked pained. "At least you'd know if those boots were made by more than one little old shoemaker. And, speaking for the government, we'd really like to make a new friend."

Nicole smiled. "Are you sure you work for *our* government?" This drew chuckles from all except Aaron.

"But," asked Aaron silkily. "Does Ms. Neale have the experience? I've been doing this kind of thing for years."

"We've checked her background." Tom's eyes held Nicole's for a moment. "You did a good job in the Peace Corps."

"Thank you," said Nicole.

"Yes, but..." Aaron began.

"We check *everyone's* background," said Tom, smiling very brightly at Steele.

"Of course," said Aaron, coloring slightly.

"An' besides," added Dwane. "She won't be settin' up production, just lookin' around for the source of them boots an' gettin' a feel for the place. For all we know those people are lazy an' might not even want to work. They had their country all this time an' never did nothin' productive with it." He turned to Nicole. "So, what do you think?"

"It... sounds interesting," said Nicole. "But, there's my son..."

"He's graduating eighth grade?" asked Tom.

"Right along with my boy," said Dwane.

"Congratulations to both of you."

"Thanks," said Dwane. "Tough school, too... book-learnin', I mean."

"Thank you," echoed Nicole. "But there's summer vacation..."

"Couldn't he could stay with his grandfolks?" asked Dwane. "Out in California? 'Course we'd pay for his flight. An' you'd only be gone..." He glanced at Tom. "What? About a week or so?"

"Probably," said Tom. "It is a tiny country. And Nicole could hire a bush pilot if she wanted to visit a village."

"Get receipts," said Meg.

Nicole's mind was suddenly flooded with things, none of which she'd anticipated. "It's just... unexpected."

"Sorry about that, Nicole," said Dwane. "We been keepin' them boots undercover till we got us a chance for a pow-wow."

"There'll be cheap copies, of course," said Nicole. "The minute they hit the shelves."

"Always are," said Dwane. "Just like our Defender dolls. But, like you said, if people can make somethin' good like them boots, they can make other things, too. Once we set up a factory, them people will realize they need us." He smiled at Tom. "An' America, too." He took a sip of coffee. "Sleep on it tonight, Nicole. ...Matter of fact, take the afternoon off an' spend some time with... er..."

"Zack."

"I like that name, it's down to earth. Got me a cousin named Zack

75

somewhere. ...Or he mighta been the one who died. But graduation's important. Dillon's makin' the speech, you know? Top of his class this year in spite of all that 'Emo' crap."

"Zack told me. Congratulations."

"I was gonna throw him a party, but he wanted to bunk with your boy tonight, so we're havin' a barbecue this Sunday." Dwane looked around the table again. "Hope y'all can be there. ...Nicole, let me know what you think tomorrow, an' if you're willin' we'll set up your trip."

Tom gave Nicole another smile. "Sounds like good advice to me."

"An' there's no rush," added Dwane, "so don't go feelin' pressured."

"Just the rainy season," said Tom.

SEVEN

The children surrounded Nathi like a cheerfully chattering escort of youth. A boy carried Nathi's flight bag, an artful object of antelope leather, while the dogs romped about escorting them all as they crossed a foot-bridge over the stream and entered the moonlit village. Cooking fires were flickering low, but scents of suppers still flavored the air.

The village consisted of twenty-three huts built of mud brick and crafted to last. All were protected by coats of pale plaster that seemed to glow in the silvery light. Once, their roofs had been thatched, but this had been replaced by tin, the older now rusted to ruddy earth tones, the newer fading to pearly gray. Fans of candle or kerosene light spilled across their little front yards from open doorways and un-shuttered windows. Acacia trees shadowed most of the dwellings, and these, like others that lined the stream, had grown uncommonly large. There wasn't an actual street, but a wide path led toward the largest hut, which naturally belonged to the chief. It stood favorably close to a bend in the stream where the tallest of trees kept it cool in summer and shielded its roof from winter rain. Most of the yards had chicken coops, along with sheds and shelters where goats and pigs were kept. Of course, the chief's were the finest, his sheds as large as family homes, his garden spread along the stream and first to get the water.

Women called greetings from doorways, while men, mostly grandfathers, asked for news, they, along with their wives and daughters, hoping to hear of husbands and sons. But Nathi had nothing to tell them.

His own hut was recently built... at least in terms of time for this land. Its yard was cluttered with boxes and crates, barrels of engine and hydraulic oil, and salvaged parts from other airplanes; a dismantled motor, a landing-gear strut, propeller blades and several tires.

Reclaiming his bag and thanking its bearer, Nathi bid the children goodnight then lifted the plank door's latch and went in. Taking a match from a box on a shelf, he lighted a kerosene lamp. The hut was one room with a smooth dirt floor and two small windows, and its white plaster walls reflected the glow as the lamp took flame from the match. In the center of the space was a wooden table and two village-made chairs. A pair of iron-framed cots with blankets stood against the far wall, and a battered British Army locker held a few clothes and personal things. A dry-sink and counter lay to the right, along with a boxy sheet-iron stove that stood spider-like on long slender legs. On various shelves around the room were piles of smaller aircraft parts, instruments, switches and flight controls, including a dismantled autopilot and intricate bits of a gyro-compass. The walls were adorned with airplane pictures, mostly cut from magazines and showing C-47s in flight.

The air was warm from the heat of day, and Nathi left the door ajar. He set the lamp on the table and tossed his bag on one of the cots, then filled the sink from a galvanized bucket and splashed his face and sweaty chest to wash off the stench of the coffin.

"*Salamu*," called a voice from the doorway.

Nathi turned to a girl of eleven, one of Akili's sisters. She wore a skirt of greens and golds, her budding breasts bare in the soft lamplight.

"*Salamu*, Nafia," Nathi replied.

"Father asks if you will join him for supper?"

"Of course," said Nathi dutifully in a tone of polite resignation. "Please tell him I'll be right along."

The girl smiled and left.

"Bother," murmured Nathi, then stripped himself naked and thoroughly washed, leaving the water a dark coffee shade.

A boy of ten strode into the room, quiet as cats in his antelope boots. He was clad in tan shorts so tightly outgrown they were more of a decoration than clothes. Although he was packing a prominent tummy, the AK rifle slung on his shoulder gave him a dangerous look. Diskman headphones were clamped to his ears, the player itself like a yellow breastplate defending his tight little chest. "*Salamu*, Nathi. Do you have any batteries? Type AA?"

"Yes, Abu." Nathi rummaged about in his bag and handed the boy a battery pack. "Are you on the hilltop tonight?"

"I was," said Abu. He replaced the cells in the player as if he was arming a mine... the shapes were disturbingly similar. "I flashed the signal when you came in. Damu is on watch until midnight when Tindo will take his place." He snapped the battery cover shut and tossed the dead ones out the door. "Rashawn was here today," he added. "He left angry, I think."

Nathi put on a clean pair of trousers and sat on a cot to don his boots. "He probably thought we'd be back earlier."

"Yes," said Abu, coming to stand before Nathi. "He wanted his jeep and the coffin. But, I think he wanted the older boys, too, and *Jumbe* Chane refused."

A woman's voice said, "Rashawn has our men, he doesn't need you." A graceful shadow appeared in the doorway, a bare-breasted, beautiful woman of twenty with skin like obsidian velvet. She wore a skirt of greens and golds, a necklace of ebony cowrie shells, and color-fully beaded antelope boots.

"*Salamu*, Fila," said Nathi.

"*Salamu*, Nathi. How was your flight?"

"...Uneventful. Please come in."

Fila crossed the room to the cot. "You must be hungry. I cooked quite a bit..."

"Thank you, Fila," said Nathi. "But I've been asked to *Jumbe* Chane's."

"...Oh." Fila turned to Abu. "If you went with Rashawn you would

79

learn only war."

"But I have to learn war," said Abu.

Fila faced Nathi. "There is no money for books and paper. The General refuses to fund village schools. His soldiers learn nothing except how to kill."

"War is manly," said Abu.

"War is childish!" snapped Fila.

"Do you think I'm a man, Abu?" asked Nathi.

Abu looked surprised. "Of course."

"*I* tell you war is a childish thing, even when it's necessary."

"I don't understand," said Abu.

"You will when you're a man," said Nathi. "I mean no disrespect, and I know you're very brave, but in the eyes of the Lion Of Life you're still but a boy with a gun."

Abu bowed hs head. "That is true."

Nathi took note pads out of his bag, along with a box of pencils.

"Thank you," said Fila, accepting the things.

"Make a list of what else you need."

"I can still teach from the radio, but..."

"I'll get batteries, too," said Nathi.

"Thank you again. ...Perhaps supper tomorrow?"

"We have to deliver some freight to the town as soon as Rashawn's supplies are unloaded."

"Oh," said Fila. "*Lala salama*, Nathi."

"*Lala salama*, Fila."

Abu remarked after Fila left, "She is quite pretty, don't you think?"

Nathi ruffled Abu's bushy hair. "Even for a teacher?"

"Some of her lessons are quite difficult."

"What comes too easy is not valued much."

"But, what use is knowledge of numbers and books if I may be killed in this war?"

Nathi gripped Abu's shoulders. "Real men think of the future, and the future of their children. And boys become men by thinking like men."

"Perhaps I will fly like you and Dakota?"

"With knowledge of numbers and books, you may."

"Fila should marry, you know."

Nathi smiled. "I would not tell her that if I were you."

"It seems a manly kind of thought." Abu put his hands on Nathi's shoulders.

Nathi nodded solemnly. "Thank you for sharing it with me."

"Inaya's father was killed yesterday while capturing an Army truck. And Shani's older brother was wounded. ...He, too, later died. Rashawn brought them back. We buried them before sunset."

"I'm sorry," said Nathi.

"I haven't heard from my father in weeks."

Nathi drew the boy close. "I wish I had news of him for you."

"This is sufficient," said Abu, pressing his face to Nathi's shoulder. "My mother hugs me but it's not the same."

EIGHT

"*Wakati gani ndege ijayo yaenda Kiwanja?*" asked Jenny.

This time it took a only moment before Nicole understood... maybe it *was* like riding a bike? "When's the next plane to Kiwanja?" she said, stepping out of the elevator. "I might be asking that question a lot from what I just heard of the place. ...Or maybe when's the next plane *out?*" Then she raised an eyebrow. "I didn't know you spoke Swahili."

Jenny smiled. "It was ethnic back in my day. Black Power and the Panthers, revolution and *Roots*. When we thought we were finally going somewhere. When our kids weren't idolizing thugs and killing each other for Walmart rags."

"You should be going, not me," said Nicole.

"I'm too old for safaris, Nicole. Adventures like that don't seem very thrilling when you've got elderly aches and pains."

"You, 'elderly,' I don't think so."

"It's not the years, it's the miles," said Jenny. "And sometimes I feel like I've walked a million."

"Did you get where you wanted to go?"

Jenny regarded her leafy glade. "Close enough for this life, I guess. Ask me again the next time around. ...Should I start planning your trip?" She indicated her monitor. "Lots of flights to Johannesburg, but nobody seems to go to Kiwanja; it's like the place doesn't exist."

"I know," said Nicole. "I just saw a map and it looks not quite there. ...Wouldn't somewhere in Zimbabwe be closer? ...Assuming I wanted to go."

"I don't think you'd want to go there now. Americans aren't very popular."

"I don't think we're popular anywhere."

"It's the price we pay for our way of life at everyone else's expense. It might be hard to believe, but ninety percent of the world's people have never ridden in a private car, or even made a phone call."

"I believe it," said Nicole. "I guess I've just forgotten I did."

"I thought you might want to visit the shop where Aaron bought those boots. Maybe find out how the storekeeper got them. Could save you some time in the bush."

"...That might be a good idea."

Jenny tapped keys like machine-gun fire. "I found a flight to Maun, Botswana from Johannesburg. Then another from Maun to Selinda. ...I've heard it's very pretty there. At the head of a delta, the Selinda Spillway. The lions hunt hippos."

"Must be big lions." Nicole crossed the room through its jungle of plants. Ducking under a palm tree, she peered at Jenny's monitor, which displayed an African map. "I don't see Kiwanja."

Jenny pointed to a dot, hardly more than a pixel or two. "This is best I could Google, and it's still listed here as a British Possession, though it was granted independence after World War One."

"Can I borrow a pencil?" asked Nicole.

"I'll get you a new one." Jenny engaged her sharpener.

"I'm not sure about this," said Nicole, as the sharpener ground away.

"Opportunity knocks once, then it catches the next plane out."

"You're making it sound like a career decision."

Jenny looked thoughtful. "There are hundreds of people in this building, but only one woman so far, Meg Tanner, can get on Floor Ten whenever she wants. I still have to use a visitor card and I've been here twenty-two years."

Nicole glanced up. "The good old glass ceiling?"

"Isn't Dwane a good ol' boy? And he's raising his son in the same tradition."

"That's hard to believe with Dillon's green hair."

"It's not what's on top of somebody's head but what goes on inside that matters."

A boy's action-figure stood near the screen, stripped to the waist in camouflage pants in a pattern of amber, black and gold. The colors went well with his dusky skin and gave him a sort of lionish look enhanced by his bushy mane. Jenny regarded the muscled man-toy. "You got Captain Keto out on the shelves. That was pretty significant, and rattled a lot of cages here."

"And hung a sword over my head?"

"Until our little man made money."

"He's still got too many muscles."

Jenny laughed. "Boys will be boys, they like manly toys. Missiles look like penises, tanks are always erect, guns and cannons ejaculate. When it comes to 'mine is bigger than yours,' some boys never grow up." She examined the needle-like pencil but found it not quite to her liking. The sharpener ground away again. "It's Zack, right? He's why you don't want to go?"

"Mostly." Nicole fingered a tree leaf. "Mud huts and yams don't bother me; I had almost a year of both. Plus a taste of a revolution. And I was lucky to get out alive." She glanced at the ceiling. "Or so I was told. But Zack has been... well... maybe feeling deserted. Feeling confused, I'm sure. First the move here, then the divorce. And now he's alone so much at home. I'm almost sure he's not doing drugs, but he's not really doing anything."

"Most kids get confused at his age," said Jenny.

"You mean about sex? Hence all the penile symbols for boys? Rockets, missiles, things that shoot?"

Jenny smiled. "That might be a little too Freudian. But, kids don't have many role models now, and boys are the most confused. Look at all the white ones who idolize black thugs... a 'man' is a brutal ignorant monkey who takes what he wants and shits on the rest." She picked up the muscular doll. "All the good cowboys done rode out of town,

84

and Superman died a long time ago... the real one, anyway."

"Along with truth and justice."

"Which leaves us with The American Way."

Nicole studied Jenny's photographs. "Did your sons have any problems?"

"Lots." Jenny returned the doll to its place beside the monitor. "Keeja played thugger games for a while. Even joined a gang for a week. Took me six months to get that off his back, and I had to buy a shotgun. Jamar wanted to play pro basketball, even though he wasn't that good. And Bilal tried being a 'player' in his junior year of high school. Bitch became his favorite word until I went upside his head."

"Any problems with drugs?" asked Nicole.

"I'm sure they all experimented, but I used to tell them that smoking weed was the perfect pacifier for slaves. It lets you accept your slavery." Jenny smiled. "And, except for giving us reggae and dreadlocks, what have the Rastafari accomplished."

"What are your sons doing now?"

"Bilal is a cruise ship officer. Jamar's an attorney... civil rights. And Keeja's a pediatrician."

"Congratulations. ...Could I schedule Zack for a checkup?"

"Consider it done." Jenny smiled. "And he's not a BMI biblebeater."

"That's good to hear. Zack's always been healthy, just... overweight."

"Depends on who does the defining of what weight there is to be over."

Nicole sighed. "I don't think Zack has any clue about what he wants to be."

"What did you want to be at his age?"

"Raising a herd of My Little Ponies."

"I'd say you did all right."

"Thanks. But, I have to talk this over with Zack."

"Why don't you take him with you?"

"To Africa?"

"It could give him a new perspective. Let him see how *most* people live, not just the lucky five percent. I'm sure you haven't forgotten."

85

Nicole remembered how Zack had looked panting and sweating with shovel in hand while digging a grave for a hamster. She also recalled a glimpse of him while passing his room a week ago, its door left carelessly half open, sprawling naked on his bed, a hand buried under his belly blubber, the other fondling his breasts, and a desperately lustful look on his face as, wobbling and quivering like an earthquake in Jell-O, he made savage love to himself. She'd supposed it was perfectly normal for a boy with nothing else to love. "That would cost the company money."

Jenny wasted another new pencil. "You're in a strong position, Nicole. I know for a fact Tom wants you to go, and he packs a lot of power."

"I noticed that," said Nicole. "Who is he anyhow?"

"Nobody knows," said Jenny. "And with his kind of power nobody asks. He doesn't show up on any web searches, and I'm pretty good at background checks."

"Zack doesn't have a passport."

"I'm sure Tom could take care of that."

"...Well... I still have to see what Zack thinks."

"I got his gifts and a card," said Jenny. "Including a model stealth bomber. They're all wrapped up on your desk."

"Thanks, Jen, that was sweet. I could have done it myself, though, Dwane gave me the afternoon off." Nicole glanced at her watch. "That was fast."

"Friends in low places."

For a moment Nicole was eighteen again, feeling the challenge of saving the world. ...Reality-check, she told herself: what was she actually doing? Or at least considering? Furthering her own career? Making more money she didn't need while fattening her company's profits? And all because of a pair of boots, probably made by a hungry child in a dirt-poor country she'd never heard of.

"At least I can spend some time with Zack before his graduation. Take him to the mall after school, then out to dinner somewhere. ...If I can figure out how to get home."

"I'm sure there's a car and a driver," said Jenny. "If not, I'll bump somebody and they can walk to lunch for a change."

Nicole laughed. "Like that joke about Las Vegas... people arriving in private jets but leaving town in Greyhound busses."

"Ted had to fly Aaron to the airport... another trip to Thailand... but if you want to wait a while I'll have him fly you home."

"I should have been afraid of you."

"The good have nothing to fear from me."

The elevator bonged and Tom stepped out. He hadn't re-donned his sunglasses and looked less mysterious without them. "Can I give you a ride anywhere, Nicole?"

Nicole hesitated a second, but mysteries had always intrigued her, and Tom wasn't wearing a ring. "...If it's not too much trouble..."

Tom tipped an invisible Stetson. "Mighty glad to oblige, ma'am."

A few minutes later, with Zackary's gifts in a plastic bag, Nicole boarded the elevator with Tom. To her surprise he tapped the Roof button.

The air was like a dragon's breath as the armored doors rumbled open. Nicole squinted her eyes in the savage glare from the towering castles of glass all around. Tom put on his glasses and escorted her to the black helicopter. She supposed she might have guessed it was his; he seemed like a man whose battles in life were a lot more important than traffic. She found herself feeling awed once more by this privileged world above the earth where people came and went as they pleased with no speed limits or metering lights, and no time lost in a plodding commute with proletarian groundlings. She remembered an ancient sci-fi book predicting a flying future for all, when everyone's family would be like *The Jetsons*. It seemed as if that future had come, but only for a few.

Tom opened a door and heat poured out, no different from a car in the sun and smelling about as familiar... upholstery fabric, metal and plastic; a kid's muscle-car in a Burger King lot. As she'd already noted, the helicopter displayed no markings, but there was a sticker on one of its windows: **Area 51 Parking Permit**. It showed a smiling alien of the Little Gray variety... which Nicole assumed was a joke.

"Give me a minute," said Tom. "I'll get the air-conditioner going." He shed his jacket, revealing a handsomely well-muscled shape in a form-fitting cream-colored shirt, though jarring Nicole when she saw

87

the gun... a sizable black automatic in a shoulder holster. She supposed it shouldn't have shocked her; *his* terrorist threats were probably real. And it explained his slight hint of leather.

She noted his underarms were wet, though his scent was cleanly male. That seemed to make him more human somehow; at least he wasn't immune to heat. She glanced at the rotor blades overhead, which seemed to be drooping uncomfortably close.

"Am I all right here?" she asked.

"I think so," said Tom, though sounding uncertain while climbing into the cockpit and seating himself behind the controls. He regarded the console and scratched his head. "I know I have to push something, but what? ...Let's try this one and see what happens."

There was a whine like starting a car, but steadily rising in volume and pitch as the rotors began to revolve, lifting and straightening as they did. The scent of burning kerosene rose above the city smells, and a wavering haze billowed back near the tail.

A few minutes later Tom helped her aboard, up front with him in a sleek cockpit that hinted of fast foreign cars. There were seats for three in the rear, one occupied by a small travel case. The instrumentation was alien, seemingly hundreds of switches and dials, knobs, buttons, and flashing displays like one of Zack's video games, but the air-conditioning was down-to-earth and furiously efficient. Tom helped her unscramble the seat belt, then fitted her with a light headset like Zack had worn that morning.

"Gets a little noisy," said Tom, as the engine's whine continued to mount like an airliner poising for takeoff.

Nicole adjusted the headphones, which didn't muss her hair too much, while Tom scanned various instruments.

"Any place out your way to get lunch?" he asked.

"There's a Chilis."

Tom made a rather boyish face. "I'm not a big fan of south-western cooking. Or just about anything else down here, including most of the natives." He grinned and lowered his glasses a bit, his blue eyes disarming above the black rims. "To be totally honest... and putting myself at your mercy... if I wanted to give the U.S. an enema, I'd stick the nozzle up Galveston Harbor."

Nicole laughed. "Are you testing my loyalty?"

"Loyalty isn't my department. That's the Homeland Gestapo."

"Meaning you're not one of them?"

"My job is defending Democracy, not suppressing it."

Nicole glanced out at the jungle of glass, its glare suppressed by the silvered windshield. "I like Texas people in general. They're usually open and honest, at least, though it took me a while to adapt. But, that's a long story."

"Too long for lunch?"

"There's a Denny's near my house, but I don't think you can land on the roof. We could take my car. ...But I don't know if I can find my house from up in the air."

"No problem," said Tom, pointing to a digital screen. "Got your address on the GPS."

"Oh," said Nicole. "My... ex-husband had one in his Hummer."

"Handy gadget," said Tom.

"Men hate to ask for directions."

"Ouch." Tom gripped the control stick. "Shall we...?"

Nicole smiled. "Please be gentle. I don't know anything about helicopters, but this one looks like a hottie."

"Nah, she'll barely do 300."

The engine's murmur rapidly rose, making a whirlwind howl. The machine lifted off, tilting nose down while soaring above the taller buildings, which seemed to shrink and spin away.

"You fly a lot?" asked Tom, his voice now reaching Nicole through the headset.

Nicole adjusted her microphone. "Mostly commercial, but small planes don't scare me."

"Because of your time in Africa?'

"One of Roger's... my ex's... friends had a small plane. A Piper, according to my son. We flew to Las Vegas a couple of times. I only flew in to my village once, then out again about a year later after the revolution started."

"Revolutions can be inconvenient."

"Thomas Jefferson said that a revolution every once in a while is probably a good thing."

"Depends on whose side you're on," said Tom. "And whether it wins or not. If we'd lost our revolution he and all our founding fathers would have been hung for treason against the British Empire."

"Am I still being tested?" asked Nicole. "I can save you some time: I'd give the U.S. an enema by sticking the nozzle up the Potomac."

"Not my department." Tom grinned again. "And none of this is being recorded."

Nicole realized she was speaking into a microphone. "Could you do that?"

"Got all the anti-terror toys. There's a torture kit somewhere in back with bamboo splints and a water board."

"You like vodka martinis shaken, not stirred?"

Tom altered their course a little after glancing at the GPS. "Please note my lack of cloak and dagger. I haven't caught any terrorists yet, but you usually don't catch the real ones. They believe too much in what they're doing."

"Not just in it for the money?"

"Guess if I was a kid and saw my family killed by bombs... 'collateral damage,' as we say politely... I'd want to bring America down." He flashed his boyish grin again, a Tom Cruise kind of naughty face that dared someone to slap it. "I don't have a flag on my car either. Even though it's a Ford."

"Oh," said Nicole. She wondered if there was an angle to this, then decided she didn't care. Like most intelligent people she assumed her email was monitored, and her past was probably filed away in some Orwellian memory bank.

Tom's chuckle came over the headphones. "If the government wants to get you, it won't need to bother with facts."

"How did you know I was thinking that?"

"Usual progression of thought."

"I guess it would be."

"So, how did you end up in Houston?" asked Tom. "If you'll excuse the rubber hose."

Nicole glanced down at the freeways, not quite as crowded at this time of day though still looking crammed to capacity. She thought of the millions of similar scenes repeated all over the civilized world.

"Roger grew up in Galveston and never really liked California. Too Liberal, I guess. So, like *Green Acres*, 'I was his wife' and he moved us here. I listed myself with a head-hunter, and Barrymore made me an offer. They haven't been bad to work for, and they're small enough where you can be noticed."

"They noticed Captain Keto. And this trip to Kiwanja could score you more points."

"I'm starting to get that impression."

"But, you don't really like it here?" asked Tom.

"Does it show?"

"Only when someone says howdy, ma'am, then you wince a little."

"My son is almost thirteen, and a boy that age needs stability. It wouldn't be fair to move him again."

Tom nodded while shifting course a bit to avoid a police helicopter that seemed to think it owned the sky. He might have traded words with its pilot, switching his mike to another channel. The other machine veered off as if swatted.

"My dad's in the Army," said Tom, switching back. "So I think I can relate. We never stayed more than two years in one place. Makes growing up hard for a kid. You just make friends then lose them again, so after a while you stop trying. ...He's why you're not sure you want to go?"

"I'd hate to leave him now, even for a couple of weeks. ...You don't think it would take any longer to find who made those boots?"

"Don't see why it would," said Tom. "I'm sure President N'dila would help. And I'm sure he'd welcome some industry so his people could have a better life instead of subsisting on yams and goats."

"Then he'd be able to tax them."

"But he wouldn't need any more help from us."

"I guess that makes sense," said Nicole.

"You'll have a letter of introduction. And we gave him a helicopter, so he might be able to show you around."

"That's a little more than trucks, fuel, and uniforms."

"It wasn't armed."

"I didn't fall off a truckload of yams."

"Query?"

91

"You're painting a picture of an unarmed Army. Or do they carry spears? Like in *The Mouse That Roared?*"

"What's a smart woman like you doing in a place like this?"

"We covered that already."

Tom glanced again at the GPS. "We've given them a few old rifles; mothballed junk from the Vietnam War. But I don't think Kiwanja is going to roar. So far it hasn't even squeaked loud enough to be noticed. But weapons are always available to any country that wants them. And they're usually cheaper than trucks and fuel. Especially flying them in."

"So, better ours than somebody else's?"

"God bless Capitalism."

Nicole looked down at the earth. "The world must be full of old war toys for new generations to play with."

"Here we are," said Tom.

Nicole was surprised again... how fast you got from here to there when free as a bird in the sky. Although they were low and hovering, she found it hard to pick out her house from all the other clones below, each with a manicured lawn and a pool. "It's the third from that corner, I think."

"Right on target," said Tom. He pointed to another screen as the helicopter swiftly sank, hatching a flock of butterflies in Nicole's unwary stomach. "We could drop a bomb in your Jacuzzi from halfway around the world."

"That's comforting to know. How about in my bathtub?"

"I could have the floor plan of your house in five minutes."

"Don't you find that a little scary?"

Tom lowered his Men In Black glasses, his other hand guiding the aircraft. "I do. ...But, so could almost anyone, from a real terrorist to a twelve-year-old hacker. And if your life was fairly routine they could guess when you'd be taking a bath. Or when your son would be in his room. And they'd know that for sure if he was online. They could even send him a message to keep him at his computer. I could find out the model and serial number of all the locks on your doors. If you had them changed and didn't pay cash... and only poor people and bad guys pay cash... I could find out who the locksmith was and what he replaced them with." Tom seemed to sigh as the ground rose up. "The genie got out of his bottle, Nicole. Just like in *Our Friend The Atom*."

"They used to show that in schools," said Nicole. "Back in the 1950s and 60s. My mother bought it on VCR to teach me about propaganda."

"Were you home-schooled?" asked Tom.

"So I wouldn't be brainwashed, according to mom. Isn't that in my secret file?"

"That'll teach me not to skim." The helicopter's skids kissed the grass.

"Nice landing," said Nicole.

"It's one we can walk away from. ...Looks like we've got company."

Nicole saw the gardener out in the flowers, a straw hat shading his coppery face. He might have been puzzled about the shovel and the fresh little mound of Freddy's grave, but now he looked ready to run. His two shirtless sons were poised by the pool, chubby brown boys in old sagger jeans. Each held a long-handled skimmer but also looked about to bolt.

"My yard service," said Nicole.

"Hope they don't think we're ICE." Tom shut off several switches as the rotors slowed to a droopy stop and the engine's whine faded to silence.

Nicole had lifted a hand to wave, forgetting she couldn't be seen. "I'm sure they're legal."

"I saw nothing, nothing, *mien Colonel!*"

Nicole opened her door and the heat burst in like a nuclear blast. "*Buenos dias*, Fernando," she called.

The gardener seemed to relax a bit, though his answering smile was wary. He called to his sons, who resumed their work, clearing the water of insect corpses.

"You also speak Spanish?" asked Tom.

"Enough to be respectful. ...You really did skim."

"Big Brother isn't quite as efficient as he'd like everyone to believe."

"Does that apply to missiles, too? Such as where they land?"

"Not my department. ...Nice pool," said Tom. "You swim a lot?"

"I'd swim a lot more, but there never seems to be enough time."

"How about Zack?"

"He hasn't been very physical lately. He used to be a soccer star, but Roger... my ex..."

"You've established his status."

"I'm sure you knew it already."

"Divorces, like floor plans, are public records."

Nicole almost asked about *his* public records, which Jenny hadn't able to find, but that might have sounded like playing coy; and besides it was none of her business. "Roger encouraged him, maybe too much."

"The Little League Syndrome?" asked Tom. "Where fathers get off a lot more than their sons?"

"It could have been that," said Nicole, removing the headset and smoothing her hair. "Sports were really Roger's thing, though he'd never played except in school. And when Roger became... well... nasty to Zack... so did sports, I guess. Zack's always been kind of passive, and I've never been much of a pusher."

"It's usually better to lead."

"But, leading takes time, and I haven't had much. Eight hours a day plus two more in traffic. And those are the good days." Nicole hesitated, hoping she wouldn't be misunderstood. "And Zack's at the age where he needs a male figure."

"I'd like to meet him," said Tom.

"You're welcome to come to his graduation. He'll be home by four."

"Think he'd like it if we picked him up?"

"You mean in this?"

"Sure, why not?"

"He'd love it. You should have seen his face this morning when the company helicopter came. I could call the school, he gets out at three-thirty."

Tom checked his watch. "Leaves us plenty of time for lunch."

Nicole slung her laptop over a shoulder while Tom took the bag of Zackary's gifts. He put on his jacket, hiding the gun -- possibly for

94

the gardener's sake -- then helped Nicole to the grass. She considered introducing him, but Fernando was gathering up his tools, while his sons had edged away to the gate, still warily eying the aircraft.

"I'd guess Nicaragua," said Tom, as they reached the patio. "So helicopters would scare them."

"You travel a lot?"

"Comes with the job."

"Are the sweatshops really that bad in some countries?"

"Sweating is better than starving to death."

The slide had been turned on for cleaning and made a musical liquid sound. Nicole remembered a brook in the hills a few miles away from her parents' house, and a rippling pond on a sweltering day like the proverbial swimmin' hole. The place had vanished long ago, the pond filled in by suburban sprawl, the brook now part of a storm sewer drain, its once verdant banks now walled with concrete, but its memory lingered clear and bright. When people dreamed of "going home" it usually meant to a *time* not a place. She tried to read Tom's expression as he gazed at the sparkling pool... was it actually wistful? "Doesn't sound as if you have much time yourself."

Tom wiped sweat from his face. "A commute's a commute, ten miles or ten-thousand. Time down life's toilet you never get back."

Nicole watched the gardener leave with his tools after setting her shovel beside the garage. She would have offered Cokes, but the boys had already fled the yard to a battered truck in the driveway. "There's plenty of food in the house, and I make a passable chicken salad. I could even shake up a vodka martini."

"You wouldn't have any plain old beer? And hopefully not Lone Star?"

"Zack seems to prefer Heineken."

"Sounds like an All-American boy."

Nicole didn't want to seem blatant, but Tom had turned back to the shimmering water, which radiated a pleasant coolness. "One of Zack's swim suits might fit you."

"Must be a husky boy at twelve."

"He's almost thirteen and a little fat. ...Actually more than a little."

"You didn't say obese."

"I don't use government-sanctioned hate-speak."

"New propaganda: '*Our Friend The Atom*, Our Enemy Fat.'" Tom took off his glasses. "That pool sure looks good."

"I suppose you're on company time?" asked Nicole.

"It's only taxpayer money, if I don't waste it somebody else will. ...Am I being tested?"

"I'll turn off my cameras," said Nicole.

NINE

Nathi walked through the moonlit village beneath the tall acacia trees that dappled the ground in silver and shadow and scented the air with their earthy musk. The children had come to escort him again, along with the ever-inquisitive dogs who capered ahead raising dust. The chief's front yard was defended by thorns, a hedge more efficient than razor barbed wire, though a nine-year-old boy stood guard at the gate, a bright bayonet on his rifle. He cheerfully greeted Nathi, who lifted the latch and went in.

Nafia answered the door to his knock, her younger sister, Aisha, beside her. The girls bowed him into the room, which had woven straw mats on its earthen floor. Draperies decorated the walls, along with hangings of shells and beads. There were also a few Lee-Enfield rifles that dated back to the First World War, but were clean, well oiled, and ready for use. Here and there were pictures, most showing lions at rest or at play. There were also many shelves of books. The room was no larger than Nathi's hut, but the house of the chief boasted several rooms, the foremost reserved for living and dining, its table now set with a lavish feast. It was custom for wife and daughters to serve, but *Jumbe* Chane's mate wasn't present tonight and his daughters now quietly left.

97

To have called *Jumbe* Chane enormous would have been understating his size. He was only a few months older than Nathi, but easily weighed at least five times as much, his body a mountain of dusky rolls clad only in a loincloth and throned upon a gigantic chair, an ancient heirloom of noble strength and no less heroic proportions. His mass proclaimed his leadership, and except for the tuft of lion's mane he wore no other adornments.

Three kerosene lamps lit the room, including one in the rafters with a circular wick and enamel shade that was almost electrically bright. The table could have seated a dozen, itself an ancient artifact with a crescent cut out for a gigantic man, while the food it displayed could have fed as many with goat, pork, roasted chicken, a steaming platter of fish from the stream, beans, corn and sweet potatoes, along with various delicacies imported in packets and cans. To drink, there was village-made beer in a pitcher.

"*Salamu*, Nathi!" boomed *Jumbe* Chane in a voice befitting his size. His face was like an ebony moon partly eclipsed by a nova of hair, while his chest was a pair of orb-like asteroids. "Come and sit down. How was your flight?"

"We were delayed as you know," said Nathi, taking a chair across from Chane.

"Mechanical troubles?" asked Chane.

"Water in the fuel."

The huge man frowned. "Sabotage?"

"I'd rather think it was accidental. Careless filter maintenance at the Selinda airfield."

"Will you report it?"

"They would want a flight plan." Nathi offered a box of Nestle bars. "Your favorites, if I recall?"

The huge man chuckled, his body an ocean of ripples and waves. "How could you have forgotten? Has it been so long since we hunted together?"

"Sometimes it seems only yesterday. Other times, a thousand years."

"I'll give the prayer."

Nathi bowed his head as Chane thanked the Lion Of Life.

"I know of the border village," said Chane after intoning the prayer. He served himself from platters and bowls, and Nathi did the same.

Nathi took a bite of roast goat. "Rashawn told you?"

"He said the Army attacked it... what the General would call a 'relocation.'"

Nathi poured a glass of beer. "Destroying people's homes so they have no choice but to go to the city and work for the General's 'social improvements.'" He sipped the thick brew and added, "Rashawn left defenders. Both were killed." He lay down his food, though his stomach protested, having been empty for most of the day. "Two against at least fifty soldiers, one of whom was also killed."

"You landed there?" said Chane. "Do you think that was wise?"

"Probably not, but it's done. At least we discovered mines and left warnings."

"You shouldn't be taking such risks."

Nathi began to eat again. "The world is full of dangers and I don't have time to fear them all."

Chane helped himself from a platter of pork. "Did you learn anything else?"

"No more than what we've suspected; the Army has more weapons than fuel. And they stripped the fallen soldier so they could be short of uniforms and maybe other equipment. Nor did they burn the crops."

Chane sipped beer. "It could also mean they have more soldiers." Then he frowned. "They didn't bury him?"

"Perhaps they feared a counter-attack. We buried all three with ceremony."

"Thank you, Nathi."

"Did Rashawn take the people away?"

"Across the border," said Chane, spearing a roasted fish. "So they are safe for the moment."

"Leaving two of his fighters to die."

"His trucks are old and slow, the Army's newer and faster. They would have caught him in a chase so he had to delay them somehow. ...What would you have done, my friend?"

99

"Rashawn could have set up an ambush. There's a narrow place in the hills nearby where the Army trucks had to come through. The trucks could have been destroyed or captured, and the village might have been saved. Now its people are refugees, and refugees are never welcome."

"They will return when the war is over."

"To find their village gone," said Nathi. "Along with everything they owned. And, I'm sure Rashawn 'recruited' the boys as payment for their rescue."

"They have their lives," said Chane.

"They could have stayed and lived in peace by meeting the General's demands."

Chane shook his head. "By growing crops that do not reproduce so they have to buy new seeds each year. And by giving their boys to the Army."

Nathi shrugged. "You asked what I would have done, my chief. May I ask the same?"

"I might have considered an ambush, but it may have been a matter of time... faster to take the people away than to prepare a defense."

Nathi took another slice of goat. "You could lead us as well as Rashawn."

"Thank you, loyal subject. But, the same could be said of you."

"I only fly an airplane."

"And I am not a warrior," said Chane. "Nor was my father, nor his father's father, nor generations of fathers before. I know when to plant our crops. I can predict a drought or a rain. And marriages I can perform."

"And burials," said Nathi.

Jumbe Chane sighed. "Too many of those in recent times. But, I know nothing of planning battles."

"You used to plan our hunts well enough."

"Animals I understand, but not the minds of greedy men." Chane sipped beer. "How is Dakota?"

"He still has the humanity to decently bury the dead."

"Akili prepared him supper," said Chane. "They seem to be very good friends."

"They have always been friends," said Nathi. He touched the tuft of fur on his chest. "Akili made his necklace."

"No doubt they are at the pond," said Chane.

"It's a peaceful place. Remember? We used to go there often."

For a moment the gigantic man looked wistful. "I've not been there for too many years. To drink beer in the moonlight and dream. To talk until dawn of the future. Of all the adventurous things we would do. And you *were* able to fly away."

"Haven't your dreams been fulfilled?" asked Nathi.

Chane shrugged a huge shoulder. "I always knew my future."

"You could have refused and come with me."

"The path not taken," said Chane, but then he shook his head. "One cannot live a privileged life and then deny his obligation to those who provided that privilege. Our people made an investment in me and I am bound to return it." He turned to gaze through a moonlit window. Beyond loomed the mass of the not-quite mountain, above it the star-studded sky. "You're blessed with a son like Dakota. He's more of a warrior than either of us."

Nathi took a sip of beer. "He has only known war in his life. But so have most of our children."

Jumbe Chane looked thoughtful. "I have, as you know, only daughters."

"As wise and kind as their father."

"Thank you. But, I must think of the future for all."

"Maybe you'll still have a son."

"But if not my son-in-law will be chief. Whoever marries Akili."

"Unless the people choose another."

"Which though permitted has never been done."

"I see where this path is leading," said Nathi.

Jumbe Chane shrugged. "A path has no choice where it leads, created by those who continually tread it; and I have a responsibility to think of our children's children. Dakota is wise for his years, and yet there is a wildness in him, perhaps from being raised in the sky. How could he ever be bound to the earth?"

"A path has no choice where it leads," agreed Nathi. "But a man does not have to follow it bound to the footsteps of others before.

101

Dakota could refuse to be chief."

"He could," said Chane. "Though that's also never been done."

"Would it be an insult to our past?"

"The past should serve as a guide," said Chane. "In places where there are no paths. At least until new ones are made."

"This may be a time for a new one."

Chane looked out the window again. "It may be a time for many new paths, but I've opened my mind to you, Nathi."

"Thank you, Chane. But what do you want of me? Is Dakota forbidden to see Akili?"

"Of course not."

"Dakota would know these things," added Nathi. "Also Akili, I'm sure."

"Of course they do," said Chane. "Let the matter rest for now." He poured another glass of beer. "How is Fila?"

"As well as can be, I'd imagine. With our children losing interest in school, and no new books or supplies."

"She has spoken to me about that," said Chane. "Books and paper require money."

"Dakota has been selling our boots."

"I've noticed," said Chane. "The music players and other toys. All of which use batteries, which seem more precious than gold. There have been several fights over batteries among the younger children... as if we didn't have enough trouble."

"You could forbid such things," said Nathi.

"One cannot lead by suppression, denying new ideas and things, or new paths created by children." Chane glanced at the antique rifles. "We adopted the best of the British ideas and we have better lights and our roofs don't leak. We have medicines to cure disease and knowledge to help the injured and sick. Our children learn to read and thus enrich their lives." He smiled. "We even improved our boots, though I wonder that other people buy them."

Nathi finished his food. "Dakota found a shop. So far he's bought only toys and beer, things that others ask for, but we could buy books with the money."

"Or guns and bullets," said Chane. "We've never made more than we've needed, but I will consider the matter." He paused, looking thoughtful again. "Fila should marry, you know."

"Abu seems to think so, too."

"Wise boy." Chane sipped more beer. "Fila is not a girl any longer."

Nathi raised an eyebrow. "Where is this path leading?"

"Don't you like her?"

For a moment Nathi was down at the pond beside an enormous fat boy. "Don't be an ass!"

Jumbe Chane laughed. "I suppose I was."

Nathi shrugged. "You're thinking about the future again."

Jumbe Chane turned to the window. "I have many things to think of these days that my father never prepared me for... such as losing a whole generation." His face grew troubled. "How long will the Americans support the General? *Why* do they help him, and what do they want?"

"I can't guess," said Nathi. "But they have a saying: 'There's no such thing as a free lunch.' And the General has been dining well."

"So has Rashawn," said Chane. "We've given him most of our men and boys. Assuming he can defeat the General, will he become our President? Or would he also become a General? Today he asked for our older boys, a request I refused. But tomorrow he might simply take them, and how could I prevent it? Order my children to fight his children?"

"We chose Rashawn," said Nathi. "A man who passed the test. So I suppose we should trust his heart."

"We chose him because of you," said Chane. "Because of the blood that beats in his heart."

"I had nothing to do with that."

"Not in words," said Chane. "But we know what speaks louder than words."

"I..."

"'Only fly an airplane,'" said Chane. "But you went out in the world and saw what it has to offer. Yet, you came back."

"So did Rashawn."

Chane nodded. "Which is why we chose him. He, too, in his way is a pilot, and I know what you say about landings."

TEN

Tom *would* have made a cool action-figure; a kinder, gentler G.I. Joe; a Rambo without a chip on his shoulder. As Nicole had guessed from his well-tailored clothes, he wasn't bulked like a comic-book hero, just male-model perfect in every proportion. Blond and tanned he resembled a surfer, especially clad in Zackary's baggies, a pair now way too small for him that Nicole had found in his dresser drawer.

She had also discovered a box of condoms. The shock had been something like seeing Tom's gun, unexpected yet logical; something she probably should have foreseen. Then she had actually opened the box to see what it "really" contained -- maybe a crack pipe, weed or pills -- but there was nothing but innocent Trojans.

In a way it didn't seem fair, as if Zack had left her behind somehow, embarked on a quest without saying goodbye. They had never discussed the birds and bees. Nicole had been meaning to do that -- or maybe waiting for him to ask -- but except for a little computer porn he hadn't shown much interest in girls. ...Or, maybe Nicole hadn't noticed.

She had suddenly felt like a clueless old fool, a typical TV American parent who couldn't do anything right; whose children were raised by the Internet while their parents only provided a place -- food, shelter, a comfortable cave -- until the young strangers were old enough to spawn their own brood of changelings.

Then she'd tried logic: maybe he'd just been experimenting? Or maybe just being neat? ...But, neat didn't seem to be his style.

That made her wonder if the rubbers were Dillon's? Dwane's muscular son, so perfectly male with his silly green hair and millions of dollars, his future as bright as a new Krugerrand. Girls almost swooned when he lost his shirt, and trailed him around like puppies in heat, watching him sweat on the soccer field and possibly wetting their pubescent panties whenever he scored for the Skins. Condoms would have been wise for him; no doubt his marriage was already planned to further the Barrymore empire.

On the other hand, Zack was a very nice boy... smelly, raunchy and sloppy, but nice. Surely there were *intelligent* girls who would want him for who he really was and not how he looked on the outside? She had tried to see him through eyes of her past: would she have dated him at his age? It was hard to imagine Zack making love to anyone but himself, and disturbing to find herself trying.

Life suddenly seemed to be moving too fast and out of control like a runaway train. But then she had tried a new tack... if those rubbers really belonged to Zack didn't that prove she had raised him right? Made him aware of the mines in his path and the traps he might be ensnared in? That made her feel a little better. She'd returned the box to the drawer as if it had never been found.

Tom swooshed down the water slide and made a big splash in the pool as Nicole emerged from the kitchen with chicken salad and beers on a tray. Tom surfaced, spit water and laughed. "You weren't supposed to see that."

"I saw nothing, *mien Colonel.*" Nicole had also dressed for swimming, choosing a modest single-piece she usually wore at Dwane's barbecues. She had studied herself in the bedroom mirror, her breasts still reasonably high and firm despite nursing Zack in the natural way, her legs and bottom quite actually good... assuming one didn't prefer Barbie dolls.

She had already been for a dip with Tom, cooling off and relaxing before going in to fix lunch. She brushed back her still-dripping hair,

105

not wanting to flavor the food with chlorine as she carried the tray to a wrought-iron table beneath a shady umbrella while Tom emerged gleaming from the pool.

"You make a mean chicken salad," he said, after seating himself and taking a bite. No wonder Zack got a little fat if this is an example of your culinary skills."

Nicole took a sip of beer. "A little more than a little fat... he won't be wearing those trunks anymore. Or a lot of other things in his closet. One of these days I'll have to go through it and call the Salvation Army. ...But, judging by the kids at his school, I guess he's not too over-weight."

"Depends on who tries to dictate what weight there is to be over."

Nicole did another appraisal of Tom -- a glistening, golden, Apollo-like man -- and wondered how he would take to Zack. Physically they had nothing in common except blond hair and indigo eyes. "I'd guess you lift weights," she added, maybe for justification.

"Just naturally blessed," said Tom. "Or cursed. People are profiled by their bodies, especially in school. Brains wear glasses, nerds are marshmallows, and muscular boys are supposed to be jocks. But, I never liked competitive sports, the kind where some anal-retentive goon gets off on pushing kids around. Makes them fight a surrogate war on the field of someone else's dreams. My dad's like that... former D.I. Tried to make me 'manly.'"

Nicole laughed. "You're saying he didn't succeed?"

"I'd never treat a kid that way. I'd find out what *he* wanted to do and try to share his interests."

"That's easier said than done." Nicole thought again of the con-doms. "Especially when..."

"They're at 'that age?'"

"They don't talk to you anymore," said Nicole. "Not about impor-tant things, things they *should* be talking about. Things they really need guidance with but don't have the life-experience to know it. And they seem to change when you're not looking."

"So you don't want to look away for two weeks?"

Nicole took another sip from her glass. "That's probably the big-gest reason. But, I'm still kind of dazed by this African thing. Going there, I mean."

Tom sipped beer. "Like I told Dwane in the meeting, I think you'd be right for this job."

"I guess it's not a Muslim country? Not that it matters to me."

"Good point," said Tom. "A country where women don't do business."

"Or can't even drive."

Tom savored another bite of salad. "Not much driving in Kiwanja unless it's a truckload of yams. I'm not even sure they have a religion, but the women aren't all covered up. Kind of just the opposite."

"One of the bare-breasted cultures?"

"Quite, as the British would say."

"They must not have suffered missionaries. And rape is almost unknown in those places."

"So is porn," said Tom. "Nothing is hidden so nothing is dirty."

"Have you been there?"

"Just seen a few pictures and read reports. We don't even have an embassy, but neither does anyone else."

"I'm sure the Kiwanjis worship something. And if they haven't had any wars, their god or gods can't be too bad."

"Two more points in your favor," said Tom. "You're not a prude or a Bible-beater, and no one could call you an ugly American."

Nicole wondered if that had another meaning. She felt Tom's eyes, and a warmth awakened, something she hadn't felt in years. "Thank you," she said, then added, "Aren't you going to say I'd be serving my country?"

"I don't wave the flag in anyone's face, it's way too bloody these days. ...Though you'd also be helping Kiwanja's people."

Nicole raised an eyebrow. "I try to be cynical, but it's hard to keep current."

"Ouch."

"Sorry, but I've read enough history... and not what they teach in public school... to know we've seldom helped anyone without a profit motive. Unless it was saving ourselves, like in the last 'good war.'"

"Which we obviously won," said Tom, "since we're not speaking German or Japanese." He shrugged. "That's why it's called Capitalism.

But it doesn't have to be greedy."

"Though it usually is," said Nicole. "Those Kiwanji boots, for example: my parents could buy them for twenty a pair from the person, or child, who made them. Money that person or child could use to build a better life. Add another twenty for shipping and import, another twenty for overhead, and my parents could still sell those boots for eighty and everyone lives a good life." She forked a bite of salad. "Yet a company like Barrymore would never pay that person or child a penny more than it had to, a dollar a day, or even less, if they set up a factory."

She took another sip from her glass. "Granted, there's advertising, marketing and distribution; expenses my parents don't have. But, Barrymore's profit would still be obscene, while its workers went to bed hungry at night... assuming they even had beds. *That's* why it's called Capitalism, and that's why everyone hates us."

"Basically true," said Tom. "But, your parents don't have to build a factory in a primitive country."

"They don't need a factory," said Nicole. "Because they buy from the bootmakers, who work at home and at their own pace. A child could make boots and still go to school for twenty dollars a pair. But they can't if they have to slave in a sweatshop for a dollar or less every twelve-hour day."

She took another bite of salad. "My parents don't get subsidies, or breaks on import taxes. Barrymore does. And since production is overseas, Barrymore won't furnish medical care, or maintain any safety or environmental standards. It can use up its workers and throw them away, and pollute their country while doing it."

"True," agreed Tom. "And I've seen those places. ...Including the Barrymore factory that makes your Defenders uniforms. Half-naked kids in dirty rags sewing cute little clothes for American dolls." He glanced around at the sprawling green yard, the huge swimming pool and the five-bedroom house.

Nicole tried not to sound defensive. "This was Roger's idea. His white picket fence and American dream."

"Mind if I ask what happened?"

Nicole shrugged. "You can take the boy out of the trailer park,

108

but... Let's just say he reverted to type and I didn't want to stay bare-foot and pregnant no matter how lavish the trailer." She glanced at the house. "Now I guess I'm maintaining stability. ...Or at least the illusion that life is stable, like training-wheels for Zack."

"Stability *is* an illusion," said Tom. "At best only an interlude in terms of world history. But Americans think it's a right. Like kids in a playpen surrounded by wolves."

"And you keep the wolves from eating the kids?"

"People die every day doing that, Nicole. Not only soldiers and 'secret agents' but harmless little underpaid people who risk their lives at computer screens all around the world. So the privileged party can keep going on with plenty of ice cream and cake."

"And damn little thanks you get?"

"Thank you." Tom was silent a moment. "But, it doesn't have to be that way. ...And I'm really at your mercy now."

"I forgot to turn on the microphones." Nicole took another sip of beer. "George Orwell predicted the present future in *1984:* people controlled by propaganda, misinformation, hate, fear and lies. Our language polluted by double-speak where bringing 'freedom and peace' to people means bombing their country to rubble first so they have to take whatever we offer. ...Which usually isn't freedom or peace but only another dictator who dances to our tune. Our wealth is spent on self-serving wars, which are always in somebody else's yard."

"Except for September eleventh."

"When a few hungry wolves crashed the party." Nicole frowned. "And how many thousands of people... men, women, innocent children, has the U.S. killed since then? Starved by economic sanctions, bombed in the name of Democracy... or 'protecting ourselves from terrorists?' Or died from lack of medicine because they couldn't pay our price?"

"That's a pretty harsh indictment."

"The truth is often harsh when you're guilty."

Surprisingly Tom smiled. "Everything you've said proves you're right for this job."

Nicole cocked her head. "Am I missing something? I'd think you'd want a patriot. At least a Pollyanna."

Tom looked earnest. "I meant what I said, Nicole. About Kiwanja being a model. An example of America's best. Everything we claim to believe but seldom actually do."

"You interest me strangely," said Nicole.

Tom took her hand across the table. "Then please hear me out. Kiwanja is like the Shire before Sauron discovered it. I've been doing what I can to protect it, but then those boots turned up last week."

Nicole raised an eyebrow again. "And 'Sauron' is after Kiwanja? ...Speaking less metaphorically, who are you trying to protect it from? We seem to have won the Cold War. The Soviet Union surrendered and seems to be drowning in Capitalism. Is the Russian Bear still a threat? Or maybe the Chinese dragon?"

Tom released Nicole's hand and sat back in his chair. "More than metaphorically, the American Eagle's a vulture; and I don't want that vulture to land on Kiwanja and rip it to shreds like a mouse."

"You've been trying to keep it hidden?"

"Just trying give it a full metal jacket before the vulture arrives."

"By helping it build an army?"

"That's usually the quickest way to pull a country together. 'Boot-camp it into shape,' as much as I hate *that* metaphor. The Kiwanjis have to be prepared when civilization drops on them... and worse the American version."

"You're afraid they'll be exploited?"

"Judging from history, what do you think? They don't even know what their boots are worth."

"Are you saying you'd want me to tell them? Wouldn't that be like betraying my country?"

"But not your professed ideals."

"Ouch."

Tom smiled. "Would it hurt a little less if I said, your *practiced* ideals? Selling war dolls doesn't hurt anyone."

"Thank you, I guess," said Nicole. "Though sometimes I wonder."

"Which proves you have a conscience," said Tom. "The alternative is Aaron Steele. Or somebody else's Gollum."

Nicole faced the sparkling pool. The trickling slide made a soothing sound, but a hawk cried somewhere high overhead, possibly spotting an unwary mouse. She shifted her eyes to the flower beds, not sure anymore where Freddy reposed without the shovel to mark his grave. "I tried that once, remember? Bringing civilization to savages... or maybe Sharkey to the Shire. And you said I was lucky to get out alive."

"I doubt there'll be a revolution."

Nicole met Tom's eyes. "But, Kiwanja isn't quite peaceful, is it? What good is an army for a country so small it's not quite even there on a map? It couldn't be used for self-defense against an outside enemy, so there must be internal problems. And you know I'll see them if I go."

Tom only shrugged. "If you came to this country from somewhere else would you say there weren't any problems? That everyone here was living in peace with freedom and justice for all? Safe, secure, and loving their neighbors? That we don't need an internal army to fight our domestic terrorists?"

Nicole thought for a moment. "I still have to talk it over with Zack."

"Why not take him along?"

"That's been suggested," said Nicole. "Which is something else to discuss with him."

The doorbell rang melodiously.

Tom laughed. "We've been talking treason. Betraying the great American dollar. Maybe it's the Thought Police."

Nicole got up. "More likely one of my unloved neighbors wetting her panties to snoop. I don't usually have helicopters landing in my yard."

She went to her room for a bathrobe, then hurried through the shadowy house, its curtains all closed to keep out the sun. She disarmed the security system, but checked the low-tech peephole. A UPS driver stood on the porch, a young black man whose dark-coffee skin matched the shade of his uniform. Without that proof of identity, along with his bubble-nosed truck at the curb, the neighbors might have called the cops.

"Overnight package, ma'am."

"Thank you." Nicole tried to remember the last time anyone had called her Miss.

Tom appeared as she closed the door, still in nothing but Zackary's shorts. "Guess it wasn't the Gestapo."

"You might have to shoot a neighbor or two... in fact I wish you would." Nicole read the package's label. "It's from my parents to Zack. His graduation present."

"I should get him something," said Tom.

"Picking him up in a helicopter should be sufficient to make his day."

"I'd still like to give him a present." Tom studied photos atop the TV. "He's a good-looking boy."

"Thank you. But those are last year's pictures; he's really gained a lot of weight."

"You said that already. Does that embarrass him... or you?"

"...You may have a point."

"Does Barrymore have a health division?"

"I don't think so. Why?"

"I'm surprised they haven't joined that party: the health hysteria Capitalists. It's a billion-dollar industry. Along with cosmetics, deodorants, hair restorers, orthodontists, plastic surgeons and diet plans. Americans might be ignorant, deluded, duped, and brainwashed, and xenophobic as driver ants, but we sure don't want to be fat, ugly, smelly, bald, or have crooked teeth."

"That's a pretty harsh indictment."

"The truth is often harsh when you're guilty. One of the signs of a decadent culture is obsession with body image. When people begin to worship themselves instead of a god or decent values. And what's an obsession with health except desperation not to die because this life is all we have and there's no god or spiritual power who's going to judge our sick little souls for all our hate and intolerance? We want a 'healthy' thousand-year Reich of our own perceived ideals of perfection. A new master race of lean, mean superior beings like Hitler's mythical Aryans; and kids like Zack are our latest mud-people to hate and persecute."

"I've thought about that a lot," said Nicole. "But maybe I needed a second opinion, especially from a manly man."

"Aw shucks, you done made me blush. What are his interests?"

Nicole considered Zack's primary pastimes. "I have to admit I don't know... I just can't seem to find the time to do anything with him." She set the box on the coffee table... probably an airplane model, judging from its plastic rattle. "I was going to take him to the mall, then out to dinner somewhere. ...Oh, and I have to order pizza for his party tonight."

"Okay," said Tom. "He can pick out a gift, and I'll cover dinner."

"Padding the expense account?"

"It's patriotic to buy and consume."

ELEVEN

"Do you love Akili?" asked Thabo, who lay with his back to the trickling sluice, his rifle leaning beside him. Headphones crowned his bushy mane, and faint music throbbed in the heat of the night. A cigarette smoldered between his fingers, and he tilted a bottle of beer to his lips. Scattered around him were various snacks; crackers, chips and crunchy things, along with CDs in their plastic cases.

"Love is a powerful word," said Dakota, who sat with a beer and a cigarette while gazing at the moon-silvered pond. "To love is an obligation. A pledge of one soul to another. But, I *like* Akili a lot." He took a drink then asked, "You love Tosha, don't you?"

"Of course." Thabo removed the headphones, letting them dangle around his neck, the wire trailing between jutting chest plates to a Diskman that lay on his stone-rippled stomach. "A pledge, as you say, of my soul to hers, as well as to the Lion Of Life, for as long as we live."

"Would you die for her?" asked Kobe, who was sprawled on his back next to Thabo, his rifle also propped to the sluice. Like the other boys he was naked, something they had always done since swimming here as children.

Thabo snorted. "What a ridiculous question! I would die for *you*, hyena-face."

"And I for you," said Kobe. "Because I love you, ass."

"And I love you, ass. But that's not what Dakota is talking about."

"Which any ass would know," said Dakota. He turned to Thabo again. "What does it feel like? That kind of love? The love you feel for Tosha?"

"As you love Nathi I'm sure."

Dakota sighed out smoke. "That is love of man for man. As I feel for you and Kobe."

"You may kiss me," said Kobe.

"I would rather kiss a drunk hyena."

Thabo's face turned sad. "I kissed my father. When he went off with Rashawn."

"I'm sorry," said Dakota, and lay a hand on Thabo's arm. "Your father loved us all."

"He pledged his soul to all," said Kobe, gripping Thabo's shoulder.

"Thank you both," said Thabo. "My love for Tosha is just like that, but also a little different now."

"How do you mean?" asked Dakota, taking a handful of chips from a bag. "Stronger, are you saying?"

"Yes," said Thabo. "Love grows like a child." He took a puff from his cigarette. "I loved Tosha more when our son was born, as if my love grew to embrace them both. Love is not like butter, it can never be spread too thin."

Kobe turned to Dakota. "Are you going to marry Akili?" He sloppily guzzled another beer, then blasted a burp that was almost a roar and might have frightened a lion.

Dakota crunched a mouthful of chips. "That's a serious thing to consider."

"Rather," said Kobe. "Then you'd be chief one day."

"I don't want to think about that."

Kobe spread his hands. "How could you fly if you were chief? We would need you here."

"Don't you think I've thought of that? Do shut up about it."

Thabo said, "A lifetime decision, marriage."

Kobe nodded. "Even if she wasn't Chane's daughter."

Thabo reached for his Diskman. "How do you turn it off?"

"Like this," said Dakota, demonstrating. "And don't get dirt on the disks."

"Her breasts are a little high," said Kobe, taking another bottle of beer from what remained of a case.

"Ass!" snapped Dakota.

"Only a little."

"Ass twice!" growled Thabo.

Kobe asked, "Why do women wear bras in the cities? To make their breasts stay high?"

"I suppose," said Dakota, and reached for a beer. "Their size and shape are exaggerated, though never publicly seen."

"Then how would you know what you're getting?" asked Kobe.

Thabo laughed. "One might get a shock on their wedding night."

Dakota shrugged. "Many things in cities are stupid. Others are often disgusting. And many more are dangerous. People try to kill you. Or try to steal what you have. Or try to kill you *and* steal what you have. One must always be on guard."

"As in war," said Kobe.

"Cities are often like living in wars."

"Well," said Thabo, sipping more beer, "we shall see for ourselves in Johannesburg."

"And eat at McDonalds," said Kobe. "And I will have sex."

Dakota smiled. "As much as you can pay for. Just like eating at McDonalds."

"I'm glad I don't have to pay," said Thabo. "At least for sex."

"When one owns a cow..." said Kobe.

"Don't be vulgar!" snapped Thabo.

Dakota laughed. "You have the manners of a drunk hyena."

"Sorry," said Kobe. "But, what will you buy with your money?"

Thabo shrugged. "I'm sure I'll find something in a place with so much."

Dakota laughed. "A green enamel teapot, at least."

"How much will I have to pay?" asked Kobe.

"For McDonalds?" asked Thabo.

"Ass!"

Dakota drained his bottle, burped, then flipped his cigarette away. "That depends on what you want. It will cost a lot more than McDonalds for a pretty girl close to your age."

"Do I have enough money?" asked Kobe. "I wouldn't want a grandmother."

Thabo grinned. "At least her breasts wouldn't be too high."

"Ass!"

"Sufficient," said Dakota. "But you'll have to use protection."

"Will it still feel as good?"

Thabo laughed. "Better than your paw, I'm sure."

"At least my paw is free and doesn't require protection."

"It's your own fault," said Thabo, blowing out a ghost of smoke. "If you're waiting for a dowry, you may be pawing yourself a long time. The war has made everyone poor but the General."

"It's not the dowry," said Kobe. "I simply can't decide."

"You can't have both, you know," said Thabo.

"Dawa and Shani, the twins?" asked Dakota.

"That seems to be his dilemma." Thabo thumped Kobe's head with his knuckles. "Dither too long and you'll lose them both. Even though you're quite a prize."

"I am?" asked Kobe, and burped.

"My wife has heard talk of a 'mighty young lion.' ...Do forgive my laughter."

Dakota laughed, too. "He still looks like a hyena to me." He patted Kobe's shoulder. "And your money might be better spent filling your belly with burgers and fries instead of a condom with cream."

"Now who's being vulgar!" snapped Kobe. He drained his bottle and reached for another. "Is that your experienced opinion?"

"My paw, like yours, is still free," said Dakota. "And, as you said... with astounding wisdom unusual for you... does not require protection."

"Ah!" said Kobe. "Then you have never had sex?"

"Have I led you to believe otherwise? And there is more in life than sex. Many great men did more with their lives than making families or just having sex."

Thabo regarded Dakota's belly. "Not to seem indelicate, but you

117

have gotten much fatter since we used to paw here together."

"Why did we stop?" asked Kobe. "Was it because Thabo got married?"

"You two never asked after that," said Thabo.

"Would you still?" asked Kobe.

"If in the mood."

"You wouldn't feel unfaithful to Tosha?"

"Only if you asked me for flowers and candy afterward."

Dakota gathered up handfuls of belly to display himself. "I assure you it's fully functional, it just has a comfortable den." He cupped his puff of chub with a hand and stroked his shaft with two fingers and thumb.

"I rather wish I could do that," said Kobe. "It looks rather intriguing."

"Despite being happily married," said Thabo, "It *does* look rather intriguing."

"How much does one actually need?" asked Kobe.

"Yours is sufficient," said Thabo, "if that's how you wish to spend your money."

"It would seem a shame to waste my first time wrapped in plastic like a sausage while having a business transaction."

"Sounds rather American," said Thabo.

Dakota added, "And your memories of McDonalds will probably be more satisfying, and certainly more substantial."

Thabo looked thoughtful. "Perhaps not the moment to change the subject, but why doesn't Nathi marry Fila?"

"Everyone does seem to wonder," said Kobe.

"It's clear that Fila loves him," said Thabo. He glanced at Kobe. "And if you say her breasts are too high I shall hit you hard."

"Her breasts are just about right," said Kobe. "Of course, she's twenty years old."

Dakota looked up at the moonlit sky. "Perhaps he loves flying more. And that kind of love doesn't bind you to earth."

TWELVE

Nicole awoke to the stirring strains of *Some Enchanted Evening*, the music still lingering in her mind like *The Song That Never Ends*. The school band had played it surprisingly well at Zackary's graduation, along with *The Yellow Rose Of Texas*, though they'd obviously practiced the latter much more.

For a moment she lay in the darkness, hearing the air-conditioner murmur, the rush of a jet through the sky overhead, while thinking of strangers across crowded rooms and wondering if she would see them again. She realized then she wasn't alone, catching Tom's masculine scent beside her, along with the slight hint of leather from the gun in its holster next to the clock on the night stand. His breathing was slow and peaceful, and she wondered what he was dreaming about. He hoped to rise in his "company" -- whatever that actually was -- and he was serving his country, but what did he really want from life?

But, what had she dreamed about lately? Climbing the rungs of her corporate ladder, soaring above the ceiling of glass on the wings of Captain Keto's sales? Piloting Zack through high school and college...

And then he'd leave home, and what would she have?

An all-American empty nest? A retirement condo in St. Petersburg or some other comfortable God's waiting room? ...Assuming there was a god to wait for. Then, would there be some great Final Judgment, an audit, perhaps, of the worth of her life and what she had *really* accomplished on earth? She had already guessed that toys wouldn't matter, and money meant nothing beyond the grave; but what *would* get her passport stamped to enter the ultimate Magic Kingdom? She pictured herself in some astral boardroom making her last presentation to God, who glowered down like Seth Barrymore. She heard herself pitching, "I got Captain Keto out on the shelves."

She glanced at the clock's ruby numbers: 1:56 though it seemed a lot later. The evening *had* seemed enchanted, for both herself and Zack. Not only had Zack been airlifted home, off-the-hooking his privileged peers and even surprising Dillon who'd flown many times in the Barrymore craft; but Tom's machine had excited Zack beyond the bounds of a Eurocopter. Zack had amazed Nicole with his knowledge, wisdom as totally unsuspected as -- maybe -- his knowledge of sex. Tom's aircraft was a Bell ARH, which in military mode was a "hunter-killer" with a Gatling gun, Hellfire Missiles, and other death-dealing accessories. Of course, it didn't have those things – "NMC," according to Zack -- but Zack seemed to know where they could have been mounted, and Tom had looked impressed.

They had gone to the mall in a mere minivan that could only slay by direct contact, and Tom had bought a model for Zack of his helicopter dressed to kill. Then they had dined on taxpayer money – Zack choosing Outback Steakhouse – returned home to fly to his graduation, and finally soared back with his friends. Tom and Zack had seemed to click, especially after a flying lesson with Zack's chubby hands on a real joystick, though he couldn't drop bombs or shoot anyone.

Nicole had wondered how Tom would react actually seeing Zack in the flesh... and there was a lot of that to see. She'd forgotten to buy him a new dress shirt, and he'd looked like a rolly-poly sausage stuffed in way too small a skin. Even his graduation gown, ordered just after Christmas, made him resemble a fat young girl with very well-developed breasts. But, Tom hadn't seemed to notice his shape – or what could have been called his lack of it -- or mind being seen with a sweaty fat boy who managed to smell despite a shower... assuming

120

he'd actually taken one. They had gotten many curious looks, this handsome muscular Man In Black -- though still camouflaged in moderate gray -- conversing with Zack about airplanes and weapons while Zack attacked the refreshment table like Slimer doing his favorite thing. Was Zack an unsuspected genius being recruited by NASA?

Tom's acceptance of size and shape had included Zack's friend, the huge Austin Colt, who had to be boosted into the aircraft and couldn't fasten his safety belt. They'd landed back home around ten o'clock, and the neighbors were probably wetting themselves... was the C.I.A. recruiting Nicole? Or had she seen a UFO?

Then she and Tom had gone out for drinks, leaving Zack and posse to video games, Dominos pizzas and clandestine beer. There was a tactful understanding that Tom would be spending the night... though presumably in a guest room.

Now, Nicole lay in the whispering darkness with Tom's peaceful breathing warm on her cheek. It had been a long time, almost two years, and Tom was perfection in all proportions, brave, clean, and reverent, too. And his suitcase had proven him well prepared... Nicole had had an uncomfortable moment, fearing she might have to call upon Zack to borrow a bit of common sense. Could this be the start of something, she wondered? And whether or not she went to Kiwanja?

The neighborhood was usually quiet, and night overflights by police helicopters were generally cause for indignant complaints instead of a sense of security. She noticed a glow through the window curtains: for a moment she thought it might be the moon, almost full and beautifully bright, especially when seen from up in the sky, but it was the lights of the pool. The power expense was of no concern, though her mother would have scolded her for wasteful American decadence. Nicole had wanted her parents to come for Zack's graduation; she would have gladly paid their way but they refused to fly these days, not supporting invasive searches based on the politics of fear. Nicole had suggested the train, but they were busy expanding their shop and couldn't take the time, though they'd promised to come for Thanksgiving. They had written a loving letter to Zack, and

121

besides a model airplane -- a harmless Piper Cub -- had included a hundred-dollar check and a fifty-dollar McDonald's gift card.

She thought about the Kiwanji boots -- her parents would probably love them -- but that was getting ahead of herself. She had to decide about making the trip and talk it over with Zack. He might not even want to come: no computers or video games, television or fast-food joints.

Did boys want adventures anymore like Tom Swift or Tintin? He'd never wanted to be a Boy Scout, though Nicole had never encouraged him: he didn't need more American values, patriotism *al a' mode* with male cold-water camaraderie and hotdogs roasted on sticks. And of course these days the Scouts wouldn't want him since he no longer fit their Hitler Youth profile... a good xenophobe was lean and mean. She had thought about taking him camping herself, but had worried about being "too strong a woman," thanks to a TV psychiatrist... supposedly, that might confuse Zack in his early years of puberty.

She and Tom had returned at eleven, finding the house was still intact with no police or firemen, paramedics or pissed-off neighbors. She had thoughtfully dialed up Zackary's phone instead of invading his space. His voice had sounded slightly slurred with the usual background of goth or punk -- his generation's regurgitation of typical teenage alienation -- but everything seemed to be under control. She had just as thoughtfully locked her door when she and Tom had retired.

The boys' brutal music had blasted till twelve, as allowed by the neighborhood council, but now there was only suburban silence. Over the sighing of Tom's gentle breaths came the trickling splash of the water slide. It made a soothing lullaby, but the pump and lights were an energy waste.

She heard her mother scolding her from several states away, and quietly eased from the bed. She half expected Tom to wake up and possibly go for his gun, but reminded herself he wasn't James Bond as she slipped on her bathrobe and crept from the room.

The cavernous kitchen was softly lit by the sapphire glow of the pool. The range was a sacrificial slab; the fridge loomed huge and vaguely forbidding while mindlessly making more unwanted ice. The patio door was open a crack, and she paused to peer out, hearing voices.

The amber lion twitched its tail, making its low-tech mechanical sounds and displaying the time as a minute past two. Yet, Zack and his friends were in the Jacuzzi. Zackary looked like a bare-breasted girl, Austin a mammoth mass of rolls, his breasts the size of cantaloupes, and Dillon a perfectly godlike boy in spite of his mane of green hair. She wondered about a circle jerk, but saw they had bottles of Heineken and were maybe discussing the meaning of life as applied to their generation.

What would that be, she wondered? That he who dies with the most toys wins? That "lesser races" existed to serve and thus were permitted to live on condition... supply them with oil, make their clothes and shoes, assemble their high-definition TVs so they could watch all the civilized people savagely raping the world?

She had *not* given birth to a monster! ... But could she be nurturing one?

And how in the world could she stop?

They lounged in the softly swirling water, which glowed a cool blue in the heat of the night. She recalled her own graduation party, rocking till dawn with ELO, Reo Speedwagon, Boston and Styx. She remembered the scent of the tall summer grass, the breeze drifting down from the moonlit hilltops, and the sparkling brook, now long defiled. The future had seemed so bright in those days, the world like a great enchanted adventure in which she was free to roam as she pleased and choose any number of shiny new dreams.

But, what kind of dreams did Zackary have? And, what kind of dreams had she given him? He had everything in the world right here.

And maybe that was wrong?

She was about to return to bed when she heard a word as sharp as nigger, one of those words that always carried even across a crowded room. For a moment she hovered in indecision, not wanting to spy though she had every right. The word had come from Dillon's lips, that splendidly muscular male of gold, the perfect All-American boy.

The wall of glass would be mirrored outside, but Nicole moved away from the door. The two other boys, Zack and Austin, seemed to be drunkenly pondering. Austin spoke first:

"Maybe it's hormones?"

"Yeah," said Zack. "Like, are you *sure?*"

Dillon stared down at the swirling blue water, a green bottle clutched in a strong golden hand. "I'm sure," he said with deadly conviction as if he had cancer and six months to live.

"But you had sex with a *girl*," said Zack, a revelation that made Nicole wince.

Dillon shrugged his powerful shoulders. "I thought it would cure me." He heaved a dramatic drunk-kid sigh. "But, I guess like they say, I was born like I am. ...I always kinda knew ever since I was about eight."

Dillon's confession was shocking enough, but his Texas drawl made it surreal... Nicole couldn't think of a drawler like that.

"Um?" asked Austin logically. "Is that why you like jackin'-off with us?"

Dillon looked surprised. "No, I just like jackin'-off."

"But, do you like *us?*" Austin persisted.

"'Course I do, but not *that* way."

"'Cause we're fat?" asked Austin.

Zack crossed his arms behind his head and struck a provocative pose. "An' 'cause I kinda look like a girl?"

"No! 'Cause you're my *friends*, dumb shit!"

"So you don't wanna bone us up our butts?"

"That's disgustin'!" snapped Dillion, then added wistfully, "I just wanna find somebody to love."

Don't we all, thought Nicole.

"Does your dad know?" asked Zack.

"Oh hell no! He'd disown me or kill me... or probably both."

"Well," said Zack, "it don't matter to me." He manfully punched Dillon's arm. "You're still the same dorky Dillon."

"Me neither," said Austin, also adding a punch. "But, what y'all gonna do?"

"Run away maybe," said Dillon. "Like to New York or San Francisco. ...Or maybe I'll shoot myself."

"Don't say shit like that!" snapped Zack.

Dillon drained his bottle. "I don't know else what to do... an' dad's gonna gimmie another damn gun for a graduation present!"

That should have sounded ridiculous, but Nicole understood well enough.

"Wow," said a voice in the shadows.

Nicole jumped as if hearing a rattlesnake... one had invaded the kitchen last year and she'd had to call Animal Rescue.

"Sorry," said Tom, clad in boxers. "I was going to get a glass of water." He looked out at the boys. "That's going to rock the Barrymore world!"

Nicole felt a twinge of unfocused fear. "I wish he hadn't told Zack. It's too much to put on his shoulders."

"Guess Dillon trusts him," said Tom.

"It's like giving Zack a bomb to guard."

"Could be," said Tom. "At least on Planet Barrymore. What about the other boy?"

"Austin? He's part of the junior good ol' boy gang; you don't shoot partners in the back for anything less than a lot of money."

"Nothing you can do about it."

Nicole sighed. "Why in hell today?"

"Guess it has been a long one for you."

"Would you like a drink?" asked Nicole.

"I'll fix it," said Tom.

"There's gin in the fridge, unless the boys got it." Nicole looked out at the pool again, but the boys had retired to Zackary's room, going in through its patio door and leaving a glistening trail on the tile. She drew the curtains and switched on the light. "How could I leave him now?" she asked. "With a secret like that on his mind."

Tom got ice and a bottle of tonic. "Maybe you're over-reacting?" He smiled. "You don't think Dwane *would* kill Dillon?"

"Probably not, though his grandfather might have."

"Or maybe just taken him to the best little whorehouse in Texas."

"Apparently Dillon tried that already... and I assume in Zack's bed."

Tom handed a glass to Nicole. "I'm a professional secret keeper. And it may not matter if Zack knows. Or won't in the very near future."

"What do you mean?" asked Nicole.

Tom sipped his drink. "Dillon must have a computer. The servers keep logs of his time on-line, including his email and messages. Also a list of the sites he visits, along with whatever files he downloads. That isn't secure information and any hacker could get it. Not to mention the Homeland gang or twenty other agencies."

"Who else could get it?" asked Nicole.

"Any of Dwane's competitors." Tom took another sip from his glass. "Dillon probably buys certain magazines, or looks at them in stores; and everyone's on camera these days. I'm sure he rents movies and pays with a card. Anybody who's watching will see a pattern... assuming they haven't already."

"The purpose of information is power. Usually over other people."

"I only evaluate threats," said Tom. "You do the same thing when you're out on the street and see a suspicious character. Do you cross the street to avoid him? Or reach for your Mace and go on?"

"I don't carry Mace."

"Might not be a bad idea." Tom smiled. "I saw you sizing up Aaron Steele, evaluating a possible threat."

Nicole frowned. "I'm not trying to be sarcastic, but is Dillon a threat to the government?"

Tom rattled the ice in his glass. "He could prove to be an embarrassment in certain situations. Probably not at the moment, but possibly in the future. Especially if he stays undercover."

"Blackmail, you mean? Him or his father?"

"Always a chance of that," said Tom, "even in this 'enlightened' age. Dwane has a government contract... those military uniforms. Then, there's this possible African deal."

"Kiwanja?" asked Nicole. "How could could Dillon's... orientation... have any effect on that?"

"Like I've said, we don't know much about Kiwanja... that's your mission if you choose to accept it. But lots of primitive cultures have taboos against same-sex relations, ostensibly for religious reasons but actually stemming from pre-history when a tribe's survival depended on numbers. It's still a capital crime in some countries. Two boys were publicly hung last year in one of those less-enlightened lands."

"I read about that," said Nicole. "But what about someone like Aaron Steele? ...Assuming those rumors are true?"

"No comment," said Tom. "But, Steele only works for Barrymore, so Dwane could throw him to the wolves. Pretend to be shocked... assuming he knows. Or really be shocked if he doesn't know, which would play even better. But, Dillon owns the company. Or will in a few more years."

"I suppose you checked on Zack for... anything like that?"

"You know I had to."

"So, I guess he's not a threat?"

"I'd call him a normal American boy with a healthy interest in sex and violence. Also airplanes and weapons."

"I never knew how much he knew. I guess I should have asked."

"You're a normal American parent, Nicole, stressed, concerned, and a little confused. But, you're doing okay, and so is Zack... assuming you trust my opinion."

"Thank you." Nicole sipped her drink and sighed. "There's that damn barbecue this weekend! All that manly cowboy crap in honor of Dillon's graduation. It's going to seem like a farce."

"Dillon could still be a cowboy. This *is* the twenty-first century."

"It's still the late nineteenth to Dwane. But I was thinking of Zack," said Nicole. "Tonight he's drunk, but tomorrow he might have a different perspective."

"About keeping Dillon's secret?"

"I'm sure he'd keep it, but it might be a burden. And I have to pretend not to know."

"Maybe he'll tell you."

"He never said much about airplanes. Though it should have been obvious... all those models. I should have asked about his interests. But, I can't ask about this."

"He might ask for advice."

"I'm not sure about that. We've never even had 'the talk.' It seems to be obsolete these days with the Internet doing it for you. Or maybe I waited too long. ...You seem to know more about him than I do."

"Then trust me," said Tom. "He's a good kid and you're a good parent. I just look at the dark side of things. Sometimes I forget there's a bright one. Zack seemed pretty hot about flying tonight."

"You're not exactly a bad role model."

"Thanks," said Tom. "I'm sure the helicopter helped. But, I really like Zack. ...And you."

"Even knowing our secrets?"

"Not all secrets are dark and dirty."

Nicole parted the curtains to gaze at the moon. "It's been a nice evening. ...More than just nice. Even after this. The best I've had in years. And for Zack. Like a genie granted our wishes."

"Therefore too good to be true?"

"The curse of being a cynic."

"If you weren't you'd be brain-dead like most of America. ...But, what do you want me to say? That going to Zack's graduation to-night, being here now... or even just taking you home this morning, wasn't part of my job?"

"I don't want you to say it if it isn't true."

Tom took Nicole's hand. "I'd really like to see you again. And Zack. Boots or no boots. It probably sounds clichéd as hell, but I wish we'd met in some other way."

"Maybe I'm seeing the dark side, too."

"Don't forget there's a bright one." Tom waved a hand around. "And maybe a way to get free of 'all this' and do what you really want to do."

"I'm not sure what that is anymore. I used to have dreams but they all flew away."

"Maybe you just need a new perspective."

"Back to business?"

"Why *don't* you take Zack to Kiwanja? Time to let Dillon's fallout settle, assuming there might be any. And stay out of range while it does. At least you'd avoid the damn barbecue."

Nicole nodded slowly. "It might be good for Zack. He doesn't know how lucky he is compared to most of the kids in this world. Maybe it's time he found out."

"I can't guarantee your safety."

"I'd be surprised if you said you could. And probably suspicious." Nicole looked out across the pool, where a thousand street lamps promised safety, along with home security systems, prowling police, a private patrol, and a rabidly paranoid neighborhood watch. "I worry about Zack when he goes to the mall, or just down the block for Circle K snacks. I guess I never bought the illusion, and he shouldn't buy it either."

"I can get him a passport tomorrow," said Tom, then glanced at the clock. "I mean today."

"Don't you need a picture?"

Tom flashed his naughty Tom Cruise smile. "Already have one. Good-looking, too."

"I think I'd be surprised if you didn't. ...What about shots?"

"We'll give you diplomat treatment."

"The same as our spies?"

"They can't do spy stuff if they're sick."

"I'll pass on the cyanide pill," said Nicole.

"You'd have to have a tooth hollowed out."

"Did you?"

"Dentists scare me. But I could wrangle a 'spy phone'... works with the GPS system... so I'd always know where you were."

"I thought you didn't watch that 'stone-age' part of the world?"

"Do you tell people everything you know? Especially in board-room meetings? The truth, the whole truth, and nothing but the truth usually isn't good for business. Or protecting a country."

"I see your point."

"You've been in the African bush," added Tom. "Things fall apart, planes don't fly, busses break down, and trains crap-out in the middle of nowhere."

"So, I push a button and the American eagle swoops to my rescue?"

"I'd have to call in a few favors. But at least you wouldn't be stranded." Tom smiled. "Think of it as Disney Mobile; I'll always know where my children are. And if Barrymore won't pay for Zack..."

"I can afford it," said Nicole. "Besides, I could write it off."

"So can Dwane."

Nicole gazed out at the nearly-full moon; the same moon that shone on Kiwanja... well, it was morning there by now. She felt suddenly weary, yet hopeful, too. She studied the handsome man beside her. Was it worth two weeks of dust and heat, probable flies, and possible danger in trade for something she might really want? ...Or at least find out if something existed?

She switched off the lights in the pool. "I'll talk with Zack in the morning."

THIRTEEN

Dawn came first to the not-quite mountain, crowning its crest with glowing gold as the morning breeze rustled its amber grass before rippling down to the still-shadowed valley. Tindo was first to see the new sun, watching it slowly spread light on the land. Tindo was ten and wrapped in a blanket to fend off the chill of the vanishing night. His rifle lay across his legs, and an ancient British walkie-talkie was slung by its strap on his shoulder. He wore old jeans and antelope boots, and sat within a primitive bunker, a circle of stones and piled-up earth, its dirt floor littered with cigarette ends and a scatter of candy bar wrappers. A wooden crate stood in the center providing a seat for the sentry, who thus could observe the surrounding land for many miles in every direction. The bunker's walls were head-high to the boy as he slid off the crate and shed his blanket to welcome the warmth of the sun. Then he sank to his knees and bowed his head, giving thanks to the Lion Of Life.

He'd taken his post as the moon had set, relieving Damu in silver starlight. His dog had accompanied him, but dogs couldn't talk of dreams or fears, so the watch had been silent and lonely. Sometimes, far overhead in the sky, he'd seen faint lights and heard jet engines and tried to imagine the people up there; pictures seen in magazines, rows of seats, pale foreign faces, and food being served on plastic trays. His thoughts now turned to breakfast: he could smell the smoke of cooking fires flaring to life in the village. The dog gave him a questioning look.

"Soon, Mbwa," said Tindo. Almost all dogs were named Mbwa and were never regarded as pets. They were always loved but seldom coddled, and talking to one was considered odd.

Slinging his rifle over a shoulder, Tindo mounted the grassy wall to study the valley below. Figures had gathered around the airplane, a wooden ramp had been set up and a jeep was being unloaded. This didn't look like an easy task; the jeep would barely fit through the doors and had to be carefully wrestled out by the muscles of many young boys.

He picked up a pair of binoculars, massive old things from the British Army, and focused them on the airplane. There was Dakota in charge of the work; and the airplane seemed to be giving birth as the jeep was coaxed onto the ramp. Various cargo lay on the ground like a sort of mechanical water-breaking... a stack of banded roofing tin, cardboard boxes, plastic pipe, drums of fuel and kerosene. Off to one side of the landing field, shunned and grim in the amber grass, lay the ominous shape of the coffin. Tindo remembered its stench roaring out like the Lion Of Death in the moonlight, and its reek had haunted his thoughts all night while sitting up here in the dark. He shuddered, and swung the glasses away. The village across the glimmering stream was hidden by acacia trees, but cooking smoke was drifting up, and Tindo's stomach growled. Mbwa gave him a puzzled look as if wondering why he was staying up here: what could be more important than food?

The sun was now bright on the hilltop, and the air was growing warm. Tindo shifted the glasses again: there was Changa leaving the trees, eight-years-old with shouldered rifle, coming to take the watch. Tindo thought of potatoes and eggs. Maybe a juicy slice of pork. Then he would take a nap until noon and might avoid the coffin.

Then, something caught his eye to the east. He lifted the binoculars and saw a distant cloud of dust. Grabbing the walkie-talkie, he pressed the transmit switch.

Down in the village under the trees, a boy stood guard at the chief's front gate. Another battered walkie-talkie hung by its strap in the hedge and suddenly crackled with static. The boy took it up and listened a moment, then ran to beat a wooden drum. Women looked up from breakfast fires, and grandfathers came to doorways. Across the stream on the landing field, boys stopped work and seized their rifles, leaving the jeep still half in the plane. They looked to Thabo, the eldest, who'd grabbed his gun and was scanning the hills. Kobe, beside him, cocked his weapon, and there were a dozen clattering echoes. The dogs had also sensed an alert and seemed to be waiting for orders.

Nathi, beneath the port side wing, had been pumping oil into the engine's tank, and emerged to scan the lightening sky. Dakota, still inside the plane, ran forward into the cockpit. He flipped a switch on the radio and waited for its tubes to warm as the dynamotor whined to life. Clamping the headphones over his ears, he thumbed the microphone: "Basenji. Simba."

High above on the not-quite mountain, Tindo aimed his binoculars at the distant swirl of dust. Mbwa poised beside him, hearing what Tindo could not… the faraway rumble of engines. Tindo sharpened the focus, straining to penetrate the dust. Finally, he keyed the walkie-talkie: "Simba. Basenji. Duma is coming."

"Very well." Dakota leaned out the window. "It's Rashawn," he called to the boys below.

Tenseness left the air. Nathi returned to the oil pump and the boys went back to unloading the jeep. At last it was out on the ramp. Dakota climbed into the driver's seat, flipped a switch, and stepped on the starter.

"May we ride?" asked Abu, as Dakota nursed the engine to life, pumping the gas and pulling the choke.

"Hurry. It's almost full day."

The jeep was instantly buried in boys, the smallest scrambling atop the hood and over the lowered windscreen. Their rifles clashed as they jostled for room.

"Careful! Don't break the glass!" warned Dakota.

Kobe clambered aboard, burrowing into the squirming boys, while Thabo claimed the passenger seat by lifting Abu onto the cowl. Kobe groaned and massaged his belly. "I ate too much last night."

Dakota laughed. "Quite usual for an hyena." He pushed the choke knob all the way in as the engine warmed and its idle smoothed out.

Thabo asked, "Do we have time for a driving lesson?"

"Not now," said Dakota. He glanced at the brightening sky. "We don't know how well they can see. But I've read they can even spot heat from an engine."

Thabo scowled. "If so, why bother trying to hide if we're all just ants for them to watch and step on if they choose?" He stabbed two fingers skyward. "Let them see this!"

"There are other things in the air," said Dakota. "Such as the General's helicopter."

Backing the vehicle down the ramp, he drove to the foot of the not-quite mountain and into a grove of acacia trees. A truck sat in shadow, a White half-track from World War II dusted with feathery gold. A skate-rail for a machine gun was mounted above its armored body, but there was no gun and the truck couldn't fight. Its heavy hood plates had been removed and it was missing its iron heart along with its fifty-caliber teeth. A hoist had been rigged from a tree branch, and a grease-caked engine lay on the ground. Dakota brought the jeep to a halt near the front of the armored machine.

"Rashawn said I might drive it," said Kobe, indicating the half-track.

"And I might command it," said Thabo.

Abu piped, "It's the closest thing to a tank in Kiwanja, and may defeat the General."

"It may at least give him a fright," said Dakota. He studied the branches overhead to be sure the jeep couldn't be seen from the air, then switched off the ignition. The younger boys avalanched out and began walking back to the airplane. Dakota called, "Unload the new engine and bring it here."

"I will command," said Abu.

"I ate too much," moaned Kobe again.

Dakota grinned. "I'm sure you'll feel better after breakfast."

"Do Americans feel like this every morning?"

"It would explain a lot if they do."

"Do you think they all hate us?" asked Thabo. "The people, I mean,

134

not their leaders."

"Perhaps their own General lies," said Dakota, "telling them we're terrorists and a threat to their way of life."

"You have the gun?" asked Thabo, scanning the half-track again. The old machine was newly painted in amber and gold with shadings of black.

"Yes, though I'm sure it's quite nasty."

"May the General find it twice as nasty!"

"Ammunition?" asked Kobe.

"It's being arranged," said Dakota.

"Will there be tracers?" asked Thabo.

"If we're not cheated again."

"Does everyone cheat in cities?"

"More often than not; they call it business."

"I should like breakfast," said Kobe.

"Go ahead," said Dakota. "But don't take a nap afterward; we have to reload the freight."

Thabo added, "Then install the half-track's engine."

"You should have it in by tonight," said Dakota. "The manual has the instructions."

The sun was clearing the eastern hills, bathing the valley in tawny shades, enhancing the gold and green of the trees and sparkling silvery bright on the stream. The younger boys had reached the plane and Abu took charge of unloading the engine, boys dragging it out on its wooden skids and onto an ancient donkey cart, although there was no donkey.

Nathi was still beneath the wing, repairing the leak on the landing gear, when Fila came over the foot-bridge.

"I brought you breakfast," said Fila.

"Thank you," said Nathi. He sat on the airplane's tire as Fila offered a platter. There were eggs, potatoes, a slice of pork, and a wooden eating utensil that looked like a marriage of fork and spoon. Nathi drew his knife to cut the meat.

"How is it?" asked Fila.

"Delicious," said Nathi. "You have the list of school supplies?"

Fila drew a sheet of paper from the top of her skirt. "I didn't ask for much. And the books can be bought second-hand."

"I know of a shop in Hillbrow," said Nathi. "Aren't you having school today?"

"Only the girls. The boys will want to be with Rashawn and learn about weapons and war."

"Those things are necessary now, but hopefully that will pass."

"Do you think we will win?"

"We have a chance if the rains come on time."

"A good chance, Nathi?"

"Even a small chance is better than none."

Fila glanced at the sweating boys pulling the cart toward the trees. "And, if we win, things will return to the way they were?"

"Not for this generation." Nathi watched the boys for a moment, then looked at the coffin grim in the grass. "War has left its stench on them. But, maybe time will wash it away. We can only hope."

"And pray."

"Only for good," said Nathi, "Abundant harvests, healthy children, a place of peace where enough is sufficient."

"But not to win the war?"

"Wars are made by men, not God. And wars are never holy."

"You're closer to God when you're flying," said Fila. "Pray for good up there."

"I often do."

Fila touched a propeller blade. "It must feel free to soar in the sky."

"It does," said Nathi. "But, one must always return to the earth and deal with all its pain and sorrows."

Fila faced the hillside burying ground as the sunlight slowly strengthened. "It's hard to forget the sorrows. But, life begins anew each day, and there is the future to think of."

Nathi was silent a moment, also watching the sunlight spread amongst the graveyard monuments. "Our men will return when the war is over... most of them, I hope. Weary, yes, wiser perhaps, but still young, and strong as lions."

"But, you are wiser now."

"Perhaps too much," said Nathi. He glanced at Dakota, who, accompanied by Thabo and Kobe, was returning from the acacia grove. "Too many children have lost their fathers, and flying is a dangerous life even in times of peace."

Fila gazed at the airplane. "She is very lucky."

"She's also very old and cross, as I have been feeling these days. We're like an old couple who constantly bicker."

"But still love each other," said Fila, then smiled. "Perhaps I should be jealous."

"She should be jealous of you, Fila... young and pretty, a whole life to live."

Fila turned toward the village. "I must begin school. Fly safely, Nathi. And always come back."

The sun had filled the valley, and much of the freight had been reloaded. Boys were pumping fuel from a drum while Dakota watched a glass-bowl filter and drained out spurts of water. Nathi was checking a landing light cover, tightening its securing wire, when distant engine sounds were heard. Dust appeared in a gap in the hills where the stream flowed out to the plain.

"Keep at it," ordered Dakota, when the other boys paused to watch the dust.

Soon, an ancient Land Rover, Series I, topless, doorless, its windscreen down, came rattling over the landing field. It was trailed by an equally ancient truck, a CCKW from World War II. The truck's lowered windscreen was starred with cracks that spider-webbed from bullet holes. Other holes riddled its body, which was painted like the half-track. Various crates, containers and tools were lashed to the running boards and fenders. Except for its ring-mount machine gun, the vehicle might have been going to market instead of fighting a war.

A boy of thirteen was driving the truck, and three younger boys sat beside him. All wore loincloths and antelope boots, the former patterned in ambers and golds with shadings of black like the vehicles. Their ebony bodies were tawny with dust, their wild hair banded by sweaty rags that mirrored the camouflage pattern. Other boys rode in the truck bed, jolted about on the wooden bench seats and sharing the space with drums of fuel and other supplies. All were armed with Russian AKs, most decorated with feathers and beads. Every boy over the age of twelve wore a tuft of lion's mane on his chest. A few of the boys were raggedly bandaged with blood-stains showing like rust on the cloth. All were lean and looked exhausted. Some were even sprawled asleep despite the jolting and bash of the truck. There was a gritty squeal of brakes as the vehicles came to a stop at the plane and dust settled slowly like weary ghosts.

A boy also drove the Land Rover. He was around Dakota's age, though his face looked several years older, partly because of a leather eye patch. His remaining eye was reddened by dust and seemed only half awake. He switched off the engine and slumped in the seat, closing his eye to the morning.

The man beside him was maybe mid-twenties, his muscles defined in bold relief, his hair subdued with a rag like the boys'. He wore antelope boots, but was clad in trousers, also patterned in ambers and golds. A tuft of fur adorned his chest, a Kalishnikov pistol rode on his hip.

The village boys ran to the Rover, though Dakota remained pumping fuel. Rifles clashed and clattered as the boys crowded up to the man. Compared to the youths in the truck, the village boys looked plump as puppies and just as energetic. Still, they made no demands of the man as they would have done of Nathi. They moved back in respect as he got out, though the dogs didn't seem at all impressed and were busily marking the vehicles' tires.

Thabo and Kobe had joined the group, but glanced at Dakota, who finished his task and pulled the hose from the airplane's tank. The younger boys now ran to the truck and began to question the dust-covered youths, most of whom were climbing down and helping their wounded companions. One of them called, "Akono is dead."

"Bury him," ordered the man.

Nathi emerged from under a wing, wiping his hands on a rag. "Without ceremony?" he asked, coming to the Rover.

"*Salamu*, Nathi," said the man. "We've grown accustomed to that."

"Leaving spirits to wander," said Nathi. "You're filling our land with ghosts, Rashawn, just as the General is doing. Ghosts who will haunt us forever."

"Surely you don't believe that?"

"I haven't become so civilized that I think I know more than God.

138

Jumbe Chane will lay him to rest." Nathi turned to Thabo. "Please go tell him. Kobe, you'll also be needed."

Thabo and Kobe hesitated, but then trotted off to the village.

"I need them, too," said Rashawn.

"No," said Nathi. "They are needed *here* to protect the village."

"You've not been attacked," said Rashawn.

"Yet."

Rashawn blew dust from his nose. "The Army fears to travel this far and camp in open country, and that's because of my men."

"Or perhaps The Lion Of Death."

"If they believe that, so much the better."

Nathi regarded the weary boys around the battered truck. "Here you have a place to rest and assemble your equipment. We also supply you with food. And you've already taken most of our men. Have you forgotten when enough is sufficient?"

"When I have enough to defeat the General, that will be sufficient."

"We buried two more of your fighters... with ceremony... yesterday. The ones you left at the border village. Also one of the General's."

"I was afraid they would die."

"I suppose it was expected of them."

Rashawn frowned. "I had to leave a delaying defense." He glanced at the ancient truck. "I could not have outrun the Army in that, especially filled with villagers. And my other broke down across the border, though fortunately it's safe. I need a six-volt dynamo. A Delco-Remy."

"I know the type," said Nathi. "Are the villagers as safe as your truck?"

"They have a camp near water, and I left all the food I could spare. You'll have to bring them more. And something for shelter against the rains."

"Permits are required to land in someone else's country."

"Were such things ever a bother for you?"

Nathi glanced at Dakota, who'd come to stand beside him. "This is becoming difficult. I'm sure the General suspects by now that we've been supplying you."

"What can he do about that?" said Rashawn. "Shoot you down with his helicopter? His pilot barely knows how to fly."

Dakota asked, "Wasn't there an instructor? A man the Americans sent?"

Rashawn smiled. "He was killed by a thief in the night. The town has become a dangerous place since the General brought it civilization."

Nathi said, "American missiles are smarter than pilots. They fly very well by themselves."

"The General doesn't have missiles."

"Yet," said Nathi.

"You'll know as soon as he does."

"Perhaps when all goes bright," said Nathi.

"We still have to fly to the town," said Dakota. "And, as my father said, we're suspected of aiding the terrorists."

Rashawn snorted. "You're only aiding the General."

"We're helping our people," said Nathi.

Dakota added, "Those in town have little. No milk for their children, no oil for their lamps. The General rations the power supply, though his compound is very well lighted at night."

Rashawn laughed. "I expect he's become afraid of the dark. And perhaps The Lion Of Death."

"I notice you still wear your honor," said Nathi.

Rashawn glanced down at his chest. "People need symbols to follow... flags, banners, idols, gods."

"What do you follow?" asked Nathi.

"My heart," said Rashawn, slapping his chest. "Isn't that why you chose me?"

"The true test of your heart will come if we win."

Dakota spoke, "Young children are begging in town. The Army takes the boys and men, leaving the women and girls to starve."

"It also takes most of your help," said Rashawn.

"Some still reaches the people," said Nathi. "And some is better than none."

Rashawn shrugged. "I suppose it must be done, if only to lessen suspicion."

"If only to help the people," said Nathi. "As a true leader would."

Dakota scanned the group of youths who were sitting around the truck. A small figure lay on the ground, and the village children warded off flies. "What happened?"

"We tried to capture another truck. We need two more to mount the attack and there's no longer time to fly them in pieces and reassemble them here." He looked at the sky. "Timing is critical now... after the airfield is flooded in town, but before the river rises too high."

Nathi studied the weary boys. "Where are the older experienced men?"

"In reserve and training the young. Too valuable to risk."

"Perhaps if you'd risked a few older men, your young would not have died yesterday."

Dakota added, "And maybe you'd have those trucks."

Rashawn frowned. "And maybe you've been too long in the sky? The view is not as clear on earth."

"I would go with you," said Dakota.

Rashawn lay a hand on Dakota's shoulder. "Your courage has never been in doubt." He faced Nathi. "Nor has yours." He glanced at the small dusty body. "And you're right, the dead should be laid to rest with appropriate ceremony."

Dakota said, "I'll get a blanket to cover him."

Nathi added, "I'll see that your fighters get food, and care for the wounded."

"Thank you." Rashawn called to the boys, "Drive the truck under the trees, then go to the village." He prodded his driver who'd fallen asleep. "Sefu! Follow the truck."

The vehicles rattled away, and the fighters trudged off to the footbridge, accompanied by the village boys.

Rashawn asked, "Did you get the jeep and the engine?"

"Under the trees," said Nathi.

Rashawn looked skyward. "How well do you think they can see?"

"On a clear day like this? I've been told they can read number plates on a car."

"When the rains come they won't see as clearly. What has *Jumbe* Chane predicted?"

"I thought you didn't believe anymore?"

"I believe God is with us. Don't you?"

"God is always with us," said Nathi.

"I meant that He is on our side."

Nathi regarded the little valley, the amber hills, the green and gold trees, the village across the silver stream. "I believe He watches in sadness when His children make war on each other."

Rashawn lay a hand on Nathi's shoulder. "I miss our talks in the moonlight, cousin."

"So do I, cousin," said Nathi.

"And *Jumbe* Chane's prediction?"

"A week at most until the rains."

"We must be ready," said Rashawn. "It's the only chance we have."

Nathi pointed across the field. "There's your coffin."

FOURTEEN

"I thought Africa belonged to black people?"

Nicole looked around the restaurant, seeing mostly shades of beige on European faces. Browns and tans were well represented -- Middle-Eastern, a turbaned Sikh, several Asians sharing a table -- but except for a handful of dark men in suits the only black people were waiters. If not for the rather foreign decor and predominance of tailored attire, they might have been dining at Dennys in Houston.

She smiled at Zack who, in baggy blue-jeans and a white T-shirt, could have passed for Canadian, or maybe an Australian boy. Both were non-aggressive nations that didn't throw their weight around despite an abundance of Triple-X youth. His shaggy mop of golden hair – he'd seen the sense of not going green in a possibly less-enlightened land -- enhanced the look of a Commonwealth kid; and the ebony waiter had said "G'day" when Zack had ordered steak-and-eggs.

"We're still at the airport," said Nicole. "It's one of the busiest in the world so there's a lot of different people."

"Oh," said Zack, his mouth full of meat. "So, this ain't really Africa yet?"

Nicole refrained from scolding his "ain't." Their plane had landed

143

around midnight, and Zack had been soundly sprawled asleep despite the I-pod headphones blasting rock in his ears. The brutal beat was a stark contrast to his face so cherubic and cute. His breasts had bobbed like Jell-O balls as the airplane bounced in the African wind, and the flight attendant had paused to ask if the "young lady's lap-strap was fastened."

Although it was two PM in Houston, the time-change seemed to have muddled his mind -- or maybe that he'd been eating non-stop ever since they'd embarked -- though somewhere over the South Atlantic he'd wobbled his way to the bathroom and joined the Mile-High Club with himself... though hopefully only she'd noticed the scent because she'd half expected it.

He hadn't really woken up, even while being searched in Customs and having his belly inspected beneath for possible smuggled contraband... the gloved officer making no comment about state of his boxers, probably having seen everything twice. In the U.S. Zack been stripped to his shorts and a scanner run over his various rolls as if fat kids were a terrorist threat.

Once through Johannesburg Customs he'd shambled along with droopy jeans puddling over his shuffling sneaks, dragging his suitcase behind on its leash and yawning like a tranquilized lion. Even a Coke from a corridor shop hadn't done much to perk him up, and Nicole had been grateful for Jenny's foresight in booking a room at the airport hotel. The place was obscenely expensive, and she doubted if even Aaron Steele would have risked his fabled expense account by lodging under its opulent roof. According to the bedside brochure...

This deluxe hotel has drawn its inspiration from the African continent, capturing the culture and spirit of Africa through the use of simple shapes and symbolic artifacts to create an African environment in a contemporary setting.

Nicole would have called it Lion King modern.

The flight had also been first-class with triple-X meals and copious snacks, which Zack had enjoyed to the fullest. She'd wondered if that was Jenny's doing, or thanks to Tom's enigmatic power.

It was now ten AM, Johannesburg time, and Nicole had been reading the hotel brochure while Zackary gobbled his overpriced food: *Guests will be treated to an entirely new taste sensation-"Aero African cuisine" - a fusion of African concepts incorporating flavours from around the world.*

Nicole had ordered eggs and toast, not feeling up to a fusion, and the coffee was not a sensation. She had typed a few thoughts on her notebook about advertising South-African style. Would Captain Keto be welcome here, or would he be seen as too violent? Or maybe revolutionary? She sipped her coffee and smiled at Zack. "We'll see the real Africa soon. But, remember what we talked about?"

"Yeah," said Zack, swiping egg from his chins. "They don't have all the stuff we do, but they don't eat people anymore."

Nicole looked around but no one had heard. "That was mostly a myth, Zack, exaggerated by Europeans. Only a few isolated tribes in equatorial Africa ever actually... ate people. And mostly because of a shortage of..." She glanced at the thick slab of steak on his plate. "...meat. Their bodies craved protein that couldn't be furnished by eating yams cooked in palm oil. It was a diet deficiency, though of course they didn't know it."

"So, nature made 'em eat each other?"

Nicole wished that subject hadn't come up... at least in their present location. "The... practice... might have started with famine. A lot of white people have... done that. Shipwrecked sailors..."

"Hannibal Lector."

"He wasn't real, Zack, only a movie."

"Would you eat me if we were starvin' an' I croaked first?"

"Of course not."

"But I'd want you to if eatin' me would keep you alive."

That was a savage innocence, and also real love. Nicole remembered an old TV ad: *Pork, the other white meat.* "Thank you, Zack, but I'm sure that won't happen."

Zack finished his steak and gulped his milk. "So, they never ate people around here? Or where we're goin'? Kiwanja?"

"No," said Nicole rather firmly, hoping to close the subject before the waiter returned. "But we're in another culture now, like guests in someone else's home, so we have to be respectful of their customs and beliefs."

"Yeah," said Zack, and muffled a burp. "Like, America made black people slaves an' stole the land from the Indians, but it ain't polite to admit it."

"That's... the basic idea," said Nicole. "But there won't be any luxuries once we're out in the bush, you know? No restaurants like this."

"Yeah," said Zack. "Like goin' campin'."

Nicole tried to picture him eating yams from an earthenware bowl in the dust. And, disregarding his diaper days, had he ever done a number-two in anything but porcelain? "I should have taken you camping."

"That woulda been cool, but we're here now."

And wherever you go, there you are. Nicole thought ahead to the next thing, the reason she'd come to Johannesburg before seeking a route to Kiwanja. She'd been dithering ever since waking at nine to an Afrikans-accented courtesy call. Should she leave Zack here with room-service, television, a swimming pool, and smiling dark-skinned servants, or plunge him into the African pot to see how well he stewed?

On one hand it could be traumatic. If so, she had a backup plan arranged with her parents and Jenny. On the other hand, it might be best to let him see the worst right now. No matter how "mud-hut" Kiwanja might be, she doubted if even its poorest village would scream of despair like a Jo'burg slum. And, despite his sheltered life, he didn't seem easily shocked. She remembered the Barrymore pilot's words: *TV and movies. Kids learn a lot and they don't even know it.*

Like, how to be strong... or just not to care?

Was that what she wanted, to know he could care?

The heat was no worse than a Houston August as, a half an hour later, they left the air-conditioned world to join a queue at the taxi stand. Zack had perfected a talent for sweating, though that was perfectly natural as far as nature was concerned, his shirt soon clinging skin-tight to his breasts and displaying his shadowy navel cave, while the lobes of his belly peeked out from below like pair of undulant marshmallow pies.

Business attire in Johannesburg was usually formal suits, but Nicole hadn't planned to stay long in the city and was clad in a casual tan cotton shirt above an olive practical skirt that would wear just as well in the bush. Her shoes were Timberland hikers, fairly new but well broken-in from treks to her neighborhood mini-mart. She had bought boonie hats for Zack and herself, but those were for out in the wilds: here they would only have marked them as tourists to be annoyed and preyed upon. A brown canvas tote was slung on her shoulder containing several bottles of water to keep Zack from getting dehydrated, along with a tube of sunscreen... she had already slathered his face and forearms. Her plastic, along with emergency cash, was safely stashed beneath her shirt in a "pick-pocket-proof" security pouch from Barrymore's Travel Adventures line... a parting gift from Dwane. Neither she nor Zack wore a watch. She hadn't allowed him to bring his I-pod, and he looked slightly naked without the headphones.

Most of the people waiting in line were better and more expensively dressed. And, many weren't obvious Africans no matter what their color. A genuine African black man, in baggy blue trousers and yellow sport shirt, a half-smoked cigar between ivory teeth, was loudly in charge of selecting the cabs and seemed to be king of his hill. He bowed to no one regardless of clothes, ethnicity, or social status, and was equally rude and obnoxious to all. His function seemed to be cramming people into each and every cab, and he loaded the various vehicles with the kind of brutal efficiency that would have impressed a Nazi packing Jews in cattle cars. Arguments were frequent, and he obviously enjoyed them. In any case he always won, though bribes were always helpful in getting a better class of ride. The vehicles ranged from respectable, fairly new but hard-used cars, to shockingly battered mini-vans devoid of all their doors.

Nicole had been watching the process, preparing herself for a confrontation and hoping to win an actual car, not one of those doorless death-mobiles. She had the address of the clothing shop where Aaron had found the Kiwanji boots, and reached in her pouch for a bribe. A well-dressed man ahead of her refused a chicken-coup on wheels and another battle began. She glanced at Zack, who'd been watching the show. He'd bought a Coke from a nearby machine, along with a Black Cat candy bar, and had obviously managed the African

147

money without any help from her.

The civilized man in front of Nicole muttered a primitive curse, but yanked some Rands from his jacket and shoved them at the grinning Shaka, who waved away the rattletrap and summoned a rusty sedan. Glancing again at Zack, who seemed to be waiting to see what happened, Nicole stepped up to the taxi king and presented the shop's address.

She was surprised when he looked surprised... she'd assumed he'd seen everything twice. He'd looked like a pit-bull ready to bite, but now his eyes seemed to show concern. He was old enough to remember Apartheid, so that was another surprise.

"Hillbrow?" he said. "Very bad place. You should not go there without a man."

Zack stepped up. "I'm with her."

Nicole had an uneasy moment, fearing the man would laugh and Zack would be embarrassed. But the man only shrugged, as if saying, "your funeral," and beckoned to one of the doorless hulks.

"No," said Nicole. She indicated a shabby Mercedes and offered the sizable bribe, but the man only glanced at the car and said:

"Driver will not go there." He pointed to the rolling wreck with its dusty, scruffy, and shirtless chauffeur, who wore a piratical head-rag and looked like a Mau-Mau terrorist. "You can trust him."

Nicole hesitated, but Zack said, "Okay."

Before she had time to argue, Zack took the money from her hand and gave it to the man. Then he escorted Nicole to the van and seated her on the ratty rear bench. Then he plopped in beside the driver as if he was going to co-pilot.

The vehicle had no seat belts, and its windshield was a web of cracks that might have come from rocks or bottles. Its radio thumped American rap Nicole recognized from a TV commercial. She gave the address to the driver, who scanned it with a curious look. Then he fired a cigarette and pulled away from the curb. Nicole glanced out at the road rushing past beyond the doorless doors, then to Zack who looked awake and even alertly observing the world while breathing the driver's second-hand smoke.

She remembered something her mother had said while telling

148

tales of marches for peace and being clubbed by cops: *what doesn't kill you makes you stronger*. She'd plunged Zack into the African pot, and so far he seemed to be stewing well. A recipe for empathy? Or maybe a dish of disaster? This could be like a video game; he'd worn so many uniforms and fought in so many environments that nothing real might ever seem real.

Johannesburg's Hillbrow district, though technically suburban, reminded Nicole of an inner-city in mid or eastern America. None of the buildings were notably tall, except the lofty Hillbrow Tower that dominated the skyline. Though graceful in style it looked forbidding, as if keeping watch on a ramshackle prison. In fact, it may have been doing just that; public surveillance was common here with cameras scanning many streets and highly praised -- by the government -- for lowering the rate of crime. Built as a glorified microwave tower, once it had boasted a restaurant, but that had been closed for security reasons.

Parts of Hillbrow resembled the Bronx; derelict rows of crumbling apartments with laundry hanging from balconies or strung over trash-littered alleys. A few of the blocks looked American-modern, with stores like The Gap and fast-food chains -- McDonalds, of course, and KFC -- but these gave way to urban despair and jumbles of even more tottering flats. The streets were filled with ebony faces, though lighter complexions weren't glaringly rare. Men and boys clustered on corners like inner-cities anywhere, some only wasting their time on earth, others alert and doing business... Hillbrow was virtually drowning in drugs like most of the civilized world. Still others were probably scanning for prey like bears on a riverbank waiting for fish.

As she had on her mission of mercy, "saving the world" many years ago, Nicole saw hundreds of homeless street kids wandering, begging, or sitting in doorways, some looking hopeful, others beaten, some enterprising in various ways -- shining shoes, touting whores, selling things that were possibly legal -- while others prowled in ragged packs ready to rob or kill to survive. Zack, she noted, was paying attention, scanning the rawness all around, these slices of life like open wounds that bled in gutters all over the world.

She wondered what he was thinking; no doubt he'd seen all this before on television or movie screens, and had probably interacted in games... Street Fighter X, Grand-Theft Auto, Death In The Ghetto, Thugger World. He'd probably heard the sounds as well; the overloud laughter and language of people who'd learned to be submissive and meek when venturing into more prosperous places and serving the power that kept them here; the yells and curses of strong young men who were trapped in cages and fighting themselves instead of raging against the machine; the ever-present scream of sirens as those in control enforced their laws while offering little protection; and once, maybe twice, a gunshot.

But now he was smelling the real world, an effect that games had yet to attain; the garbage rotting in slimy gutters, the sweat of children with nowhere to wash, the reek of overloaded sewers, the piss on walls, the shit in alleys, the landfill stench of too many people trying to live in too few corners.

All these sights and sounds and smells were only *déjà vu* to her, though time had blurred their memories, softened their stink, muffled their roar, and dulled their jagged edges. This *could* have been a safari, she thought, into human jungle-land. But the tour bus didn't have any doors, and there were no fences, glass, or bars to keep the wild things away.

The streets grew rough and narrow as the battered little van rattled on, jolting over gaping holes and trailed by swirling ghosts of dust. Zack's shirt had morphed from white to gray with zebra streaks of something like soot; a kind of urban camouflage like one of the optional uniforms for the Defenders toys. The rows of flats grew more rundown, the drying laundry ragged. The gutters displayed more sewage than trash because there was little to throw away. Words of anger screamed from walls; of revolution unfulfilled, of threats against an unknown power that never showed its smirking face. A scrawl in bloody red screamed

GET OUT OF AFRICA

but didn't specify who. The people were mostly men and boys, many clad in hip-hop styles, which seemed ironically pathetic. A few women managed sidewalk stands, but except for obvious prostitutes, no girls or women walked alone.

Nicole regarded the shirtless driver avoiding the worst of the crater-like holes. The taxi man had said she could trust him, but while she'd been prepared for slums, she hadn't thought they'd be slumming *this* deep. What if this wreck of a cab broke down? They were many long blocks from the last light face.

She told herself not to borrow trouble and looked around again. It was hard to believe Aaron Steele had braved this neighborhood. She had noted a few younger boys on the streets, most bare-chested and cheaply jeweled, who might have been available... assuming the rumors were true. But, Aaron could have afforded better; certainly cleaner, and possibly safer with AIDs running rampant like modern Black Death. But, that sort of thing was frowned upon here, even by the most desperately poor, and Aaron may have had to search.

She glanced around at the crumbling buildings shimmering under the blazing sun. Many eyes watched the doorless van as it clattered along trailing dust. No matter what Aaron did for a living, or how he entertained himself, she couldn't call him cowardly.

It came as a shock to realize that nobody knew where she and Zack were. She regretted bringing him along and putting him in this kind of danger. She'd wanted him to see the real, but this was becoming way *too* real.

Tom had provided a "spy phone." Nicole had expected a military thing like an action-figure accessory, but it looked like a common wireless and had passed through all the airport checks without a second glance. Tom had said she was free to use it... he'd given her his number, which she assumed was a government line. She also assumed it was monitored, and had used an airport telephone to call her mom in Thousand Oaks. She had also called up Jenny and thanked her for the first-class trip... it *had* been Jenny's doing. Nicole had the phone in her pouch. She hadn't imagined using it, actually pushing the panic button, she just hadn't wanted it left in her room. She wondered if it was working now. Was someone tracking her on a screen, a tiny blip on a radar grid? She pictured a dim-lit room somewhere with rows of glowing monitors, a man in shirtsleeves muttering, "what the hell is she doing *there?*" Would he pick up a phone and notify Tom... *Houston, we might have a problem.* Would Tom think she was brave... or just incredibly stupid?

Whatever he thought -- assuming he knew -- it wasn't any comfort now. No SEAL team was going to drop from the sky like G.I. Joe or *Blackhawk Down* the minute she pressed that button. Still, she thought of calling Tom if only to hear his confident voice. But, what would she say? That she was scared in Africa because the people were black?

She was just about to tell the driver to turn around and take them back -- she could find the source of those boots in Kiwanja, the wild Africa she didn't fear -- when the man brought the car to a squealy stop in front of a three-story building. Its upper floors were dingy flats with the usual lines of sad-looking laundry, while the street level housed a grocery store of the tiny inner-city type, and the shabby little clothing shop where Aaron had said he'd bought the boots.

She scanned around for possible threats... "evaluating" as Tom had said. The neighborhood was quiet as the driver cut the engine, leaving only the radio's bump. From windows above came other music, a news program in English -- the U.S. was threatening Iran again -- someone cooing a lullaby to soothe a crying child. There were some men on a corner who'd watched as the van rattled past, but they didn't seem interested now. A woman came out of the market with a wicker grocery basket. She was clad in a clean but threadbare dress, and gave Nicole a curious look but didn't seem to resent her. The shop and the market's windows were barred, but dusty produce was on display beneath a tattered awning. A near-naked boy of maybe eleven was sitting under the patch of shade and munching Simba Chips. The arrival of a taxi here didn't seem remarkable, judging by his casual glance.

Maybe he was guarding the veggies? If so, he didn't look concerned that anyone would boost a yam. A burlap sack lay beside him, apparently full with lumpy things that might have been more yams. Or, he could have been homeless and those were his worldly possessions. But, though far from being American clean and wearing only grimy shorts, he didn't look cannibalistic.

"Can I get a Coke?" asked Zack.

"...Er..." said Nicole.

"Want one, too?" Zack asked the driver.

The Mau-Mau terrorist smiled. "Thank you." He turned to Nicole. "Shall I wait?"

"...Yes. Please," replied Nicole. She reminded herself that all she had seen was an everyday part of life in this place; the men on the corners, the rowdy street scenes, the homeless children, the poverty, and the ever-present smoldering threat of violence on the verge of erupting. But, the woman doing her shopping was also a part of this world. As was simple courtesy. How could she have forgotten that? Especially after drilling Zack.

She studied the little market, the boy crunching chips in his patch of shade, his head nodding now to the radio's beat. "Go ahead, this shouldn't take long."

Zack peeled off his sweat-sodden shirt as if going naturally native, though his peaches, cream, and pale pinkness seemed as vulnerable in this dark place as an innocent lamb staked out for bait; but in the driver's presence Nicole couldn't think of a subtle excuse to tell him to put it back on, and watched as he tossed it on the seat and jiggled into the market.

The clothing shop was a second-hand store and smelled like most such places, a dusty, musty, rodent scent that always seemed a little sad. A rusty bell clanked as she opened the door. Two small light bulbs hung from wires, but they were dark and the room filled with sha-dows. She paused to let her eyes adjust. Uncertain shelves were sagging with junk, old boom-boxes, ancient TVs, cooking utensils, rusty lamps, and mournfully battered household things. A few racks of clothes were on display..."dead white people's clothes," as they were sometimes mockingly called. A middle-aged man, obsidian-skinned, looked up from behind a counter where he'd been reading a book... maybe one from shelves of many that lined the wall behind him. Like the woman out on the street, he gave Nicole a curious look but didn't seem to resent her. Pale was the faceless face of power, but maybe hers was a little more human.

"May I serve?" he asked in English, laying his book aside. The title

153

was *Great Expectations.*

Nicole decided to play it cool and maybe a little spyish. After all, she was on a mission. "We were just passing..."

The man's smile turned ironic. "Of course."

Nicole had been looking around for the boots while feigning a casual browse. Then she saw them up on a shelf, standing like savage but disciplined soldiers among a rabble of shoes and sneaks that the poorest of America's poor wouldn't have worn in a Welfare line. There were a dozen pairs of the boots in various sizes from child to adult. Nicole pretended to notice them and casually went to the shelf.

"What are these?" she asked, selecting a pair about her size and again enjoying their friendly feel. They almost begged to be put on her feet, and her expensive Timberlands now felt like cloddish clogs. She fingered the supple leather and examined the truck tire soles. They smelled brand-new as if made yesterday, a primitive, earthy, exotic aroma that hinted of sun-shimmered veldt. "Are they locally made?"

Again, the man's smile was ironic. "You are the second American to ask such a thing about those boots."

"Oh?" said Nicole, pretending surprise, though suspecting her cover was blown. "I haven't seen anything quite like these. Do people around here wear them?"

"Wise people do," said the man. He glanced at the other derelict shoes... ancient oxfords curled from the heat, zombies of Nikes, Cons, and Adidas. "The young of today are not so wise. They only want things of the moment. Of times here today but gone tomorrow. Things of great price but of little value."

Nicole reinspected the boots. "They seem very well made." *Déjà vu again.*

The man got up and came to the shelf. "They are the real Africa. Something of value that will endure when worthless things have fallen to dust."

Nicole made a mental note of that for possible advertising. "Wise people buy them?"

"People who respect the past as well as value a future."

"I try to do both," said Nicole.

"Is that why you brought your son?" The man smiled when Nicole

154

looked surprised -- genuinely this time -- and glanced to the grimy windows. "One must pay attention to life, or much of it passes when one is not looking."

"To be safe?" asked Nicole.

"Life should not always be safe," said the man. "Without knowing danger and hardship, one never appreciates peace and comfort."

"Or values it," said Nicole.

"Yes," said the man. "Peace for yourself and peace for others."

"We're going into the bush," said Nicole. "On to Selinda from here."

"I have heard it's a beautiful place," said the man. "The lions hunt hippos there."

"I've heard that, too," said Nicole.

"Very large lions no doubt," the man added. "Not like those of neighboring lands."

Was he on to her? wondered Nicole, recalling what Tom had said of Kiwanja... that even the lions were small. She tried a new tack: "These boots should wear well in the bush."

"Quite well," said the man. "All the wise people who buy them here say they wear quite well everywhere. It is sad that more youth do not wear them."

"But they're not made locally?" asked Nicole. "You import them from somewhere else?"

"You may safely buy them here. Somewhere else there may be danger."

Nicole wondered if she should sweeten the pot. But Aaron had already tried that. For her to try seemed ugly. And maybe very American. Was she giving up too easily? Going down without a fight at company expense? But, Kiwanja was a tiny land. And, she would have its President's help -- all the king's horses and all the king's men -- to find the wise people who'd made these boots.

The rusty bell clanked and Zack wobbled in, a Coke in one hand, Simba Chips in the other. "These are good, mom. Chutney flavor, whatever a chutney is."

The man selected a pair of boots. "These are just his size."

Zack spotted something on a shelf. "Check this out, mom, it's an

155

eight-track player. If it works I could sell it on Ebay for like a hundred bucks."

The storekeeper chuckled. "Your son is not yet a man of business."

Nicole smiled. "Obviously not."

"I'm sure he would wear these boots quite well."

"Zack," called Nicole. "Do you like these?"

Zack jiggled between the racks of clothes, raising a ghostly swirl of dust and toting the eight-track player, a dusty but bright yellow plastic box branded Panasonic. "Yeah, they're like Africa cool."

The man indicated a wooden chair. "Please sit down."

Zack's girth made it hard to reach over himself, but the man knelt to untie his sneaks, surprisingly also removed his socks, then slipped the brown boots on Zack's pale chubby feet.

"Hey, these rock!" said Zack, standing up with less of a struggle than he usually required. He took several light steps and poised like a dancer. "Totally atomic, mom! You gonna get some, too?"

"How much are they?" asked Nicole.

"In American dollars, twenty a pair." The man gave Zack a wink. "Fifty for the tape machine so we will share the profit. There are also several cartridges, but batteries are not included."

"They never are," said Zack.

The man turned to Nicole. "If you wish...?"

"Thank you," said Nicole, sitting down. Like the pair she had worn in the boardroom, the boots seemed to joyfully welcome her feet. Again she felt as if she could run. She wondered if Zack felt the same, even if his running days seemed to be far in the past.

A few minutes later she and Zack came out of the store into savage sunlight. Both now wore the Kiwanji boots, their civilized shoes and the eight-track player toted by Zack in an old paper bag. The Mau-Mau terrorist lounged in his cab, eating a Twinkie and sipping a Coke. The radio thudded another rap song, though this one had an African flavor... maybe like chutney potato chips. Nicole took her ratty seat in the rear, while Zack climbed in to co-pilot. The driver reached to start the engine, when three young teen boys emerged from the market.

"Wait!" called one to the driver.

Nicole recognized the boy's command, spoken in Swahili, though his accent was hard to decipher. But it *was* a command in a tone of command and could have implied a threat. Nicole realized they'd been lucky so far, and this was not a wise place to be. She flicked her eyes to the driver. Would he help if there was trouble? Or, should she grab Zack and run to the shop?

Her eyes returned to the trio of boys, who were sauntering up to the cab and toting brown bottles of Chibuki beer. All were shirtless and shiny with sweat as if they'd been prowling the streets. The eldest was maybe fifteen, a stark-muscled ebony panther. The second boy was slightly younger, solidly-built but awkwardly bellied, a black hyena stuffed from a feast. Nicole regarded the third boy, the one who'd called the command. If he had an animal avatar it might have been a fat meerkat who could have been Zackary's midnight twin... or maybe his African doppelganger. His boy-breasts bobbed as he strode to the car, while his belly hung over the crotch of his jeans in the same sort of pendulous double-lobed shape.

Despite her initial flash of fear it was hard to be frightened of him. Of course, his face was different from Zack's -- mostly the wide and bridgeless nose -- though just as roundly chipmunk-cheeked and equipped with a slight second chin. An American orthodontist could have sent his kids to Harvard by taming the boy's front teeth, which might have opened bottle-caps. Like the two other youths he looked scruffy, though somehow not in an urban way. He wore ancient jeans at an indecent level so only his belly concealed his sex. His companions were clad in canvas shorts of the kind often worn in the bush. The fat boy sported a complex watch that rivaled the Barrymore pilot's... and might have been a trophy from some unlucky mark. His other wrist boasted a bracelet of brass. All the boys wore tufts of fur on leather strips around their necks, which could have been tribal I.D. tags, or maybe religious charms.

Nicole also noted the boys had knives in brightly beaded sheaths... big knives. She shifted her eyes to the driver again, but relaxed when he didn't look worried. The fat boy asked him a question, his voice amazingly like Zack's on the cusp of choir-boy cracking. Again the accent was hard to decipher, but he seemed to want a ride to the airport. ...Or, maybe she hadn't understood? These boys may have ridden a truckload of yams, but how in the world could they fly?

The other two boys had joined the first. Their scents were raunchy and rankly male but slightly less bitter than Zack's... maybe lacking civilized additives. The fat boy studied her and Zack. It was hard to imagine his chubby face ever showing malice, but his foxy eyes, up-turned at the corners, narrowed in something like anger. Again, Nicole struggled to translate his speech. Her Swahili was rusty anyhow, and her basic Peace Corps language course hadn't included strange dialects, but the word, "American," came out like a curse. Zack had also heard it. He'd been watching the boys in a friendly way, maybe checking his ebony twin, but now he looked confused.

Then the driver spoke, though Nicole was too distracted to translate. But, the fat kid gave her a sudden smile that might have charmed a rural girl -- or maybe scared a lion -- and also smiled at Zack. Then he turned to the big-bellied youth. Nicole missed most of whatever he said, but "hyena-boy" went back to the market, where the kid with the sack still sat in the shade. Rumpled Rands changed dusky hands, and hyena-boy shouldered the sack.

Nicole decided it *was* full of yams, and maybe these boys had just come to shop. It still seemed strange they would go to the airport, but maybe that food was bound for a village and being flown in by bush-pilot freight?

Then she saw the boy's footwear... the beautiful Kiwanji boots! All three boys were wearing them, though only the toes of the fat one's showed beneath his ragged tumble of cuffs. Were these boys from Kiwanja?

"You may put it in back," said the driver, glancing at the lumpy bag.

The fat boy indicated the roof. "It will be better up there."

"Mom?" asked Zack. "What's goin' on?"

The driver murmured, "They do not like Americans. I told them you were from Canada."

"Thank you," said Nicole, then added to Zack in a whisper, "Remember, we talked about this?"

"Yeah," said Zack. "A lot of people hate us."

"I do not," said the driver. "My cousin is in your country and makes a lot of money. With luck I will join him next year."

Nicole watched the booted trio of youths surround the doorless van. They seemed to have come prepared with a length of nylon cord. It didn't seem wise to leave yams in the sun, but there wouldn't be much room inside with everyone aboard. She listened carefully as they talked: "the hyena" remarked in his odd dialect that, "she was very pretty although her breasts were a little high."

Nicole almost smiled... until the ebony meerkat said, "He's a boy, you ass."

The driver went on in a murmur: "I could have refused to take them, but one I have brought here before... the boy with the watch. I do not think they are dangerous, and now I have three more fares."

"I understand," said Nicole. She could have offered more money so she and Zack could ride alone, but that also seemed ugly American.

"I think it is safe," added the driver. "But you should not speak to them. Perhaps you are Canadian-French and do not understand English."

"Do they talk English?" asked Zack.

"I do not know." The driver glanced at the fat boy, who also shared Zackary's plump pudendum lolling out of his half-buttoned jeans with only the ebony tip of his shaft protruding as he stretched to tie the sack on the roof. "But he is wiser than he seems."

How dammed ironic, thought Nicole. These boys must have known the source of their boots -- assuming they hadn't bought them here -- and now she couldn't talk to them! ...But why would they hate Americans if the U.S. was aiding their country? Was there a fundamentalist group that wanted to cling to a primitive past? Or maybe courted Communism despite it being obsolete? She recalled her conversation with Tom... Kiwanja wasn't quite peaceful. But Tom would have known about serious threats and wouldn't have wanted Zack to come if there was significant danger. And any nation, no matter how small, always had some dissidents, wannabe rebels and terrorists, especially among their young. She turned to Zack. "You understand?"

"Yeah," whispered Zack. "Like, we're spies."

159

The driver smiled. "You are James Bond."

And I'm Pussy Galore, thought Nicole. How ironically Freudian, like cannibalizing her son.

FIFTEEN

"It's, like, Thomas The Tank Engine, mom."

Nicole regarded the locomotive, which was clearly of antique British design. In the U.S. it might have been on display in a children's park or railroad museum, but here it stood panting and hissing, waves of heat shimmering up from its boiler, and presumably going somewhere. Coupled behind it were six flatcars, two loaded with lengths of iron pipe, possibly for a water project, while three carried lumber, sacks of cement and other construction supplies -- wheelbarrows, shovels, picks and hoes -- which also suggested progress. The sixth car bore rows of steel drums, which were probably filled with diesel fuel, gasoline or motor oil... all had flammable warnings. Last in line was a passenger coach, another shabby Victorian relic resembling Annie and Clarabel, though with a platform at each end and missing most of its window glass. It didn't seem especially safe behind the flammable liquids, but maybe the fuel or oil was safer away from the spark-throwing engine.

Zack had been scanning the locomotive... all young boys liked trains. The thing looked about to explode any moment, a steaming, dribbling, time-bomb on wheels, but neither the engineer or fireman -- sooty, soot-colored, shirtless men -- seemed concerned as they oiled

161

things with long-nosed copper cans. Resisting the urge to pull Zack away, Nicole lay a hand on his shoulder.

"As you said the other day, they don't have all the new things we have. But they take care of their old things, which is something most Americans don't."

"Like, they recycle better than us?"

Nicole glanced again at the hazardous relic. "That's a good way of putting it. ...Maybe we should get on board." She gently took his hand and led him away from the dangerous thing. "This is the only train for a week so we don't want to miss it."

"Yeah," said Zack, holding a Coke he'd bought in the station. As always, his jeans were about to fall off, their tumble of cuffs dragging over his feet and hiding all but the toes of his boots. He'd abandoned boxers yesterday, complaining they chafed in the heat, and the moons of his bottom were partly displayed along with the pendulous lobes of his belly lolling from under a souvenir T-shirt which featured the friendly face of a lion obviously bootlegged from Disney, and though supposedly size XL but having been made in China, clung to his breasts and bulges like paint. He also wore one of the brown boonie hats Nicole had brought for the trip, while Nicole was topped with the other.

Zack's face and forearms had coppered a bit despite her warnings to use sunscreen, and his body was also lightly tanned from an afternoon spent in the hotel pool, comfortably sprawled on a floating lounge chair, where he'd punished Nicole's expense account by ordering tons of overpriced snacks. He gulped from the can and wiped sweat from his face. "Too bad we couldn't find a plane, but ridin' this train should be cool."

The little border station was simply a shack of rusty tin. The sun beat down on its wooden platform while heat shimmered up from the narrow-gauge tracks. It was only about nine in the morning, but already close to a hundred degrees. Nicole eyed the ramshackle passenger car, thinking this trip would be far from cool. "They said a plane was coming today that usually went to Kiwanja. I know how much you like airplanes."

"*Cool* airplanes," said Zack. "Passenger planes are borin'. Like gettin' stuffed in a big metal tube an' nothin' happens between here an' there."

"Bush planes are usually interesting. What did you think of Selinda?"

Zack took another gulp of Coke and politely half-smothered a burp. "The hippos were cool, but there weren't no lions. I wish we coulda seen some lions eatin' them big fat hippos."

"*Any* lions, and *those* hippos, Zack."

"Sorry."

"I wish we could have stayed longer, but this is a business trip."

"Maybe we can come back."

"Do you like Africa?"

Zack pulled a half-melted Nestle bar from his jeans' back pocket. "The food's real good an' the people are nice."

"Remember we've stayed in hotels so far." Nicole had a vision of facing Meg Tanner and trying to justify all her receipts. Except for the Hillbrow "safari" and taking a hippo tour in Selenda, Zack had done little but eat and sleep and self-love himself in bathroom showers. "Dammed expensive hotels."

"Yeah," said Zack, and burped again. "I guess when you're rich, everything's nice."

"What did you think of Hillbrow?"

"I guess there's, like, ghettoes all over the world, an' lots of poor people who have to live there."

"But, you knew that already, didn't you?"

Zack licked chocolate from his fingers. "Kinda. But it's different when you see it for real. Makes you sorta sad, an' like you wanna do somethin' to help."

Nicole smiled. "I'm sure we'll see lions in Kiwanja."

"Hey!" said Zack, suddenly pointing. "Are those, like, African Boy Scouts, mom? ...They get to carry M-16s?"

Nicole turned around and tensed a bit as a dozen boys ranging from ten to fifteen rolled up in a dusty army truck. All were clad in sand-and-tan that matched the vehicle's camouflage paint but didn't quite work in this lion-colored land... Captain Keto's ambers and golds would have blended in much better. But, now it was suddenly clear why most of the Barrymore uniforms being sent to Kiwanja were small.

There was something a little ironic about it; a company making toy soldiers also making soldier suits for real soldiers of toylike size. The boys and their uniforms may have been small, but all were packing big black guns. As Zack had observed, they were M-16s... Defenders Of Democracy optional accessories. Or, as Tom had said, leftover junk from the Vietnam War.

Could Tom have known about this? No, she decided, he couldn't have... surely he would have told her. Countries that forced their children to fight were usually suffering civil wars, and sometimes ethnic cleansing. She watched the boys clamber out of the truck, raising more dust as they hit the ground, then realized Zack was waiting for answers.

"They're Kiwanji soldiers, Zack."

"But they're only kids like me."

"Remember what we talked about? Other cultures?"

"Yeah, I know," said Zack. "But, they have *kids* in their army?"

"Many nations do, Zack. And not just in Africa."

"Those kids fight wars an' kill people?"

"Kiwanja isn't at war, or I wouldn't have brought you along."

"So why do they need to have kids in their army? Like, where are all the men?"

Nicole scanned the camouflaged, gun-toting boys, who looked rather grim for their ages. Or maybe they were tired. There was no horseplay or childish chatter. What words they exchanged were in Swahili, the same archaic dialect of the boys who'd shared their Hillbrow taxi. "It might be... community service."

Zack raised an eyebrow. "You mean if you're bad... like get busted for beer or smokin' weed... you get put in the army in Africa instead of pickin' up trash?"

Nicole felt as if she was pitching a product she didn't believe in. This hadn't been in her job description: she'd agreed to look for some bootmakers, not plunge herself and her son in the middle of somebody's war. She thought of the phone in her tote, a direct line to Tom for a few direct questions. Or maybe some revelations for him. He wouldn't blame her for backing out now.

164

Then she pictured herself facing Dwane Barrymore in another boardroom meeting; explaining to him and the rest of the gang why she'd aborted her mission. Aaron Steele would likely be there, and would probably drop the biggest bombs... *maybe taking her son had been a mistake? Understandable, of course... a woman did have maternal feelings... but what had she accomplished to benefit the company?*

Of course she would pay for Zack's trip, but she would have accomplished nothing and wasted the company's money. It would take more than a Captain Keto to put her back in the glass-ceiling game.

She thought of Tom again... *the alternative is Aaron Steele. Or somebody else's Gollum.*

Would Aaron have retreated, she wondered? Been scared away by a few little soldiers? She had already seen the risks he would take... assuming the rumors were true. And, even if they weren't, he'd still put himself in danger to possibly profit his company.

What had she done so far? Asked her boss to pay her son's way on what should have been a business trip. Stayed in obscenely expensive hotels and wasted a day watching hippos. And now she was thinking of bailing her butt because she'd seen a few boys with guns. Jenny had probably seen many more, and not in a disciplined Army.

She considered alternatives... she could send Zack home with her backup plan and keep to her company quest. But, what would he have learned? That, except for a glimpse of an urban slum, Africa was luxury inns, lavish food and smiling servants, a banquet spread for the color of privilege. He hadn't even seen a lion.

"We can talk about that on the train."

"But, like, could they shoot us?"

"Not everything is 'like' something else. Lots of things are just what they are."

"It's just an expression."

"I know, I used to say it myself, but it's a hard habit to break, and it makes you sound..."

"Retarded?"

"...Yes." She glanced at the soldiers again. "An American cop

165

could shoot us. Or all those guards in the airports."

"But, those are adults," said Zack, finishing his candy bar and washing it down with Coke. "They're supposed to know who to kill."

Nicole remembered the letter she carried; a genuine U.S. Government letter addressed to Kiwanja's President. She assumed at least some of those soldiers could read. "I'm sure those young men are well-trained."

"Guess you wouldn't give guns to kids unless you made sure they knew how to use 'em."

"Have you ever smoked weed?"

"I checked it out, but I like beer better."

"Me too," said Nicole.

"How come they're not ridin' inside with us?"

The soldiers were boarding the freight cars. Two carried an olive-drab wooden box that might have contained ammunition. "Probably for security."

"Do they have terrorists here?"

"The world has never been safe, Zack."

"Don't people have a right to be safe?"

"Too many people think they do, and that's something else we can talk about. But no one is going to be safe in this world until they start giving instead of taking."

"An' we're here to give 'em somethin', right? A chance to make money by sellin' their boots?"

"Yes," said Nicole. "Do you feel okay?"

"I'm gettin' a little hungry."

"I mean you're not upset, are you? Or maybe a little scared?"

"Oh. No, mom," said Zack. "This is like educational."

Nicole pressed his hand. "Yes, it is."

She gazed across the sun-shimmered land, amber-grassed and mostly flat except for occasional humps of hills that looked like sleeping camels. The sky was clear and brilliantly blue, and the tracks seemed to dwindle to the horizon like a lesson in vanishing-point perspective. According to the stationmaster the trip would take about six hours. Maybe Kiwanja wasn't as small as Washington, or Tom, seemed to think? More probably the train was slow: it was already over an hour late simply getting started, though apparently had been waiting for guards. She noted canteens on the soldiers' web belts.

"Did they have any water for sale in the station?"

"Nah, just a Coke machine."

Nicole had sandwiches packed in her tote -- big submarine "safari" types of roast beef, ham and cheese purchased at the fancy hotel, sealed in plastic and presumably safe -- along with four bottles of water, but she should have been better prepared. "I'll buy us a few more sodas," she said. "You get on, stow our luggage, and find good seats. Okay?"

"Sure, mom."

There were no good seats, Nicole discovered, boarding the coach a few minutes later. In George Orwellian New-Speak terms, all the seats were "un-good," some just double-plus. Most of the cushions were bleeding stuffing of scratchy-looking horsehair, and more than a few displayed rusty springs. The floor was covered with dun-colored dust, and the single washroom had no water, she found after trying the tap. Nor was any paper provided for the rusty tin funnel that passed for a toilet and dumped on the rail-bed below, though she had come prepared for that. Yet, all this neglect seemed recent. This antique car, like the train itself, could not have survived a hundred years without a better class of care. She wondered when that care had stopped and, more importantly, why? President-General N'dila was supposedly bringing progress, yet his trains didn't even run on time.

Zack had chosen a pair of seats near the forward end of the car, which were less un-good than most. He'd stowed their suitcases up on a rack, and that surprised Nicole; she wouldn't have thought he was strong enough. But there was no shortage of space; there were only four other passengers at the opposite end of the car. They seemed to be native people, a twentyish woman with two small boys, and a man who might have been their grandfather. They could have been urban Kiwanjis -- if that wasn't an oxymoron -- residents of the capital town, though obviously not upper-class.

The man and woman were shabbily dressed in the second-hand, civilized-castoff look of many Third-World people… "dead white people's clothes." Nicole noted ancient sport shoes on their feet, while the kids wore nothing but ragged shorts. The adults didn't seem to resent her, but avoided making eye-contact, though the big-eyed boys were openly staring as little kids did everywhere.

Nicole smiled at the woman, who returned the smile but looked nervous. That was probably logical; she couldn't have seen many white people, and certainly not on this battered old train. The woman noticed her children staring and made them switch seats so they faced away. Nicole had been hoping to practice Swahili and learn the Kiwanji dialect -- not to mention the subject of boots -- but this didn't seem like a promising start for what would be a long, hot trip. The train's whistle blew, not the deep mellow blast of American trains, but a shrill-pitched, almost hysterical scream.

"Hey," said Zack. "It's like that movie, *Murder On The Orient Express.*"

The train gave a jolt and began to move, couplings clashing, huffing, puffing, gathering speed, clanking away from the tiny station and chugging across what now seemed to be an endless expanse of lion-colored land.

"James Bond rode that train," said Nicole. *And Sherlock Holmes might have ridden this one.*

"I seen that movie, too," said Zack. "Some Russian spies were tryin' to kill him. ...It was fun playin' spies, wasn't it, mom? Pretendin' to be from Canada 'cause them dudes didn't like Americans."

"*Those* dudes," corrected Nicole. "And I wish we hadn't had to."

"But it's cool now, ain't it?" asked Zack. "To be ourselves again?"

"*Isn't* it."

"Sorry."

"I'm sure it is."

"'Cause Kiwanja is on our side? Against all the terrorists in the world. So everybody will like us here?"

Nicole thought again of the three scruffy boys, and the angry, possibly hateful, look the fat one had given her. "That's what Tom said."

"Too bad he couldn't come with us."

"That would have been nice," agreed Nicole.

"You really like him, huh?"

"I do."

168

"Think it could get, like, serious?"

"...Well... how would you feel about that?"

"He seems cool."

"I'm sure the helicopter helped."

Zackary laughed. "Def."

Dust swirled in through the glassless windows, along with bitter black coal smoke, as the train finally reached a cruising speed of maybe thirty-miles-an-hour. It had a kind of pulsing motion, while the car rocked and pitched on the uneven rails, wheels clicking and clacking over the joints, its woodwork creaking and rattling as if it might fall apart. The forward door swung back and forth, its latch apparently broken, revealing glimpses of the soldiers riding the swaying freight cars. One boy around Zackary's age was dozing atop an oil drum, his rifle across his legs. Heat shimmered up from the other drums so he seemed to be surrounded by ghosts.

"I'll fix that, mom," said Zack. "Keep some of the dust an' smoke outta here." He got up and flattened his empty Coke can beneath the tire-tread sole of his boot, then wedged the can under the door, which still had a cracked pane of glass in its window. "Better, huh?"

"Thank you, Zack."

"Can I have another Coke?"

"You'd better drink water, too. Sodas don't keep you hydrated."

"I'm gonna give it to him," said Zack, pointing to the dozing boy. "He looks hot out there. ...Is that okay? Like, it's not against regulations?"

"...I'm sure it's all right," said Nicole. "But he probably doesn't speak English."

"Coke is Coke in any language."

Nicole thought of adding a warning -- *don't surprise the soldier* -- but Zack had already opened the door and called to the uniformed boy. The kid jerked awake, clutching his gun, but then studied Zack and relaxed. He slid off the drum and accepted the can across the clanking couplings.

"He said *asante sana,*" Zack reported, returning.

"That's thank-you very much."

"Is it hard to learn African?"

169

"Africa has many languages, but Swahili is fairly easy to learn: it was basically a trading language. I brought a phrase book; it's in the side pouch of my suitcase."

Zack stretched up to the overhead rack, baring his chubby "cream puff" and the rosy pink tip of his shaft, reminding Nicole of his midnight twin as he'd tied the sack of yams on the cab. Zack found the book, then unzipped his case for the eight-track player, along with a bag of Simba Chips, a candy bar and a Coke. Zack had bought batteries at the hotel and created his own little boy-cave, popping a tape in the player -- a Rolling Stones album, *Out Of Our Heads* -- and plugging in his I-Buds.

Nicole's parents had that album, which featured the song, *Satisfaction (can't get no)*. It had been one of the favorite tunes played by troops in Vietnam, usually when dropping bombs or spraying napalm on villages. She recalled a line from some old movie -- *napalm sticks to kids* -- like an advertising slogan.

"Is it cool to lose my shirt?"

Nicole turned to look at the other people through dust and smoke like dirty fog. The children had opened the car's rear door and were standing out on the platform watching the track dwindle behind. It didn't look safe to be riding out there, but safety was a relative thing in a land where kids carried guns. "It's cool," she said, while thinking, *this is a bare-breasted culture.*

Zack peeled off his sweaty shirt and settled back in the worn out seat as if he was on a first-class flight. Nicole hadn't thought he'd adapt so fast... he didn't look very adaptable. He opened the chips and the book. "Tell me if you see any lions."

"You watch, I'm going to take a nap."

"Think we'll stop somewhere for lunch?"

"If we don't, you know where the sandwiches are."

"That's why you can't starve on a beach."

"Why's that?" asked Nicole.

"'Cause you can eat the sand which is there."

Nicole was snapped awake by a scream. At first she thought one of the children had fallen off the back of the train. She squinted through the haze of smoke, but both little boys were sleeping in seats, along with the man and woman... the scream had only been the whistle. Zack was also sprawled asleep, his breasts and belly lolling about to the rattling rock of the train, his hat pulled over his face like a cowboy. The bag of chips was empty, along with three Cokes and two sandwich wrappers. His body was lionish brown with dust; and Nicole wasn't any cleaner, she found. She wiped the dust from her watch: two hours had passed. The country looked the same outside, shimmering plains of amber grass crossed by beds of meandering streams, dry as bones at this time of year. There were scattered groves of acacia trees, little islands of gold and green, and distant clumps of camel-like hills against the clear blue sky. She saw a small herd of small antelope, but if there were lions they must have been napping, possibly in the acacia shade.

Risking a face full of cinders, she leaned out the window to scan ahead. The train was approaching a huddle of hills, and there was a long wooden trestle across a waterless riverbed that would probably be a roaring torrent during the rainy season. Most of the soldiers seemed asleep in the blazing sun on the clattering cars, though several were smoking cigarettes and gazing across their land. Maybe they were thinking of home, of villages not too far away, a few days walk at most. Had they joined the Army willingly? Did it offer opportunities, education, social status... or simply regular meals? Many had lost their shirts like Zack, including the boy on the oil drum whose tummy was healthily round. They were probably taking turns on guard, though there didn't seem much to guard against. Assuming there were any terrorists here, they would have been seen for miles away.

But, what would they get for attacking the train... wheelbarrows, pipe, lumber, cement? No weapons of mass destruction; the U.S. supplied all the war toys. But, terror was also destruction on any kind of scale, disrupting a nation's economy and keeping its people in fear. Terrorists wouldn't want any progress under the current government; no water systems or modern housing... and certainly not a boot factory.

The train started over the trestle, which creaked and swayed beneath its weight. Zack opened his eyes, glanced out, and yawned. "Are we there yet?"

171

"Still a long way to go," said Nicole.

Zack closed his eyes again. "Wake me up for lunch."

Nicole looked down at the dry riverbed thirty feet below... jagged with rocks and savage thorns; not a happy landing place. The hills rose up on the other side where the tracks made a curve and climbed a slope then vanished into a cutting. The engine slowed and began to puff harder, reaching the end of the rickety bridge and starting up the grade.

Suddenly there were gunshots! Ragged blasts of auto-fire! Bullets twanged off iron and crackled into wood. Splinters flew from flatcar decks, ricochets whining away. The train whistle screamed hysterically, and the soldiers scrambled for cover amongst the rattling freight. Bursts from their rifles ripped the hillside, tearing up dirt and clumps of grass, though Nicole couldn't see any targets. More splinters burst from a window frame a few seats down the aisle.

"Mom!" In a second Zack had grabbed Nicole and tumbled them both to the floor. She didn't have time to be surprised... Zack was actually sheltering her beneath his rolly mass.

"Stay down, mom!" he yelled.

Dimly through the smoke and dust, Nicole saw the woman and elderly man also down and protecting their kids. Then there was an explosion, more like a gigantic WHUMP than a blast, and the car seemed to leap in the air. The floorboards smacked Nicole in the face, spewing dust in her eyes. The automatic fire increased. Young voices yelled in Swahili. The whistle continued to scream. More bullets ripped the roof of the car and shafts of smoky sun stabbed in.

"Stay down, mom!" Zack yelled again.

If the car had really been blown in the air it must have landed back on the rails. The train was still moving, whistle screaming. The day went black with smoke... they must have been pouring on the coal trying to get away. The gunfire lessened a little, shorter bursts, single shots... maybe the smoke was hiding the train? Trying to wipe the dust from her eyes, Nicole caught a hazy glimpse through a window of three young boys in loincloths firing down from the hillside. Their loincloths were amber and gold that blended into the waist-high grass. Their dusky bodies were shadows. Then the smoke closed in again.

"I don't think they're shootin' at us," puffed Zack.

"...What?" Nicole gasped stupidly. Zack's weight on her back made it hard to breathe.

"They're shootin' at the soldiers."

There was another air-slamming WHUMP, and again the car seemed to leap off the rails. The door window shattered and more smoke poured in. Through the rattle of gunfire and ricochet screams Nicole heard the engine's chugging speed up. Yet the car suddenly lurched to a stop, throwing them both against a seat. Then she smelled burning oil.

"Zack! We've got to get off!"

"Stay down, mom!"

Between the smoke and her grit-filled eyes, Nicole could hardly see. She felt Zack scramble to his feet. The engine was chugging faster now... racing *away* from the motionless car! She heard a roaring rush of flames. Grabbing the back of a seat, she struggled onto her knees. "ZACK!"

The engine's puffing was getting fainter. She realized the shooting had stopped. She couldn't see a goddamn thing; her eyes were streaming tears. There was a clanking sound, and a hiss. The car began moving, slowly at first, wheels squealing over the rails.

"ZACK!"

The smoke was thinning a little. Through burning eyes she saw a shape approaching from the front of the car... but it seemed to have more than two legs! "...Zack?"

"It's okay, mom, I unhooked us."

The smoke was rapidly clearing now as the car began picking up speed. The reek of burning was fading away, the crackle of flames growing fainter. "...What?" said Nicole.

"I unhooked us," Zack repeated. "The oil drum car was on fire. It's probably gonna explode. They always do in movies."

Nicole stopped rubbing her eyes, letting her tears wash the dust away instead of stupidly grinding it in. Zack was still a blurry shape, but somehow too large... and with too many legs. "...You... unhooked...?"

"Like in movies, you pull a handle. We're rollin' backward away

173

from the fire."

"...Oh..." said Nicole. "...Where's your hat?"

"It got kinda burned. Sorry."

"...Burned?"

"The handle was hot 'cause of the fire. I wrapped my hat around it."

"...Oh."

"The rest of the train ran away."

"...Oh."

"You okay, mom?"

Her vision finally began to clear, and Zack morphed into a pair of boys... he stood supporting a child soldier, the one who'd sat on the oil drum, the boy's arm drawn over his shoulders and one of Zack's arms around his waist.

"He got shot in the leg," puffed Zack. "We gotta stop the bleedin'."

The boy was younger than Zack by a year, and didn't look much like a soldier now -- shirtless, capless, tears on his cheeks -- even still clutching his big black gun. Smoke curled out of its muzzle as Zack eased him down on a seat.

The car was still gaining speed, clicking and clattering over the rails, starting around the hillside curve. They were aboard a runaway train -- part of a train, anyhow -- but were getting away from the fire. They were actually going faster than the ancient engine had gone. But the land was flat across the bridge so they would eventually coast to a stop. After that... Nicole didn't know. But at least they were safe for the moment.

Then she remembered the other people. The man, woman, and kids were gone. The car's rear door was open, revealing only the curving tracks around the amber-grassed hillside.

"They jumped off," said Zack. "...Mom, this dude is bleedin'."

"...Get a bottle of water. There's a first-aid kit in my suitcase."

Zack stretched up to the overhead rack, almost losing his jeans. But then he suddenly stared down the car and pointed to the open door. "Mom! They blew up the bridge!"

SIXTEEN

"They were wearing our boots," said Thabo, thoughtfully regarding his own, which were comfortably propped on the instrument panel. "The Canadian boy and his mother."

"I noticed that," said Dakota, who lay relaxed in the pilot's seat, his boots resting clear of the rudder pedals. The auto-pilot was in command, its phantom hands moving the steering yokes as the airplane plodded the sky. The engines sang their droning duet, the altimeter showed three-thousand feet, and the airspeed hovered at 130 knots. Wind rustled past the open windows, making its soothing waterfall sound as the Akan doll and lion's fang gently swung above the compass.

Thabo lounged in the co-pilot's seat, smoking a Players cigarette. "You were right."

"About what?" asked Dakota. "Though you'll notice I often am."

"We could make a lot of money if we made a lot of boots."

Dakota sipped from a bottle of Coke. "*Jumbe* Chane is thinking of that. Such money could buy many bullets."

"*Jumbe* Chane would think of that."

"Which is why he's our chief."

Thabo flipped his cigarette stub into the clear blue sky. "What

175

would you do if you were chief?"

"Please don't bring that up again."

Thabo tapped his chest with a thumb. "*I* am thinking ahead." He looked over his shoulder at Kobe, who was sprawled asleep on the cockpit floor. "The future belongs to us, you know."

Dakota glanced at the oil pressure gauges and tinkered a bit with the mix control. "And what of our children's future?"

"I haven't even lived *my* future so how can I think of my children's?"

"Because you have a son."

"You already talk like a chief."

"Do shut up about that," said Dakota. "The future is what we make it beginning every day. And, unless we win this bloody war it's not going to be very bright."

Thabo frowned. "The old make wars for the young to fight."

"Try to remember that when you're old."

Thabo glanced into the cargo bay, where Nathi lay asleep, resting atop a stack of boxes that bore the labels, BARRYMORE. "We're helping the General steal our future!"

Dakota shrugged. "Dressing boys in soldier suits doesn't make them men."

Thabo spit out the window. "It still angers me to carry them."

"It must be done," said Dakota. "To lessen suspicion upon us. Even Rashawn agrees."

"Would you fly weapons to the General?"

"The General wouldn't trust us with weapons. We're only flying the uniforms because they arrived too late for the train."

Kobe stirred on the dusty floor, then groaned and rubbed his belly. "I ate too much at McDonalds."

Dakota laughed. "That is a hazard of having money, when more than sufficient becomes too much."

"Maybe I should have had sex." Kobe made a hideous face. "The coffin smells worse than last time!"

"If you're going to lose your lunch, please step outside to do it."

"How can you stand it?" asked Kobe, clamping a hand to his nose.

Dakota adjusted the trim wheel. "One grows accustomed to unpleasant things, even the stench of death."

Thabo offered a cigarette. "This will help."

"Are we almost there?" asked Kobe, taking a light from Thabo.

Dakota glanced at the landscape below. "We will soon reach the town. We'll have done with those bloody uniforms and should be home by suppertime." Then he stared ahead. "Smoke!"

"Where?" asked Thabo, squinting through the bug-spattered windscreen.

"A little to starboard… to the right. Use the binoculars."

Kobe scrambled to his feet. "A village?"

"No villages left in those hills," said Dakota. "The General 'relocated' the people."

"It's the railway line," said Thabo, aiming the heavy glasses.

Kobe peered over Thabo's shoulder. "Did Rashawn blow up another bridge?"

"Apparently someone did," said Thabo.

Dakota unlocked the auto-pilot and banked the plane to starboard. "Maybe this one won't be easy to fix."

"Most of the middle is gone," said Thabo. "But the fire is up in the hills."

Kobe asked, "Shall I wake Nathi?"

"Not yet," said Dakota. He eased the yoke forward and lowered the throttles, putting the plane in a slow descent.

"Look!" cried Thabo. "A coach is rolling down the hill! …It's going to run off the bridge!"

"One less coach for the General." Dakota banked tighter to starboard and dropped the nose even more.

"This will be cool!" exclaimed Kobe.

"Can you go any faster?" asked Thabo. "We don't want to miss the crash!"

*　　　*　　　*

Nicole was kneeling on the floor between the child soldier's legs. She had unbuttoned and pulled down his trousers; the bullet wound was in his thigh but seemed to have missed an artery. She turned when

177

Zack yelled, and stared out the door. The runaway car was still gaining speed, rocking, rattling, rounding the curve. The long wooden trestle lay ahead...

And the center section was gone!

"Zack! Jump off!" she yelled, and grabbed the soldier's arm, pulling him onto his feet. But, Zack ran in the wrong direction, dashing down the swaying aisle and out the door at the downhill end.

"Zack, no! The other way!"

The car lurched onto the trestle.

"ZACK!"

Suddenly, there was grinding screech of steel skidding over steel. The car jerked savagely side to side, pitching, bucking, wheels screaming, locked and sliding along the rails. Nicole and the soldier crashed to the floor, tumbling over the rattling boards to slam against a seat. Suitcases shot from the overhead rack, flying the length of the skidding car to burst open against the wall at the end. Clothes and things spewed onto the floor. The tote bag followed the luggage, and Coke cans exploded like chemical weapons, spraying gouts of amber foam. But the car finally squealed to a shuddering stop, leaving only the hiss of spurting sodas.

Nicole coughed dust from her throat. "Zack!"

"It's okay, mom."

Nicole was lying halfway down the car, the terrified boy-soldier clutched to her, crying. Zack was out on the platform gripping a big iron wheel.

"I put on the brakes," he panted. "Just like in the movies."

Nicole gave the soldier a comforting hug. "Are you all right?" she asked in Swahili.

"...Yes," he replied, though looking bewildered.

Nicole helped him onto a seat. "Press on the wound like this." Then she shakily went to the end of the car. They had stopped six feet from the dangling rails... just like in the movies. "Zack, are you all right?"

"Yeah, mom." Zackary's body was gleaming with sweat, striping the dust like a brown-and-white zebra. His jeans had tumbled to his feet, but somehow he didn't look funny.

178

Nicole scanned around. "The water bottles survived. ...And there's my first aid kit."

Zack hoisted his jeans. "Is the soldier okay?"

"For a twelve-year-old boy who's been shot."

A Coke can gave a final sputter, sounding like a sniffly nose. Then Nicole heard a distant hum. At first she thought of a swarm of bees, maybe enraged by the bridge explosion... African killer bees! But, no, it was an engine. A diesel locomotive? Maybe help was on the way? But, Zack looked up at the sky.

"Woah, mom! It's a C-47!"

The humming grew to a vibrating roar. Nicole joined Zack on the platform as a lion-colored airplane swooped over the bridge. She caught a glimpse of dusky faces peering from its cockpit windows.

The plane climbed into the sky once more, trailing smoke from its thundering engines. Nicole saw the face of a friendly lion painted on the nose. Did Kiwanja have an air force? According to Tom they had one helicopter... but he hadn't known of the child-soldiers. Again, she thought of the phone, now on the floor and soaked with Coke, though it seemed designed to survive a lot worse. Would this be a good time to use it?

* * *

"It's the Canadian boy!" cried Kobe, pointing to the railway coach on what remained of the trestle.

"Get your paw out of my face!" snapped Dakota, pulling back on the steering yoke, his other hand advancing the throttles.

"And his mother," said Thabo as the airplane climbed away. "Fortunately they stopped the coach."

Kobe said, "I would have liked to see it crash. ...But not with them in it, of course."

"Get away from the throttles!" yelled Dakota. "Thabo sit down, I can't bloody steer!"

Nathi appeared in the doorway. "What's going on?"

Thabo and Kobe began to explain.

"One at a time!" shouted Nathi above the engine roar.

179

"Shall I land?" asked Dakota, banking to circle around. "There's a place along the riverbed."

Nathi took the binoculars. "Thabo. Kobe. Out!" He dropped into the co-pilot's seat and scanned the land below. "What of that fire?"

"I don't know," said Dakota. "But there must have been an attack on the train."

Nathi shifted the glasses. "Take us over the hills. ...Why would you want to land?"

"There's a woman down there and her son. In the railway coach. We met them in Hillbrow two days ago, and they were wearing our boots."

"...Interesting," said Nathi. "And now they're here on the General's train."

"Is Canada against us, too?"

"From what I know of Canada they don't terrorize anyone." Nathi turned the focus knob. "The fire is oil and fuel on a flatcar... half derailed it seems."

"Less for the General," said Dakota.

"But none for Rashawn if that was his plan. ...The rest of the train must have escaped... yes, there's its smoke beyond the hills."

"But the General can't repair the bridge before the rains begin."

"Probably not," said Nathi, shifting the glasses again. "The damage is extensive. ...I don't see anyone near the fire."

"You wouldn't see our fighters."

"They wouldn't stay long, it's too close to the town."

"So what of the boy and his mother?"

*   *   *

"Mom! It's gonna land!"

Nicole looked up from tending the soldier. The bullet had gone through his thigh as cleanly as a bullet could, and she'd washed the wound with bottled water, sprinkled antiseptic powder and bound it with a bandage. "Be at peace," she said. "Maybe they will send you home."

For a moment the boy looked wistful, but then his face turned grim. "It would have to be much worse than this. I wish they had shot my leg off!"

"Don't be..." Nicole had almost said childish. She patted the boy's sweaty shoulder. "Is that an Army airplane?"

The boy peered out a window. "No. It brings supplies to the town."

Nicole watched the airplane settle to earth along the waterless riverbed, bouncing over the uneven ground, kicking up clouds of amber dust and finally rocking to a stop near a golden grove of acacias.

"Cool!" exclaimed Zack. "They built those planes in World War Two. They're one of the best ever made. They also used 'em in Vietnam."

We lost that war, thought Nicole. *And haven't really won any others since surrendering Saigon.* "We'd better start packing our things."

She tensed when Zack picked up the gun, and almost told him to put it down. She remembered when he'd been about five and she'd caught him playing with matches. But he handled the weapon carefully and gave it to the soldier.

"*Asante,*" said the boy.

"*Karibu,*" said Zack, surprising Nicole, until she remembered the phrase book.

"Um..." Zack added. "*Jina langu ni* Zack. Um...*Jina lako... nani?*"

"Jabari," the boy replied.

"His name's Jabari," said Zack.

Nicole smiled. "*Asante*, Zack."

Zack checked the disemboweled suitcases. "What a fuckin' mess!"

"Zack!"

The boy soldier giggled... apparently "fuck" needed no translation.

"Sorry," said Zack.

"Just stuff it all back in," said Nicole. "Now's not a time to be neat."

Zack looked out a window. "Some dudes are comin' from the plane. ...Are we still Canadians?"

"It might be safer to say we are until we know more about them."

"Like we're spies again?"

"We're not spies, Zack, we're just being careful."

Nicole heard voices out on the bridge. Then puffing breaths like Zack's whenever he had to walk anywhere. Someone mounted the platform steps at the opposite end of the car. A shadow darkened the doorway and there was Zackary's African twin, the fat scruffy ebony meerkat.

The muscular panther followed, then the big-bellied hyena. All had guns slung over their shoulders, nasty-looking AK-47s... Defenders Of Democracy Terrorist Accessories.

Nicole recalled her blurry glimpse of three young boys in the hillside grass shooting down at the train; they'd had the same kind of weapons. But, they'd been wearing loincloths. These almost anthropomorphic boys were dressed the same as they'd been in Hillbrow; the fat one clad in droopy jeans, the other two in canvas shorts, the beautiful boots on their feet. Nicole wasn't sure how to greet them... was it wise to reveal she spoke Swahili? But the soldier already knew that; and Zack took the matter out of her hands.

"*Habari,*" he called.

The fat boy smiled. "*Habari. Unazungumza Kiswahili?*"

"...Um," said Zack. "*Kidogo... tu...*"

Nicole said, "I also speak a little."

The soldier cried, "We were attacked by the terrorists!"

For an instant the boys looked... Nicole wasn't sure. Maybe predatory. Whatever the look it was quickly masked, and the fat boy's voice sounded neutral. "We will take you to town."

The muscled youth added, "And you can tell the General his bridge has been destroyed."

The fat boy smiled. "Hopefully, he won't kill the messenger."

The wounded boy asked, "What happened to the other soldiers?"

The fat meerkat shrugged. "They ran away on the train."

"Like jackals from lions," said the muscular panther.

"And left you," laughed the hyena, sounding a bit like one.

Nicole wondered if there were other boys lying wounded, maybe dying, up in the hills where the fire still burned. ...But, they were soldiers no matter how young. Their government made them risk their lives, and their government should have been caring for them. Then she remembered the two little kids. "There was a family. They jumped off back in the hills."

"I'm sure they're safe," said the fat boy. He gave the soldier a meaningful glance. "The 'terrorists' will help them." He turned to Zack again. "I am Dakota. This is Kobe and Thabo."

"I'm Zack," said Zack, who'd found the phrase book. "This is my mom... um... *mamangu.*"

Dakota smiled. "It might save time if we spoke English."

"Cool," said Zack. "This is my mom."

"Nicole," said Nicole, noting Dakota's British accent, which had flavored the archaic Swahili. "This is Jabari."

Dakota gave a short nod to the soldier, then smiled again at Zack. "We'll carry your things. ...Is that an I-pod?"

About ten minutes later they were trudging along the dry river-bed nearing the idling airplane. Dakota was leading, always about to lose his jeans and looking all the more like Zack, at least in wobbly shape. The hyena, Kobe, followed; the panther, Thabo, carried the luggage, while Zack supported the limping soldier, and Nicole came last with the soda-soaked tote.

The scene, she thought, was almost surreal -- the gun-toting boys, the tawny airplane, the ambers and golds of the heat-shimmered land, and the clear indigo of the sky -- like something out of a fantasy game set in an alternate universe and starring half-animal characters. Even Zack looked like a Rambo hamster helping a wounded warrior. She often glanced at the boys' dusty boots -- they were the reason she'd come to this place and gotten herself and Zack in this game -- but it didn't seem an appropriate time to ask about native footwear.

It was clearly a cargo airplane with big double doors near the tail. Like many bush planes it was showing its age and not in the best of repair. Nicole noted oily engine soot on the undersides of the wings, and the fuselage had a battered look enhanced by many patches. The engines clattered like washing machines spinning loads of marbles, spitting out puffs of gunmetal smoke behind their revolving propellers. Then, Captain Keto appeared in the doorway!

...Well, not quite.

Of course he wasn't the action figure, cartoonishly bulked like a comic-book hero... boys wanted masculine mass. Instead, he was the

183

ideal image, the model that she and Jenny had drawn. Like a picture-negative Tom, he was realistically perfect... high, jutting pecs, rocky biceps, and a narrow waist like an *Elfquest* male. He wasn't wearing amber and gold, just shabby brown trousers blackened with oil. She noted the antelope boots on his feet, along with a tuft of fur on his chest, the same as worn by the trio of boys.

Dakota said, "This is Nathi, my father."

The man's onyx eyes looked tired but kind, large, and up-turned at the corners. They didn't harden while scanning the soldier, and may have even saddened. Then he raised them and smiled at Nicole. "Welcome," he said in English. "Despite the bothersome circumstances."

Zack was puffing and pouring sweat from the effort of helping the wounded boy, but grinned and glanced back at the wreck of the bridge. "Any landing you can walk away from is a good one."

"Spoken like a pilot," said Nathi. He jumped to the ground, landing light as a cat.

"Are you a pilot?" asked Dakota, turning to Zack.

"Not in realtime so far, an' I only flew in passenger planes. Boeing 737s, a 387, a 727, an' an Airbus 380. An' once... no twice... in a helicopter, a Bell ARH."

"Please come aboard," said Nathi. "I'm sorry there aren't any passenger seats." He noted the look of shocked surprise that blanched Nicole's face as she neared the doorway. "I'm afraid you'll have to tolerate that; we carry a coffin for burial."

Which is long overdue! thought Nicole. She had never believed much in omens, but they'd been in Kiwanja less than a day, gotten attacked by terrorists, were almost killed in a train wreck, and now they'd be sharing a flight with a corpse! But she made herself smile despite the stench. "Thank you for rescuing us. Of course, I'll pay..."

"That isn't necessary," said Nathi. "And it was my son who noticed your trouble."

"He seems like a fine young man," said Nicole.

"Thank you."

"Thabo, Kobe," said Dakota. "Fix something for them to sit on."

Thabo tossed the suitcases in, hoisted himself through the door-

184

way, then offered a hand to Kobe. Nathi boosted Dakota aboard by grabbing the back of his jeans, then gently lifted the soldier, and Zack got a boost like Dakota. Then he made a sling with his hands and nodded to Nicole. "I'm sorry there aren't any steps."

Zack offered a hand from the doorway. "Here, mom, grab on."

"He seems like a fine young man," said Nathi.

"Thank you," said Nicole.

SEVENTEEN

Another omen, wondered Nicole? ...Or maybe her past catching up to her present? Dakota, Thabo and Kobe had arranged some boxes to sit on... boxes labeled BARRYMORE. She recognized the division; the factory in Mississippi that made the little uniforms. She remembered a Biblical quote: *The sins of the fathers shall be visited upon the sons.* Did that also apply to mothers? But, it wasn't as if her company was making *guns* for children. ...Not real ones, anyway.

She made her way up the slanted floor and past the reeking coffin, resisting the urge to hold her nose. Nathi closed the cargo doors, entombing them with the stench of death in a broiling aluminum oven. Nathi must have seen her face, which might have gone as green as the smell.

"It will be less in the air."

Nicole made a smile that might have looked ghastly and tried to breathe through her mouth. "It's better than walking, or even that train."

"The train was once in much better repair."

"Before your new government?"

"Yes," said Nathi, latching the doors. He glanced at the soldier, who lay on the floor uncomfortably close to the coffin. "Our government does not serve its people."

Nicole saw some flats of canned milk and other food items amongst the cargo. "Is this for the people?"

"What the government doesn't steal."

Nicole sat on one of the Barrymore boxes, and Hyena-boy sat on another. "What is snow like?" he asked.

The muscular panther settled beside him. "Yes, please tell us."

Dakota was in the cockpit, and Zack was peering in through the doorway. Dakota squeezed into the pilot's seat and flashed his bottle-opener smile. "Would you like to co-pilot, Zack?"

"Def!"

Nathi went forward to stand in the doorway as Zack wiggled into the co-pilot's seat, while Dakota readied the plane for takeoff.

"That is the landing gear lever," Dakota said to Zack. "Please pull it up when I ask. When that light goes out, center the lever."

"Roger, Captain."

Nicole tried to explain the concept of snow while glancing into the cockpit as Dakota throttled the engines up and swung the plane around, Zack intently watching his moves. The engines' rumble increased to a roar. The airplane started to rattle and creak, slowly gathering speed. The wings seemed to flap alarmingly outside the dusty windows. The floor leveled out as the tail left the ground. Then the jolting rattle stopped, leaving only the engine thunder.

"Gear up," ordered Dakota.

"Roger, Captain."

Nicole watched the amber land fall away. For an instant she saw a shape in the grass that might have been a lion.

"Would you like to fly?" asked Dakota, when they seemed to reach a cruising speed and the engine roar dropped to a deep-throated drone.

"Yeah!" said Zack.

Nicole watched her son take control, his chubby hands on the steering yoke, his booted feet on the rudder pedals. He made a few careful adjustments, obviously getting the feel of flying just as he'd done in Tom's helicopter. She remembered a line from a John Steinbeck story: *A boy becomes a man when a man is needed*. Was that

187

why America seemed full of boys? Men on the outside but children within; greedy, narcissistic, self-centered children acting out meaningless Hollywood roles.

Dakota indicated the compass. "This is our course at three-thousand feet."

"Roger, Captain," said Zack. "But, ain't that kinda low? The ceiling for a C-47 is 24,000 feet."

"24,440 with these Pratt and Whitney engines. But we prefer to stay off radar. Unscheduled landings must be explained. And I mean no offense, but isn't 'ain't' rather bad English?"

"Yeah."

"Would you like a Coke?"

"Sure. *Asante.*"

"Are you hungry? I have a ham sandwich."

"*Asante sana.* Is Dakota an African name? It's also what these airplanes were called. Like, in England in World War Two."

"That's why my father named me Dakota." Dakota patted his wobbly belly. "A bit slow and clumsy but I always get there."

"Cool."

"Rather like ice-cream but without any flavor?" asked Thabo.

"...Oh," said Nicole. "...More like a snow cone."

"What is a snow-cone?" asked Kobe.

Nicole explained as best she could while glancing at Nathi from time to time. He was watching the boys as they flew the plane, but might have been listening to her, a smile occasionally touching his lips. The coffin's stench had thankfully lessened, behind them now in the wind of their flight. Faintly above the engine drone, she heard Dakota instructing Zack. "...fuel mix controls, propeller pitch, manifold pressure..."

For the moment all seemed safe... though a long way from American safe. But, maybe that was America's problem? Make a culture foolproof and it became a culture of fools; a country of car seats and child-proof caps, of parental controls and bicycle helmets, where kids could be taken away from their parents just because they weighed more than the government said they should.

Yet, also one of the few "great nations" where kids could be sent off to war and die but not be allowed to legally drink. A country constantly building new prisons to prove how much it cared for its kids and what kind of values it taught them. A nation obsessed with bodily health that left its children's brains to rot in a sanitized dump of material trash. A country that exported its violence, both Hollywood fiction and brutally real; where murder and terror were called "shock and awe" in the U.S. version of New-Speak.

She looked at the soldier lying alone beside the ominous coffin, clad in her company's little war pants, one leg soaked with his little-boy blood. He hadn't been mistreated by the anthropomorphic trio, though being left alone back there might have been a subtle torture. It seemed that Nathi and his crew were trying to keep a neutral stance in what must have been a civil war. But, it also seemed clear where their sympathies lay.

Nathi turned from the doorway, speaking above the engine drone. "You seem to like our boots."

"They're beautiful things," said Nicole, "and seem very lovingly made."

"Anything in life worth doing should always be done with love."

"Can you tell me about them?"

Kobe said, "I should like to hear more about Canada."

Thabo gave Kobe a poke in the side and pointed to the wounded boy. "Perhaps we should have a chat with him. I'm sure he could tell us some interesting things."

"...Oh," said Kobe. "Yes."

Nathi took Kobe's place on the box as Kobe and Thabo went back to the soldier. "The style is an ancient tradition, unchanged for many hundreds of years, though the rubber soles are a recent improvement." He smiled. "The British brought in motor trucks after the First World War and their tires often disappeared, though now old tires are free in almost any country."

Nicole made a mental note of that... one component was virtually free except for shipping costs. "Are they made in your villages?"

"In happier times, in every village. But, the government wants to 'civilize' us and many old ways are now discouraged. Often under penalty. From traditional crops to traditional clothing. And traditional values. ...May I ask why you have come here? We seldom see any tourists, and none in recent years."

Nicole suddenly felt like a spy, and that wasn't clean. She shifted her eyes to Zack for a moment, hoping he wouldn't make a mistake and tell Dakota something he shouldn't... blow their cover at three-thousand feet in a plane full of terrorist sympathizers. She remembered something her father had said: *the best way to lie is tell part of the truth.*

But, how much truth should she tell? That her company wanted to buy those boots? The same company that made uniforms for a government that oppressed the people? "My parents have a leather goods shop. ...In a mall."

Nathi laughed. He had a nice laugh, kind like his eyes. "We have been to malls, and also McDonalds."

The plane banked sharply, throwing Nicole against Nathi. His arms went around her, steadying her as curses burst from the cockpit. "Dammit, you ass, get out of my way!"

A clattering shadow flashed past the windows.

"It's a Huey UH-1!" cried Zack.

Dakota's voice broke like most boys' his age as he shouted into a microphone. "You bloody son of a painted whore!"

The airplane swiftly descended, and butterflies hatched in Nicole's surprised stomach. Nathi kept hold of her shoulders. "That was our government's air force." He chuckled. "All of it."

"Where did you learn to fly!" bawled Dakota. "In a fucking video game?"

"Dakota," said Nathi. "We have a lady aboard."

"Sorry."

Nathi turned back to Nicole. "We are landing now in the town." He laughed again. "Please return your seat to an upright position and fold your refreshment tray."

Nicole laughed, too. "Do you fly out of there often?"

"Usually at least once a week."

"Is this plane available for charter?"

"You have seen enough of Kiwanja by rail?"

"I... wanted my son to see Africa. The *real* Africa," said Nicole.

190

Truth-flavored lies came more easily now. "We'd like to see one of your villages, and your boots being made."

Nathi seemed to consider. Unlike Tom he didn't smell neutral -- disregarding the reek of death -- and maybe not nice by American standards. He smelled like... well, a tired, sweaty man. "I'll give you the name of someone in town and he will be able to contact us."

There was a sudden double jolt, squeals of rubber hitting dirt, and the airplane was rattling over the ground.

"Cool!" exclaimed Zack. "But it wasn't a three-point."

Dakota replied, "One does not make three-point landings in a C-47. The fuselage is weakest around the cargo doors, and such landings cause a strain upon it."

The airplane bumped to a dust-shrouded stop. Dakota began instructing Zack on various things to check and shut off. Nathi released Nicole's shoulders. "Thank you for flying Simba Air Freight."

EIGHTEEN

"Where can I buy one of those?" asked Zack. He touched the tuft of lion's mane between the soft shapes of Dakota's chest. "Like at a souvenir shop in town?"

Dakota gave him a curious look as they stood in the airplane's doorway. "I should hope not."

"Did I say somethin' wrong?" asked Zack. "I know I'm a guest in your country an' I don't wanna offend you."

Dakota fingered his charm. "I'm not offended, Zack. But these can never be bought. And would mean nothing if they could be."

"Are they magic?" asked Zack. "Like your boots?"

Dakota cocked his head. "Why do you think our boots are magic?"

"I'm not sure," said Zack. "I never believed in magic, except when I was little... like, Peter Pan an' The Wizard Of Oz." He leaned over his belly to look at his feet. "Wearin' 'em just makes me feel good."

"Perhaps because they are made with love." Dakota thought for a moment. "So many things are made with hate by people who must trade their lives for money. Perhaps that hate seeps out of those things and makes the people who buy them feel bad. ...If it would not be rude of me, may I ask your age?"

"I'll be thirteen in two days, havin' my birthday in Africa."

192

Again, Dakota seemed to consider. "Perhaps, if your mother charters our plane, you may come to our village and see our boots being made." He fingered the charm on his chest again. "And you may earn one of these, if you wish to try."

"What would I have to do?"

"A simple thing, yet one of courage. A thing every boy in Kiwanja must do." Dakota glanced at the wounded soldier. "Though some don't anymore."

"Like a native ritual?"

"One might call it that."

"That would be cool, I'd wear it forever."

Dakota smiled. "I'm sure you would. And you could tell me about your country. I have heard it is cold, yet your people seem warm in their hearts."

Nicole, out on the hot dusty ground, tensed a bit before Zack replied, hoping he wouldn't blow their cover. But he only said, "Thanks, I like your country, too." Then he laughed. "Even gettin' shot at."

"That is not the fault of our people." Dakota touched Zack's chest. "Our hearts are as kind as your own, and perhaps you will see that in time."

"Thanks for the flyin' lesson, Dakota. Do Kiwanjis shake hands?"

"We usually hug our friends."

"Wanna?"

"Of course." The boys seemed to meld into each other's bodies. "I hope we meet again," said Dakota. "And in happier circumstances."

"So do I," said Zack. "See ya, man." He jumped to the ground, his belly rebounding, his jeans slipping comically low.

"Pull up your pants," murmured Nicole. "Here comes a jeep."

She gazed across a shimmering flat that would probably be a muddy lake during the rainy season. The town was about a mile away, its buildings blurred by ghosts of heat, but looked like it had in Tom's presentation, partly old American West, yet also spaghetti-western foreign. The "airport" itself was a red-rusted barn with a ragged wind sock hanging limp as a dishrag – or a used condom -- and there were several derelict airplanes which would obviously never fly again. At the

193

edge of the baking landing field was a big, van-bodied Army truck painted sand-and-tan. On its roof was a radar antenna... yet more American Aid?

"That ain't a real jeep," said Zack as a smaller vehicle neared, trailing dust. "It's an M151. They called 'em MUTTs... Military Utility Tactical Trucks. They're what we used before HumVees, like in Vietnam. An' the M-16 Jabari has, an' the Huey that buzzed us comin' in, they're all old Vietnam war stuff."

Recycled war toys, thought Nicole. Was that America's contribution to saving the environment? Zack was scanning the ancient airplanes, shading his eyes with a hand. "Woah! That's a Ford Tri-motor! An' a Tudor 688. An' what's left of a C-54."

Thabo and Kobe were helping Jabari out of the airplane's doorway. Zack assisted the boy to the ground and offered a shoulder to lean on, taking the weight off his wounded leg, as Dakota handed Jabari his gun with a smile that looked ironic, while Nathi was checking the landing gear. Nicole saw oil dripping here and there from various places under the wings, making tiny atomic explosions as they hit the amber dust. She felt a little uneasy as the jeep-like vehicle came to a stop... had Tom contacted the government saying she was coming? That wouldn't look good for her and Zack in present company. But, Tom couldn't have known she'd arrive in this plane...

Or could he?

She thought of the spy phone again, of monitor screens and radar grids and satellite eyes in the sky; of faceless men with tasteless coffee paranoiacally spying on everyone in the name of defending Democracy. And maybe Tom looking over their shoulders.

She raised her eyes to the cloudless sky: they could have been on camera now. Tom might have seen the attack on the train. Might have watched her watching hippos. But, there was nothing she could do except be very careful.

She was getting used to child-soldiers – "normalizing" in New-Speak – and driving the MUTT was a boy of fourteen dressed in a Barrymore uniform that badly needed washing. The passenger was an actual man, hippo stout and maybe mid-forties, his uniform clean and pressed. He wore the rank of Major, but looked like a typical minor

194

official, a paper-pushing pompous ass, instead of an African warrior. Thankfully, he seemed surprised at seeing her and Zack. He gave them both a second-glance, then got out and marched up to Nathi. They spoke in Swahili of course, and Nicole listened carefully.

"Your cargo list," the Major demanded, reminding Nicole of a DMV clerk.

"I'll get it," said Nathi.

"You have the shipment for me?"

"You have the payment for me?" returned Nathi.

"Yes, but it does not please the General that you demand payment in Krugerrands."

"I would think it would be convenient for him since they comprise his treasury... at least according to rumor."

"You should not listen to treasonous rumors!" The Major wrinkled his nose as they walked to the airplane's doorway. "*Another* bloody coffin?"

"The war, you know," said Nathi. "As Joseph Stalin said, 'One death is a tragedy, but a million is just a statistic.'"

"Who is he?"

"Someone who knew quite a bit about death and how to reduce it to meaningless numbers."

The Major snorted. "The people should just put their dead in the ground! What do they need of coffins?"

"Perhaps they wish to become civilized as the General tries to teach us. ...Of course you'll want to inspect the contents?"

The Major scowled. "You say that every time! Do you think I can't look death in the face?"

"You will know when he comes for you."

The Major snorted again. "I do not believe in The Lion Of Death!"

"Tell him that when you meet him. ...Dakota, please open the coffin. And try not to let out the maggots."

"No!" snapped the Major. "You'd like that, wouldn't you? Making my duty disgusting."

"It's quite disgusting already," said Nathi. "All the things you confiscate that never reach the people."

"I only follow orders."

"Others have said that in the past, but it didn't save them at their trials for crimes against humanity."

The Major scowled again, but clumsily hoisted himself through the doorway. "You should get some bloody steps like the American airplanes!"

"No doubt their steps are bloody indeed."

The Major slipped and almost fell, and Nathi boosted him aboard by the back of his trousers. Zackary laughed and got a glare.

"Who are these people?" the Major demanded, recovering like a ruffled hen. "This young white girl and the woman?"

"Guests in our country," said Dakota. "They were coming by the General's train, but the terrorists blew up a bridge. Very uncivilized of them. We also brought back your soldier, and only slightly damaged. ...And our young guest is a boy."

"...I see," said the Major. "You," he added to Jabari. "Report to your Captain."

"He's been shot," said Zack.

"What did he say?" the Major demanded.

"Your soldier has been shot," said Dakota.

"I have eyes. Tell the boy... ask if our young guest will help the wounded soldier into the jeep... if he pleases."

Dakota translated.

"Sure," said Zack. "But it's not a real jeep."

The Major added, "Tell... direct our the guests to the terminal. Someone must look at their passports."

"You would make our guests walk?" asked Dakota.

"...Invite them to ride with me."

Nicole breathed a sigh of relief: she wouldn't have to show their passports where Nathi and his crew could see. She smiled at Nathi and said in English, "Civilization has come to Kiwanja."

"Mostly the worst of it."

Zack assisted Jabari into the back of the MUTT, waited for Nicole to climb in, loaded the luggage Nathi brought, then raised a palm to Dakota. "*Kwa heri*, Dakota."

"See you, Zack."

Nathi stepped close to Nicole and pressed something into her hand. "This is how you may contact us. But, please say nothing to anyone, and don't keep this paper for long."

"I understand," said Nicole, feeling uncomfortably spyish again.

"I hope your son sees the real Africa and the best of Kiwanja's people."

Nicole smiled. "We've already seen some of both."

*   *   *

"Dakota's dad is cool, huh?"

"He is," agreed Nicole. She smiled at Zack as they stood in a street of tawny dust. Kiwanja didn't have taxis, but they'd gotten a ride in the back of a truck, an ancient Bedford... coming to town on a load of yams.

Zack looked up at the sky as the C-47 climbed away over the distant hills. "I didn't like lyin' to him an' Dakota."

Nicole also gazed after the plane. "I didn't either. But, sometimes the truth can be dangerous."

"Or not good for business?"

"Life isn't a Disney movie, Zack."

"I figured that out a long time ago."

They were standing in front of the town's hotel, a shabby building of plastered brick with a British Victorian look. It was two-stories tall, a Kiwanji skyscraper, with a rusty tin roof and iron balconies. The sign above the doorway was the only thing that looked fairly new

N'DILA HOTEL

Nicole had suggested Zack put on a shirt, even though dirty and sticky with Coke, before they'd gone through Kiwanji Customs... a rather bewildered-looking old man who had searched neither them nor their luggage but had to thoroughly search his desk to find an ancient passport stamp that still said **British Kiwanja**... Tom must have been right that tourists were rare. He also seemed to be correct that there was little for tourists to see. The "city" looked more like an old mining camp, probably built as a company town to exploit

197

Kiwanja's coal reserves; which, according to Tom, had not been enough to justify the British hanging on to this land. The town lay at the edge of a plain that had probably been a shallow lake back in the days when dinosaurs ruled. On a hillside a mile away was a seemingly half-abandoned mine, though workers appeared to be toiling there. It was too far to see them clearly, but all were shirtless and some were small.

Near the mine was a grim-looking building with a tall iron stack that was spewing black smoke. Sagging wires on tottering poles led from the structure into the town but didn't seem to go anywhere else.

In typically African fashion the town looked deserted at this time of day, its people indoors out of the sun, except for the laboring miners. The few Nicole had seen on the streets were mostly sad-looking women in bargain-basement cotton dresses that somehow seemed unwillingly worn, along with some near-naked pot-bellied kids whose tummies weren't round from McDonalds. Nicole had traveled enough in her life to learn to trust her feelings, and this didn't feel like a magic kingdom.

It didn't seem to be growing either, despite the construction supplies on the train. The only thing new was an Army compound about a quarter mile away. Its concrete walls were topped with barbed wire, and powerful floodlights were mounted on poles. Watch-towers loomed at the corners, and little soldiers guarded the gates. No doubt she would have to go in there and meet the President-General. Then she would have to talk about boots. She wondered how often Aaron Steele had done those things in these kinds of places.

But, thankfully, that would have to wait; both she and Zack were filthy. First on the list were a room and a bath, then arranging for laundry service. Then a dinner and a good night's sleep. Those boots had waited for centuries to be discovered and exploited; they could wait another day.

Zack picked up the suitcases. "This place looks worse than Hillbrow. I wish we could stay in Dakota's village. I'm sure their huts are better than this, even if they're made of mud."

"We might," said Nicole. "But..."

"Yeah it's a business trip."

198

"Are you feeling upset?"

Zack gave her a patient look. "I don't get upset that easy, mom. Maybe you just think I do."

Nicole remembered the morning when Zack had announced that Freddy was dead; the morning she'd really looked at him and... yes... hadn't liked what she'd seen. ...Or maybe what she thought she'd seen. "I'm sorry things didn't work out between your father and I."

"He wasn't very strong, mom. Not on the inside where it counts. An' he wanted me to be like that, all outside an' no inside."

"...Maybe he did," said Nicole. "But don't you miss having a father sometimes?"

"Like for campin' an' 'manly stuff?'"

"Well, yes."

"Dakota's dad would be cool, but I guess he's taken. ...Or did you mean Tom?"

"...It's a little early to think about Tom. That way, I mean."

"Yeah," agreed Zack. "We hardly know him."

Nicole recalled the Houston night, waking up with Tom beside her. "Well," she said almost playfully, "we know even less about Nathi."

"Does him bein' black make a difference?"

It seemed like a logical question, and yet Nicole was surprised... Zack seemed to be full of surprises ever since he'd donned those boots. "I've never thought much about that."

"'Cause we never knew any black people? Like, personally... like *people*, I mean. They're just kinda like things."

"Things?"

"Or actors in movies," said Zack. "You see 'em, an' you hear 'em, but you never get to... I dunno... touch 'em."

Nicole thought of Zack and Dakota hugging, then of Nathi holding her shoulders, and then how she'd held Jabari. "I know Jennifer Walker. And I was in the Peace Corps."

Zack looked patient again, like a child explaining the Internet to a cyber-challenged adult. "But you never brought Mrs. Walker home. Or go shoppin' an' stuff with her. Or ever gone to where she lives. An' when you went to Africa it was only to help black people. Like, sure

199

you lived with them, but you always knew you were comin' back to where there wasn't any. ...Like, not for neighbors an' real friends... like not for people to really touch."

Nicole realized she could smell Dakota, his wild-boy scent from hugging Zack. "I guess that's true. ...But we both need a bath and clean clothes. We can talk later, if you want."

"Like over dinner?" said Zack. "An' with beer?"

NINETEEN

Kobe was in the co-pilot's seat gazing down at the lion-colored land as the airplane droned through the sky. "It seems quite sad," he remarked, "to not have a father at such a time."

"What time?" asked Thabo, standing behind him. "It's always sad to not have a father. I will miss mine for the rest of my life."

"Yes," said Kobe. "But sadder still being almost a man. They must have a manhood rite in Zack's country."

Dakota was flying the airplane, a cigarette between his lips, the sunglasses low on his nose. The not-quite mountain lay ahead, gold against the lowering sun. "Many boys in Kiwanja do not have fathers because of the war."

"Still, they have men to prepare them," said Thabo. "In our village they have Nathi and us. And, there are many grandfathers, as well as *Jumbe* Chane."

Dakota scanned the instruments. "There are many more people in Zack's country, therefore there are many more men. And of course their rites are different."

"Of course," said Thabo. "And they don't have lions except in zoos."

"They have polar bears," said Kobe.

Dakota laughed. "I'm sure it's much more complicated becoming a man in his country. But Zack is surely brave enough to pass whatever the test."

"And kind as well," said Thabo. "He helped the wounded soldier."

"Wouldn't you have?" asked Dakota. "Kindness is part of being a man."

"Perhaps in the same situation," said Thabo. "Jabari is still of our people, though his mind has been poisoned with lies. I hope I don't have to kill him."

Kobe asked, "But, why would Zack want to become a man here?"

"Because he *is* here," said Dakota. "And, because it is time."

Thabo said, "I'm glad I wasn't in his country when it was my time; I wouldn't have known what to do."

"You can drive a truck," said Kobe. "Driving must be part of their rite because everyone there has a car."

"What happened to his father?" asked Thabo.

Dakota eased the steering yoke forward and lowered the throttles a bit, putting the plane in a slow descent. "We mostly talked about flying, but I think his father left him."

"Abandoned his wife and son?" asked Thabo in something like shock.

"It's often done in civilized lands. ...Switch to cross-feed, Kobe."

Kobe reached for the fuel-selectors. "Why would a man leave a son like Zack?"

Dakota glanced at the airspeed. "Their lives are much more complicated. And women often raise their sons."

"I'd think that would be confusing," said Thabo.

"Zack didn't seem confused." Dakota studied the valley as the plane cleared the top of a hill. "Rashawn must have come."

Thabo took up the binoculars. "If so, his trucks are well hidden."

"But not their tracks," said Dakota. "He should have obscured them across the field. It's not the time to get careless, even with the rains so near."

"He must be almost ready," said Kobe, "to launch his attack on the General. The railway line is cut, and he now has sufficient ammunition."

Nathi looked in through the doorway. "All the more reason for caution. The General isn't a fool. He knows the time for Rashawn to attack is when the Americans can't help."

"Kobe, gear down," said Dakota.

"Right," said Kobe. "...Green and latched. Tail wheel locked."

"I smell supper," said Thabo. "Despite that bloody coffin."

*　　　*　　　*

"What do you think they'll have for dinner?" Zack was barefoot and shirtless in jeans after taking a bath. Despite the day's stimulation – or perhaps because of it – he'd also made love to himself again, revealed by the primal earthy scent above that of Pears Transparent soap. His body had darkened a bit more to copper, enhancing the indigo of his eyes and the sandy shade of his hair. He was comfortably sprawled on a tarnished brass bed, reading the phrase book while sipping Chibuki. The eight-track player had survived the attack -- things had been made to last in those days -- and the headphones were clamped to his ears. The sounds of Country Joe And The Fish, an anti-war song from the 1960s, echoed faintly in the air... *be the first mom on your block to have your boy come home in a box.*

Nicole stood facing a cloudy mirror, brushing tangles out of her hair. She noticed three new strands of gray but didn't pluck them out. The hotel clerk, an elderly man, had summoned a woman to wash their clothes -- by hand, no doubt, in a tin washtub, and dried outside in the afternoon sun -- but they'd come back folded and hospital spotless.

"I doubt there'll be many choices, Zack."

"Guess it'll be real African food. I didn't see a McDonalds in town."

Nicole sighed. "That will come with civilization. Our so-called brand of better life... fast-food, new clothes, and trashy TV." Nicole glanced down at the boots on her feet. "This week's style of new sport shoes. And all the million other things that people are told they can't live without. Including all the propaganda to make them feel ugly, fat... or old. With yellow teeth and nasty breath." She regarded herself in the mirror again. "When everything natural about ourselves has to be improved or fixed... lost, gained, enhanced, disguised, dyed, whitened, or covered up. And not enough toys to ever be happy." She turned to her son. "You know that, don't you?"

"Kinda," said Zack. He took off the headphones and shut down the player. "But, Dakota is cool without all that stuff. An' I don't think he ever gets bored."

"You haven't looked bored since we bought the boots."

"Guess that's why you brought me, huh?"

"Kinda." Nicole looked out the second-floor window as an Army truck rumbled past in the street, small soldiers bouncing around in its bed like camouflaged peas in an oversize pod.

"That's an M35A1," said Zack. "With an LDS multifuel engine. Vietnam era like all their war stuff."

"You know a lot," said Nicole.

"But I never thought I'd use it for real."

"I'm glad I didn't put parental controls on your computer."

"I woulda just hacked 'em out." Zack put down the book. "But, civilization ain't all bad. There's computers, an' history channels. Like, to make people smarter. An' medicine to save their lives."

"True," said Nicole. "But you have to learn what improves your life and what's just basically I-want-it junk that only makes you want more junk."

"Guess I got a lotta junk."

"But you're smart enough to know it's junk."

The room was like a Victorian junk-shop, its faded wallpaper of English moss roses. The furniture might have been valuable with proper restoration, but like the old train had been sadly neglected. Two balconied windows looked over the street, and the slanting rays of the evening sun were softened by yellowed lace curtains. Only one faucet worked in the bathroom, but "cold" was sufficiently hot. Nicole had warned Zack not to drink the water, and had ordered two beers brought up to the room, delivered by a small timid girl in a sadly ragged calico dress. Apparently, as Nicole had noticed, going bare-breasted was not done in town. By government order?

She watched the truck lumber away trailing dust. The remains of the train had finally arrived, and across a vista of rusty tin roofs more little soldiers worked to unload it. Others were standing guard, though there wasn't anything to guard except the building supplies. Both sides had obviously lost the fuel.

Two boys unloaded the olive-drab box Nicole had seen at the border station, but she didn't see an ambulance or any small bodies on stretchers, so maybe there hadn't been other wounded. She thought of the loinclothed boys in the hills and wondered if any of them had been hurt. Men, it seemed, were in short supply; and no matter who won this child-sized war, Kiwanja would suffer for years to come.

Could a boot factory help? Giving its people something to sell, branching into more industries, enabling them to rebuild their land. A land that... yes... *she* had helped to ravage by doing her part to do basically nothing except support a corporate system that preyed on people's ignorance and profited from war.

She'd been hoping to call her parents, but telephone lines to the outside world had been cut by the terrorists, as the old clerk had explained. That didn't seem to bother him, but who would he call. She'd considered using the spy phone... and why should she care if the call was recorded? She wasn't betraying anyone.

"*Pombe*," said Zack. "That's Swahili for beer."

"I'm glad you're learning more useful stuff. Get dressed and let's see what's for dinner. Judging from the ambiance it might be toad-in-the-hole."

"With real toad?"

There was a muffled squeaking sound. Nicole's first thought was a rat in the room, but it was the phone in her tote.

Zack smiled while puffingly donning his boots. "Bet it's Tom."

Nicole had oddly mixed feelings; welcome surprise, a bit of relief, and yet a twinge of fear. Was Tom calling to warn them of danger? That terrorists were coming to town with weapons of mass destruction? She unzipped the tote and took out the phone, sticky with Coke and crusted with dust. She sat on the bed and Zack squiggled close. "Hello?"

Tom's cheerful voice brought reassurance... that despite a few problems the world was okay and people were working to make it all good. "How's your safari? See any lions?"

Resisting an urge to open her heart -- of course this was being recorded -- Nicole tried to sound businesslike, yet still let Tom know she was happy he'd called. "No lions yet. But the trip was... exciting."

"Problems?" asked Tom.

Nicole wondered how much he knew. Also how much she should tell him. Or, was she being paranoid? They had never discussed any secret codes, or what not to say if she used this phone. "I thought you could watch us?"

"Wish I could," said Tom. "But the big boys have big wars to watch."

"You said there wasn't a war in Kiwanja."

"Not officially," said Tom. "We knew they were having some terrorist troubles, but most countries are these days."

"Then I shouldn't depend on the panic button? If nobody's watching this war."

There was concern in Tom's voice. "Did you think you were going to need it? You know I wouldn't have put you in danger, or let you bring Zack if things were bad. But, we don't know the situation there. What's your experience so far?"

"Somebody blew up a railroad bridge. I guess you could call that a terrorist act."

"You took that antique train?"

Nicole ruffled Zack's hair as he pressed close to listen. "We were hoping to see some lions." She slipped an arm around Zack. "But, we got here okay, and just slightly soiled."

"How's the other man in your life?"

"Hey, Tom," said Zack.

"Hey, pilot. Been fighting any terrorists?"

"They shot up the train with AK-47s."

"Jesus, Zack! Did you get hurt?"

"Nah. But a soldier got shot in the leg. An' they blew up a car full of gas an' oil."

"That must have been scary."

"I didn't have time to get scared."

"That's a good pilot... handle the situation first. Plenty of time to get scared later."

Zack laughed. "Or just have a beer with mom an' chill out."

"That's a manly attitude. Been taking good care of your mom?"

"I'm tryin'."

"Good man. Can I talk to her again?"

"Hi," said Nicole.

"So, you're in the town? How does it look?"

"Like an abandoned museum of British colonial rule. But it might be quaint if they fixed it up."

"Thinking ahead already? But, what's going on there now?"

"We've only been here a few hours, and that was the quietest time of day."

"Power plant still working?"

"Yes. And the water."

"Shops and stores?"

"They seem to be open. And the hotel cafe... such as it is."

"Hope it doesn't serve fried locusts with a side order of flies. What about the people? Normal activities?"

"I guess you could say that. They don't look happy or prosperous, but nobody's shooting here. Soldiers patrolling the streets. ...Child soldiers."

"I suspected that. But it's common enough in that part of the world. Another problem that needs to be fixed. ...But you've seen terrorists?"

"I saw three kids with guns," said Nicole. "Just like the soldiers but not as well dressed."

"Talked with any people?"

"One or two," said Nicole. Why should she mention Nathi and crew? They seemed to be having their own problems trying to run a little business between the claws of government graft and the teeth of terrorism. "Are you asking me who they sympathize with?"

Tom might have shrugged wherever he was. "Poor people usually back revolutions. They think any change will be better."

"Third-World 101," said Nicole. "What they usually get is another dictator, along with a wreck of a country. Which leaves them worse off than before."

"Which is why we're trying to help them. N'dila promised a free election as soon as peace is restored."

"Don't they all?" said Nicole.

"Freedom is mostly in people's minds. As long as they're not being bombed or shot, have enough food and a few basic things, they really don't care who runs the zoo."

"Well," said Nicole. "We haven't had time to meet many people. But I did learn a little about the boots."

"Listen, Nicole," said Tom. "I don't want to run your battery down in case you have to use that thing for something really important. If you feel you and Zack are in danger... more than it sounds like you've already been... get out by any means necessary. One of our transports is coming tomorrow, and it might be the last before the rains. And there seems to be an air-freight service... Simba, I think... so you might be able to charter their plane. If you can't get out, then find a safe place and push that button. I'll get someone there as soon as I can. Understand?"

"Yes," said Nicole. "And thank you."

"For what?" said Tom. "Getting you and Zack in a mess?"

Nicole drew Zackary closer. "We're not in a mess at the moment."

Tom seemed to hesitate... maybe because this call wasn't private. "I've been thinking a lot about both of you."

"We've been thinking a lot about you."

"Give Zack a hug for me," said Tom. "And hey, pilot, I'm going to arrange for flying lessons as soon as you get home."

"Cool!" said Zack. "Maybe at Area 51?"

"Hey, I'm good, but not that good."

TWENTY

The airplane sat in moon-dappled shadows near a grove of acacia trees. Its metal and engines ticked now and then, still cooling down from the heat of the day and its afternoon flight, its radio tuned to a shortwave station and rock music softly throbbing the night. Dakota was in the pilot's seat, his arms around Akili, she pressed to him girl-breast to boy-breast, their half-naked bodies tightly entwined, lips met and tongues gently questing, their breathing fast and deep.

Across the moonlit landing field beside another grove of trees the coffin sat in shadow. In deeper shadow beneath the trees were three old trucks and Rashawn's Land Rover, along with the jeep and half-track, their camouflage patterns of ambers and golds only black and grays in the dark. The half-track's hood had been replaced, and a heavy twin-barreled machine gun was mounted on the skate-rail above the armored body. Although the night was just settling in, many small figures were lying asleep, most on blankets spread on the ground, while others slept in the beds of the trucks. All were clad in loincloths, and most clutched rifles like grim teddy bears.

A group of men in their twenties and thirties were gathered around the coals of a fire where scents of supper still lingered. Cigarette embers glowed in the dark, and shafts of light from the cloud-mottled moon reflected from eyes and gleamed on teeth, while two young boys in loincloths, rifles slung on their shoulders, patrolled the camp's perimeter.

Across the stream in the village, cooking fires were flickering low, and fans of candle and lantern light spread from windows and doorways. Children still played their nighttime games amongst the joyfully romping dogs, though mothers were calling for younger ones to come inside to bed. Up on the not-quite mountain, Tindo sat with Mbwa, his rifle across his legs. From far overhead came a faint rush of jets; a red winking light appeared through a cloud, and Tindo imagined the people up there. Did they ever wonder what lay below when soaring high above the world?

"We will have many children," murmured Akili, pressing her lips again to Dakota's, her breasts melding into the orbs of his chest, her ruby necklace entwining his charm.

But Dakota drew away and switched the radio off. "That was an American song, *Get Together* by The Youngbloods. Some of their youth still hope for peace and sing about building a better world."

"Then there *is* hope," said Akili. "Because the future belongs to the young."

"But the young are often deceived by the old. As Thabo said today, the old make wars for the young to fight."

Akili still clung to Dakota. "Perhaps we can change that when we are old. I never want my children to have to fight in a war. But, maybe that's always a woman's wish."

"The English Queen Victoria sent many young men to war. War is not always the fault of men."

"Not of men like you." Akili stroked Dakota's cheek, but Dakota only sighed.

"I can't marry you, Akili. ...Surely you must know that?"

"...But, the war may be over soon." Akili gazed out though the windscreen. "Clouds have been gathering today just as my father predicted." She turned her eyes to the camp in the grove. "Nature gathers her forces just as Rashawn has gathered his. He's with my father and yours now making the last of their plans."

"The last of their plans," said Dakota. "Because if we fail there will be no more. There will be only the General's future, and that's not a future I want for my children." He pointed toward the village. "To forget that places like this existed, where people were happy without many things and respected the earth as the mother of all."

"And if we win...?"

"Win or lose, I may not return."

Akili regarded him. "I think I understand, and I think I've always known, though maybe I didn't want to admit it."

"There is no other," said Dakota.

Akili smiled. "Of course there is." She touched the leather-wrapped steering yoke. "But I ask you to give me a gift. The greatest gift a man can give."

"...Oh," said Dakota. "But, that's not done."

"Our people never made war," said Akili. "Fighting each other was also 'not done,' and so we did not stop the General before he grew so powerful. We can't just blindly cling to the past or none of us will have a future." She gestured toward the fighters' camp. "Too many men have died on both sides. And far too many children. The final battle is yet to come and who knows how many more will die. Our land will need men for its future." She smiled at Dakota. "Your kind of men."

Kobe called from the ground, "They want you at the council, Dakota."

Dakota sighed. "Very well."

"Will you give me your gift?" asked Akili. "Which will also be a gift to our land?" She kissed Dakota again. "Tonight."

"At the pond?"

Akili regarded the lion's fang and doll above the compass. "Here... if that will not make her jealous."

Dakota embraced Akili once more. "I'm sure she will approve."

211

TWENTY-ONE

Nicole awoke to the scent of a man, thinking again of that night in Houston waking with Tom beside her, but then realized it was Zack. She turned on her side to see him asleep in the other brass bed near the windows. The night had been hot and he lay naked, the sheet kicked down to feet. As she had a few days before, she tried to remember herself at his age, and wondered if she would have loved him then... or rather a boy like him. That would have depended on how smart *she* was.

She looked at her watch on the bedside table: 8:13 Kiwanja time. The morning air seemed almost cool compared to yesterday's heat. The streets were still fairly quiet, though there were sounds of a wakening town and people going about their lives; a few women's voices, the chatter of kids, and the rattle of a chain lock being opened. There was also the rumble of Army trucks passing in the street below, a sound now almost familiar, and diesel smoke drifted in through the windows. Drawing the sheet around her, Nicole sat up and looked out. Gunmetal clouds were gathering above the distant hills. A plane was at the airfield, huge and painted desert tan, which must have been the transport Tom had mentioned yesterday. ...The last plane out before the rains.

Somebody knocked on the door. *They come for you in the morning.* She rose and put on her robe as Zackary sleepily stirred, then crossed the room and opened the door. A boy-soldier stood in the hallway, a comically pot-bellied boy of fourteen who looked like he'd swallowed a basketball, his uniform spotless and smelling new, maybe from yesterday's shipment, though his shirt couldn't be buttoned over his bulbously bulging bulge like a Don Martin *Mad* magazine cartoon. He seemed a little uncertain despite the big rifle slung on his shoulder, maybe at seeing a bathrobed woman. And maybe her color -- or lack of same -- added to his uncertainty. He mumbled a sort of Swahili "um..." then announced that President-General N'dila would like to have them for breakfast.

Zack sat up. "Who is it?"

Nicole recalled a book she had read: *Dining With The Dictator.* Word must have reached the President-General that there were "guests" in his town. "We've been invited to breakfast."

"Cool," said Zack, and yawned.

The soldier smiled at Zack and spoke.

"What did he say?" asked Zack.

"He heard what you did from Jabari, saving us on the train. He said you're very brave."

"Oh," said Zack, and smiled at the boy. "Thanks... *karibu.* How's Jabari?"

"All right," said Nicole after asking. "His duties will be light for a while."

The boy added that he was Corporal Akida, and had a jeep waiting to take them away.

"We'll just be a minute," said Nicole, recalling one of Zack's eight-track tapes, the Beatles' *Magical Mystery Tour.*

Zack rolled from the bed and looked out a window. "It's not a real jeep, it's a MUTT. ...An' that's a Hercules C-130 over at the airport. It can carry four MUTTs or three HumVees."

It could also carry us out of here, thought Nicole as she closed the door... which Corporal Akida, waiting beyond, now seemed to be guarding.

213

*   *   *

"It was the work of children," said Nathi. "I know little about such things, but I wouldn't have used a land mine to blow the wheels off a car full of fuel. Not when I needed that fuel."

Rashawn frowned. "I ordered them to stop the train. To blow up the tracks ahead of it after destroying the bridge behind so it could not escape. Kiwanja will need that train again to help us build a future. But they set off the mine too late."

"Perhaps you should have been there?"

"No doubt," sighed Rashawn. "And everywhere else, doing everything else. My Army is farmers, hunters and boys. ...To think if I only had *one* missile! *One* missile aimed at the General's compound and this bloody war would be over!"

"When all goes bright," said Nathi.

"Bright begins a new day," said Rashawn, turning toward the eastern hills to face the rising sun. "A bright new day for our people."

"With you as our President?" asked Nathi.

"That will be the choice of our people."

"Would you vote for yourself?"

"I would if Kiwanja needed an Army after our freedom is won, but that would be absurd. An army of mice... a handful of mice... in a world of hungry cats. Kiwanja can only protect itself with wisdom and diplomacy, by allying itself with peaceful nations who know the value of human life and when enough is sufficient... which is not America. If we win, I will vote for *Jumbe* Chane."

"Forgive me for ever doubting your heart."

Rashawn fingered his charm. "My heart has not been tested since I became a man."

"Once a man has passed the test no one should ever doubt his heart."

"Thank you, cousin."

They stood beside the airplane, its propellers revolving slowly at idle. Rashawn looked across the landing field, shadowed in patches by gathering clouds. A fire burned in the acacia grove, and loin-clothed boys were gobbling food provided by the village. He raised his eyes to the sky. "What has *Jumbe* Chane predicted?"

"Rain the day after tomorrow."

"Then we leave tonight," said Rashawn. "We can make it as far as the river with the fuel we have. ...You know the place? The abandoned village?"

"How could I forget," said Nathi. "It was your birthplace, cousin."

"And the first village the General destroyed."

"No doubt for that reason," said Nathi.

Dakota leaned from the cockpit window. "We can land near the river."

"At night in the rain without lights?" asked Rashawn.

"My father can."

Thabo and Kobe came trotting up. "The half-track is running well," puffed Kobe. "I adjusted the carburetor."

"I should like to test the guns," said Thabo.

"When there are more clouds," said Rashawn, gazing up at the sky. "We can't risk them seeing the tracers. And only a few short bursts; we haven't a bullet to waste."

"Yes, sir," said Thabo.

Rashawn faced Nathi again. "The fuel has been arranged for at the Selenda airfield. And one more load of ammunition. Everything now depends on you." He looked up at Dakota. "Both of you."

TWENTY-TWO

"Have some more sausage, Zack. It's Jimmy Dean's from America."

"Thanks, Mr. President," said Zack. "Or should I call you General, sir?"

The huge man smiled from across a vast table that looked like a Denny's breakfast commercial with platters of eggs, bacon and toast, sausage and hash-brown potatoes. A boy, maybe ten, in a white waiter's coat, loaded more links onto Zackary's plate and topped off his glass with orange juice.

"President-General is proper, but here we are simply friends. And you are a hero, young man."

"I just put on the brakes," said Zack, stabbing a juicy link with his fork.

"You saved a valuable thing for me. There are only three such coaches, and all will be needed when peace is restored." The President-General turned to Nicole. "Do you think there will be tourists then? Many nations such as mine profit greatly from tourism."

"Well," Nicole said carefully, as the white-coated boy hovered with coffee and seemed as determined to refill her cup as to keep piling food on her plate. "You would probably need to restore the hotel."

"I plan to build a new hotel with all the modern features. This will generate many new jobs and make my people productive."

"The old one might still have charm," said Nicole. "Like your... vintage train."

"Indeed?" said the President-General, helping himself from a mountain of toast before the boy could scurry around. His English put Nicole's to shame and suggested a British boarding school.

Nicole had expected an illiterate thug, the typical Hollywood stereotype of a brutal African dictator, a gorilla who ruled by jungle law and ate raw meat with a bloody machete. She should have asked Tom for more information, assembled a client profile. Did the President have a family? Even that would have helped.

They were breakfasting in his quarters within the Army compound. It was built like a bunker with thick concrete walls. The windows were small with steel shutters, and anything less than an atom bomb might have bounced off the reinforced roof. The furnishings were lavish, though man-cave things of leather and wood in adolescent American style. And, though there were plenty of boys around -- messengers, the white-coated server, a sentry standing outside the door -- nothing she'd seen suggested children. ...Unless they played with real war toys. Of course, the place was a terrorist target, a wild-west fort on Indian land, so if the President did have a family they might have been living abroad.

The huge man forked a bite of eggs, also using his knife in the British way. "Your country has offered a diesel engine."

"Then you would need to buy fuel," said Nicole.

"That is true," said the President-General. "My coal mine is much more productive now since I began a policy of encouraging people to work in my city instead of subsisting on hunting and crops. Though I also encourage *productive* crops with genetically engineered seeds."

Nicole was making mental notes: the man had a passion for progress, and Barrymore could profit from that. He looked like he had in Tom's presentation, probably close to six-hundred pounds and stuffed in a camouflage uniform, an oversize version of Baby Doc, Haiti's infamous dictator who'd ruled by "shock and awe." ...Or, in pre- New-Speak terms, murder and intimidation. She wondered if he had dress

217

uniforms or always wore his battle gear like a warrior protecting his people. Fidel Castro came to mind.

"You suggest keeping some of our old things?" he asked.

"It could be a good selling point," said Nicole. "Something to make your country unique. And, it's cheaper to work with what you have than trying to make everything new."

"Old things and ways are not efficient."

"But they're often labor-intensive."

"I see your point," said the President-General, spreading strawberry jam on buttered toast. "My people would still be productive repairing and maintaining the old."

Nicole went on, "You'd need ads in travel magazines, and a website with pictures. The acacia groves are beautiful, gold and green on the amber land."

"Yes," said the President-General. "I had almost forgotten that."

"And photos of typical village life... though we haven't seen a village yet."

The huge man nodded. "No doubt picturesque in their primitive way. Some harbor terrorists at the moment, but they will soon be dealt with." The President-General looked thoughtful. "I would need a Minister of Tourism. Someone to do all those things for me... pictures, a website, travel brochures. But, what would you say about my country?"

"Just off the top of my head," said Nicole. "...'Kiwanja is the *real* Africa. Unspoiled by civilization.' ...Or too much civilization. '...Benignly untamed. ...Kiwanja is for real explorers, not an air-conditioned safari." She hesitated a moment: the bunker was well air-conditioned. "'See lions from a steam train, both cherished national treasures.'"

"But we didn't see any," said Zack, around a mouthful of Jimmy Dean.

The President-General speared a link. "The terrorists have frightened them just as they've terrorized the people. When I have brought peace they will come out of hiding." He turned to Nicole once more. "Your friend Mr. Reynolds called this morning... I have a satellite phone. He told me of your arrival and the purpose of your visit. Please accept my apology for the unpleasant incident occurring on the train. The terrorists are savages with no regard for human life. Had I known you were coming, I could have sent my helicopter to meet you at the border."

"That woulda been cool," said Zack. "To ride in a Huey UH-1. But, like mom said..."

"Yes. Lions. They seem more valuable than I had thought. ...As are the primitive boots. It's really rather ironic to think my country might profit from them."

"Ironic?" asked Nicole.

"That means kinda funny," said Zack.

"Thank you," said Nicole.

The President-General looked thoughtful again. "Those boots are a bit of a bother, though I have not forbidden them... many of my less-fortunate subjects cannot afford modern shoes. Yet, I've questioned my wisdom in allowing them to still be made. The terrorists have adopted them... primitive symbolism... to make the ignorant believe they are right in trying to cling to the past."

"Well," said Nicole. "They might also help your country's future."

The President-General considered. "During the Cold War period, Nikita Khrushchev once remarked that the Soviet Union should hire the Americans to build them a better Communism."

"We probably would have," said Nicole. "If the price had been right."

The President-General sipped coffee. "More sausage, Zack? Eggs, potatoes? Orange juice? It is Minute Maid, flown in this morning."

"No thanks, sir." Zack patted his belly. "I'm totally stuffed."

"More coffee, Mrs. Neale? It is Folgers."

"No, thank you," said Nicole, almost snatching her cup away as the boy tried to refill it. "It was a wonderful breakfast."

"It rocked," said Zack, and muffled a burp.

"Thank you," said The President-General. "I have grown to love American food. It may lack sophistication but never fails to satisfy. I hope we will share many meals together." He glanced at his watch, a massive Rolex. "But, this is a rather unfortunate time. Had you arrived a week ago I could have had boot-makers brought to my city for you to conveniently question."

"...Well," said Nicole. "I was hoping to see the boots being made. Some of the work is labor-intensive and might be efficiently done by machines. On the other hand, there are still some crafts better done by people... American baseballs are made overseas because they have to be stitched by hand."

"I understand," said the President-General. "I could have put my helicopter at your complete disposal. Unfortunately, as you have seen, the terrorists have increased their threat. ...I believe you have 'levels' in your country?"

"Yes," said Nicole. "Though we're not sure what to believe. But, I could charter a plane."

"Simba Air Freight?"

"They seem to be available."

The huge man frowned a little. "They are not safe. And they would demand Krugerrands, not American dollars."

"I brought a few Krugerrands," said Nicole, "for just such contingencies."

"That was wise," said the President-General. "How would you contact them?"

"I..."

Zack kicked her leg.

"...suppose at the airport. The message board."

"Oh. Yes." The President-General picked up a napkin and patted his lips. "You understand, of course, that I cannot be responsible for the safety of you and your son? Not if you chose to go into the wilds."

"That's cool," said Zack. "The world ain... isn't safe."

"You are indeed a brave young man."

"Thank you, sir."

The President-General got to his feet after a bit of struggle. "I will put a jeep and driver at your disposal while you are in my city. I hope your stay is productive."

"Thank you," said Nicole, as Zack also struggled to rise.

The President-General turned to his server and ordered in Swahili, "Notify Corporal Akida." Then he reached into a pocket. "Zack, I have something for you. A token of my appreciation for saving a valuable

220

thing." He brought out a small ribboned medal. "I give these to my soldiers for demonstrating bravery. Please allow me to present it to you."

Zack stood at sloppy attention as the medal was pinned to his T-shirt upon the balloon of a breast. "Thank you, sir."

The President-General saluted. "I'm sorry there wasn't a ceremony."

"That's okay, sir, you've got a war."

"Spoken like a soldier." The President-General turned to Nicole as the sentry opened the door. "Please feel free to see the sights. However, the coal mine is off-limits, as well as the power station. Security reasons, you know?"

"Of course," said Nicole. "And thank you again."

"Thank you for your interest in helping my country. If you are able to visit a village I hope you will share your impressions with me. As your son so wisely said, I do have a war on my hands, and I haven't been as close to my subjects as all great leaders should be." The President-General smiled. "They are, after all, my children, and deserve what you call quality time, even if some are misbehaving."

"It ain't a jeep, it's a MUTT," said Zack, as they emerged into mid-morning heat, young sentries saluting as they left the bunker. Ghosts shimmered up from the dusty ground and the barbed-wired tops of the compound walls. The MUTT stood waiting at the gates with Corporal Akida at the wheel unsoldierly munching a Snickers bar. From above came a thunder of engines, and Nicole saw the transport climbing away. Zack watched the plane disappear in the clouds, then pointed to another vehicle sitting in a three-sided shed.

"*That's* a real jeep. An M38A1. They used those in the Korean War an' some in Vietnam."

Nicole gave the jeep a casual glance. Unlike the other vehicles -- ten-wheeled trucks and a handful of MUTTs in desert camouflage patterns -- it was faded olive drab with dim white stars and other markings, including

U.S. ARMY

and had what looked like an old-fashioned cannon mounted in the

221

back.

"It looks like it came from the Cold War and hasn't been used since then."

"It was probably mothballed," said Zack. "Before we gave it to the General." He stopped to study the vehicle as a troop of young soldiers marched by. A man in his thirties was drilling them, barking orders for left and right. "Hey, it's a Davy Crockett jeep."

Nicole smiled. "That sounds very American. Like baseballs and McDonalds."

"It was a kind of missile," said Zack. "A way small atomic bomb. It was fired from a recoilless rifle like that one, an' had a kill radius of about two miles."

Despite the heat, Nicole felt a chill. "That doesn't sound very small."

"It only vaporized everything for five-hundred feet from wherever it landed. But the thermal shock an' radiation would kill everybody for two miles around."

Nicole shuddered, recalling pictures of Hiroshima. "Did we ever use them?"

"Nah," said Zack. "They were scrapped a long time ago 'cause there was a problem. The rifle could only fire the bomb about one-point-seven miles. So, whoever was in the jeep woulda got toasted, too." He looked down at his chest. "But they might have got a medal."

* * *

"Green and latched," called Nathi. "Cowl flaps trail. Tail wheel locked."

Dakota nodded, a hand on the throttles, the other guiding the steering yoke as the airplane gently descended. His foxy eyes behind the green glasses quickly roamed the instrument panel, then flicked to the ragged wind sock on the rusty building below. "It's sad that Zack will become thirteen and not be able to prove his manhood."

"Their customs are different," said Nathi, his own eyes scanning the gauges. "Their boys become men by slower degrees and no one acknowledges it."

222

Dakota adjusted the flaps. "Then how do they know when they're really men and not just older boys?"

"I would say Zack is already a man, judging from what he did on the train."

There was a double-bump of wheels, and dust billowed out behind the tail as the airplane kissed the earth. Dakota gently toed the brakes as they rattled toward the airport building. "His mother also seems quite brave. Like our women, don't you think?"

"She has courage," Nathi agreed.

"And she is kind."

"I would say so, though our meeting was short."

"What did you talk about?"

"Mostly our boots."

"Does she think they're magic like Zack seems to think?"

"She seems to feel the hands that made them."

The tail touched down with a lesser thump, and Dakota pressed the brakes again, producing gritty squeals. "Someone awakened Zack's courage, and also taught him kindness."

"Then he's well on his way to becoming a man."

Dakota glanced down at the charm on his chest. "It still seems sad not to celebrate that on the most important day of his life."

Nathi raised an eyebrow. "Our rite of passage? Who would prepare him?"

"I would."

"I doubt if his mother would consent."

Dakota throttled back the engines. "Surely she would if she knew the importance."

"She would also know the danger," said Nathi. "Besides, it's the day before the attack."

"But still a day that comes only once." Dakota looked toward the town, where clouds had mottled the sky in a camouflage pattern of blues and grays. "Will Zack and his mother be safe?"

"Rashawn has no wish to harm innocent people."

"War often harms innocent people." Dakota brought the plane to a stop and cut the clattering engines. "I wish we could warn them."

"So do I," said Nathi. "But that would be dangerous, both for them

223

and us."

"They would be safe in our village."

"Only if we win."

*   *   *

Inside the barn-like terminal building Zack kicked an ancient Coke machine and a can finally dropped in the tray. He performed the ritual a second time as Nicole returned from the message board, where she'd posted a note to Simba Air Freight.

"Stocking up for safari?"

"One's for Corporal Akida," said Zack. "He ain't supposed to leave the MUTT."

"Isn't," said Nicole.

"Sorry." Zack set the Cokes atop the machine and stripped off his shirt, going native again. "Can you put this in your tote?"

Nicole took the sweaty shirt and examined the ribboned medal. Tiny letters on the reverse said

ACME TROPHY COMPANY
CLEVELAND, OH, U.S.A.

"Do you think you'd want to join the Army? ...Our Army?"

"I couldn't pass the physical." Zack laughed. "I couldn't even join the Boy Scouts... not that I ever wanted to."

"But you could, you know? ...If you wanted to."

"You mean, like, get in shape?"

"...Well, yes."

Zack spread his arms. "What's wrong with this shape?"

Nicole smiled. "Nothing as long as you're happy in it."

"I think I'd rather fly a bush plane."

"Like Dakota?"

"Yeah. He's cool. ...Can a white kid have a black role model?"

"I don't see why not."

"I hope we can find 'em." Zack glanced out through a grimy window, where Corporal Akida sat in the sun behind the wheel of the jeep that wasn't while eating another candy bar. "What about our contact?

224

The paper Nathi gave you?"

"It's a truck mechanic in town," said Nicole. "I memorized the address then flushed the paper down the toilet."

"Cool spy move."

"Thank you, James. But we have a soldier for a chauffeur."

"We could lose him," said Zack. "Go back to town an' say we don't need him. ...Or, you think we're bein' watched?"

"The thought crossed my mind," said Nicole. "What do you think?"

"If I was the General I'd watch us. To see what we saw an' who we talked to."

"Why?"

"'Cause that's what Generals an' Presidents do to keep control of their countries. Like, everything's a threat to them, includin' their own people. Even Tom hacked my computer."

"...How do you know that?"

Zack looked patient. "I don't know for *sure* it was him. But I know for sure somebody did a day before you met him."

"...You're right," said Nicole. "But he had to check us out."

"That's what I figured... just following orders. But, I didn't have anything dirty on it."

"I'm sure you didn't. ...What do you think of President N'dila?"

"I don't think I like him."

"Why not?"

"He's kinda like the health-nazis: like, nobody has a right to be happy unless they get skinny an' exercise. Only with him it's bein' productive. Like, bein' the people *he* wants them to be so they can make money for him."

"I got that impression, too," said Nicole.

"Then why would you wanna work for him?"

"I wouldn't actually be working for him."

"You'd still be helpin' him," said Zack. "I don't know what Kiwanja was like before he got in control, but I don't think it had wars an' terror. An' none of the kids in town look happy. You can tell a lot about a place by whether the kids are happy or not, an' I don't mean just havin' a lot of stuff."

"I'd agree with that," said Nicole.

225

Zack spread his hands. "So, why would you wanna help the General? I know it's your job to make people want stuff, but it's somethin' you don't believe in. ...An' I know you hate our house, an' don't like workin' for Dillon's dad."

But I got Captain Keto out on the shelves. Nicole was silent a moment, then smiled. "You're really a smart young man."

"That's 'cause I got a smart mom. I'm glad we came to Africa. It's like quality time for real." Then he turned to the window. "Hey, there's Dakota an' Nathi."

Nicole joined Zack at the window. The lion-colored airplane was out on the field, and there was a rusty tanker truck that seemed to be refueling it.

"Want me to charter 'em?" asked Zack.

Nicole smiled again. "More quality time."

*   *   *

The tanker truck had a platform in back to carry extra drums of fuel, and Dakota and another boy, the latter sixteen in oily trousers, were wrestling barrels into the plane, while Nathi filled the wing tanks.

"You have a long flight ahead?" asked the boy.

"Yes," puffed Dakota. "The burial of a Kenyan chief."

The boy eyed the coffin and wrinkled his nose. "I hope it will be very soon!"

Both came to the doorway and sucked deep breaths.

"*Habari*, Dakota!" called Zack, puffing up to the plane.

Dakota smiled. "What's up, Zack?"

TWENTY-THREE

"So, what do I gotta do," asked Zack, "to earn a magic charm like yours?"

The airplane sat on the landing field near the grove of acacia trees. Across the stream in the village, cooking fires were flaring to life and children trudged in bearing armloads of wood. The gold light of evening was dappled by clouds and dimming now toward amber dusk as Dakota inspected the landing gear and showed Zack how to insert the pins.

Dakota fingered his necklace. "This isn't magic, Zack. It won't protect you or give you strength beyond what you already have. Nor will it give you any more courage than what it took to earn it. A boy becomes a man at thirteen as nature always intended, and this is only visible proof that you have become a man."

He lifted a palm toward the sky. "A man protects the world around him... women, children, other men, animals, and the earth itself." He touched his tuft of fur again. "This, as I said, is merely a symbol that one has demonstrated their courage and accepted a man's obligations; proof that others may trust you to help or protect them in need."

"I kinda felt some of that," said Zack. "Like, something important was happenin' to me." He patted his chest. "Like, inside, I mean." He

227

smiled. "An' not just jackin'-off. But, nobody cares in my country. Thirteen only means you can get on some websites... like, you couldn't anyway. An' have to pay more to see movies. You don't get to drive till you're sixteen. You can't smoke till you're eighteen... legal, anyhow. Or join the Army an' kill anybody. The law says you're not allowed to drink until you're twenty-one. An' then you're supposed to be a man, but you didn't have to *prove* it... like, it didn't cost you anything."

Dakota looked thoughtful. "It must be hard to become a man after twenty-one years of being a boy."

"I guess that's true," said Zack. "'Specially when nobody tells you what bein' a man is all about."

"Would you like a beer?"

"Sure," said Zack. "What's your drinkin' age here?"

"When you become a man."

"But I'm not one yet."

"You are in your heart," said Dakota, leading the way to the cargo doors. "Age is only a number. A symbol on a calendar. A passing of so many seasons. I have seen many aging boys who will never be men as long as they live."

"You mean I'm a man in my heart 'cause I stopped that runaway train car?"

Dakota struggled to climb through the doorway, his jeans slipping off his bottom, and Zack gave him a boost. Dakota leaned out and offered a hand. "You did what had to be done, Zack. You took the responsibility of protecting others in need. That is the real test of a man no matter what his age."

"I didn't think about none of that."

"Which again proves you're a man," said Dakota, helping Zack aboard.

The lowering sun disappeared behind clouds and the light through the windows grew dim. Zackary glanced at the coffin amongst the many drums of fuel, then wrinkled his nose and made a face. "I'm sorry whoever's inside is dead, but I wish they were dead somewhere else."

Dakota had gone up the sloping floor and opened the rusty ice chest. He pulled out a pair of warm bottles and studied Zack in the shadows. "Death somewhere else is also a number, and therefore has no meaning." He regarded Zack a few moments more. "A man is always faced with choices. And every choice one makes in life decides what future choices one has. That's why the choices one makes when they're young are often the most important."

"Too bad there's no flight manual."

"That's what parents and elders are for." Again Dakota studied Zack. "I must now make a choice, and then you must choose."

"You mean about takin' your manhood test?"

Dakota came down to where Zack stood. "That is a choice you must make for yourself which may decide your future. ...Or even if you have a future. But this choice I will ask you to make now could decide if my people will have a future."

"Then maybe you shouldn't ask me to make it."

Dakota handed Zack a bottle. "I already have in a way, when my father and I brought you here. But that choice we made has put you in danger, so it's only right that you should know all."

"Is it about the war?" asked Zack. "Like, choosin' sides?"

"A man must often choose sides in life. If he chooses the right one, so much the better."

*   *   *

In the village Nicole was surrounded by children. Compared to the kids she had seen in town, all looked healthy and happy, all round-tummied, some even chubby. She'd been jolted at first by the gun-toting boys -- at least the child-soldiers had uniforms -- but these were simply kids with guns. She had naturally thought of the terrorists, but none of these boys wore loincloths; the older males in trousers or jeans, the younger clad in canvas shorts. The girls were dressed in colorful skirts, though bare as the boys above the waist. And, every child wore the beautiful boots.

She had noted the absence of Thabo and Kobe... the panther and hyena. This made Dakota the eldest young male, and again she thought of the horror of war in which young men were sacrificed. Yet, this little place seemed peaceful and safe.

229

Zack had stayed at the plane with Dakota, while Nathi, toting the luggage, had led her across a wooden foot-bridge into the tree-shaded village. The earth here was lightly dusted with gold, which made her think of *The Wizard Of Oz* and Dorothy's quest in a magical land. The children had formed an escort, their cheerful chatter a strange contrast to the death-rattle clatter of weapons.

"This is for guests," said Nathi, leading Nicole to a whitewashed hut, its tin roof rusted to ruddy earth tones. "Guests were frequent in happier times, before people feared to leave their homes because their villages might be attacked."

"By the terrorists?" asked Nicole.

Nathi lifted the door latch. "You've met the General. Who do you think has brought terror?"

"Not all progress is bad," said Nicole... she still believed that much.

"Not if people are wise enough to choose how they wish to progress."

Nicole turned to look at the village over the heads of the children. "Your people seem very wise."

Nathi smiled. "Noble savages?"

"I think *I'm* wise enough to know that's a naive philosophy. Romanticism by privileged people who've never really been hungry or had to survive in the wild. ...'The life of man in nature is solitary, poor, nasty, brutish, and usually short.'"

"Thomas Hobbes," said Nathi.

"But I see no evidence of that here. Your children seem happy and well cared-for, and a few of the elders must be in their nineties."

"We have a civilization," said Nathi. "Which has usually been sufficient; education, medicine... though some would call it primitive... and a decent system of values grounded upon religious beliefs that don't require unquestioning faith in unlikely events or improbable myths. We have love of family, respect for elders, and a sense of community, so we share what we have and help one-another. What more does a civilization need? And we don't automatically fear new ideas. But, we would be children in your country, our noses pressed to your toyshop window."

230

"Children easily learn," said Nicole.

"Only if they are honestly taught by those who are free to speak the truth instead of a government's propaganda of patriotism, morality, or even what is beautiful." Nathi looked up at the cloudy sky, fading to gold as the sun disappeared. "I have been to many other lands and seen the results of civilization dropped like bombs upon children. This often creates a cargo cult where people try to imitate a life they think is better."

"Where enough is never sufficient?"

Nathi nodded. "Because they are taught by self-serving systems that happiness comes from money and things. They forget the true meaning of life." He paused to regard the cluster of kids. "Children, a home, a village, and friends. Even work that is meaningful if sometimes hard or unpleasant. Instead, they imitate people with money, believing those people must be happy because they have so many things."

"And because they have power."

"Yes," said Nathi. "Might must be right... and usually white... so they mimic those in power; how they dress, what they own, often even their appearance, believing this will reveal the secrets of how those in power became powerful."

"It is like a cargo cult," said Nicole. "Building idols of junk to material gods... imitation airplanes... in hope of enticing a real plane to land."

Nathi nodded again. "Like many Pacific Islanders after World War Two. Who saw so much wealth being dropped from the sky for the powerful people who fought on their land."

Nicole looked up at the golden sky. "It must have been very confusing to see all those men who had so much fighting and killing each other. Wasting their wealth making war."

Nathi looked again at the kids. "*They* are just as confused as the General builds his idols of junk and orders them to worship so material wealth will come to this land. But of course, unlike the children, he knows it will have to be paid for, and they are the ones who will pay."

Nicole hesitated a moment, then asked, "Would you call the attack

231

on the train an act of terrorism?"

Nathi shrugged. "Terrorists are anyone with no regard for innocent lives. Who justify murder, destruction and war in the name of their gods, ideals or greed. Those who would rule by any means, even destroying the world. The American revolutionists fought a war of terror. ...What was the Boston Tea Party if not an act of terror? But, what is also called terror is often the only weapon left for people oppressed or exploited. Just as the British oppressed the Americans and they fought back with terror. It's sad they have forgotten that and now export their own kind of terror."

"Do you hate America?" asked Nicole.

"No doubt its people are being misled by their own self-serving Generals." Nathi entered the hut and set down the luggage. "Our chief asks you to dine with him in about an hour. I hope you and Zack are comfortable here."

"Thank you," said Nicole. "And, thank you for bringing us."

"It seemed the right choice," said Nathi.

The hut was one room about twenty feet square. In the center was a table and chairs, primitively but lovingly made, and there were four cots with iron frames. On the table was a kerosene lamp, a box of matches, a pitcher of water, and Mason jars for glasses.

The water appeared to be crystal clear, but Nicole had purification tablets... better to be safe. There were two windows, open but screened -- not all civilization was bad -- but the evening light was fading to dusk so she struck a match and lit the lamp. The door, she noted, couldn't be locked. She seemed to have found the source of the boots, and this was the real Africa.

She put Zack's suitcase on one of the cots, then took out the eight-track player. Among the bulky, old-fashioned tapes was one by Crosby, Stills, Nash and Young. A song she remembered was *Wooden Ships*. Her mother still played it a lot. Airplanes had once been called ships in the early days of flight... Zack had told her that. And many had been made of wood. She slipped in the tape and turned on the power. Haunting lyrics filled the room...

If you smile at me, I will understand.

232

*'Cause that is something everybody everywhere does
in the same language.
I can see by your coat, my friend, you're from the
other side.
There's just one thing I got to know,
Can you tell me please... who won?*

The door latch lifted and Zack came in bringing a faint scent of beer. "Rats," he said.

"Rats?" asked Nicole.

"In the coffin, mom, dead rats. They paid that boy in Hillbrow to collect dead rats in a sack."

"...I don't understand," said Nicole.

"To make the coffin smell bad so nobody wanted to open it. It's full of ammunition. That's how they always flew it in. Same with the guns." Zack pointed out at the peaceful village. "*These* are the terrorists, mom."

TWENTY-FOUR

"I'm not very strong," said Zack, flexing an arm that drooped underneath instead of bulging above.

Dakota secured a loincloth below Zack's pendulous belly with a strip of antelope leather that also held his knife. Except for the boots Zack was otherwise naked, his body pale gold in the cloud-dappled light. They had left the village just before dawn on a trail around the not-quite mountain that led through the amber grass of the plain. Both puffing a bit from the half-hour walk, they had stopped in a small acacia grove where the scent of lions was strong.

Dakota uncapped an earthenware jar about the size of a jelly glass. "As I said, this is not a test of your strength, and even Thabo could not fight a lion. ...And, you don't have to do this, Zack. You have already proven your manhood to us; and who in your country would care?"

"But I'm here," said Zack. "I want all your people to know I'm a man so they can trust me to help them."

Dakota nodded. "There must be many boys in your land who only grow older without growing up. And maybe inside they will always feel cheated that no one honored their manhood."

"Or explained what it meant like you did."

"It should have been your father... I mean no offense," said Dakota.

234

"It's cool," said Zack. "He wanted me to be manly, but he didn't know what manly was."

"Perhaps because no one explained it him."

"I think you're right, but I don't hate him."

"Hate is not a manly thing."

"I think I already figured that out, an' I kinda feel sorry for him." Zack spread his arms. "Check out what he missed."

Dalota gripped Zack's shoulders. "I would be proud to have you for my son."

"Even if I don't come back?"

"Men always come back."

Zack took a breath. "Guess I'm ready."

Dakota reached to a thorn bush and pulled off a tuft of dusky-brown fur. "This is what you must earn. A symbol of your manhood that you will wear for the rest of your life."

He scanned the slowly lightening land, where shadows of clouds made camouflage patterns. "Lions will return here soon as they have for thousands of years." He gripped Zack's shoulders again and looked full into his eyes. "And we have lived in peace with them."

"Is that important to know?" asked Zack.

"I can't tell you any more. From here you must trust your heart." Dakota dipped a hand in the jar and began to rub an oily mixture over the orbs of Zack's chest.

"What is it?" asked Zack. "It smells kinda wild."

"It pleases the Lion Of Life," said Dakota. "But hopefully keeps his brother away."

"Does his brother have a name?"

"That shouldn't be hard to guess."

"Guess he's the lion I don't wanna meet."

"Do not be afraid, he will smell your fear."

"But, shouldn't I be afraid of him?"

"He, too, has a purpose in life, and we will all meet him sooner or later; but fear only weakens the fearful, as hate only weakens those who hate."

"If I don't come back, you can have my I-pod."

Dakota gave Zack a hug and gently kissed his cheek. "See you at

235

your feast."

"But, how would anyone know?" asked Zack, as Dakota turned to leave. He gazed around the golden grove at the many signs of lions... lions who'd slept and played in this place, who'd probably mated, snuggled their cubs, eaten their prey and scratched their itches.

"Know what?" asked Dakota, turning around.

"That I didn't just take a piece of fur, like that one on the bush?"

"Only you will know, Zack, and for a man that is sufficient."

*   *   *

A squeaking sound awakened Nicole, and again her first thought was a rat. She opened her eyes to the soft glow of dawn that brightened the hut's pair of windows. Zack's bed had not been slept in, but he'd probably stayed with Dakota.

She remembered his graduation party, the boys drinking beer in the heat of the night, which was only the ghost of a ritual that civilization had made meaningless, and recalled Dillon Barrymore's anguished confession. No doubt the pain was real to him, yet how many boys of his age in the world would gladly trade their pain for his?

These thoughts were replaced by a welcome warmth as she reached for her tote on the floor, though again she felt a twinge of fear: Tom wouldn't be calling to just say hello... as nice as that would be.

Still, his voice was cheerful. "Finally see some lions?"

"You know we're not in town anymore?"

"Just guessing," said Tom. "You're a do-something person and so is your son."

"Apparently, when he has something to do."

"How is our brave young pilot?"

Nicole glanced again at the empty cot. "He seems to have made a new friend. Maybe even a role model."

"Guess I'll have to try harder."

"It's someone his age so there's no competition. I'm sure you're still the man in his life."

236

"Which is what I want to be. So, where are you now?"

"I found a bush plane."

"So, you're in a village?"

"...Yes." Nicole remembered what Zack had said: these people were technically terrorists. They had dined last night with the *Jumbe*... a man who certainly was. He and Nathi must have known Dakota had shared their secret with Zack, but their talk had been mostly about the boots; and again Nicole had lied a bit, telling the chief of her parents' shop instead of her company's interest. She had justified that by reminding herself she had to stay neutral in this little war.

They had also talked of a manhood rite... dammit, today was Zack's birthday, and what could she give as a gift? She hadn't really understood what Zack might have to do... her mind had been focused on business. But any test Dakota could pass couldn't have been very dangerous, and certainly not very physical so there didn't seem much to worry about: these were a kind and peaceful people who seemed to make boots a lot better than war. Whatever the Kiwanji rite it seemed important to Zack. What else did he have to prove his manhood... a middle-school graduation diploma?

"Still there?" asked Tom.

"Sorry," said Nicole. "I forgot the power of maize beer, but I found the source of the boots."

"Great," said Tom. "Mission accomplished, and none too soon. I just saw a weather report; the rains might be starting later today so you'd better get back on that plane and out of there by tonight."

Nicole got up and went to a window. The sky above the acacia trees was almost totally gray. "It's going somewhere else tonight. They have a big load of cargo."

There was a moment of silence, as if Tom was carefully choosing his words because his bosses were listening. "You should be on that plane, Nicole."

"Do you think the rains will be that bad?"

Again there was a pause. Nicole pictured Tom in the "radar room" ... the glowing screens, the faceless men, the sour scent of indifferent coffee. "It's more than the weather."

The air was muggy and growing hot, but Tom's next words

237

brought a chill: "We think someone there has a bomb."

Nicole wasn't sure what to say. ...Finally, "I guess you mean a... big one?"

"Too big for Kiwanja," said Tom. "But we're still trying to figure out what."

"Are there things I shouldn't say on this phone?"

"Not if you think they're important. Are you alone?"

Nicole glanced at the door with its primitive latch that couldn't be locked... because for several thousand years there had never been a need for locks. "At the moment," she said, but lowered her voice. "Does Davy Crockett mean anything?"

"A whole lot more than an old Disney movie."

"Zack saw it first," said Nicole, before realizing how childish that sounded. "But I thought it was just an old jeep with a cannon."

"That's basically all it is," said Tom. "Or all it *should* have been, anyway... an old piece of junk we found in a warehouse and gave them as part of an Aid consignment. We should have taken the launcher off, but there wasn't supposed to be anything still lying around it could shoot."

"Zack said the bombs... or whatever you call them... were scrapped a long time ago."

"The Cold War died a long time ago, but its bones are still rotting all over the planet. One of those things got away somehow... stolen, sold, or just plain lost... and it's been loose in the world ever since."

"And nobody worried?"

"I'm sure somebody did," said Tom. "Long before my time, of course; but the worst-case scenario was, maybe someday, somewhere in the world, a little pop might go off."

"A pop with a two mile kill-radius."

"Zack knows a lot more than I thought," said Tom. "But, that's the reason to be on that plane."

"In case the General drops his big one?"

Again there was a moment of silence, as if Tom was either thinking, or maybe awaiting a nod from his boss. "There's another problem, Nicole. We know N'dila has the launcher, but we don't know which side has the bomb. The terrorist leader... they call him The

Cheetah. ...Dumas, or something."

"Duma."

"He's been getting his guns and ammunition through... call it the Walmart of weapons. With finance from folks who don't like us... who, we're not sure, the list is too long. I doubt if N'dila's security could keep a kid out of a cookie jar."

"I... think I understand," said Nicole. "If someone... a spy... saw that old jeep..."

"Right," said Tom. "And if Duma figured out what it was, he might have gotten what it shoots. ...We don't know much about him. But, doing a Google would tell anyone all about a Davy Crockett."

"So, if he stole the jeep...?"

"He doesn't actually need it," said Tom. "It wouldn't take much technical knowledge to set off the warhead in some other way. ...Put it in town with a timing device, or maybe a willing martyr. But, having the launcher and staying mobile would make him a lot bigger threat. If I was President N'dila and knew that thing was aimed at me, I'd get out of Dodge before high noon."

"And the terrorists would win," said Nicole. "Without firing another shot."

"You can't think that's a good thing."

"Of course not," said Nicole, then realized she had lied. Not a half-truth, or a bit of the truth, but bold-faced lied to Tom.

"You've been in the compound," Tom went on. "Would it be hard to steal that jeep?"

"...Well, the soldiers are mostly kids. And the jeep is in an open shed. And no one seemed to be guarding it. Zack could have pro-bably climbed right in."

Tom seemed to consider. "Might mean N'dila doesn't know what it is."

"Why don't you tell him so he could guard it?"

"Then he'd know there was a bomb. ...Assuming he doesn't have it."

"I thought we're on his side. ...Or he's on ours."

"We don't give our little friends big-boy toys. We know he's at-tacked some villages... suspected terrorist strongholds... but the people have been relocated."

"To make them more 'productive.'"

"Exactly what we want," said Tom. "It's for their own good. ...You do think so?"

"You said I was right for this job, but I didn't come wrapped in red, white and blue."

"Understood," said Tom. "But we can't let N'dila have *that* much power. Conventional warfare is bad enough; most of the men have already been killed and now they're fighting with boys. The terrorists only have one chance left; assemble somewhere and attack the compound after the airfield is flooded. Of course N'dila knows this... the village you're in, for example: if he thought they were gathering there, he could wipe out half his country's future. ...Again, assuming he has the bomb."

"So, come take it back," said Nicole.

"And what if he won't give it back? We invade yet another little country and call it protecting ourselves?"

"Or bringing it Democracy."

"The world's getting tired of that joke."

"But this time there's really a... WMD."

"With a range of one-point-seven miles. We could hardly call that a threat to ourselves and justify a preemptive strike."

Nicole pictured screens lighting up, men speaking into microphones, and satellite eyes being aimed. "So there's no way to stop this?"

"It's Africa, Nicole."

"And there's no profit in saving black lives."

"This started with the best of intentions."

"I won't even go there," said Nicole.

"But you did," said Tom. "And that's my fault."

Nicole sighed. "At least you tried to do something good, which is more than I've done in a long time." Then she had a new thought. "What if I could find the bomb? Or maybe at least who has it?"

"No," said Tom. "Too dangerous. And think of Zack... and I know you are. Please, Nicole, get on that plane tonight with him no matter where it's going."

*   *   *

Zack scented the lions before he saw them, a wild kind of smell like the oil on his chest. He'd seen lions once, up close in a zoo, though safely behind the bars of a cage. But these lions knew they were free. They came silently through the amber grass, a tawny male with a dusky mane and two sleek mates of golden-brown, one with a small antelope in her jaws.

Zack's first instinct was to run. But he couldn't run far, and not very fast. He backed against a tree trunk... should he try to climb? Could he reach the first branch? But, he'd gotten a D in P.E. last semester for not being able to do a pull-up.

The male raised his head, coming alert. Then, three pairs of eyes like molten gold were suddenly aimed at Zack. The male made a sound, though not quite a growl, and moved in front of his mates... protecting them like a manly thing.

Slowly, his back to the tree trunk and feeling the smoothness where lions had rubbed, Zack sank down to the earth and drew his knees up to his chest. He couldn't meet those soul-seeing eyes, and lowered his head as the king approached.

Again a deep rumble, and not quite a growl. Breath hot and moist and smelling of meat. The feel of something powerful seeming to nuzzle his hair. Then, a huge paw on his shoulder. An almost gentle rake of claws, yet a touch that cut rivulets of blood.

Zack felt for the knife, but then told himself this wasn't a movie and he wasn't Tarzan! Was this the Lion of Life... or his brother?

It didn't seem right to die with his eyes closed. He opened them and raised his head. If he really had a soul -- he'd never much be-lieved in a god -- those golden eyes were seeing it naked. What had he done in thirteen years that gave him any right to live? ...Or, maybe what would he do with his life if it wasn't taken now?

Those eyes seemed to search his soul a long time. Then the lion turned to his mates, who also came forward to gaze at Zack, the antelope's body dripping blood within the grip of crimson jaws. Now the women were judging him.

241

"I never had a girlfriend," he said. "I don't even know how to talk to girls. I'm still tryin' to learn how to talk to my mom."

Then he turned to the king. "I never really liked my dad. He didn't teach me anything a real man should know. ...But, maybe it's not too late to learn?"

The lioness dropped the antelope, warm and heavy upon Zack's boots. Then all the lions lay down around him. The king's hot body was pressed to Zack's side, his sooty mane brushing against Zack's legs as he sank his teeth in the kill.

Gently, Zack drew out the knife.

TWENTY-FIVE

Nicole was putting her boots on when there was a gentle knock at the door. "Welcome," she called in Swahili.

A young woman entered, proudly bare-breasted and quite beautiful. "Good-morning," she said in English with the ghost of a British accent. "My name is Fila. Did you sleep well?"

"Good-morning, and yes, thank you," said Nicole. "It's very peaceful here."

A shadow crossed the young woman's face. "This is the last peaceful place in Kiwanja."

"Maybe in the world," said Nicole. "At least from what I've seen of it."

Fila looked sad. "We hope our village will survive this war. ...Do you mind if we speak English? I am a teacher and need to practice."

Nicole would have liked to refresh her Swahili, but then she wondered why: she would probably be leaving tonight, and from what she'd learned about the bomb it didn't seem likely she would return. But she said, "Of course. Please sit down."

"Thank you." Fila took one of the chairs at the table. "I would have brought you breakfast but the feast of your son is being prepared." She laughed. "That did not come out quite right."

Nicole laughed, too. "I didn't think he was on the menu." She took a breath of the cooking aromas drifting through the windows. "And he probably wouldn't smell that good." She saw a slim strip of leather in one of Fila's hands, and thought of the lion's fur charms. "Did he complete your rite?"

"We don't know yet," said Fila. "But Dakota said he had a good heart, and those with good hearts always return."

"...Return?" asked Nicole.

Fila looked surprised. "You do not know the rite? I assumed it had been explained to you."

Nicole tried to remember what had been said during dinner last night. Had she been so involved in the business of boots that she'd missed something really important? "I... didn't think it was dangerous."

There was concern in Fila's eyes. "You don't know what your son has to do?"

Foolishly, Nicole recalled what she'd felt when finding the box of condoms... Zack had no right to become a man without her parental approval!

A few minutes later, Nicole was running across the footbridge, the village children following and looking concerned and confused. Nathi was at the airplane up on a wooden ladder. One of the engine covers was off and tools were laid out on the wing.

"Where's my son?" Nicole demanded.

Nathi looked as surprised as Fila. "Dakota prepared him at dawn. ...Surely you knew?"

Nicole remembered when Zack had been five and had wandered away in a mall. How helpless she'd felt, and so afraid. She stared around the little valley darkened now by the gathering clouds. "I *didn't* know!" she almost screamed. She turned toward the not-quite mountain. "He's out there with lions!"

"It was his choice," said Nathi, laying down a wrench.

"He's only a child!" yelled Nicole. "He's not qualified to make life and death choices!"

Nathi descended the ladder; and despite her fear and fury, Nicole saw how tired he looked, a man who faced danger and death every day in a land where children killed each other. ...yet he had honored her son.

The anger that had sustained her now died away like a fire in the rain. She tried to fan it back to flame... *he had no right to let Zack do that!* The children had clustered around them, and Nicole had a sudden crazy thought, of grabbing a rifle from one of the boys and running to rescue her son. But she'd never shot a gun in her life... despite supplying a million war toys to little boys all over the world. Then, like a woman -- or maybe a weak one -- she simply burst into tears.

Nathi gathered her into his arms.

*   *   *

Zack scented cigarette smoke on the breeze as he came along the ancient trail that led around the not-quite mountain. He was puffing a bit from the walk, and the loincloth barely clung to his hips. His chest and face were smeared with blood, and some it was his.

He rounded a bend and saw Dakota lounging under a tree. Dakota smiled. "*Habari*, man."

"*Habari*, man," Zack returned, raising a palm in the sign of peace every human being knew... see, I don't have a rock in my hand. "You look like you knew I'd come back."

Dakota got up and hoisted his jeans. "As I said, men always do." He came to Zack and hugged him, smearing his own chest and belly with blood, and kissed Zack's cheek, then looked at the tuft of fur in Zack's hand and noted the cuts on his shoulder. "The Lion of Life has marked you as one who will do something noble."

Zack touched his bleeding gashes. "Like, this is a bonus point?"

"One might call it a medal." Dakota took the tuft of fur. "Your mother will make your necklace. Fila, our teacher, will show her how, and *Jumbe* Chane will present it to you with the whole village present." He looked at the sky. "We'd better get back before the rain starts, your manhood feast is waiting."

"I feasted a little already," said Zack. He turned to look back at the distant trees, the golden grove in the amber grass where something

245

wild and very old had judged him worthy of life. "It was like they shared with me."

"Waste is not a manly thing, so you must eat a lion's share of your feast."

Zack's smile suddenly died. "Lyin' ain't manly neither. You told me the truth last night an' trusted me with your people's future. But I been lyin' to you. ...I'm an American, Dakota. I guess we're the ones who started your war... 'least we're helpin' the General... so maybe you should hate me."

"I also said that men do not hate." Dakota smiled. "Despite being a terrorist savage I know a bit about the world, and your country is one of the few where the drinking age is twenty-one. In Canada it is eighteen or nineteen depending on province or territory. More sensible but still too high."

"...So you knew I was lyin'?"

"Say rather I knew you were being careful and protecting your mother. That is also a manly thing."

TWENTY-SIX

The rain had begun as a whispering rush like the sound of a distant waterfall. Silver droplets freshened the air and drew a rich fragrance from dry summer grass. It was late afternoon, perhaps four o'clock, in a place where time wasn't measured by clocks, and the rain had been falling for maybe an hour, gently quelling the cooking fire where the meats of the feast had been roasted, and Zack had eaten a lion's share to the admiration and praise of the village while seated in honor beside *Jumbe* Chane.

Grandfathers now sat in doorways, as if watching the rain brightened old memories, and *Jumbe* Chane was enthroned on his porch perhaps contemplating the future. The kids had resumed their childhood play, the youngest discovering glorious mud, the older reinventing wet games, the boys taking care with their rifles.

Rain pattered down on the airplane, washing the amber dust from its wings and making a soothing, sleepy sound as it drummed on the cockpit roof. Zack was in the co-pilot's seat wearing only his boots and jeans. Dakota was in the pilot's seat, and both were sipping from bottles of beer while smoking Dakota's Players. The ancient eight-track player sat atop the instrument panel, and a song by the Youngbloods softly pleaded to, *smile on your brother and love one-another.*

247

Zack patted his still-bulging belly and sighed. "That feast really rocked." He fingered the tuft of lion's mane nestled between the spheres of his chest on the leather strip his mother had made. "Thanks for everything, Dakota."

Dakota also sighed, watching raindrops run down the windscreen. "I remember when there were many such feasts, but there have been far too few this year."

"'Cause so many kids have been killed in the war?"

"On both sides." Dakota turned to the open window and gazed across the landing field where drops hit the dust like tiny explosions and the coffin lay empty near glistening trees as if waiting to serve its true purpose. "It will take many years to heal our wounds." He regarded the wounds on Zack's shoulder, the four bloody medals bestowed by the king. Then he touched the Akan doll, caressing its sensuous feminine shape. "I suppose I should marry and do my part."

"Get married?" said Zack. "But you're only... Oh, yeah." He sipped from his bottle. "I saw you with a girl after the feast was over. You an' her were holdin' hands. She's really pretty. ...'Course, I'm still gettin' used to girls with no tops."

"She is very pretty," agreed Dakota. "Also very wise and strong. Her name is Akili."

"Are you gonna marry her?"

"Perhaps I should, and yet I cannot."

Zack's hand strayed under his belly. "Um, it's not 'cause... you know?"

Dakota laughed. "No, as I discovered last night... though it does require some adaptation on the part of both parties involved."

"...Oh... I didn't mean to get personal, but it's somethin' I been wonderin' about."

"It's okay, Zack, as I'm sure you'll find when the time comes." Dakota watched the sparkling drops patter on the glass. "Some choices are right and some are wrong, and sometimes only the future can show if we chose correctly."

"Um... is there another girl?"

Dakota fingered the steering yoke. "Perhaps the same my father loves."

248

"...Oh," said Zack again. He touched the twin yoke on the co-pilot's side. "Is it like a freedom thing?"

"Freedom is never free, Zack. Like everything else of value in life, one must give up something to get something else."

The player switched tracks and Zack turned it off as the song, *Darkness, Darkness*, began. Then he looked at the pair of AK rifles cradled on the bulkhead. "I wanna help you fight... to take down the General an' win back your country. I know a few things about guns, like how to cock those, an' put in the clip, an' how to take off the safety."

"Because of the war in your land?" asked Dakota. "In which black people are being killed? And for reasons I can't understand."

"I don't understand it either," said Zack. "I wish I could stop it but I don't know how."

"The world has many wounds," sighed Dakota. "Neither you nor I can heal them all."

"I guess it's like my mom said; you can't save the world, only little pieces." Zack gazed across the rain-dimpled stream to the village amongst the glistening trees. "I wanna help you save *this*, Dakota." He struggled out of the seat, very nearly losing his jeans, and took down one of the rifles. "I have a lot of war games. You only fight 'em with your fingers, but I think I could fight on the real. ...Like, I know these kick. An' the muzzle climbs up when you're shootin' full-auto."

"Have you ever actually fired a gun?"

"A few times with one of my friends. He's got a Winchester 30-30, an' a bunch of six-shooters."

"He sounds like a cowboy."

"He is," said Zack. "Rides horses, drinks beer, an' spits an' swears... which is funny, I guess, 'cause he's gay."

"He must be quite brave."

"I guess he is," said Zack. "He'll have to fight all his life just because he is who he is."

"But, you have never shot anyone? Or killed anyone?" asked Dakota.

"Have you?"

"I see their faces sometimes in my dreams."

249

"But you had to, it was war."

Dakota also got to his feet. "Aim at me, Zack."

"...But, this thing is loaded."

Dakota gripped the gun's muzzle and pressed it to his chest. "Look at my face, could you pull the trigger?"

"'Course not!"

"Imagine I am Jabari."

"Huh?"

"He will be your enemy if you make that choice. Could you kill him?"

Zack lowered the gun. "Maybe if he was gonna kill me. Or my mom. Or you."

"Most people could kill under those circumstances, to save a loved-one, themselves or a friend, but could you kill for a concept?"

"I don't understand," said Zack. He tried to put the weapon away, but Dakota thrust it back into his hands.

"Could you kill for *your* President-General if he claimed there were terrorists who wanted to steal or destroy all you had? Could you kill for your religion, believing your god approved? Or, could you kill because people weren't free, even if you didn't know them?"

"Maybe the last one," said Zack.

"But, freedom is only a concept."

"I don't understand," said Zack again.

"Would you say black people in your country are all as free as you?"

"No," said Zack. "We fought a war to stop slavery, but we never really let them be free."

"The General has his concept of freedom, and he has convinced some of our people that they should kill for it." Dakota patted his chest. "Perhaps I *am* a terrorist." He pointed toward the village. "And so are all the people here. But *our* concept of freedom will bring us nothing except to live as we've always lived. And even that will have to change. Could you kill for our concept of freedom, Zack? Could you look Jabari in the eyes... a boy who has never harmed you... and kill him because you're on our side?"

"...I don't know."

"I didn't either," said Dakota. "Until that moment came."

"I guess it was like with the lions," said Zack.

Dakota nodded. "A man faces many moments like that, and each requires a new decision while not always knowing which choice is right."

Zack was quiet a moment, then said, "I know you're flyin' somewhere tonight, an' I think it's to fight the General." He pointed into the cargo bay. "All that gas in barrels, an' all the ammunition. An' Thabo an' Kobe are gone."

Dakota nodded again. "This is our last chance to win our freedom and bring an end to this child-killing war. The rain will increase throughout the night, and by morning the airfield in town will be flooded. The American planes won't be able to land and bring the General supplies. Perhaps they could come to his aid if they chose, mount an invasion with helicopters, but we don't think they will... too much expense for too little profit. Rashawn, our leader, is waiting with all his men at a river. With the fuel we bring and the last ammunition, he will attack the General at dawn."

"An' you'll be fightin' with 'em?"

"I will do what I can, as will my father. The General may use his one helicopter to defend his compound. We hope he doesn't have missiles, but he can arm it with soldiers to fire on our men below."

"Fight a Huey with a C-47?"

"Perhaps at least we may give it a fright."

"...You could lower the landing gear," said Zack, "an' hit the main rotor."

"That's a wise idea."

"I wanna go with you," said Zack.

*　　　*　　　*

Raindrops made a cat-footed patter across the rusty roof of the hut. Acacia trees dripped softly outside, and the air was rich with the smells of wet earth and the seminal scent of awakening life. Nicole stood at one of the windows watching naked children at play, belly-flopping and sliding in mud, while dogs capered joyously with them. Would Zack have ever done that, she wondered? Of course she would never

251

have let him... *Oh no, Zack, you'd catch the sniffles!*

Just as she wouldn't have let him face lions.

But he had, she thought. And he'd come back a man, though not without scars. And she had felt a sense of great pride seeing him standing before the chief to receive his proof of manhood, a symbol she had made with her hands; a crude and worthless thing to the world, yet something that could never be bought.

She watched the women hanging out clothes to benefit from a natural rinse, giving real meaning to "rainwater fresh." Had they felt as she did now after a ceremony like Zack's, losing a boy yet gaining a man? But, Zack would always be her son, and she would always worry about him.

The day, already darkened by clouds, was growing darker as evening drew on. Shadows were gathering in the hut like dusky spirits haunting the corners. She glanced at the lamp on the table: at home she would have been turning on lights. The rain was getting heavier, and yet its sound was peaceful. It made her think of winter days when she'd been a girl, of My Little Ponies and Barbie Doll games... and dreaming of the perfect Ken.

She went to the table, picked up the pitcher and poured a glass of water. She thought of her purification pills, but took a sip unprotected, tasting the natural flavors of earth. A new pair of boots stood on the table, a pair she had watched being lovingly born. They were only made by women and girls... which might present a cultural problem if Barrymore built a factory. Men hunted, farmed and maintained the village... or had before this goddammed war. Women ran the households. Not exactly liberated, but honored and respected.

But things would change with civilization: there was already a shortage of men, and then the women would start making money. She remembered the streets of Hillbrow, the hundreds of men and boys on the corners, no longer hunters or farmers, no longer needed to maintain a home; angry, confused, and made obsolete since women were easier to control and thus were more productive.

Someone knocked on the door. Nicole thought it might be Fila, but Nathi appeared when she called a welcome.

The rain, like the air, was pleasantly warm, and he was still clad in

252

trousers and boots, his cheetah-like body glistening. For a moment Nicole thought of Tom by her pool, but these men were different in so many ways that had nothing to do with their color. Nathi seemed kinder somehow: she remembered when he'd held her that morning when she'd burst into tears.

Of course, Tom's kindness was civilized; one didn't instantly drop their guard or open their hearts to strangers. She wondered how Nathi *could* be kind, because he had probably killed other men... and probably boys. It was hard to believe Tom could have killed. He must have been in dangerous places, and surely knew how to use his gun, yet she couldn't imagine him taking a life. A man who slid down water slides. Who'd guided Zack's hands in a flying machine. And guided her body in love.

Then she remembered she'd lied to him: she *did* sympathize with the "terrorists" and hoped in her heart they would win. But she had also lied to Nathi, first about her country -- though Zack had somehow made that clean -- but then about her real purpose in coming to Kiwanja. She remembered Tom's warning to get on that plane and out of this village tonight. But, how could she do that without more lies?

Night was slowly filling the hut, and Nathi's dark face was a shadow. "May I light your lamp?" he asked.

"Thank you," said Nicole, her mind now turning to strategies and ways to manipulate people... while hating herself for doing it. She watched as Nathi lit the lamp and a golden glow brightened the room. "And, thank you for everything you've done. First the rescue, then bringing us here. And for honoring Zack."

Nathi smiled in the lamplight. "The first was simply the right thing to do. The second... it was practical. And the third no more than your son deserved."

"It was something he needed," said Nicole. "Something I could never give."

Nathi touched the charm on his chest. "You gave him what a mother should give; you gave up a boy to gain a man and the world will be better for that."

"I'm sorry I got angry this morning."

"That was also a motherly thing. And it was my fault for not explaining."

"And mine for not asking more questions."

Nathi smiled again. "Any landing you can walk away from..." He put the chimney back on the lamp and the golden glow brightened still more. "Fila will bring you supper."

Nicole wondered how to make her pitch... truth with an ulterior motive? She assumed the plane was flying freight, obviously fuel, to some other place... another village, a neighboring country. Why would she want to come along, her and Zack, on a cargo flight? Until Tom had called, she would have been happy to stay a few days in this peaceful place, maybe recharging her batteries to battle the civilized world again. Would she have to choose sides to get out of here now?

She would have to tell Nathi about the bomb; and assuming his side didn't have it, at least they would know it existed and might be used on this village. That could save lives; the people could be evacuated beyond the two-mile kill zone. If Nathi's side won she would be a hero... at least in a tiny African country that most of the world had never heard of. And maybe its grateful people would become willing slaves in a boot factory.

If they lost she would be a traitor to President-General N'dila. She and Zack might be shot. And, even if they got out alive, she would have betrayed her own government, her company... and Tom.

She opened the door and stood looking out. Night had come to Kiwanja. Lamps and candles lit windows and doorways, and cooking fires were flaring to life beneath little shelters of thatch or tin. It was hard to believe that somewhere in this land men were plotting to kill each other and using their children as weapons.

Then she heard footsteps splashing through puddles. She turned toward the bridge and saw two figures. One was Dakota, no more than a shadow. It took her a moment to recognize Zack. He should have looked ridiculous, a bobby-breasted marshmallow boy dressed as Rambo for Halloween. Like Dakota he wore only jeans, and the beautiful boots now sullied with mud. ...And a headband of amber and gold. He also toted an AK rifle. He was puffing a little as always when moving at more than an amble, but his voice sounded deeper than she remembered:

"I'm going with them tonight."

* * *

Up on the not-quite mountain, Tindo and Mbwa sat in the dark as rain pattered down all around. Tindo was wrapped in a piece of canvas, and Mbwa was sharing the shelter, though probably thinking how foolish men were to be sitting up here in the rain tonight instead of at home in a comfortable den. Then he suddenly came alert. Tindo had almost been dozing, his belly still full from Zack's manhood feast, but he jerked up his head and watched the dog, no more than a shadow beside him. Mbwa went to the bunker's east wall and stood peering up at the sky.

Then Tindo heard it! Gabbing the ancient walkie-talkie, he keyed the transmit switch.

TWENTY-SEVEN

The words were almost on Nicole's lips: *You're not going any-where, Zack!* It was time to be an American parent, and boys of thirteen didn't fly off to war!

But then a drumbeat sounded, and the village peace was suddenly shattered. Cooking fires and lights went out. Water steamed on glow-ing coals. Women called for their children, and boys yelled to each other. Rifles clattered, being cocked. Behind her, Nathi doused the lamp, and Nicole was suddenly blind.

"Zack!" Hands stretched out to reach her son, she stumbled from the doorway.

A violet-colored shooting star fell hissing from the sky.

There was an explosion and everything went white!

A blast of heat smashed into Nicole. She staggered back and almost fell. Pictures flashed across her mind; grainy 1950s films of buildings bursting into flames and then disintegrating. Trees like wooden matches flaring. Probably in secret vaults were images of human beings burned to blackened skeletons before their bones were blown away. She marveled she had *time* to think before her brain was vaporized.

Something heavy, soft and wet slammed her to the ground. That was almost funny: she'd stood against an atom bomb, but Zack had knocked her down! His rolly mass protected her from wreckage raining all around... a twisted sheet of roofing tin, spears of smoking, splintered wood and razor shards of pottery. She felt his body tense in pain as something hit his back.

"Mom!" he yelled. "Are you okay?"

Nicole spit mud. "I... think so."

Zack rolled off but stayed in a crouch. There was Dakota, also crouching, staring at the sky. Nicole wondered how she could see -- *when all goes bright, don't look* -- then realized there was a fire.

Women and children were running past, boots and bare feet splashing mud. Some were cut and bleeding. Boys and grandfathers urged them on, waving them to the foot-bridge. Mothers and girls carried infants, and little children ran beside them. All were streaming over the bridge and vanishing amongst the trees. Above the roaring crackle of flames a mighty voice was booming commands.

Nicole looked dazedly around: the chief was standing in front of his hedge, his mass supported by two young boys, his wife and daughters at his side. It took Nicole a moment to translate... "Help the wounded! Run to the cave! Stay off the landing field!"

Dakota yelled to a small naked boy, whose rifle seemed longer than he was tall. "Abu! Was anyone hit?"

"Bilal and his mother are dead!"

Nicole remembered a boy, maybe six, who'd been at Zack's feast. She must have met his mother, too. She started to rise but Zack held her down. "No, there might be more!"

"...But, there was only one," said Nicole.

Zackary's face was spattered with mud like camouflage paint on a boy's war doll. "What you mean only one?"

"That old jeep you saw yesterday... the General has the bomb it shoots."

Zack looked amazed. "He's got a Davy Crockett?"

New visions of horror filled Nicole's mind -- pictures of Hiroshima, radiation poisoning -- but Zack shook his head.

"That wasn't it or we wouldn't be here." He rose again to a crouch and gazed up at the sky. "It was some kinda missile, maybe a Hellfire, laser-guided an' fired from a plane."

Dakota added, "Or the General's helicopter." He cocked his head and listened, peering into the sky. "I think I hear a helicopter."

Nathi emerged from the hut, his body seemingly bathed in blood by the crimson glare of the rising flames. "What is a Davy Crockett?"

"A little atom bomb," said Zack. "The launcher's on a jeep, but the General ain't used it yet or we wouldn't be talkin' about it." He paused to look around. "It would have be less than two miles away to fire on this village, an' if he was gonna do that, why did he send the helicopter an' shoot us with a missile."

Dakota asked, "You saw this... Davy Crockett?"

"Just the launcher. ...But I thought all the bombs had been scrapped."

Nicole sat up. "Tom said one got loose."

"Who is Tom?" asked Nathi.

"A friend," said Nicole, then added, "Who would be on your side if he knew the truth."

Dakota glanced toward the not-quite mountain. "We would have known of a jeep approaching long before the sun went down: Tindo would have seen it. And now the night and the rain would slow it. ...Could this bomb be dropped from a helicopter?"

"If it was modified," said Zack. "But you'd lose the helicopter. ...An' why use a missile first? The bomb woulda killed everybody here."

"Would the people be safe in the cave?" asked Nathi. "From this atom bomb?"

"Probably from the blast," said Zack. "But then they'd have to get out fast 'cause of the radiation... like, at least two miles away."

Nathi faced Nicole. "Go with the women and children. The cave is at the foot of the mountain where the stream comes out. Tell *Jumbe* Chane about this bomb."

"Yeah," said Zack, grabbing his rifle. "You should be safe in a cave."

Dakota asked, "What of these missiles, Zack?"

"Hellfires have to be targeted... like usin' a laser pointer. An' that don't work good when it's rainin'."

"What else do you know about them?"

258

"The pilot has to paint the target to guide the missile in. That means he has to see it, so he has to be below the clouds." Zack turned toward the flames, a burning hut... a family's home. "He probably aimed at a cookin' fire."

Nicole saw another picture... a woman preparing her children's meal.

Nathi turned to Abu, who looked more naked without his boots. "Take her to the cave."

Nicole remembered the wounded. "I have a first-aid kit in my tote."

"I'll get it," said Nathi, then faced his son. "Go to the airplane and start the engines. Turn her around for takeoff." He rose to return to the hut.

"DOWN!" yelled Zack.

There was another shooting star, its tail an eerie violet. Zack flung himself on Nicole again as another explosion blasted the village. The earth seemed to punch Nicole in the stomach. Jagged wreckage and splinters of wood razored the air and ripped the ground, tearing leaves from the branches of trees. Then, something -- somebody -- crashed to the mud. Nicole stared in horror at Nathi. He was lying face-down. ...Dead? Almost shoving Zack away, she scrambled up on her hands and knees and scuttled to his side.

"Dad!" yelled Dakota, also scrambling to his father.

Abu pointed skyward. "There!"

The roar of flames was louder -- the guest hut was also burning now, part of its roof collapsed -- but Nicole heard an almost familiar sound... the chopping of blades overhead. There were bursts of auto-fire as the village boys shot at the sky. Abu aimed his gun, but Dakota yelled, "Don't waste bullets! ...All of you! Wait until you can see it!"

The women and children had all crossed the bridge and disappeared into the trees. The chief had taken charge of the boys, calling to some to search for wounded. High overhead was the scream of an engine that seemed to be climbing away, the aircraft's pilot maybe surprised that kids were shooting back.

"Dakota! Zack! Help me!"

With Zack and Dakota assisting, Nicole turned Nathi onto his back. For a moment she almost panicked. A spear of wood like a vampire

259

stake had pierced the upper part of his chest. She didn't know much anatomy, and her Peace Corps lessons in basic first-aid hadn't covered missile attacks, but the wound seemed too high to have punctured a lung. But wasn't it close to an artery?

"Zack! Get my tote!"

Zack scrambled up and lumbered away. Nicole had a ridiculous thought; of being questioned at some future time by Child Protective Services: *You sent your thirteen-year-old son into a burning building?*

"Here, mom!" puffed Zack a few moments later, his rain-wet hair and body steaming.

"Can you help him?" asked Dakota, on his knees at Nathi's side.

"I think so," said Nicole. Her first impulse was to pull out the stake, but that was only instinctive, a reaction to something that shouldn't be there. Where were the arteries close to the neck? The wound wasn't bleeding a lot. Would it be safer to leave it in and pack a bandage around it until...?

Until what? There was no 911 to call, no ambulance or emergency room... and the only helicopter was raining death on them! She looked into Nathi's eyes, relieved to see them clear. "I'm not sure what to do."

Nathi struggled to rise, but Nicole took his shoulders and held him down. "Don't move! I don't know how bad that is yet, but you'll only make it worse."

Nathi sank down but turned to his son. "You must get the fuel to Rashawn."

"I will," said Dakota.

"Can you land in the dark? In the rain, with no lights?"

"I will try."

"Go, then. Hurry!"

Dakota leaned down and kissed Nathi's cheek.

"I'm goin' with you," said Zack.

Dakota turned to Abu. "Get them to the cave!"

Nicole almost made a grab for Zack as he rose to his feet with Dakota, but that was instinctive, too. Instead she reached in her tote. "Zack, take the phone! Tom can't help you now, but maybe he can do something later."

Zack crouched again and kissed her cheek. "I love you, mom."

"I love you." Nicole watched Zack and Dakota as they splashed away through the rain. Then footsteps approached from another direction. Abu aimed his rifle, but relaxed as Fila appeared.

"Nathi!" Fila dropped to her knees beside him and faced Nicole across his chest. "How can I help?"

"Maybe I should be helping you." Nicole studied the spear of wood in the glare of the burning hut. "Should we take it out?"

Fila examined the wound. "It may be best to wait. There are medical supplies in the cave." She winced as several village boys fired again at the chop of blades. Abu also fired, somehow controlling the bucking gun though it seemed to take all his strength.

"We must get out of here!" he cried. "The pilot can see us because of the fires!"

"I think I can walk," said Nathi.

"No," said Nicole. "Don't move until we can get that thing out."

"Yes," agreed Fila. "Stay still."

Nicole looked back at the burning hut. "But we have to get away from these fires."

"I'll get a cart," said Fila. "Abu, help me."

*   *   *

Zack and Dakota were crossing the bridge, both panting from the run. "I'll take the locking pins out," puffed Dakota. "Can you begin the engine start? It's the reverse of shutting them down."

"I think so," puffed Zack.

"Set the mixture auto-rich."

They ran onto the landing field and there was a rushing sound overhead. "DOWN!" yelled Dakota.

They threw themselves to the muddy ground as a third shooting star hissed out of the sky. Zack rolled onto his back and watched the violet trail. "I think it was aimed at the plane, but the pilot didn't paint the target long enough to hit it."

The missile wavered toward the stream. Missing the bridge, it hit the water. Another explosion erupted. It had not rained enough to

261

soak the trees, and several burst into flame.

"There!" yelled Dakota, pointing up. "It's coming in for another attack!"

Zack aimed his gun at the sky but yelled, "I can't see it!"

"Fire at the sound, but lead it!" Dakota's rifle spit yellow flame. Zack's gun joined it a second later. There was the scream of a full-throttled engine, a straining clatter of thrashing blades as the helicopter pulled out of a dive and veered away toward the mountain.

"Is it the General's?" panted Zack.

Dakota yanked the clip from his gun and pulled another from his jeans. "It must be, there is no other."

Zack replaced his clip. "The pilot's not comin' in low enough."

"That would take courage." Dakota got up and screamed at the sky: "How much courage does it take to push a button from up in the air!"

Then he ran to the plane and pulled the pin from the starboard landing gear as Zack splashed to the doorway and struggled to hoist himself in.

* * *

Jumbe Chane was crossing the bridge, a pair of boys helping him walk. Other boys ran ahead. Behind came Nicole and Fila, pulling a cart with Nathi aboard. Last came Abu, his rifle clutched ready.

Jumbe Chane boomed, "Malik! Asanni! Taji! Defend the plane while it's taking off!"

Three boys ran for the landing field.

* * *

Now in the airplane's cockpit, Zack had found the light switch and the little space was lit ruby-red. He stretched to reach the ignition switches. Behind him in the cargo bay, Dakota was closing the doors.

"Dakota! Hurry!" yelled Zack above the rattle of rain. "The 'copter's comin' back!"

*   *   *

Atop the not-quite mountain, Tindo was scanning the sky. Mbwa was pressed to his legs, half in fear, half in defense. Below, the village was burning. Flames were leaping above the trees and lighting up the landing field. Tindo had seen the helicopter, a darker shadow against the clouds. He'd fired his gun but seemed to have missed. He grabbed the binoculars and focused them on the plane in the valley, clearly seen in the glare of the fires and now a helpless target. One propeller began to turn. Black smoke puffed from under a wing.

*   *   *

"Too rich," panted Dakota, plopping into the pilot's seat.

"Sorry," said Zack.

Dakota adjusted the throttles and mix, turned on the instrument panel lights and reached to the starter switches. "Watch the tachometers. Call out the readings."

*   *   *

Tindo heard the scream of a turbine. He spun to see the helicopter diving out of the clouds. He aimed his gun and fired.

*   *   *

Both engines sputtered to life, spitting, smoking, one backfired. Dakota worked the throttles and the clattering rose to a vibrating roar. Slowly the plane began to move. The rain hadn't penetrated deep, but there were inches of mud on the field. The tail wheel skidded instead of turning. Dakota held the port side brake and fed the starboard engine fuel. It coughed and faltered.

"Come on!" cried Dakota.

There was a violet flare in the sky. "Another missile!" yelled Zack.

The starboard engine roared again, and the airplane slowly swung around, its wheels plowing ruts in the mud.

263

"Ready for takeoff!" shouted Dakota, throttling up the port side engine. "No time for an engine test!"

"Tail wheel locked," called Zack. "Cowl flaps trail. Mix, auto-rich. RPMs, twenty-seven-hundred."

"We need more," said Dakota. "She's heavy and the field is wet."

"Twenty-seven-fifty. ...Twenty-eight-hundred."

There were bursts of rifle fire as boys outside tried to target the missile. Dakota thrust his head out the window. "Aim at the helicopter!"

The boys swung their guns and flames spit from the muzzles. Somewhere above a turbine screamed. The missile suddenly veered to the left. An instant later came an explosion blasting the acacia grove. Bits of branches and coffin wood flew.

"Twenty-nine-hundred!" called Zack.

The airplane was trembling, rivets creaking. Its tail lifted slightly out of the mud. Dakota released the brakes. Nothing happened. The engines roared, the tail lifted more. Dakota leaned from the window. "Clear the wheels! Watch out for the props!"

The three boys ran to the struggling plane, dropped in the mud and dug with their hands.

*   *   *

Tindo heard the helicopter diving for another attack. Jamming another clip in his gun, he aimed at the sky and fired. There was another violet flare.

*   *   *

The airplane's tail dropped back in the mud. It gave a lurch and started to move. "Three-thousand!" yelled Zack.

"Hold the throttles!"

The plane began to gather speed, rocking and jolting down the field, splashing up sprays of water and mud. Zack peered through the streaming windscreen, the wipers fighting to keep it clear. There was only blackness ahead as the fires in the village were left behind. "How

264

do you know when to roll out?"

Dakota's hands were clenched on the yoke, his boots now guiding the rudder. "Hopefully she will know."

* * *

Beside the stream among the trees, Nicole and Fila pulled the cart. Abu came slogging behind. Ahead was the puffing of *Jumbe* Chane and the panting of the boys helping him. There were more bursts of gunfire, then another explosion.

"I hear the plane!" cried Nathi. "Stop!"

He rose up on his elbows, squinting into the rain. Nicole remembered Zack once saying that pilots always watched a takeoff until a plane was safe in the air. They were too far away to see the field, but she heard the thunder of engines.

Abu pointed up. "The helicopter is coming back!"

There was distant gunfire, and all eyes turned to the mountain. Suddenly, it seemed erupt like an ancient volcano wakening.

"Tindo!" screamed Abu.

A yellow glare flooded the valley. Nicole saw tears in Nathi's eyes. Also in the eyes of the chief.

So this was war, she thought. No rousing patriotic music. No civilized History Channel hype or *Modern Marvels* wonders of better ways to kill human beings. No brave and noble *Band Of Brothers* fighting for Democracy. Here was only savage death, suffering... and *murder*.

Nathi cocked his head and listened. Above the patter of rain in the trees and the distant crackle of fires came a droning, deep-throated roar. Nicole thought of lions in duet.

"They will make it," said Nathi.

"Of course they will," said Fila. "You taught Dakota well." Then she turned to Nicole. "As you taught your son."

Abu stared up at the burning mountain. "Tindo shot the helicopter!"

Again, Nathi cocked his head to listen. "Maybe," he said. "The engine sounds rough."

265

"Will it crash?" asked Abu.

"I hope to God it does!" cried Nicole.

Jumbe Chane spoke: "Don't call upon God in the name of war."

Abu spit at the sky. "Killer of children! Cowardly *boy!* Fall to earth and face me!"

Nathi listened, gazing up. "The damage may not be serious, he may pursue the plane."

Abu snarled. "May the Lion Of Death find him tonight!"

TWENTY-EIGHT

"Help me, Zack!" yelled Dakota.

Zackary grabbed the co-pilot's yoke. The engines roared at full RPM, drowning out the rattle of rain as drops exploded against the windscreen and pelted the creaking fuselage. There was only blackness ahead, but they must have been close to the end of the valley. The boys strained back on the trembling yokes, fighting to pull the plane into the air. At last the rumble of wheels cut off, but the plane tilted right as it left the ground. One wheel struck the earth again, throwing up a spray of mud.

"Gear up!" yelled Dakota.

Zack yanked the landing gear lever. The airplane's nose tilted slowly up. There was a jolt, rocking the plane.

"What was that?" panted Zack.

"The top of a hill," puffed Dakota, his muddy face and glistening body bathed bloody red by the instrument lights.

Zack wiped his own muddy face. "It's raining in here!"

Dakota smiled a little, his foxy eyes scanning the instrument panel. "That is a C-47 feature. It always rains on the inside whenever it rains on the outside. Can you see if the starboard gear is up, and hopefully undamaged?"

Zack rose to look out his window. "Yeah, an' it looks okay."

Dakota looked out his window. "Port side also."

"Another missile!" yelled Zack.

"Which side?"

"Mine!"

Dakota banked hard to the left. The missile shot past with a violet glare beneath the starboard wing.

"Hellfires are anti-tank," said Zack. "Supposed to be air to ground. They're not very good against other planes."

"Maybe that's all they would give to the General so he could destroy more villages."

"How fast can we go?" asked Zack. "A Huey can do about 185."

Dakota adjusted the pitch controls. "She could go 220 when new. I once had her up to 195, but we are heavily loaded and there is the rain."

"Can we get above the clouds?"

"We have to stay low. The Army has a radar, and we can't let them see where we're going."

Zack checked the red-lit compass. "Is that why we're goin' west now? You said Rashawn's camp was east of here."

"Yes. We can't let the helicopter trail us."

"He's gonna be hard to lose." Zack stuck his head out the window, gritting his teeth as the rain lashed his hair, while searching the night behind the plane. "I'm sure he's got radar, too!" he shouted above the roar of the engines and waterfall rushing of wind.

Dakota turned the airplane north. "How many missiles do you think he has?"

Zack pulled in his head. "Depends on the system. Some have six, others have eight."

Dakota was watching the compass. "He fired two at the village, and two at the plane on the landing field. Then one at the mountain, and one just now."

"Then he's out if he only had six, so he might be just tryin' to follow us." Zack looked at the fire on mountain top. "Tindo...?"

"This is what war really is."

"There's the 'copter!" cried Zack. He grabbed his rifle and fired out the window. Smoking brass spewed from the hammering gun to clatter across the cockpit floor. Then the clip clanked empty.

Dakota banked away from the mountain. "Did you hit it?"

"I don't know," Zack jammed in another clip. "I only saw it for a second." He thrust his head out the window again, slitting his eyes against the rain. "But, it didn't look right."

"What do you mean?" asked Dakota, leveling the plane.

"I couldn't see enough to be sure... just a shadow against the fire... but it didn't look like it was flyin' right. Like, it was hard to control. I got a game like that."

Dakota watched the compass, bringing the plane around the mountain then heading on an eastward course. "We must get this fuel to Rashawn! The river by his camp is rising. Soon there will be no place to land."

Zack was still looking back, his long hair streaming in the wind. "Can we outrun it?"

Dakota gripped the throttle levers. "We can try."

*   *   *

The cave beneath the not-quite mountain had been prepared as a refuge with blankets and medical supplies. The stream flowed through the middle, gleaming in candle and lantern light. Lions may once have denned here, but a wall and door had been built at the entrance.

Nicole had been tending the wounded; cuts and gashes from flying debris along with many cruel burns. Abu's little sister had died in her arms. She supposed that should have shocked her, but she didn't have time to be shocked. With Fila's help but with no anesthetic, she'd removed the wood from Nathi's chest, an ordeal he'd borne in silence. Then they had treated the other wounded. *Jumbe* Chane was a healer, too, assisted by his wife and daughters.

Nicole lost track of time amid blood, pain, and children's cries. Then, while bandaging a boy, she remembered she hadn't thought about Zack. Where was he now? Had the helicopter pursued the plane? Faintly, while tending Nathi's wound, she'd heard the sounds of engines above; the deep-throated drone of the old cargo plane and the thrashing chop of the helicopter. Maybe Tindo had damaged it before he'd been killed on the mountain? Even to her inexperienced ears its engine sounded ragged.

She gave the boy a comforting hug, a reassuring smile to his mother, checked on Nathi at rest on a blanket, then went to the mouth of the cave and opened the heavy plank door. Two boys, maybe seven or eight, were standing guard outside... she had warned them not to look if everything went bright.

The rain had increased to a steady fall and the fires in the village had all gone out. The boys regarded her curiously as she stood there letting her eyes adjust from the candle and lantern light in the cave. She wondered what they would think of her if they knew she was responsible -- ignorantly, indifferently, complacently, what did it matter -- for bringing this death and destruction to them.

"Your son is very brave," said one.

Nicole raised her eyes to the sky: even with the falling rain it wasn't totally black. She thought of stars above the clouds, and maybe Zack could see them. "Thank you," she said.

The other boy added, "We think our airplane got away."

The first boy pointed eastward. "The helicopter was following it, but we think it had to land... just there beyond the hills. Its engine was on fire."

Nicole lowered her eyes to the trees, where smoke from the village still ghosted above. Although it looked like a vine-tangled forest, she knew the land was open and grassy a few hundred yards beyond the stream. Dimly, she could see a trail. Was that where Zack had gone to face lions? "Have you told *Jumbe* Chane?" she asked.

"Yes," said the first boy. "He will send someone to look."

Abu emerged from the cave, no longer naked though still nearly so in only a loincloth of amber and gold that now proclaimed his allegiance to what Nicole's leaders called terror. He also wore Kiwanji boots, his rifle in one hand. "I'm going to find it," he said. "And I will kill the cowardly boy who murders from the sky!"

Nicole didn't know why -- maybe she wanted to see for herself what kind of man could murder children -- but said, "Let me go with you."

270

"Do you want to see me kill him?"

"Yes," said Nicole.

*   *   *

"I think he's goin' down!" called Zack, his head out the window again. "His engine's spittin' flames."

"Do you think he will crash?" asked Dakota, watching the compass and altimeter as rain pelted the windscreen.

"He's still under control... MISSILE!"

"Which side?"

"BOTH SIDES!"

Dakota shoved the yoke forward and the airplane almost stood on its nose, the drums of fuel in the cargo bay straining against their straps. Two missiles shot past just missing the wings. A moment later came the explosions, blasting the ground not far below. The airplane rocked in the fireball. Dakota yanked back on the yoke and gave the engines full throttle. "Zack!"

Zack dropped back into the co-pilot's seat and fought along with Dakota to pull the plane back into the sky. Slowly it came out of the dive, leveled, and finally began to climb. "Guess he had eight," panted Zack. "...Damn, we were close to the ground!"

Dakota lowered the throttles a bit, watching the altimeter. "We have to stay low or be seen on radar. But there are no hills between us and the river." He watched the compass and came back on course. "We should be there in about twenty minutes."

"Then land with no lights?" asked Zack, wiping the rain from his glistening face.

"They will signal us, but one or two flashes is all they can risk. The place is not many miles from the town, and the Army has patrols. ...Would you like to fly?"

"Guess I better," said Zack. He placed his boots on the rudder pedals and gripped the steering yoke. "This might be my last chance."

Dakota fired a cigarette, shielding his match from the windscreen leaks. "Are you afraid?"

"Aren't you?"

271

"Mostly of landing, that's my scary place."

Zack watched the compass and altimeter. "I hope your dad is okay."

"Your mother seems very capable."

"She can be brave when she has to. ...Can I have a smoke?"

Dakota gave Zack his cigarette and lit another for himself.

"Funny," said Zack.

"What is?" asked Dakota.

"Bein' scared, like facin' them lions..."

"Those lions."

"Yeah." Zack blew out a ghost of smoke. "It's like you don't know how lucky you are... to be alive, I mean... till you *really* got somethin' to be scared of."

*   *   *

Nicole was surprised she could see. For most of her life she had never known darkness, not in the natural way. The civilized night was never quite dark, lights always burning somewhere outside as if to deny that night existed, or was an enemy to be fought. Yet here, without lights, the whole sky seemed to glow.

It wasn't much more than a pale shade of black, but Nicole had no trouble following Abu, a little black shadow in waist-high grass -- her waist, not his -- as they left the trees and climbed a hill. The rain was falling steadily but like the night was warm. Steam ghosted up from the life-scented earth, and it might have been a pleasant walk, climbing a hill in the rain with this boy... except they were hunting a dangerous thing; the only animal in the world that killed for country, gods, or greed.

They reached the rounded top of the hill. Abu dropped to a crouch and waved Nicole down while scanning the shadowy land below. Nicole moved up beside him: there was little to see in the not-quite dark, only a vague and empty expanse with deeper shadows here and there of scattered acacia groves. Somewhere in the distance she heard a growl, but Abu seemed to pay it no mind.

"There," he whispered, pointing.

Nicole leaned over his glistening shoulder, sighting along his arm. At first she saw nothing but more shades of black, shadows of shadows too dark to be grays. But then she noticed the ghost of a glimmer, rain-wet metal or maybe glass, and a shape that wasn't natural. It wasn't far from the foot of the hill, and close to an acacia grove.

Abu whispered again, "Look beside it, not at it."

Nicole shifted her eyes and the shape became more distinct... low, streamlined, long drooping rotors. It didn't seem to have crashed. Still, it didn't look quite right and may have come down hard. Its pilot may have been injured... she found herself hoping he was.

"This way," said Abu. "We'll circle around and come through the grove."

"Could there be lions in there?" asked Nicole.

"They are on our side."

Nicole wished she had the boy's faith, but followed him as he led the way just below the crest of the hill. They descended its gentle northern slope and approached the aircraft through the trees, crept to the edge of the rain-pattered grove and peered out through the dripping leaves. The helicopter sat in the open about a hundred yards away. It did look like it had come down hard; one of the landing skids was bent and a rotor blade almost touching the grass. Was the pilot lying injured inside? If he was, did he know that -- formerly the hunter, shooting fire and death from the sky -- he was now hunted here on earth?

"Wait here," whispered Abu. Clicking something on his gun -- the safety, Nicole assumed -- he left the trees and approached the aircraft, his rifle aimed at the door. Nicole held her breath, wishing she could protect him somehow. Reaching the door on the damaged side, his gun poised ready to fire, Abu found the latch and yanked it open. After a long wary moment, he turned and waved to Nicole.

"The cowardly boy has run," he said, pointing to a trail in the grass as Nicole came up beside him.

Nicole peered into the cockpit, which gave her an eerie *déjà vu* feeling. It was clearly a military machine, though painted flat black with no markings, yet it seemed somehow familiar. A tiny amber eye was alight on the instrument panel. A Thermos bottle lay on the floor, and the scent of coffee lingered. That awakened new rage in Nicole, as if murdering children was only a job. You dropped your bombs, had a cup of coffee, and then flew home to a comfortable bed.

"I know nothing about helicopters," she said. "But this isn't the one I saw from the plane before we landed in town."

"This is not the General's?"

Nicole studied the aircraft: smoke curled from the engine exhaust, and raindrops hissed on hot metal. There was the scent of kerosene, and maybe fire-retardant. "My son said the General's was a Huey, an old one from the Vietnam War, and it was olive-drab. This one is different and looks almost new."

"I have read of that war," said Abu. "The Americans lost, and they are still bitter."

"I know," said Nicole.

There was a shot!

Abu pitched forward, face-down in the grass! His small body quivered and then went still. Nicole almost dropped to his side, though already knowing the boy was dead. But a figure rose from the steaming grass maybe fifty feet away. From what Nicole could see in the dark, the shape was clad in flight coveralls -- Defenders of Democracy Optional Accessories -- and wore a kind of Borg-like helmet with goggles that covered part of its face. ...Defenders of Democracy Optional Night Vision Gear. One gloved hand held a pistol.

Nicole pressed her back to the aircraft as the faceless figure approached through the rain. The night vision goggles glowed eerily green. She had vague thoughts of Terminators. Her eyes flicked down to Abu's rifle, but then the child-killer spoke:

"Don't even think about it, Nicole."

TWENTY-NINE

The airplane droned through the rainy night, its wipers creaking rhythmically as drops exploded against the glass and rattled along the fuselage. Zack was flying, watching the compass. Dakota was leaning forward, scanning ahead through the windscreen, his eyes slitted against the leaks that sprayed around the frame. The eight-track player was on, and Barry McGuire's *Eve Of Destruction* echoed accompaniment to the engines.

Dakota looked at his watch. "We should be nearing the river, and we're probably south of the camp."

"Should I turn north?" asked Zack.

Dakota switched off the player. "We must sight the river first, then we'll know where we are."

"Can we radio the village?"

"You are worried about your mother?"

"I got a creepy feelin', but I'm worried about everybody there."

"Because of the Davy Crockett?"

Zack eyes flicked to the altimeter and he pulled back a bit on the yoke. "They should be safe from the blast in the cave as long as it's not too close, but then they gotta get outta there fast 'cause of the radiation."

"I'm sure your mother has warned them, and *Jumbe* Chane will know what to do."

"But so many people were hurt," said Zack. "How could they move 'em all?"

"Maybe the General won't bomb the village. He's already used those missiles on us, which should be sufficient even for him." Dakota glanced at the radio. "They only have the walkie-talkie, and we are out of its transmitting range. They would hear us but we couldn't hear them, and the Army may be listening."

Zack pulled the phone from his jeans. "I wish there was somebody we could call, but even Tom can't help us now." He put the phone on the instrument panel.

"Who is Tom?" asked Dakota. "Your mother said he was a friend."

"He's been tryin' to help your country, but he don't know you're the good guys."

"Then he has been helping the General."

"Yeah," said Zack. "By givin' him guns an' war stuff. But he don't know what's goin' on or he'd be on your side."

"Ignorance is no excuse for supporting dictators and wars."

"Then I was guilty, too... just playin' my games an' watchin' TV while all this shit was goin' on."

"But obviously your heart was kind or you would have met the other lion." Dakota pointed ahead. "There is the river."

Zack wiped rain from his eyes. "Yeah, I see it... sorta shiny."

"I recognize this bend," said Dakota. "We are south of the camp."

"You better fly. What should I do?"

"Prepare to become very busy." Dakota took control. "They will hear us and flash two lights where we are to land... one at the start of the landing place and the other to mark the end. We have to make it the first time; the General has soldiers on patrol and they may hear us coming in. Rashawn must fuel his vehicles and get his men across the river before the General learns where they are and musters a defense."

"Or shoots the Davy Crockett," said Zack. "...This is gonna be scary, huh?"

"My very scary place."

276

*　　　*　　　*

The claws of a beast seemed to clutch Nicole's stomach as if to rip something out of her. Two children had died in less than an hour, the girl in the cave from brutal wounds, and now Abu shot in the back; and suddenly all the horror of that seemed to bore into her body like some monstrous parasite laying eggs. She felt sick with every evil thing, loathsome, vile and despicable, that one human being could do to another; with every wound they could inflict for king, queen or president, for country, race or fanatic cause; with all the suffering they brought in the name of all their glorious gods or nobly professed ideals; with every disease they wouldn't cure, with all the starvation they wouldn't prevent because there was no profit. Even with all her cynicism of how and why the world was run, she had always believed in a *few* good people, people who actually wanted to help, to share what they had because it was *right*, a pure and human thing to do; to build a sane and peaceful world where no one died because of wars, hate, greed, or poverty: that small percentage of each generation who seemed to evolve a little bit higher, a little bit kinder, a little more loving. Maybe she wasn't one of those people, but she had always believed in them like a child believed in fairy tales... or wanted to believe.

The figure had stopped about ten feet away, holding the gun professionally, the way a mechanic would hold a wrench, a carpenter would hold a hammer. A thousand curses flashed through Nicole's mind, but none were enough -- *all* weren't enough -- to vomit the absolute loathing she felt as Tom removed his helmet.

"You bastard," was all she could say.

Tom nudged Abu's body with the toe of his boot, a master craftsman inspecting his work, though his voice sounded tired: "I expected more than that, but maybe I shouldn't have."

Nicole supposed she should have been scared, but even the sickness was passing away, leaving her empty and hollowly cold. Whatever the beast had ripped out of her was something she didn't seem to need. "Of course you're going to kill me. And please don't say it's just your job."

"I have to, Nicole. And it is my job."

277

"Murdering children. Innocent people."

Tom shrugged. "You just never got close to your work. ...Kind of like selling your little war dolls but ignoring who suffers to make them. How many kids have *you* killed, Nicole? By living in the big playpen, being part of the great American party with all the ice cream and cake."

He glanced down at the body again. "I pull the trigger, but *you* made the gun and furnished the bullets, and you chose the targets. You and millions of other people who think it's their right to have all their toys. You could almost forgive a lot them... like Jesus said when they nailed him up, 'they know not what they do.' But you're more guilty than most, because you're smart enough to know there *have* to be people like me. People who do your dirty work, who'd willingly die for their country...or you... if I was ordered to."

Once more he looked down. "Or him."

He shook his head. "The good townsfolk were terrorized so they hired a few gunfighters to do what they think they're too good to do... too kind, enlightened, or just plain yellow. Then they go to bed feeling pure because they think their hands are clean."

Almost against her will Nicole looked down at her hands: the rain had washed the blood away... Nathi's, the children's.

Tom kicked the rifle away and slipped his gun in its holster. "One of my accessories to keep the wolves from eating the kids."

"So, everything was a lie," said Nicole. "And only a few hours ago I was feeling guilty about lying to you."

It was hard to see in the dimness, but Tom's eyes may have saddened. "Not everything, Nicole. It wasn't supposed to work out this way. ...You believe that, don't you?"

"Why would you lie now," said Nicole. "The truth can't hurt you anymore. Or the murderers you work for. ...What exactly was my job?"

"Shouldn't be hard to figure out."

"Find the 'terrorists' for you."

"Call them freedom fighters, I would. ...*If* I had that luxury. Not a big budget for this operation. Too many other threats in the world... to the great American party. Duma was smart. Never assembled all his men. Kept them scattered all over. But N'dila isn't a total fool; he knew Duma's only chance to win was to attack the compound when the rain

278

started. Duma would gather all his troops... mostly kids like the great General's Army."

"That's what the bomb is for," said Nicole. "You knew all the time N'dila had it."

"We gave it to him," said Tom. "After a little dusting. The smallest nuclear bomb ever made. Almost, but not quite too small to go off. ...Correction: we arranged for N'dila to find it on the weapons market after we gave him the launcher and made sure he'd find out what it was by including all the manuals. 'We' would have given him something much better... *if* we did dirty deeds like that. And officially we don't know he has it. ...It was on your train the other day. We sent the fuel as a decoy; something Duma would go for and not look for anything else."

"An olive-drab box," said Nicole.

"Very observant," said Tom. "But I never thought you'd take the train."

"I wanted Zack to see lions. ...How long have you been here?"

"A day before you arrived. When you and Zack were watching hippos." Tom glanced at the helicopter. "Brought this in on the last transport. I arranged for Simba Air Freight to pick up the Barrymore uniforms so the plane would be at the border for you, but..."

"We took the train. How much did N'dila know about me?"

"No more than I wanted him to. I didn't tell him you were coming until I knew you were already here. And he still thinks you're here about the boots."

"In other words you pull his strings." Nicole sighed. "Like you pulled mine from the start. You knew I'd sympathize with the 'terrorists' after I saw this child-killing war... that's why I was right for the job. And you wanted me to bring Zack because it made good cover... what kind of spy would bring her young son. You tracked us everywhere with the phone, so you wanted us on the plane tonight because it was flying fuel to Duma. Then you would know where he was. Then you'd drop the bomb."

"I would have gotten you out of there first." Tom looked sad again. "But, they changed the game plan."

"Your bosses," said Nicole. "The degenerate murderers you'd die

279

for decided we were expendable. Or another threat to their precious party. ...But, why did you shoot at the plane tonight? You didn't...?"

"No," said Tom. "They got away. That Kiwanji kid is a damn good pilot." He glanced at the wounded helicopter. "And that kid on the mountain was a pretty good shot."

"But, if you'd shot the plane down, how would you know where the 'terrorists' were?"

"N'dila had pretty much narrowed the field to where they would probably be. If the blast didn't take them out, the radiation would. After all, this is his country, though he didn't spend most of his childhood here. Went to a British boarding school."

"He never took the manhood test."

Tom cocked his head. "Did I miss something?"

"Maybe. Or your masters did. When they chose what side they wanted to win."

"The lion thing?" said Tom. "Could have been the deciding fa-tor. America is scared of men. Especially men who can't be bought."

"What was your price, *boy*?"

Tom shrugged. "As bad as we are, I've seen a lot worse. If I was one of my opposite numbers we wouldn't be having this conversation."

"That's just happenstance," said Nicole, "so don't try to come off as noble. You would have killed us all on the plane... Nathi, Zack, Dakota and me. 'Just following orders, *mien Colonel.'*"

"Somebody has to follow them or there wouldn't be an America."

Nicole looked down at Abu. "If this is the only way to protect it, then there shouldn't be."

"It's not the only way, but that goes back to following orders."

"I suppose we 'know too much?'"

Tom sighed. "Especially Zack. He's a damn smart kid. If he got a good look at this helicopter he knows it isn't the General's, and he knows something American attacked the village tonight."

"Why did you do that?" demanded Nicole. "Are you trying to kill everybody here? You've already been supporting a war... probably even started it... that's killed off most of Kiwanja's men. And now you're going to kill more boys. Why did you attack the village where

there's mostly women and children?"

"Because we're learning from our mistakes. ...Better ways to be hated, at least. Americans whine 'protect us from terror,' but they can't be bothered about how it's done. Terrorists are savages. They worship evil gods. They teach their kids that war is holy. They're not our kind of people, dear, so they shouldn't be allowed to live."

"Don't you have a conscience?"

"That's why we're having this conversation." Tom glanced at his watch. "After we won 'the last good war' we started making mistakes. Got careless and full of ourselves. And one of our mistakes was leaving wars unfinished. Not teaching our enemies that no one messes with us. And if they do, they'll pay the price, and it won't be cheap."

Nicole gazed around at the nighted land beneath the softly starlit clouds and faintly silver rain. The drifting mist looked like gathering ghosts. "How could Kiwanja threaten us?"

"Not my job to plan the party, only to protect it. Maybe we want our own sweat-shop; a little country all our own where people work for a dollar a day and don't bother us about pension plans, safety standards or pollution. Or maybe we want another black site."

"Black site?" asked Nicole.

"A place to torture people without violating our constitution. Like an Area 51 that really doesn't exist."

"So, no one cared about the boots?"

"The boots will be Barrymore's little reward for being a good American business. ...Too bad you couldn't have set that up. I'm sure you would have done a good job."

"What if I had? If things had worked out differently?"

"I like you and Zack," said Tom. "I never lied about that."

"We might have been... together?"

"I would have liked that."

Absurdly, Nicole asked, "You really don't care that Zack is fat?"

"Just more of him to love. And I would have. ...Wish I could have."

"And you would have just had a government job. One that kept you away a lot. A job you couldn't talk about."

"Lots of people do, Nicole. It's called defending democracy. Our version of it, anyway."

Again, Nicole looked down at Abu. "You believe this much in America?"

Tom's voice hardened. "You don't think I enjoyed that, do you? I'd rather have brought him an ice cream cone, maybe the first he'd ever had. I could have brought him indoor plumbing. Or books for his village school. He might have grown up liking me because I helped him build a future. But that's not what America wants me to do. I'm part of the terror America made. I'm part of the power *you* put in control and won't do anything to stop because you're too busy playing with toys, driving your car, watching TV, or 'battling childhood obesity.'"

"I accept that guilt," said Nicole. "But it's the same power you're working for, and you know it much better than I do."

Tom spread his hands. "What do you want me to say, Nicole? That I couldn't turn my back right now and let you walk away? Do you think it would matter if I did? That you and Zack would get out alive?"

"I suppose not," said Nicole. "...So, what happens now? You kill me here? And Zack will die when you drop the bomb. Which, of course, will be right on target because he has the phone. ...But *you* won't fire it, will you? Because whoever does will die."

"I would if I'd been ordered to."

"A boy wants to die for a noble cause, but a man wants to live for one."

"Where did you hear that?"

"From a real man."

Tom looked at his watch again, his voice becoming professional. "The General's Huey is on its way... assuming the pilot can fly a straight line and follow a blip on a screen." He glanced into the helicopter, where the yellow eye glowed on the instrument panel. "As soon as he gets here I'll blow this up... could prove to be an embarrassment. I usually can't give options, but maybe you'd like to be with Zack?"

"When all goes bright?"

"Believe me, Nicole, you won't feel a thing."

"I'd want to be with him no matter what."

"I'd be surprised if you didn't." Tom cocked his head and turned toward the east. Above the whispering patter of rain came a distant

282

chopping of rotor blades. "Please step back a little, Nicole. Have to set the timer. ...And please don't run and make this messy."

THIRTY

"There!" cried Zack, above the engines' rhythmic roar and the rattle of rain on the windscreen. "Those must be the lights!"

Dakota leaned forward to gaze ahead at two tiny sparks in the distance. "...Yes! Gear down!"

Zack grabbed the lever. There were thumps and the plane balked a bit. "The lights went out!"

Dakota's hands were clenched on the yoke. "That's all they could risk. I have the compass heading and I think I've guessed the distance." He noted the airspeed indicator and reached for the wing flap control. "Switch to cross feed. Cowl flaps open."

Zack turned the fuel selectors. "Roger, Dakota. Tail wheel locked."

"You will be a good pilot, Zack."

"I just wanna walk away from my landings, startin' with this one. ...How can you tell where the ground is?"

Dakota glanced at the altimeter. "Sooner or later we'll hit it. The trick is not to hit it too hard."

"What can I do?"

"Take hold of your wheel, I may need help. Feel what I do."

There was a jolt that rocked the plane as one of the wheels struck the earth. "Port!" yelled Dakota.

Zack pulled left. The other wheel struck and the plane bounced back in the air.

"Damn!" yelled Dakota. "Push forward!" He cut the engines' power.

"This is flyin' into the ground!"

"I know! Push!"

Both wheels struck. The plane careened over uneven ground, creaking, rattling, slewing in mud. The drums of gasoline thudded together, straining their nylon straps. "Keep her straight!" yelled Dakota. "Port! ...No, starboard!"

"We're goin' into the river!"

"It's just a flooded place, I hope!" Dakota jammed down on the brakes and there were teeth-gritting screams from the wheels. The plane began to nose-over. Dakota let up on the pedals and the tail wheel finally thumped down. The airplane hit the flooded ground and water sprayed from the props. The tail came up again with the drag. "Push!" yelled Dakota.

Then they were out of the water. The tail wheel thumped down again, and Dakota trod hard on the brakes. A drum broke loose and tumbled forward, crashing against the cockpit bulkhead. There was a sudden reek of gas. Both boys battled to steer the plane as it jolted and bashed along in the dark. Finally it lurched to a rocking stop, and dimly seen through the shroud of rain was the corpse of a burned-out village. Dakota cut the engines, then the battery switches. The ruby instrument lights went out and there was only darkness. Rain rattled loud on the roof. "Thank you," sighed Dakota.

"You're welcome," said Zack.

Dakota touched Zack's shoulder. "Thank you, too."

"...Oh," said Zack. "You were thanking the Lion Of Life. ...Thanks, Mister Lion... again."

"There's a flashlight by your seat," said Dakota. "We have to stop the leaking fuel."

"Is it explosion-proof?" asked Zack.

"Switch it on and we will find out."

* * *

285

The chopping of blades grew louder approaching through the night. Nicole stepped away from the helicopter as Tom had ordered her to, backing toward the little acacia grove and stopping when he said, "Far enough."

Despite his warning not to run, she glanced to the glistening trees, but reminded herself that the boots she wore only made her think she could run, no matter what Zack had said about magic. And even in her teenage years she doubted if she could have outrun Tom. Besides, he would shoot her in the back.

And even if she got away she could do nothing to stop this mass-murder she had helped to orchestrate. She couldn't contact Zack and Dakota, nor could she warn the freedom fighters. She wanted to hold Zack's hand when they died. And Dakota's, too.

Tom had pulled a microphone out of the helicopter's cockpit. Nicole heard his voice above the rain and the thrashing of blades overhead: "Right above me now. Come down. Don't use your lights."

Nicole saw a shape against the dark sky. A rush of wind and spraying rain buffeted her face. The Huey came clumsily down, jolting hard as it landed, a faint green glow in its cockpit. Tom pointed toward it with his gun. "All right, Nicole."

A shadow burst from the trees! It parted the glistening grass like a scythe, flashing silently past Nicole. Tom tried to aim, but the lion was on him!

Nicole expected a roar, snarls, but there was only a wet crunching sound… one, and very final. The lion turned to look at her, its eyes glowing eerily pale in the dark… a very old lion, seemingly no more than skin over bones with mane hanging lank and bedraggled. Too old and feeble to hunt, Nicole wondered, but seeing easy prey in Tom? …But, why not her? Then she recalled its deadly speed… old, but far from feeble. Then it simply walked away and vanished in the mist.

Nicole blinked… had this really happened? Or, had her mind just made it up like a desperate escape in a nightmare? …But, Tom lay on the ground near Abu.

Only seconds had passed. The other helicopter was waiting, rotors spinning, engine whining, scenting the air with hot kerosene. Nicole hesitated unsure what to do. Run back to the cave? But that wouldn't help. She dashed to Tom's body, smelling hot blood as she snatched up the gun. It was an Army .45, another Defenders accessory though obsolete by American standards. Maybe it had belonged to Tom's father? A sentimental weapon of death. She assumed the safety would be off. She didn't want to look at Tom, but wondered if he had a phone. She might be able to call Zack.

She forced herself to look anyway, avoiding where his face might have been. Would his phone be monitored? Probably, and also tracked. Calling Zack would alert Tom's masters that something was going wrong with their plan. ...Could they fire the bomb by remote control?

She pictured the shabby old jeep and its 1950's technology. The gun -- launcher -- would probably have to be manually fired. The jeep would be out in the country now, less than two miles from the fighters' camp... assuming N'dila had guessed the location. There would have to be a radio, final aiming directions, and then the order to fire. Who would be giving that order? General N'dila safe in his bunker? But how would he know when to fire? Had a time already been set? Or, was he waiting for orders from Tom?

The latter seemed most likely... there was only one bomb, one chance for N'dila to win this war by killing all the men who opposed him... men no matter their calendar ages. Tom would have wanted the target confirmed; would have wanted to actually see the camp, get the final range or something, then give the order to fire.

She studied the waiting Huey: its pilot was probably wondering why Tom hadn't come to it yet. She had to do something fast! Assuming Tom's phone was being tracked, they expected him to be moving soon. She peered into his helicopter; ruby digits were flashing a countdown and less than five minutes remained. She knelt, and searched his flight suit pockets: there was a phone like the one she'd been given. She looked at Abu. "I'm sorry," she said in Swahili.

Then, holding the gun concealed at her side, she went through the grass to the Huey. She saw a sliding door on its flank and remembered old movies about Vietnam; M-16s blasting, troops leaping out, with a Rolling Stones song in the background. There might have been boys with guns inside... in which case she was probably dead. But the cockpit door clicked as she approached as someone released the latch. She

287

yanked the door open and aimed the pistol, gripping it double-handed.

A boy of maybe seventeen, his ebony face looking rather corpse-like in the green glow of the instrument panel, blinked at her in surprise. He was clad in sand-and-tan, another Barrymore uniform, and his young chest bared by his half-open shirt displayed dog tags but no proof of manhood. A cigarette hung from his lips and the cockpit was hazy with smoke. Tom had been speaking to him in English, so Nicole ordered, "Take off the headset!"

The boy looked more confused than scared, but after a moment complied. "Where is Mister Reynolds?"

Nicole kept the gun aimed. "Defending the devil's democracy."

THIRTY-ONE

The fuel drum had been punctured and was spewing gasoline down the floor. By the glow of the flashlight Zack and Dakota wrestled it so the hole faced up. There were voices outside calling above the rattle of rain echoing in the cargo bay. The double doors creaked open and another flashlight beam stabbed in. "Nathi? Dakota?" called Kobe.

"It's Zack and I," said Dakota.

Thabo's voice cried, "There is fuel running out!" Another flashlight beam shone in.

"Put out those lights!" yelled Dakota. "They are not explosion-proof!"

"You have such a light?" asked Kobe.

"So far, anyhow," said Zack in English.

"We're bringing a truck for the fuel," said Thabo.

Other boys were gathering, peering in through the doorway, all in loincloths and antelope boots, rifles slung on their shoulders.

"Get away!" yelled Dakota. "One little spark and we're dead! Stop that truck! ...Kobe! Thabo! Come and help! Tell the others to stay away! Send them for buckets to wash out this mess."

"We must hurry," said Kobe. "The river is rising fast. Soon it will be too deep to cross."

"Then hurry, dammit!"

Thabo and Kobe gave orders and small figures ran to obey. One of Rashawn's battered trucks, its blackout lights like tiny pale eyes, stopped about forty feet away. Kobe and Thabo climbed into the plane. "Where is Nathi?" asked Thabo.

"He got wounded in the village," said Zack.

"Our village was attacked?" asked Kobe.

"Destroyed," said Dakota. "But most of the people are safe."

"Most?" asked Thabo.

"Many were wounded, and some were killed by missiles from a helicopter."

"But we think it went down," said Zack. "Maybe Tindo shot it. But there's somethin' else to worry about."

A man's voice spoke: "Who are you?" Rashawn climbed into the airplane and, taking the light from Thabo, shone it full on Zack. "...A girl?"

Dakota came down the tilted floor, towing Zack by an arm. "This is Zack. He is with us." He touched the charm on Zack's chest. "And a man as you see. ...Put out that light!"

Rashawn switched it off, leaving only the glow of Dakota's light at the forward end of the cargo bay. "There is another danger?"

A rat-like squeaking came from the cockpit. Zack looked at Dakota. "It could be Tom tryin' to help."

"Then you'd better answer it."

Rashawn grabbed Zack's arm. "Who is Tom, and how could he help us?"

"He might be tryin' to warn us," said Zack. "The General's got an atom bomb! If he knows where we are he can kill everybody!"

*   *   *

"I hear a lion," whispered Jabari, staring into the rainy night while clutching his M-16. He was sitting in the back of the jeep, his bandaged leg stretched out. In the driver's seat was Corporal Akida, an old American walkie-talkie pressed to one of his ears. The vehicle sat on a low hilltop, its

WHEN ALL GOES BRIGHT

U.S. ARMY

and faded stars glistening pale in the darkness. Its engine was running at idle, exhaust pipe ghosting steam. The little blackout lights were on, and the instrument panel was dim-lit red. The windscreen was down on the hood, and the cannon-like weapon was aimed southwest.

Akida reached for his gun. "When I was younger we didn't fear lions."

"Because we lived in peace with them." Jabari lay his gun aside. "Do you think that will ever be again? If the General wins his war?"

"Our old ways are gone," said Akida. "As the General has said, men of today do not live with lions. Lions are locked away in zoos. Or kept in animal preserves for wealthy tourists to photograph. ...And of *course* the General will win!"

Akida indicated the launcher. "This is his secret weapon. And you should feel honored to be here tonight, chosen by the General to shoot it."

Jabari looked down at his wounded leg. "Perhaps I was only chosen because I can't do anything else." He glanced at the gun's mechanism. "Just follow orders to aim and fire. Turn that wheel and pull that lever. A little child could do it. ...And perhaps you were chosen because you can drive."

Akida frowned. "This is an important mission! This weapon will kill all the terrorists and we will be heroes for winning the war. The General will give us medals. ...Straighten your cap, Private Jabari! At least try to look like a soldier!"

Jabari sighed. "I do not want a medal, I will just be glad to go home."

*   *   *

Nicole held the gun to the young pilot's head as the Huey thrashed its way through the night, its wipers creaking across the windshield, while her other hand pressed the phone to her ear. There were warbling pips as Zack's phone rang, but seconds passed without an answer. Wasn't he carrying it? ...Or was it already too late?

291

No, she thought. If the bomb had been dropped all would have gone bright across this tiny land.

"What was the plan?" she asked the pilot above the vibrating engine drone. "After you picked up Tom?"

"I do not know any plans." The boy seemed too intent on flying to worry much about the gun. "I was told to meet Mr. Reynolds and to follow his orders. That is all I know."

He was probably telling the truth, thought Nicole: Tom would have been careful with information...

There was a distant explosion!

Nicole almost screamed, but then realized it was Tom's helicopter blowing up behind them. She recalled a song by The Doors on one of Zackary's eight-track tapes... *This is the end*.

The phone continued to pip in her ear. She studied the instrument panel... compared to Tom's it looked very low tech, more like Nathi's airplane. But something new had been added. She remembered when Tom had flown her home; the little screen he'd been watching. She pointed to another such screen. "Is that how you found him?"

The boy had been startled by the blast. The aircraft tilted and seemed to slip sideways, but then he recovered. "...Yes. It tracked the phone you are holding. See, the blip is now centered."

"What about tracking another phone? ...I guess it's on a different channel."

The pilot hesitated, but eyed Nicole's gun and finally said, "I was given another frequency." He carefully tapped a keypad. The display grid changed, and now the blip was off to one side.

"How far is that?" asked Nicole.

The pilot studied the screen. "About fifty kilometers east."

"Is that near a river?"

"Yes."

"Take us there fast."

"Hello?" said Zack's voice in Nicole's ear.

Along with a million other things, Nicole had been wondering what she could say that wouldn't alert anyone who might be monitoring the phone.

292

Tom had been ordered to kill her and Zack, but how and when had been left up to him. For all his masters knew he might still be playing the role of their "friend," a man who'd made gentle love to her, who'd wanted Zack to be his son... until he'd been ordered to murder them in the name of defending Democracy.

"Hi, Zack. Are you having fun?"

The pilot gaped at her as if she'd lost her mind. For a moment the phone was silent except for a rustle of static. Nicole pictured Zack's puzzled frown, like when she had found him a "pin." She remembered Tom's words... *he's a damn smart kid.*

As if to confirm that, Zack's voice turned cheerful. "Oh, yeah, mom, it's really cool here."

Nicole tried to think of the right things to say. She had to warn Zack to get rid of the phone. And, the freedom-fighters' camp was a target. ...And Tom had not had been their friend. "I... don't want to spoil your fun, Zack. But Tom said to remind you about your diet."

"...He said *what?*"

Nicole went on, "He's *always* said you were obese. ...He's here right now and he said it again... you're *dangerously* obese."

"...He's with you?" asked Zack.

"He came with his own helicopter... you remember it, don't you?... but there seems to be something wrong with it. We're in the General's now, and on our way to meet you."

"...You know where we are?"

"You know Tom can follow your phone." Nicole considered, then added, "It was supposed to be a surprise, but I wanted to warn you Tom isn't happy. He knows you haven't been watching your weight."

"...What did he say?" asked Zack.

"What he's been saying all along ever since he met you. You're obese and it's *dangerous*. ...He's already set a target weight. ...And you're going to have to start running, and the sooner the better. ...How do you feel about that?"

Zack's voice turned adolescently squally. "I think it sucks!"

"But, your health is really in danger, Zack. ...Don't you dare hang up on me!"

There was a pause, then the phone went dead. The pilot was still staring at her. Then he said, "I have heard that was an American problem."

"It's what we're supposed to worry about, instead of what's really wrong with the world."

*   *   *

The cargo bay was filled with boys working in near-darkness by the glow of Dakota's flashlight. Some were washing the gasoline out, others un-strapping and wrestling barrels, rolling them to the doorway. Dakota called to Rashawn outside, "It should be safe to bring up the truck."

Zack burst out of the cockpit. "We gotta hurry!" he yelled. "Fill up the trucks an' get outta here! The General knows where we are! An' we gotta get rid of this phone! They're usin' it for the target!"

Thabo had been pushing a barrel. "Smash it!" He made a grab for the phone, but Dakota caught his arm.

"No! They might suspect we know of the bomb, and that could make them fire it."

Rashawn was outside directing the truck as a boy backed it up to the plane. He thrust his head through the doorway. "Zack! What is the range of this bomb?"

"It can kill for two miles, but it has to be fired from less than that."

"...Who fires it will also die?"

"Yeah, but they probably don't know it."

Kobe said, "Put the phone in a plastic bag and throw it in the river."

Rashawn shook his head. "It might be caught on something. Or wash ashore nearby."

"I'll take it away," said Zack, "an' run as fast as I can."

"You would do that for us?" said Rashawn.

"I'm part of the reason for all this shit."

Rashawn glanced at Dakota. "He is a man."

"I mean no disrespect," said Thabo, laying a hand on Zack's shoulder. "But I think I may run a bit faster than you."

"No," said Dakota. "I'll take it. I'll fly a few miles upriver and circle, and they'll aim the bomb at me."

"I'm goin' with you," said Zack.

"Why do you do this for us?" asked Rashawn. "America will call you a traitor."

"That's America's problem," said Zack.

Dakota called to the other boys as the truck eased up to the door. "Hurry with the fuel! Soon there won't room to take off."

"Want me to start the engines?" asked Zack.

"Yes. And..."

"Yeah, I know, not too rich."

*　　　　*　　　　*

"Private Jabari!" snapped Corporal Akida. "You could be shot for sleeping on duty!"

Jabari jerked his head up. "I wasn't alseep, I was thinking of home. Don't you?"

"Of course I do. But we are defending our homes tonight."

"Would you shoot me?"

"I would have to if the General ordered... but I would rather not." Akida pulled a candy bar from the pocket of his rain-soaked shirt. "Here is a Milky Way. We will have many American things after we win the General's war. Think of those to stay awake, and how much better your life will be."

"Is that why we're fighting? For American things?"

"Of course," said Akida. "Don't you want an I-pod? And a television? And a computer, and a car?"

Jabari took a bite of candy. "A car would get stuck in the rainy season. ...Perhaps a Land Rover."

"Those are made in England. Americans have jeeps."

"I hope they are better than this one."

"Of course they are. This is old. Americans always have new things."

"What do they do with their old things?"

"Throw them away."

"Could I have the Internet?"

"That comes with a computer."

295

"That would be good," said Jabari. "I could talk to other people, then I could understand them. ...But that would require electricity."

"We will have that, too," said Akida. "In every village across our land, as the General has promised." He pulled out a candy bar for himself.

"But, who will pay for all these things?"

"We will have jobs," said Akida. "And make lots of money to buy all we want."

"But, I have to hunt and fish. And grow food for my family."

"Those are old ways," said Akida. "Just like living with lions and worshipping things of the earth."

"So, we will worship American things?"

The walkie-talkie sputtered, and Akida pressed it to an ear.

Jabari reached to the launcher. "Shall I fire?"

*   *   *

"The General is calling," said the pilot, indicating his headset. "What should I do?"

"Answer," said Nicole. "But, be careful what you say."

"If you shoot me, we will both die."

"You assume because I'm a woman I can't fly a helicopter?"

"If so, why haven't you killed me?"

"Because I'm not a boy like Tom."

The pilot put on his headset. "The General wishes to speak with Tom."

"...Tell him... Tom's busy. ...There's a problem. He's trying to fix it. Make believe you're talking to him."

The pilot spoke into the microphone then listened for a moment. "The General has the target painted and awaits your order to fire."

"Tell him I want to... confirm the target." Nicole looked at the monitor: the blip was almost centered now, the tiny dot that might be Zack... unless he'd understood her and gotten rid of the phone. "How long before we get there?"

The pilot studied the screen. "Perhaps another five minutes."

"The General will wait for my orders."

296

The pilot relayed her words. "He thanks you for your help in ending terrorism."

"Just following orders," said Nicole.

*　　　*　　　*

"Woah," said Zack, peering from the cockpit window as Dakota swung the plane around, throttling up the starboard engine, his boot on the port side brake. "That's a White half-track from World War Two. ...An' those are CCKW trucks. An' that's a Willys MB jeep. An' a Land Rover Series One. It's kinda like a museum."

Dakota was watching the compass, aligning the plane for take-off. "Hopefully they will soon be in one as part of Kiwanja's history, even though a sad part."

Zack watched the vehicles as they rumbled past and into the river, steam ghosting up from their hot exhaust pipes. The river had risen noticeably, and the vehicles' black-out tail lamps vanished under the water, but all drove slowly on. Their shapes soon vanished in the rain as they neared the opposite shore. "How far is it to the town?"

Dakota was testing the pitch controls and checking various gauges. "They should be there by dawn... assuming they get away from here before the bomb is fired."

Zack glanced at the phone on the instrument panel as Dakota ran up the engines. "I almost forgot we're the target now."

"Can we survive the blast in the air?"

"Depends on how high an' close we are. An' we have to stay low an' fly real slow or they'll know the phone ain't on the ground."

"Has Tom now chosen to be on our side?"

"No," said Zack. "It was mom who called. Tom betrayed us. ...I used to think he was a hero. The kind of man I'd wanna be. Like, a good American. But, I guess it was all a front."

Dakota touched Zack's arm. "*You* are a good American who is really fighting to make people free." He checked the compass heading again, then gripped the throttle levers. "Ready for takeoff."

*　　　*　　　*

297

"Shall I fire?" asked Jabari again.

"No," said Akida, the radio still pressed to an ear. "Take your hand off the trigger! There are new orders. ...We drive northwest. ...Down to the flats near the river." He pulled a compass out of his pocket.

Jabari sighed. "I wish this was over."

"It will be soon," said Akida.

*   *   *

Nicole was watching the monitor. "Is the... target... moving?"

The pilot scanned the screen. "It has moved, though not very far. Do you wish me to go there?"

"Yes," said Nicole.

The pilot hesitated, then asked. "This bomb? Is it atomic?"

"Very atomic," said Nicole, recalling an old children's movie. "And dirty... full of radiation. It will poison much of your land. And it could kill half your people. ...That's what your General has brought you."

The pilot gazed ahead at the night. "My brother is a terrorist. He is with them now."

"Your brother is not a terrorist. You've just been taught to think he is." Nicole studied the boy. "Why did you choose to fight for the General?"

"So I could learn how to fly."

"What good is being able to fly if you don't have a home to come back to on earth?"

*   *   *

"I could throw the phone out," said Zack. "Rashawn should be more than two miles away from the target site by now."

Dakota was holding the plane in a circle. "But, what if it is broken? As long as the bomb is aimed at its signal Rashawn and his fighters are safe."

"Won't they be seen when the sun comes up?"

"But the jeep with the bomb will still be out here. And once Rashawn is close to the town they can't fire it at him."

298

"Yeah, they'd be shooting it at the General."

"Dawn is nearing," said Dakota, scanning the rainy sky to the east. "When it becomes light enough to see we will land and leave the phone on the ground. I know a place by the river."

"If they don't shoot the bomb at us first."

*   *   *

"Listen!" said Jabari, as the jeep crawled along in four-wheel-drive, splashing its way through a muddy stream.

"To what?" asked Akida, as the jeep clawed its way to higher ground. Akida stopped and peered ahead beyond the dim beam of the blackout lamp.

"Turn off the motor," said Jabari, cocking his head and listening again as Akida switched off the ignition, but there was only the patter of rain and the gurgling of the stream behind them.

"Did you hear another lion?" asked Akida.

"I thought I heard a motor. Maybe a truck… perhaps more than one… but I can't hear it now."

"You are tired," said Akida. He started the engine, checked his compass, and put the jeep in gear. "We're almost there. Just over that hill is the river. I used to play there as a boy." He studied Jabari a moment. "You may sleep for a while."

*   *   *

The pilot checked the monitor. "We are nearing the source of the signal. What do you wish to do?"

Nicole had been wondering about that. Had Zack understood her warning and gotten rid of the phone? But if so why had it moved? If he hadn't understood, he might be with the freedom fighters and all were still in danger. Should she risk another call? That could make Tom's masters suspicious… he probably should have killed her by now.

And they might tell the General that something was wrong.

She gazed ahead at the darkness beyond the creaking wipers. Was

299

it just her imagination, or was the sky a little lighter? She recalled her eighth-grade graduation and the party in the grassy hills and watching the sun come up by the pond. She remembered something her mother had said when she'd come home that morning: *This is the first day of the rest of your life.*

How many hundreds of new days had come since watching that peaceful sunrise? And what had she done with those days that contributed anything good to the world? All she could think of was raising Zack. "Is it getting near dawn?"

"Yes," said the pilot.

"Can you circle around the signal? Until we can see what's going on."

"We only have fuel for about thirty minutes."

"Will it be light enough to see by then?"

"Sooner than that, I think."

"Then circle," said Nicole. She was startled by the phone's sudden squeaks. Her first thought was Zack and she pulled it out... but what if it was one of Tom's bosses? She passed it to the pilot. "Tom is still busy with something, keeping us in the air. ...Could there be a problem like that?"

"One of many," the pilot replied. "This aircraft is very old. ...*Ndio?*" he said to the phone. He listened a moment. "It is the General."

"Be careful," warned Nicole.

The pilot pressed the phone to his chest, covering the speaker. "I have no wish to die." Then he spoke into the phone, saying there was a fuel leak. He listened once more, then said, "yes, sir," and gave the phone back to Nicole. "The target is stationary and painted, and the bomb is ready to fire. The General knows we are near the target and warned he will fire in ten minutes, with or without your order."

Nicole looked at a clock on the instrument panel. "Just circle for now. We have to know where that phone is. ...If all goes bright, don't look."

The pilot drew something from his shirt pocket... a tuft of fur on a strip of leather. "May I wear this?"

"Of course, young man," said Nicole.

300

*   *   *

"Wake up, soldier!" snapped Akida. He stopped the jeep near a grove of trees, switched off the engine and blackout lights, then pressed the radio to an ear. "Make these adjustments," he said to Jabari.

Jabari eased himself to the ground out of the rear of the vehicle, wincing from his wounded leg. Stretching up to reach the controls, he aimed the launcher as ordered.

"Stand by," said Akida.

"I'm hungry," said Jabari. "Do you have more candy bars?"

"Hush." Akida looked across grassy flats, now becoming more defined as the sky slowly lightened above. Faint in the distance was a river glimmering like polished gunmetal. He peered intently into the rain. "I see something. ...Perhaps a big truck." He turned to Jabari. "I have no more candy. But we should be back in time for lunch. And a victory celebration. And, of course, our medals."

Two small shadows rose out of the grass. "Don't move!" ordered Dakota, sighting his gun on Akida.

Zack, beside him, aimed at Jabari. "Get away from that!" he yelled in Swahili.

"FIRE!" ordered Akida.

"NO!" yelled Zack.

Jabari hesitated, a hand on the firing lever.

Dakota yelled, "If you shoot that we'll all die!"

"What do you mean?" demanded Akida.

Dakota jerked his jaw toward the river. "Your target is a kilometer away. You're aiming at my airplane, but the bomb will kill for twice that far."

"Yeah!" said Zack in English. "But your General didn't tell you that, did he? Wanna die for an ass-hat like him?"

"What is an ass-hat?" asked Jabari.

Akida looked confused, but finally turned to Jabari. "Stand down, soldier."

Jabari backed away from the jeep. "Shall I put my hands up?"

"Yeah," said Zack. "On top of your head."

Jabari looked startled.

301

"*Kichwa,*" said Dakota, and Jabari obeyed.

"What did I say?" asked Zack.

"On top of his *kuma*... vagina."

"I knew it started with K."

Dakota jabbed his gun at Akida. "Out of the jeep, and put your hands up!"

"Terrorists!" spat Akida.

Dakota shook his head. "I think we shall tire of that word fairly soon."

Akida looked around. "Where are the others of your kind?"

Dakota shook rain from his eyes. "They should be nearing the town by now. We heard your engine and waited here. If your General is not an absolute ass he will surrender without a fight."

"Why would he do that?"

"Because we're going to take a jeep ride."

"An' aim that thing at him," said Zack.

EPILOGUE

"So, you really don't think I'm too fat?" asked Zack.

"Just more of you to love," said Nicole, laying a hand on his shoulder.

Dakota laughed. "Especially in Kiwanja."

Zack put his gun on the hood of the jeep and pulled a rain-soaked Nestle bar from the pocket of his sodden jeans. "An' Tom didn't think so either?"

Nicole gazed west though silver rain, across a land of golden grass where shades of new green were already appearing. "He wasn't an evil man, Zack; he... just believed in his country, I guess. Like, 'my country, right or wrong.' Millions of people have died for that concept in too many countries all over the world."

"That is strange," said Dakota. "To love one's country more than people." He sat behind the steering wheel and munched a Nestle bar. Jabari was in the passenger seat: he'd thrown away his uniform and now wore only a loincloth, and was also eating a candy bar. Corporal Akida sat in the rear, hands behind him tied to the launcher. He tried to look like a prisoner of war, though his eyes often strayed to the candy.

Zack turned to Dakota. "What if you had to make a choice?

303

Between your country an' your people?"

"You already know the answer to that. A country is only a concept. God and the earth recognize no borders. Nor do animals, birds, or the wind. Borders are drawn by men on a map to keep some people apart. Family and friends... friends like you... are all one really has in life. If one must kill or die for something, it should be for the ones they love, not for a line on paper."

The jeep was on a hilltop that overlooked the town to the east. The airfield was now a lion-colored lake, and work had stopped at the coal mine. The antique train was at the station, smoke curling up from the engine's stack. It was hooked to every car in Kiwanja, and people were getting aboard. Battered old trucks and a few Land Rovers were taking more people and children away, many driven by loinclothed boys. No soldiers were visible anywhere, presumably all in the Army compound... or maybe walking home.

Corporal Akida's walkie-talkie blipped atop the jeep's lowered windscreen. Dakota pressed it to an ear, listened a moment, then looked at Zack. "It's Rashawn. Will eight kilometers be a safe distance to evacuate the people? ...About five miles."

"That should be sufficient." Zack ate the last bite of chocolate and frowned at the rusty launcher. "If we have to use this thing."

The Vietnam Huey sat nearby, its motionless rotors drooping. The pilot stood beside the jeep. He'd lost his Barrymore uniform shirt, and the lion's mane charm swung free on his chest. "You would actually do that?"

"The choice is the General's," said Dakota. He glanced at his watch. "And he has less than an hour to make it. High Noon as cowboys say."

There were squeaky rodent shrills, and Nicole took Tom's phone from her pocket. "Hello?"

Everyone watched as she listened. The only sound was the patter of rain. Finally she spoke to the phone. "Your title doesn't impress me. ...I expected more than being exiled. But maybe I shouldn't have. You want this over quietly. I guess that's understandable; things that plot and scheme under rocks don't like being seen in the light."

She looked at Zack. "I *am* thinking of my son. A hell of a lot more than you were when you gave the order to murder him. ...Oh, you

304

could invade Kiwanja. Murder more people and children; and this time there really is a 'Weapon Of Mass Destruction.'"

She glanced at the jeep. "Has shamefully made in America painted all over it... and we have lots of pictures."

"...Of *course* you'd make up a story, but I'm pretty good at that, too. It used to be my job... lying to the American people, brainwashing them to want what you want and never ask why they should want it... or who has to suffer so they can have it... and I'm sure that's in my file. Not that you'd actually need any truth. ...Yes, I know what I'm doing. I'm being a good American. I'm bringing Democracy to Kiwanja... and without murdering anyone. Or wrecking their country any more than you and your boys already have."

She looked at Zack again. "I think we have a bright future here. And even if we did come back I'd always worry about him becoming another Amber Alert. ...Not to mention being blown up every time I started my car."

The radio sputtered. Dakota listened a moment, then turned to the Huey pilot. "The *former* President-General is waiting. I assume he has packed all his things, including the Treasury."

Nicole dropped the phone on the ground and crushed it under her boot. "I think I can make us some money. It's the one thing I've always been good at."

"Besides raisin' me," said Zack.

The pilot went to the helicopter but paused before getting aboard. "May I come back?"

"Men always do," said Dakota.

Zack pointed toward distant acacia trees. "I see lions!"

ABOUT THE AUTHOR

Jess Mowry was born in 1960 near Starkville, Mississippi. When he was only a few months old his father took him to live in Oakland, California. Mowry's father was a voracious reader who introduced his son to books at a very early age. Jess attended a public school, but despite his love of reading, dropped out at age thirteen, part way through the eighth grade and worked with his father in the scrap-iron business. In his late teens, Jess moved to Arizona to work as a truck driver and heavy equipment operator. He also lived and worked in Alaska as an engineer aboard a tugboat and as an aircraft mechanic on Douglas C-47 cargo planes, as well as at a children's refuge in Haiti.

Mowry has written twenty-five books and many short stories about black children and teens in a variety of genres, ranging from inner-city settings to the forests of Haiti, the wilds of Alaska, the Arizona desert, the Caribbean Sea, and the African veldt. While some of his novels are set in Oakland and deal with social issues, such as poverty, violence, drugs, gangs, teenage sexuality, and school drop-outs, Mowry has also written ghost tales, as well as novels featuring Voodoo and African magic, in addition to sea stories, and compiled an anthology of Victorian ghost stories.

Jess Mowry lives in Oakland, California.

THIS BOOK IS ALSO AVAILABLE IN A KINDLE EDITION

OTHER ANUBIS BOOKS

AVAILABLE ON AMAZON